Readers love ELLE E. IRE

Reel to Real Love

"*Reel to Real Love* is nothing short of fun. If you're after something easy, exciting, thrilling, and unexpected, then absolutely check out this book."
—QueeRomance Ink

Dead Woman's Pond

"Psychics, ghosts, and supernatural events, sign me up!"
—Quiet Fury Books

Vicious Circle

"I'd recommend this story to readers who enjoy descriptive, action packed, sci-fi stories, regardless of character gender or sexual orientation."
—Love Bytes

By ELLE E. IRE

Harsh Reality
Reel to Real Love
Vicious Circle

NEARLY DEPARTED
Dead Woman's Pond
Dead Woman's Revenge
Dead Woman's Secret

STORM FRONTS
Threadbare
Patchwork
Woven

Published by DSP PUBLICATIONS
www.dsppublications.com

HARSH REALITY

ELLE E. IRE

DSP PUBLICATIONS

Published by
DSP PUBLICATIONS

5032 Capital Circle SW, Suite 2, PMB# 279,
Tallahassee, FL 32305-7886 USA
www.dsppublications.com

This is a work of fiction. Names, characters, places, and incidents either
are the product of author imagination or are used fictitiously, and any
resemblance to actual persons, living or dead, business establishments,
events, or locales is entirely coincidental.

Harsh Reality
© 2022 Elle E. Ire

Cover Art
© 2022 Tiferet Design
http://www.tiferetdesign.com
Cover content is for illustrative purposes only and any person depicted
on the cover is a model.

Mass Market Paperback ISBN: 978-1-64108-430-7
Trade Paperback ISBN: 978-1-64108-429-1
Digital ISBN: 978-1-64108-428-4
Mass Market Paperback published May 2023
v. 1.0

Printed in the United States of America

To my spouse. May we keep sharing so many wonderful adventures.

Acknowledgments

WITHOUT A doubt, this is the most "out there" book I ever attempted to write. It's what happens in a writer's brain when she sees *Cowboys and Aliens* and eats spicy food after 8:00 p.m., then goes to bed and dreams up a badass female Old West sheriff who ends up on reality TV. Special thanks go to Amy Boggs for her suggestion of alternate methods of time travel and Elizabeth Winick Rubinstein for encouraging a bigger, more explosive ending.

Additional thanks to my former writing group: Mark, Amy, Joe, Evergreen, and Gary who critiqued early chapters of this with a mixture of "This is awesome!" and "What on earth are you doing?" and "How do you come up with this stuff?" throughout the process.

Thank you to my agent, Naomi Davis, who found just the right home for this, and all the amazing folks at DSP Publications who gave it that home. Thanks to my editing team: Gus, Brian, Yv, and Katie—any remaining errors are entirely my own. Thank you to Gin for the blurbs. Thank you to publicity guru Naomi Grant and the entire art department but especially Anna Sikorska for consistently exceeding my expectations when it comes to my covers.

Finally, thank you to my friends and readers. Your positive feedback, encouragement, and support are why I do what I do.

HARSH REALITY

ELLE E. IRE

CHAPTER I

Oblivion, Territory of New Mexico, Circa 1891

"*SHEE*-IT, THEM miners don't usually head *into* the saloon drunk."

Those miners, I thought, Ma's voice carrying to me from the grave. Being raised by a schoolmarm meant proper speech stuck with you. I resisted the urge to correct my deputy. Again.

Shifting my weight, I let my chair thump forward onto all four of its legs. The porch bore the indentations from years of my abuse, and I rubbed the sole of my leather boot over its uneven surface. Lowering my hat brim against the setting sun, I followed Deputy Baylor's gaze. Sure enough, a trio of men shambled their way up the main dirt street of Oblivion.

Nothing new about miners coming into town, but as my deputy had pointed out, these three weaved from side to side like the mayor after one of his benders. They dragged their gear behind them in the dust, adding unnecessary damage to picks and shovels. Where were their horses?

Maybe they'd been robbed—which made them my problem, regardless of whether or not they started any trouble.

A sigh whooshed out of me, and I pushed myself up by the arms of my faithful chair.

"Think we should have a chat with them, Cali?" Baylor's blue eyes twinkled beneath the brim of his hat and dirty-blond bangs.

My stare fell on Baylor like a bucket of river water in January.

Suddenly, the rail post at the edge of the general store's porch seemed particularly interesting to him. "Sorry, Sheriff McCade."

Everyone knew I preferred to be called "Sheriff" while on duty. Hard enough to maintain authority as a woman without drawing extra attention to my too feminine first name.

I rested a hand on Baylor's shoulder. "No, I'm sorry, Jake. Just hoping for a nice quiet Monday. That's all."

He stood, his lanky frame too thin for his six feet of height, and watched the trio of miners disappearing through the saloon's swinging doors. The tinkling of piano keys I'd barely been aware of ceased drifting across to us on the faint breeze.

"Don't think you're gonna get it."

Hank never stopped playing the saloon's old upright. Not in the late afternoon while trying to draw in the evening crowd.

"Neither do I." Tucking my shirttail into my dungarees, I set off at a brisk pace down the board-walk lining the street. Baylor kept pace behind me.

We paused for two horses pulling a creaking wagon to pass, and I took the opportunity to tighten the strip of rawhide holding my long hair in a plaited braid that hung heavy between my shoulder blades. The wagon lumbered on, its noise drowning out any trouble that might have been erupting in the saloon.

"Miss Cali! Deputy Baylor!"

Dang it.

I glanced at the unmoving wooden doors. No sign of real trouble except the silent piano. I didn't want to stop. I really didn't. But there were certain citizens one couldn't ignore without consequences.

I closed my eyes, counted to three, then pasted on my best Sunday school smile and turned to face the man who'd called to us, aware of Jake doing the same.

To Preacher Xanthis, I would forever be Miss Cali, and Jake would be Deputy Baylor. Shiny stars, especially on a woman, meant nothing in the face of religious propriety. Besides, who could argue with a man whose sanity got called into question more often than a bartender poured whiskey?

I finished my turn, my nose ending up three inches from a bird's beak, and jerked back to avoid losing a nostril or two.

"Whoops! Sorry, Cali. You startled her, is all. You know how much Pandora likes you." A harsh squawk begged to differ. Xanthis put a couple of feet between us, pulling his black-sleeved arm against his chest, the perched bird along with it.

Bright gold-and-scarlet feathers stood out stark against the dark coat fabric. Intense black eyes studied me, head cocking from side to side, giving the impression of a creature of much greater years than the average pet's lifespan. Whether Pandora "liked" me or not, she certainly found me intriguing. Or maybe tasty. I hoped I'd never find out. That beak looked sharp.

Not for the first time, I wondered what kind of bird she was. Not a parrot, and nothing I'd seen in these parts before.

"Dangerous animals should be kept in cages," Jake drawled, keeping well clear. I noticed his hand rested on the grip of his six-shooter. Seriously? He was going to shoot a twelve-inch-tall bird that hadn't actually harmed anyone? We needed to have a little chat later.

"Nothing dangerous about Pandora. You live right by the Lord and she'll leave you be." The preacher stroked her ruffled feathers. "She might speak her mind, but she's never bitten another good soul. Believe me, I'd know it. If she ever did, it would have a Purpose."

No humor there, and from the tone, it was Purpose with a capital P. I wondered if our crazy preacher thought he'd trained Pandora as some sort of godly guard bird. He carried the darn thing everywhere, even up to the pulpit on Sundays. Why Oblivion's townsfolk put up with such shenanigans was beyond me, but he was the only preacher we had, and souls, after all, must be saved.

Speaking of saving souls…. I looked over my shoulder at the saloon across the street. No one had exited or entered the swinging doors after the three miners, and I still didn't hear any sounds of distress—no breaking glass, no shouting. Maybe I was worried for nothing.

The piano remained silent.

Preacher Xanthis cleared his throat for attention. "I noticed you weren't in church yesterday."

Of course he had. I'd hoped with all the miners and their families attending (dangerous work made for pious folk) he might have missed my absence. No such luck. Of course, even when I was there, I wasn't. Not really. In body maybe, but not in spirit. And he always noticed that too.

Someone screamed.

Jerking my head up, I followed the sound, right into the saloon.

I exchanged a quick glance with Jake. My hand found the rawhide loop keeping my pistol in its holster and released it. "Sorry, Preacher, gotta go." Without waiting for a response, I raced my partner the rest of the way across the street.

Finally.

"I'll expect your attendance next Sunday, little lady," Xanthis called after us.

Sometimes I wondered if, despite my discretion, he knew about some of the other "unladylike" things I did beyond being the sheriff.

That's when the first body flew through the saloon's front window.

Glass, expensive and hard as hell to get out here, shattered in all directions. One of the miners I'd seen earlier hit the boardwalk with a thud, then rolled until he dropped off the edge and settled in the dust. Sounds of fighting poured into the street.

I ran the last few steps, crouching on one knee beside the stranger, who lay faceup, eyes staring at nothing in the darkening afternoon sky. Cuts crisscrossed his pale cheeks, presumably from the broken panes, but no blood welled up from the wounds. My nose wrinkled at the foul stench, well beyond that of unwashed male, rising off the body—spoiled meat. Reaching out, I placed two fingers against his neck, just to be sure, and recoiled at the chill of the miner's skin.

I swiped my hands over the sightless eyes to close the lids, but they popped open again, startling a screech out of me that I covered with a clearing of my throat. So much for that idea. I tried not to look in them as I scanned the rest of the body, noting dark dry stains, some flaking into the dust, but further inspection revealed no wounds. The blood spattering this miner's clothing wasn't his own.

Which meant another body somewhere.

"Hellfire," I whispered.

"What?" Jake said from my right shoulder.

From within the bar came crashing and yelling accompanied by the high-pitched shriek of one of the "upstairs girls." But not Arlene. Her shriek, and any other excited sound she could make, I knew. Intimately. Whatever was going on, she would be smart enough to stay out of the way. I hoped.

A couple of whiskey bottles followed the miner through the window and into the street. I ducked as one missed my head by inches. At least it was empty.

"Go on, get in there," I shouted over the din. "Put a stop to that before someone else gets killed."

"He's dead?" Xanthis asked from my left.

"Good and," I assured the preacher while Jake vanished through the swinging doors. Should have been me, I knew, but all my attention focused on the body in front of me. By all reasonable assessments, this guy had been dead for days. What the hell?

Maybe the other two had been carrying this one. That would explain their lurching approach. But why on earth would they go to the saloon with a dead man? And why toss a corpse out a window?

Whatever the explanation (and I had to believe there was some reasonable one somewhere in all this), I needed to get ahold of the doc, right quick, especially if there were other victims.

A flash of motion caught my eye, and I reached up and yanked Xanthis with his bird down beside me as a chair flew out the new opening. Pandora flapped wildly, several red feathers floating to the ground beside us. "Might want to wait a bit on prayers for the dead until we get these folks under control."

"God doesn't wait," Xanthis said, passing his hands over the body while he muttered religious phrases the poor bastard would never hear.

God didn't have to duck flying chairs, either.

"'Scuse me." I stood to go help Jake. As an afterthought, I turned back. "Don't move him." If God didn't wait for prayers, who knew how long he'd wait for burial.

CHAPTER 2

PUTTING ON my best no-more-nonsense face, I stomped onto the porch and pushed through the swinging doors. Maybe not the smartest move, but I hadn't heard any gunfire in the chaos, and sometimes the best stance to take in quieting a fistfight was an authoritative one.

A swinging pickax missed my head by about an inch.

Okay, definitely not my smartest move.

I threw myself behind an overturned table while the pick's owner staggered about like a blind man, still swinging his weapon wildly. That bought me a minute to survey the insanity.

Only a handful of patrons and employees were scattered about, shielding themselves with tables, the much-too-narrow stairway railings, anything they could find. One of the serving girls, Cindy, lay facedown on the floor, her tray's shattered glassware and spilled liquor all around. Her spine rose and fell with labored breathing.

Alive, thank God.

At the top of the stairs, two other gals peeked between the slatted rails, eyes wide and frightened. No sign of Jake.

No sign of Arlene, either. Good.

Al had the shotgun he kept behind the bar trained over the counter's flat surface, his sights on the third miner across the room. I made eye contact with Al and shook my head. Never a good idea to use gunfire in close quarters. Stray shot could end up in an unintended target.

Like me.

I jumped at the delicate hand on my shoulder, shooting a quick glance back to see the last person I wanted to in the last place I wanted her to be. Arlene—leader of drinking songs by the bar, lady of the evening, and my occasional secret bedmate—finally showed herself. The sweet red-painted-lips smile that attracted most of the men in this town was missing from her expression, and she sported a deep gash across her left shoulder, marring her velvet-soft skin. Her eyes went wide, and I let her push me lower, ducking the sluggish swing of the pickax one more time.

Swinging at the sheriff. Had this stranger lost his damn mind?

Arlene gathered her frilly white petticoats in her other hand and tucked them in behind the table so she could squat next to me. Her breath came fast and hot in my ear. The scent of lilacs and lavender muddled my senses for a moment. I shook my head to clear it.

"Don't let me distract you, Sheriff," Arlene said.

Like locking the barn door after the horses have run out. I hadn't let her "distract" me in quite a while. Which was probably why every one of my five senses and a couple more I hadn't been aware of prior were firing off like an unruly six-shooter.

"Shoot him!" someone yelled, bringing me back to my more immediate concerns—probably Hank from behind the piano.

Maybe I should have, but while the pick looked sharp and deadly and he'd destroyed plenty of furniture, the miner didn't seem anywhere close to actually hitting me.

"Any idea what's got into them?" Arlene said, pressing corset-covered breasts against my back. My legs burned from the extended crouch, but I didn't want to risk standing, even with his bad aim.

"Don't know. Don't care. Gonna stop it." I stood, grabbed at the pick in midswing, and caught it just below its metal points. Shoving hard, I drove the handle into the miner's rib cage, forcing him back several feet. He had muscle, though, and wrenched the weapon away from me. I focused on my assailant, meeting the miner's blank gaze while he again swung the pick from side to side, well out of range of me. He never blinked, and I found myself drawn into his empty stare, unable to break away until the uneven motion of the pickax brought the weapon between us.

"This guy can't hit the broadside of a barn. Can he even see you?" Arlene asked. She stood behind me, and her painted nails returned their soft grip to my shoulder.

"Don't think so." I thought a moment. Maybe sound would snap him out of it. I pulled my gun, pointed it at the planked floor, and, ignoring Al's shouts to not shoot up his place, I fired it. The women on the stairs screamed, Al cursed, and splinters of wood shot up, flying out in all directions.

One, I counted. Never lose track of your ammunition. My father's personal motto. Too bad it hadn't been one to live by.

The miner didn't hesitate and took a step forward to close the distance between us. His body now blocked my view of the rest of the room, but I could hear sounds of struggle and breakage. With one hand, I aimed my pistol at my attacker's chest. The other I held palm out in what I hoped was a calming gesture, though if he really couldn't see me, there wasn't much point. The threat of getting shot didn't work. Time for a gentler approach. "Let's all take it easy," I said, pitching my voice low and even despite the pounding of my heart and the racing of my pulse.

Swoosh. The pick passed in front of my face, close enough for the breeze it made to flutter stray strands of my hair.

"Cali...."

I shifted to the side, giving Arlene a chance to get clear while I took a shuffle-step toward the center of the saloon. In my peripheral vision I could see the other miner, this one armed with a shovel, bearing down on Al. He slammed the tool, edge first, into the bar, leaving a deep gouge in the polished wood. The clang resounded through the room, carrying over the whimpers of the women on the second floor.

Where the hell was Jake when I needed him?

My attacker took another swing at me and I backpedaled, the heel of my boot catching in the skirts of the fallen serving girl. One arm pinwheeling, I clung to my pistol and fought to avoid a wild shot as I toppled over the body. My spine met the hard floor, air whoofing from my lungs.

The miner loomed over me, cracked yellow teeth visible in the open mouth that now worked like he was trying to say something but no longer had the capacity to form words. He hauled the pickax up, raising it above his head in preparation to bring it down on my skull. A chair shattered on his shoulders, Arlene holding the remaining sticks that had been its legs, her deep brown eyes widening when it had no effect.

Enough was enough. I brought my Smith & Wesson to bear.

The pickax fell and I fired, then rolled, awkward in my struggle to propel myself over the body of the server. Shards from the broken glassware cut into my skin where my shirt and vest had ridden up. A large piece bit deep into my back, and warm wetness flowed.

Two.

The gunshots I'd fired had my ears ringing, and disorientation kept me from tracking the other people in the bar.

The floorboards beneath me trembled with the miner's impact. I released the breath I'd been holding, letting my eyes close for just a moment, relief draining away the rush of my near death.

Something moved in front of my closed eyelids, blocking out my perception of light beyond.

When I'd killed my attacker, I'd lowered my gun. I raised it once more, opening my eyes at the same time, and got a yelp in response.

"Whoa, Cali!"

Arlene. I jerked the pistol away from her ample chest. Using my elbows, I propped myself up, focusing on the fallen miner with a messy hole in his forehead. Arlene caught me under one arm and pulled, giving me the assist I needed to stand on shaky limbs.

"You all right, darlin'?" Accent slow and sweet as honey, she pressed her snug-fitting bodice against me, the one I'd peeled her out of Christmas the year before. My arms went around her as if they had a mind of their own. She was shaking. So was I.

For just a moment, I indulged in her warmth and the sheer femininity of her. Man's profession and masculine needs. Sometimes I forgot just how *wrong* I was and what would happen if my neighbors found out I sought female company when nights got long. In the heart-pounding exhilaration of survival, I took a quick look around, saw no one was paying us any mind, and leaned in for a reckless kiss.

The blast of Al's shotgun made us both jump. We whirled in unison, Arlene's skirts twirling in a wide flare, to watch the second miner drop his shovel and topple into one of the few remaining upright tables, cracking it down the middle with his weight.

Sanity returned. I gently pushed Arlene away. "You lost the right to call me darlin'," I growled, low and bitter. Last week, on one of my "inspection tours," I'd caught her upstairs with Lucinda, one of the other girls. Sleeping with men to earn her keep I understood, though I'd been trying to convince her to increase her daytime hours working at the general store. Quite another thing to sleep with other women for pleasure when she was supposed to secretly be my girl. Arlene had been a born flirt from the moment she arrived in town, but she could have been discreet enough not to let me walk in on them, whether I had any legitimate claim on her or not.

Instead of getting riled, her grin returned. Rather than make me want to despise her more, it actually worked to disarm me, as usual. Dang it. Maybe I didn't have any claim, but she didn't have to flaunt the fact.

Arlene didn't leave my side as I picked my way to the last miner. "Damn," I said, glancing at Al, "I wish you hadn't had to do that."

He shrugged, knowing I couldn't blame him. Man had a right to defend himself. So did I.

I nudged the miner with the toe of my boot. No response. Didn't expect one. What I *had* expected was a pool of blood forming beneath the corpse, but I wasn't getting that any more than I was getting the nice, quiet Monday I'd wished for.

"What in tarnation?" Arlene had noticed it too.

"Anyone seen Doc?" I glanced at the fallen serving girl, then toward the shattered front window where a third corpse lay beyond. "We're gonna need his services."

A step creaked under the tread of heavy foot-falls. "I'm here, Sheriff." Doc Wilson trudged down the stairs, black bag in one hand, the other pulling up suspenders over his white undershirt. Guess the commotion had caught him with both boots under the bed. Alongside Lucinda's shoes, no doubt, since she hadn't been one of the girls on the stairs. He snapped the suspenders into place and ran a hand through his long beard, effectively combing it out.

I gestured toward the bodies, pointing an index finger at the barmaid. "Her first. She's the only one still breathing."

Doc grunted and went to work, kneeling and gently rolling the girl over. "Not anymore," he said, deep sadness in each word.

My jaw clenched, and I suppressed a growl of frustration. Not his fault.

I knew Doc's emotions mirrored my own. He might come off gruff and unsociable (except with the upstairs ladies), but he cared about his patients, each and every one. We were damn lucky to have him in Oblivion. Not a lot of good medical care in the New Mexico territory. Probably wouldn't be until we gained statehood and more folks decided living in the middle of nowhere might be worthwhile.

I turned from the dead woman's body, trying not to picture all the welcoming smiles, bawdy jokes, and free drinks she'd slipped to me when Al wasn't looking. "Where the hell is Jake?"

Someone groaned behind the bar. I heard a thud as Al put the shotgun back in its hiding place. "He's back here. Got hit upside the head with the backside of a shovel the second he stepped in. Arlene and me dragged him behind the bar when things really started to fly."

I nodded to him, then Arlene. "That's two I owe you," I said quietly.

She waved the gesture away. "Just don't arrest me if you catch me workin' outside the saloon."

My gaze narrowed. "You make house calls?" Exchanging sexual favors for money was illegal everywhere in town except the saloon's second-floor bedrooms. It was in the bylaws.

Arlene raised an eyebrow, and my face flushed—not a common occurrence.

Of course she made house calls. She'd been in my bedroom a time or two. Why should it surprise me that I hadn't been her only after-hours acquaintance? But it did. And it hurt. She'd never asked me for payment. Said we had something special. We'd even talked about running off, starting a farm or ranch of our own as "friends," but I guess those had been just fantasies. For her.

"Maybe," she admitted. "I just don't get caught."

Doc cleared his throat, and I shook off my embarrassment. The physician finished up with Cindy, closing her eyes and crossing her hands over her chest. Something about her position bothered me.

Cindy lay in the center of the room, the area the townsfolk used for dancing in the evenings. There was nothing in the vicinity for her to hit when she went down, except maybe the floor itself. I scanned her forehead for signs of injury and found none. No bumps, no forming bruises, no blood.

"What killed her?"

Doc rocked back on his heels. "Not sure yet." He turned to the others in the bar. "Anyone see what happened?"

"It was the darndest thing," Al said, face paler than fresh cream. "When them miners first came in, she tried to offer them chairs and drinks, and then she stopped. Just stopped. And stared like she couldn't look away." He shook his head. "Next thing I know, she's lyin' on the floor and the miners start swinging axes and shovels."

"Heart attack, maybe," Doc muttered. He didn't sound convinced. "Lips are blue. I checked her throat. She didn't choke on anything, but…." He shrugged.

When doctors shrugged, I knew I had reason to worry.

I remembered the way the miner's gaze had held my own and shuddered. Blind or not, that stare had power.

Hank crept out from behind the piano so as to help Al carry the server outside, presumably to lay her out next to the other body and let Preacher Xanthis perform his duties. Then Doc took his medical bag behind the bar to tend to Jake.

"After the deputy's head and Arlene's cut shoulder comes you," Doc told me.

I blinked, the piece of glass in my back all but forgotten in the excitement. Now that he'd gone and mentioned it, though, it ached and throbbed. I gently probed the area around it, only to have my hand come away sticky and red. Nothing wrong with *my*

bleeding, that was for sure. It half soaked my shirt
and ran down my dungarees. And blood was even
worse to get out of fabric than pig shit.

Arlene returned to my side just as a wave of dizziness hit, threatening to send me to the floor. She
caught my arm, dragging me to a fallen chair and
kicking it upright with a practiced move of her high-
heeled boot. With extreme gentleness, she settled me
in it and took an adjacent one. Didn't matter how
gentle she was, the shifting hurt like hell. Air hissed
out between my teeth.

Arlene covered the hand resting on my knee
with her own. Its warmth drove away some of the
chill settling in my body. "Be still, Cali. I know it's
not in your nature…."

Good thing Doc showed up before I went into
detail about *Arlene's* nature.

"Tend to the sheriff first," she said, pressing a bar
rag against her own cut. "Mine's nothing much."

I would have argued, but she was right. The gash
on her shoulder wasn't nearly as deep as I'd first
thought, and it had almost stopped bleeding, whereas
the trickle down my back had turned to a flood.

Ten minutes later the bloodied glass hit the floor,
a much bigger piece than I'd pictured. Large, callused hands wrapped bandages around my midsec-
tion and tied them in place, then carefully readjusted
my shirt and vest over them. He gave a satisfied hm-
mph at his handiwork and headed out the swinging
doors to check the miner lying in the street.

Jake appeared from behind the bar, looking as
unsteady as I felt and carrying two shot glasses of

whiskey. He also sported white bandages around his head.

Some of the liquid sloshed on the table when my deputy set them down. Sinful waste.

Drinking with the sun high went against my code, but today I'd make an exception. I wrapped thumb and forefinger around the glass, hand more unsteady than I would have liked, and downed most of the shot in one gulp. The whiskey burned a path down my throat, melting the ice encasing my bones.

Everything froze over again when I took in Doc's expression from where he stood in the doorway.

"Sheriff, we need to talk."

I motioned him over, ejected Arlene from her seat with a jerk of my chin, and shooed her toward the bar. She pouted at me. I swallowed down a gulp of guilt. Maybe it was time to give her another chance. Maybe. Nights got cold and lonely in Oblivion, especially for someone with my proclivities. Finding a like-minded woman wasn't easy in these parts.

Doc eased down beside me. He kept his tones hushed, words carrying to Jake and myself alone. "I didn't come out on the upper landing till the shots started," he confessed. The heavy scent of beer wafted across the table. No wonder he hadn't heard the fight start.

I peered closer at him. Bloodshot eyes met mine. Jesus, I hoped he hadn't been too hungover to patch me up properly. Twisting, I tried to get a good look at the wound. Neat strips of white covered the injury, and there was no sign of blood, but I couldn't see everything without a mirror. I'd need help changing the bandages too. An image of Arlene sliding her palms across my bare skin rose unbidden in my mind's eye, and I shoved it away.

"No one expected you to get involved, Doc," I assured him. "Least not until the shooting stopped. Not much use to anyone if you're dead."

He favored me with one of his rare smiles. "Not my point. My point is," he said, staring out the saloon door, "am I supposed to believe these miners died here, today, just now?"

"Lord's truth," I said, already knowing where this conversation headed.

"Not possible."

"You callin' the sheriff a liar?" Jake's voice dipped dangerously low.

I laid a hand on his wrist. "He's not. He's just as confused as I am."

Doc nodded, his beard waggling as he did so. He'd gotten some gray in there. No doubt this situation would add a few more strands. "No blood, at least not their own. Plenty of stains on the clothing, though. I haven't seen this much death in town since…." He trailed off in embarrassment, realizing I wouldn't appreciate *that night* being brought up.

"No fresh blood," I agreed, sticking to the problem at hand. The past could stay in the goddamn past. "And they're cold."

Al stepped back inside. With one finger, Doc signaled him for a drink. "By my reckoning, those men departed this world at least two days ago, maybe more."

I shook my head as Al approached with Doc's beer. "They walked and talked their way in here." Not to mention swinging a pickax and a shovel. Outside of the horror dime novels I'd sneak-read when Ma buried me in the classics, dead folks didn't do those things.

"Not talked," Al interrupted, handing off the bottle. "Just walked. That's why Hank stopped the piano playin'. Them miners just stopped in the doorway, staring at nothing, then staring at poor Cindy."

"So, who tossed that one guy out on his ear?" Not that I'd be charging anyone with murder. Clearly any action the patrons had taken had been self-defense, and a big advantage of being sheriff in a small town meant I could judge things as I saw fit.

Arlene stepped forward. Often I'd wondered if she could read lips. Her perceptiveness served her well while working with her customers, I was sure. Didn't mean I had to like it.

"Katy and I threw him out," she said. One of the girls on the stairs offered a weak wave. "He wasn't too big for the both of us together. Grabbed him by his suspenders and tossed. You gonna arrest us, Sheriff?"

I grinned. "Not today. Way I see it, eliminating a public threat is community service."

"Oh, we're all about community service," Katy called between the stair railings. The men chuckled.

I held my peace and returned my attention to Doc. "So, what're we lookin' at?"

"No idea," Doc admitted. "Let me send a wire to a friend of mine in Chicago. He's a highfalutin coroner with the police force there."

"Why not use the store's telephone? Don't we need an answer right quick?" Jake asked.

I shook my head. "We also need to rightly keep this quiet." And making a call from the very public general store was no way to do that.

"Besides, the dang thing isn't working, almost never is," Doc put in. "Newfangled inventions." He spat on the floor while I hid a grin. Telephones had been around for more than a decade, working just fine in the major cities, even if Oblivion only boasted one.

"Charge the telegram to the sheriff's office," I said. Sooner we got this cleared up the better.

"Or," Jake added, "you might want to give a little more credence to those old Indian tales about the mines being haunted."

I sat bolt upright, the motion stretching my injury and making me wince. Draining the final sip of my whiskey took the edge off the pain. "Keep that under your hats, gentlemen. Last thing we need around here is folks worrying about hoodoo and stirring up troubles by blaming our problems on the tribes." The local natives were peaceful but as emotionally prickly as cacti. It was an uneasy peace, mostly due to a lot of talking, trading, and general hard work on my part. I would not let three dead miners ruin all that.

But Doc shook his head, his cheeks flushing a faint pink above the line of his beard. "'Fraid that ain't gonna happen, Sheriff. Preacher Xanthis was next to me while I was trying to determine the time of death. I'm afraid shock kept me from being as discreet as I should have been. He took off, screaming about demons and black magic, that damn bird of his squawking up a storm. He's probably organizing special services already."

"Just wonderful." I signaled to Al for another shot. "Add that to the fact that we might have another victim somewhere around here. All that blood on their clothes didn't appear out of thin air, and it's too dry to be from this fight." On second thought, I held up two fingers to Al and ignored Arlene's frown of disapproval. My drinking was nothing compared to her profession. She could go to hell on this one. Besides, way things were headed, we might all join her soon. "Put that on the mayor's tab," I told the bartender. Fighting walking dead men went beyond the call of duty. Behind me, Hank dusted glass off the piano bench and started to play, trying to get things back to normal, but any tune, even a melancholy one, seemed out of place.

Al poured me the double shot of whiskey, including one for my deputy as well. "On the house," he declared. He had to be really rattled to give away liquor.

"*Shee*-it," Jake muttered under his breath.

I couldn't have put it better myself.

CHAPTER 3

WE DIDN'T find another body in Oblivion. Combing the outskirts of the town turned up no further clues, even when we repeated our search the next morning in full daylight. I enlisted the aid of some of the local boys, sending them out on horseback to the outlying farms and ranches, folks who mostly stayed out of touch except to trade goods and attend church, but the riders returned with no new information. That left us one more place to look for the source of the blood—the mining camp. Maybe we'd find some answers there.

I certainly hoped so. Every glance, every inquiry as to my progress seemed accusatory. With my reputation for getting things done, Oblivion's citizens expected me to pull conclusions out of thin air.

The once productive mine lay about a mile east, and a steady stream of hopeful men had increased to a flood since the last reported gold strike, even though that had been almost a year back and nothing since. I had no idea how they managed to survive so long without income. Maybe they were hiring themselves out to the local farms and ranches. Hell if I knew. The mine was outside my jurisdiction. Maybe greed just kept a man going. Even after death.

Six of us headed out; Jake, Doc, Arlene, and I had guns. Could hardly believe it when she volunteered, decked out in riding breeches and a white lace top that revealed her shoulders—probably bought it off one of those Mexican traders that came through from time to time. The sidearm also caught me by surprise, since she rarely carried it, but a saloon girl being able to defend herself wasn't so surprising. When I asked her why she wanted to come along, she said, "Those miners have wives and children out there. If there's been trouble with their menfolk, someone will need to see to them. You aren't exactly the homemaker type, Sheriff."

True enough.

I also brought Sam, one of the ranchers living on the outskirts of Oblivion. He gave me a grim smile from his wagon's driver's seat—a wagon big enough to transport wounded, or more corpses, which seemed the likelier possibility.

Normally, I wouldn't involve a family man like Sam, but I needed him, and he owed me. In my first week on the job, I'd kept his cattle from being rustled.

And the rustler taking liberties with Sam's daughter? I'd shot him.

In the head.

Twice.

I dragged Preacher Xanthis along, too, as much to offer prayers for the dead as to keep the man of

God from spreading more demon tales and stirring up further trouble. He'd held two special services since the saloon incident, and I could hear the singing and the "Praise the Lords" all the way down the street on my porch. I'd had over a dozen visitors to my tiny office before breakfast, from the mayor to the schoolteacher, all asking what news I had and what they should do to protect themselves.

Good Lord, people. I'm not your guardian angel.

I'd been half tempted to recommend Sunday school and clean living, or make up some fool procedures for them to follow—radish tops hung in doorways and walking backward, naked, to the outhouse, but hell, I didn't know what was going on any more than they did.

Besides, no one wanted to see the mayor walking around naked.

I took point in our little posse, with Chessie, my chestnut mare (I'd never been real inventive with names), unusually skittish beneath me. The volunteers rode in pairs behind, and Sam's wagon brought up the rear, wheels clacking over stones and dirt. Xanthis had the damn bird with him, and it squawked every ten yards or so, setting my teeth on edge and adding to a headache behind my eyes that the whiskey had started the night before. When we came within sight of the encampment, Pandora took off from the preacher's shoulder, flew around the distant circle of tents, a blur of red and gold in the midday sun, vanished from sight for a brief spell, and returned to her owner with a pitiable little cry.

She hunkered against him, and I would swear her tiny body trembled.

A fearful vise closed around my heart and squeezed. If the bird's reaction was a predictor, we were in for some bad times.

We'd ridden a little farther when Arlene spurred her palomino up beside my horse. "You smell that?" All I could smell was her sweet perfume—honeysuckle and maple sugar today—making my head spin. Then the breeze shifted and I caught the stench she referred to—one of rot and death.

"Yeah. Dammit." Using profanity around a lady wasn't my habit, but I knew she wouldn't scold me for it.

I called a halt at the edge of the ring of tents, a dozen or so haphazard peaks of canvas, two or three leaning or toppled inward. By this point, all my companions were covering their noses and mouths with their hands. Xanthis pulled his collar up against the putrid odor, and the horses shifted their weights beneath us, snorting and pawing at the ground. Someone gagged. I thought it was Jake but didn't want to embarrass him by checking. "A few had their families with them," I reminded everyone. Arlene looked grim. I thought back to the clusters I'd seen entering the church. "Wives, kids." Not the most common practice, but sometimes everyone in a family got into the mining. The men would break up the rocks, and the women and children would sort through the bits, searching for gold dust. Having a few wives along made for better meals, too, most likely.

I studied the scene in silence. A loose tent flap blew in the wind, slapping in frustrated repetition, but that was the only motion or sound. No cooking fires, no women hanging out the wash, no kids playing. Nothing. Nothing but the smell. Oh God, the smell. It hung heavy in the air like pig carcasses left too long at the butcher's.

Jake lost it, leaning over in the saddle and spewing his breakfast across the dirt. Arlene reached over from her saddle and patted his back. I was proud of the other men for not giving him a hard time about it, and after a moment he wiped his mouth on his sleeve and nodded his willingness to carry on.

Five of us rode forward. I left Sam behind. His team of mares looked ready to bolt, and the last thing we needed to deal with was spooked horses and a runaway wagon. Been there. Done that. Still had the scars on my right leg to prove it.

In the center of the tents, we stopped again. All of us dismounted, the impact of our boots stirring up more dust than the wind already had. "Spread out," I called to Jake and Arlene. Though I was reluctant to send her away from me, searching separately would speed things up and get us away from here faster. "We'll search every tent. Then I'll check the mine. Maybe some took refuge there." A shiver made its way up the back of my neck. I did not relish the thought of investigating that dark, cold shaft. Even before they'd discovered gold, the caves made their way into my nightmares.

I'm so sorry, Mrs. Pendleton. We found your boy. He must have gotten lost... couldn't find his way

back out. I'm so sorry. I loved my job, loved when I
helped folks get their lives in order, when I was successful at protecting my people, but on days like that
one and this, it could be the worst career on Earth.
I did not want to tell any more families they'd lost
their loved ones.

I licked suddenly parched lips, wishing I had a
drink and not thinking of water. Damn, I didn't need
to start that habit again. One indulgence last night.
That's all it had been. Now I wanted another. I'd
thought that demon long dead.

But now the dead could walk.

I needed that drink.

With Doc and the preacher hanging back, ready
to provide two very different kinds of comfort to
whomever we found, Jake, Arlene, and I began pulling aside tent flaps. Nothing in the first tent except
discarded clothes, bedrolls, and some metal pots and
pans. I glanced over at Arlene standing beside the
second tent. She shook her head at me, long brown
curls swinging back and forth. No one there, either.

Jake's shriek of fear made all the hairs stand up
on my arms, and I had my pistol in my hand before I
even realized I'd drawn it.

Easy, Cali, I warned myself. *You're on edge.
Don't want to accidentally shoot the good guys.*

Whirling, I spotted my deputy staggering away
from one of the tents, something large, black, and
feathered clawing with sharp talons at the bandages
on his head and screeching up a storm. Using one
hand to shield his face, he batted at the buzzard with
the other until it landed and retreated, hopping away,

then taking its bulky form awkwardly to the air and flapping off into the distance.

I followed the black dot across the bright blue sky until I was sure it had fled, then ran the few steps to my deputy, the others hot on my heels. "You all right?"

He turned wild eyes to me, but at least he still had two of them. "And you wonder why I want to shoot birds."

Pandora let out an offended screech behind us.

"Next Christmas, I'll let you kill my dinner, all right?" I said, laying a hand on his shoulder.

"If you let me cook it, you've got a deal."

I gave Jake a good-natured shove. "My cooking's not that bad."

"No deal."

I turned to Arlene. "You pull the flap, I'll shoot anything that tries to scratch our noses off."

She nodded, holding her gun in one hand, delicate fingers wrapping around the grip, and reaching with the other to grasp the canvas and tug it aside.

What I saw within brought my free hand up to cover my mouth, though whether it was to hold back a scream or vomit, I wasn't sure.

Four bodies in various states of being eaten lay in a pile in the center of the dirt floor of the tent. A cluster of buzzards circled the corpses on their knobby talons, staring each other down for dominance, though from the looks of things, they'd taken quite a few bites out of the exposed arms and faces of the victims. In one or two spots, I could see bones. Cheekbones, wrist bones, and skeletal fingers. Of children.

I stumbled away from the opening, sucking in lungfuls of hot, dry, cleaner air, and waved Doc and Xanthis inside. Maybe Doc could tell me what happened, and the preacher's duty was obvious. Arlene's palm came down to rub my back in soothing circles, but I shook her gently off. I still had my own job to do, and I wasn't a deputy. I was the sheriff.

Seven standing tents later, we thought we had all the camp's inhabitants accounted for, based on the number of bedrolls we'd found. Xanthis said he recognized most of them from church and didn't recall anyone missing. Of course, that didn't take into consideration those who might have followed other faiths or any newcomers to the mine. It did give me a temporary excuse not to explore the dark cavern looming at the opposite end of the encampment like a mouth ready to swallow me whole.

All the victims had died violently. All bore grievous wounds. And every single man, woman, and child had his or her eyes wide open. Well, those whose eyes hadn't been buzzard food.

We loaded the bodies into Sam's wagon, covering them with empty wheat and flour sacks from the general store. To satisfy my conscience, I forced myself to march up the slight rise and stop before the opening to the mine. But I wasn't going in. Nope. Not unless something gave me a definite reason to.

"This is the sheriff," I shouted. "Anybody in there?"

"…in there… in there…," my voice echoed back to me.

As if in response to my call, a frigid wind howled out of the pitch-black tunnel. I sucked in a breath as its force blew my hat clean off my head and whipped my braid around to thwack my cheeks.

What the hell?

An inhuman howl accompanied the gust, undulating in pitch and volume before it faded away. My throat closed on anything else I might have said, and I swallowed hard. The primal fear churning through my intestines threatened to send me running. I wanted to look and see if any of the others had heard the sound, but I knew they were likely too far away, and I couldn't turn my back on that opening. Instead, I unglued my boots from the dirt and walked backward until I stepped on the brim of my hat. I bent down to retrieve it while still watching the entrance, and then retreated as fast as propriety and my position would allow.

Just the wind, just the wind blowing through the tunnels, like organ pipes in a cathedral, I told myself. Yeah, a cathedral in hell.

But where had the wind come from?

The others were kneeling around one last body hidden by brush at the edge of the camp. Jake covered the mauled boy with a grain sack while Doc shot me a bleak look.

"Fresh," he said when I'd crouched beside him.

I dug one hand into the dirt and sand, small pebbles driving under my nails. "How long?"

"A few hours, maybe."

So, after we'd taken care of the three in the saloon.

"There's tracks," Arlene put in, pointing. "Looks like the kid ran away, then doubled back at some point."

Looking for survivors, maybe. Found another killer instead.

We loaded him with the others onto the bed of the wagon.

The preacher headed our procession returning to town, mouth moving in silent prayers only a lip-reader could interpret. With one hand on the reins, he held his cross outstretched before him in the other.

I couldn't work up the energy to tell him to calm down and put it away before he riled up the town again. Besides, it looked like we might need all the help we could get.

CHAPTER 4

IF ANYONE told me I'd head onto Paradise Found ranch alone and unarmed, I'd have called him crazy. But here I was, solitary and shotgun-less, sliding between two boulders bigger than me and trying not to make too much noise doing it. Not that I needed to sneak in or catch them unawares. These people knew me. I just had a faint hope to speak my concerns to their leader without the entire enclave overhearing the tale and thinking I'd lost my mind. I had enough panic going on in Oblivion.

No such luck. The perimeter guards "Robert" kept on patrol could have detected the passage of a snake. I'd been foolish to think I might slip past without them knowing it, and the rustling I heard in the brush confirmed my suspicions. The guards shoved through the spindly branches, ordering me to keep still. I hid a smile of amusement. They'd pitched their voices low, and they wore men's clothes with their hats pulled down over long lashes and shortened hair, but I knew them for who they were.

Women.

Women who felt as I did but had found a way to live, and love, as they chose. Women who'd been living off the land, surviving, creating, since before Oblivion had been built. Generations and generations of women who heard about this place and traveled far and hard to reach it. Women who now owned a sizable ranch under a man's name, who wore their manly disguises to come into Oblivion after sunset, catching the general store just before they closed up for the night to purchase their supplies, or stopping in the bank to deposit earnings once most everyone else was home having supper.

Women who'd come to me for help when drought turned times hard and nearly killed off their livestock. I'd organized a group of generous citizens to donate what they needed. Oblivion's God-fearing folks never learned quite whom they were donating *to*.

In an instant, I found myself flanked, one handsome woman angling a shotgun at my ribs, the other testing the sharpness of a knife with the tip of her thumb. Both bore fierce expressions as they searched me for weapons and found none. Cold chills whispered down my spine. I had to remind myself that this was standard procedure. No weapons allowed on the ranch other than their own. They were prickly, with short tempers, and had every right to be. The world hadn't treated them well.

"Gentlemen," I acknowledged them, nodding to each in turn.

Some of them preferred to be referred to as men. Didn't matter to me one way or another, and it earned me their respect. And reminded them I was on their side.

We held our respective positions, sizing one another up, though at two against one, there wasn't much for them to size. The morning sun beat down, and sweat formed beneath the brim of my hat. I'd had a few too many whiskeys with Jake and the boys. Arlene had joined us too, until she'd had to leave for work, and I couldn't stand to be in the saloon knowing what she was up to on the second floor. This was followed by a long night of restless sleep and bad dreams, and a longer morning putting out more panic fires amongst Oblivion's residents. The lingering hangover had set my head to throbbing, and the sunlight sent splinters of pain through my eyeballs. All that meant little patience for posturing.

"Sorry for the surprise visit. I should have sent word. I need to talk to Robert," I said, the formalities dropping easily from my lips. We might not be enemies, but they still didn't entirely trust me, even being a woman in a man's job. Pa had taught me when to tread lightly. "You gonna keep me out here dripping sweat all day?"

Then again, I'd been known to run my mouth at inopportune times.

One grunted and sheathed her blade, pointing forward to indicate I should precede them. The other kept her gun trained on me. Even facing away, I could sense the double barrels aimed at my back.

Stop it, Cali. Showing fear was not going to win me any points here.

Head held high with a faked confidence one of the big-city vaudeville performers would envy, I parted some scrubby bushes and entered the cluster of low buildings that made up the ranch compound.

A half dozen single-family homes, a large stable, a barn, and a bunkhouse stood in a rough cluster, one- and two-story light-colored structures of adobe or wood sheltered on one side by the mesas—reddish tan monsters protecting them all. In spring, the brush would hide the structures almost completely, but for now, they were a bit more vulnerable. On the opposite side stretched their fields, where a number of horses and a good-sized herd of cattle were grazing or lying down under a few scattered trees in the brutal heat. They had crops, too, wheat and corn, and some smaller gardens of vegetables with a few fruit trees thrown in for good measure.

I preceded my guards past the remnants of communal cooking fires, cooling after the morning meal, and women, dressed as women, sewing, cleaning up, washing clothes, and performing any number of other necessary tasks to make the ranch run. No children, though. But they'd gotten word to me that if we had any orphans needing to be raised, loved, and cared for, they were willing with open arms. If circumstances presented such, I intended to take them up on that offer.

Robert, formerly known as Roberta, stepped from the door of the largest of the homes, her sharp gaze finding me in an instant. She had short-cropped dirty-blond hair, the brightest blue eyes I'd ever seen, and a kindly wrinkled face that reminded me of my long-deceased grandmother, or in this case, maybe more like my grandfather. Unlike the guards, she greeted me with a warm smile and a wave of her age-spotted hand, then wiped her palms over her dungarees and held her right out for a firm shake. "Sheriff!" she said in an only slightly wavering alto. "What brings you out all this way?"

"Trouble," I said, unwilling to mince words. And just like that, my bravado disappeared, the exhaustion and worry caught up with me, and I had to lean a hand against the porch railing to steady myself.

Robert's smile vanished. She shooed the guards off with another wave, then gestured for me to sit upon one of two handcrafted rocking chairs outside the door, turning one to face the other. Excellent workmanship. Alexandra, "Alex," their carver, was really something with woodworking, and she sold the chairs at the general store from time to time, including the ones on my office porch.

I acknowledged her invitation with a nod and dropped into the chair, noting she studied me for a long moment before seating herself. A sudden memory struck me, of story time upon my father's knee, only today I was the one telling a story, and it was no fairy tale. More like the works of Edgar Allan Poe.

"Does this trouble involve us?" Robert asked.

"No, ma'am. Um, sir. I mean—"

She laughed. "I'll answer to either with no offense taken. So if it doesn't involve us, why bring it here? Don't you think we have enough troubles of our own?"

I met her gaze head-on. "More than your share. But our troubles may become yours if things keep going the way they have been. And besides, I value your experience. Maybe you can answer some of my questions."

Robert laughed harder. "You mean you value the fact that I'm old and I've seen a few things. Go on, ask your questions. Let's see if I can't help you some." She folded her hands over her stomach and waited.

Where to begin? I cleared my throat and dove in. "Oblivion had some… strangers visit us two days ago." Briefly, I outlined the events from the saloon and the mining camp, leaving no gory detail unspoken. I watched her face, waiting for the patronizing smile or a grandfatherly chuckle, and got neither.

Fixing her dark gaze on me, she nodded, then rattled off a few words in one of the local Indian languages. Something "look" and something-something "death." I didn't speak much of it myself, but I'd learned considerably more than most white folks in these parts. It helped in keeping things peaceful and carrying out trade.

"Eye Killers," she clarified when I continued to wait for an explanation and said nothing in return.

"Pardon?"

Robert leaned forward, resting her palms on her denim-covered knees. "That's what the Indians called them. A legend, but not one of theirs. Something they picked up from travelers and traders dating back generations, and then the Indians passed it along to our predecessors, the women who founded this commune, which became the ranch you see around you today. No idea where it originally started, a legend about demons born to cursed women. Women who slept with no man, yet birthed children."

I swallowed the snicker that threatened to escape my pursed lips. In my world, we didn't call those women "cursed." We called them "liars." In Arlene's line of work, she had to be extra careful timing her monthlies. If she got with child, no one would believe she was cursed, that was for sure.

However, I had thoughts. Lots of them. Such as, were those early women settlers looking for a way to have children of their own, and did they think the local tribes might have had a solution. Lots of folks thought Indians had some sort of magical abilities, but I'd never seen anything of it. They were people. Different beliefs. Different traditions. But people. And people didn't have babies unless the process involved both a man and a woman.

"According to the legend, the demons leave the newborn babes at birth, kill those closest to hand, and replace their spirits within their bodies. Then the dead walk, sometimes murdering others through brutal force, sometimes killing with their eyes. They never blink, and you cannot turn from them. They are violent in their rage." Like those she described, Robert's eyes never left mine, and I could read concern in them. Concern for me.

So, if Robert and this legend were to be believed, those miners who'd attacked us *were* already dead? Somewhere along the line, babies had been born possessed by these demons, which then left the babies, killed the miners, and transferred to the miners' bodies? I thought I had it all straight, but I wasn't sure. One point came through clearly, though. Walking dead men. That by itself was a lot to swallow, though it explained Doc's concerns. And mine.

To believe or not to believe. It fit, but it was quite the tall tale. Xanthis would tell me only belief led to salvation, though I doubted he had old travelers' legends and Eye Killers in mind. I made no indication of my doubts to Robert. She seemed to take this seriously, and I had no desire to cause offense.

Visions of my encounter with the miners rose in my memory. I'd wanted to look in their eyes—felt compelled to. And Cindy, the waitress, she'd faced them before she died. Belief was winning. I forced my attention back to my host. "Did the stories say where they came from initially? The caves?" Not sure why I made that leap, but the howling wind coming from the mines had haunted my nightmares.

She nodded. "I've heard different versions of the tale and read them in the journals of our founders here, but they all claim that since the start of time, these Eye Killers called the mesas their resting place. Generations ago, some of the tribes angered them by making their homes in the stone caverns. So the demons invaded their women. They made atonements by abandoning the caves, building their own pueblos, and leaving offerings of part of their harvest in the cave mouths until the Eye Killers left them alone." She broke eye contact with me, her gaze resting in the distance, in the past. "Then, years later, a few of our women tried their hand at mining, not where the mines are now, but the same general area of cliffs and caves. They worked alongside the men there, in disguise of course."

Of course.

"Some went missing. A few of their bodies were found, but others… our leaders of that time never knew what happened to them. They heard the stories and started leaving a small portion of what was earned here, putting it up on the rocks where the site had been to try to repay the damage caused, and we carry on that tradition. Maybe passing travelers take it. Maybe not. But it's always gone in the morning, and we sleep better at night." She focused on me again. "And no one else has disappeared. We tried to warn the newcomers when the mining started up again. The rock feels pain. It does not care for man's gold fever. It does not want to be…" She trailed off, gaze clouding. "…stripped, in this way. But they wouldn't listen, said we were fools. I believe their damage angered the demons who inhabit the rocks. At some point, the demons were reborn to untouched women, invading them in the way the men invade the earth." Robert paused, considering, her weathered face turned toward the sun, eyes squinted against the glare.

Not for the first time, I wondered at her age. That face, those eyes, they could have seen eighty or more years with the intensity they held, the sorrow.

"Then they must have left the children's bodies to kill and inhabit your… unexpected visitors," she went on. "Isolated as they are from the rest of

Oblivion, the miners would have been convenient. And once dead, they have no will of their own."

"Once born, they jump bodies, you're saying? Move to better... hosts?" I asked for clarification.

Robert nodded. "According to the legend and the entries in the journals we pass on from leader to leader. I've never encountered them myself and glad not to have."

I thought back, trying to add more specifics to what I thought I understood about the process. We'd had a number of births since my installation as sheriff in Oblivion, and probably quite a few more since the opening of the mine seven years before that, though I hadn't kept track of our citizens then. But none of the mothers I'd known had claimed immaculate conception. A couple had been young, though, and unwed. Maybe they knew better than to tell their fathers a wild tale like they were the next Virgin Marys.

I shifted on the rocking chair. "And it's only these rocks? This area?" We didn't get a lot of good communication out in the wasteland surrounding Oblivion, but passing travelers earned many a meal telling their wild tales and ghost stories when they came through. Surely, if other mines and miners had suffered a similar fate, we would have heard about it. Then again, I'd never heard this Eye Killer story until today.

"If all this is to be believed, these are the rocks the demons call home. I have never heard of their like elsewhere," Robert confirmed.

"So how do I get rid of our Eye Killers? Grain and corn and a few coins?" Oh, Xanthis would love that. Pagan offerings and rituals. He'd never let me live it down if I succumbed to "heathen ways." I could imagine his impromptu sermon already.

Didn't matter, because Robert was shaking her head again. "Your miners have given greater offense than ours once did." She swept a hand out in the general direction of the mines. "That first gold strike was small, nearly worthless. Very little was found, so very little was removed. And all they had back then were picks and axes. No dynamite, so no great destruction. Yours," she said, pointing a finger straight at my chest, "dug much deeper, blasted to get at what they couldn't easily reach, and I heard quite a bit was found before it ran dry. You'll need to offer something of equal value or replenish what you have stolen, and you'll have to replace it at the heart of the damage, wherever that may be."

The gold. She meant the gold.

My heart sank. No way would I convince anyone to return that. Though she had indicated something of equal value would also suffice, so it didn't have to be *that* gold. Didn't really matter. Oblivion barely got by, what with droughts, river floods, and the occasional cattle rustler or horse thief. Money got spent as fast as it got made. When gold did get found, folks celebrated, and rightly so. Not much to celebrate out in Oblivion. But that meant the riches went right quick. Even if I took up a collection, I'd never gather enough to appease these Eye Killers. And besides, what on earth would I tell my people I was collecting *for*?

Then came the issue of the "heart of the mine." I avoided the mine as much as possible. I had no idea where the diggers had first struck gold. Hoping our crazy preacher would have better ideas, I stood to leave.

"Wait, Sheriff McCade." Robert gestured toward one of the smoldering cooking fires. "Fire. According to the tales passed down, fire distracts these creatures. Forces them to blink. It won't stop them, and it works only for a short time, but you may need that time to live until you find a way to banish them." She rested a careful hand on my shoulder. "Be careful. Your people, and mine, need you. And you know, you would always be welcome here. Permanently."

I nodded my thanks, a warmth blossoming inside my chest. Yes, here I would be welcome, and I wouldn't have to hide anything about myself, anything at all. And if I could convince Arlene to come with me....

But right now, I had a job that needed doing. Reaching into my pocket, I produced a small paper bag of peppermints I'd picked up at the general store on my way out of town and offered them as thanks for the advice. They were Robert's favorites, and I always tried to bring her some. She took the sack in her wrinkled hands, peeked inside with some caution, and smiled.

"May God be with you," she said.

The guards returned, and I followed them to the edge of the ranch, nodding to each of them and thanking them for the escort.

On my return trip to Oblivion, I thought about Robert's final words. I hadn't been with God too much of late. Hopefully he didn't hold the same kind of grudge the Eye Killers had.

CHAPTER 5

BY THE time I got back to Oblivion, all of Robert's words were swirling around in my brain like flies over sour milk. Hundreds of half-formed plans jumbled around in there too: curfews for the residents, hopeless pleas to close the mine. The camp might be deserted for now, but more would come, driven by the gold fever that had claimed many a reasonable man. Even my authority as sheriff couldn't shut the operation down permanently. Oblivion didn't own the land where the cave rested. It sat too far outside the town proper. And sneaking in to dynamite the whole damn thing would probably send the rock-protecting demons into the ultimate frenzy.

Then came the doubt, pure and simple. We'd had three crazed killers on the loose, nothing more. No demons, no dead men walking around, no howling caves longing to be whole. My parents hadn't raised a child given to flights of fancy.

Superstitious myth and nonsense. That's all it was. And it was over.

Except for that last little boy. Who had killed *him*?

I settled myself at the desk in my tiny office, lighting the oil lamp standing on the corner of its scratched wood surface. I yanked open the drawer that always stuck and withdrew the bottle of whiskey buried deep within it. For a long moment, I contemplated it. Booze could be a demon for me, but dammit, I needed a drink. The cork came free with a pop, and I sloshed some of the amber liquid into a glass sitting beside my leather-bound journal.

I'd left the book out, something I never did, but the past couple of days' events had disrupted my usual routine. Turning to where I'd last stopped writing, I skimmed those events and sighed. I took a long pull on the whiskey bottle, not bothering with what I'd poured in the glass.

Damned if I knew what to do next.

The lamplight fell over a scattering of notes littering the rest of the desk—messages Jake had taken for me in my absence. I spotted one from the preacher, another from the mayor. If the hour wasn't so late, nearly ten o'clock, they'd be crowded around me, demanding to know what I intended to do about the current situation.

Brushing a couple of the slips of paper toward me with the heel of my hand, I saw several reports of folks gone missing over the last twenty-four hours: a rancher and his wife, the hotel desk clerk, and a little girl from one of the outlying farms. Well, that was just dandy.

I took another swig of Old Grand-Dad, its fire burning down my throat, and stared into the two empty cells on the opposite side of the office. Didn't get much trouble in Oblivion, really. At least we didn't before. The cells grew blurry as the night wore on. So did the words I scratched in the journal with a dull pencil.

Miners, Paradise Found ranch, the Eye Killers…. Arlene. Words and inspiration failed me, and I found myself sketching the saloon girl's pretty face, penciling in the high cheekbones and long eyelashes. Not a bad likeness, either, though that could have been the whiskey's influence on my inner art critic. I flipped through the pages, studying other pictures I'd drawn over the years. Ma had once thought to pay for lessons, but there'd never been anyone in town qualified to teach them. I jotted a few more words and drained the glass I'd poured when I first sat down.

I'd drunk enough to wonder if I could make it to my upstairs room without help, and I'd finished writing down everything I'd learned about the Eye Killers. I fumbled the leather-covered book into the safe behind my desk and spun the lock. Ridiculous precaution, but the locals had enough curiosity about the "lady sheriff" and little enough to do that they might go prying. I didn't need more gossip about my private life, and my last entry would only stir up the town gossips' hornets' nest. We didn't have much important paperwork in Oblivion. There was plenty of room in the safe.

I'd made it up a couple of steps, with generous support from the handrail, when the door to the office swung open and banged against the interior wall.

One of these days, I'd fix the hinges so it'd stop doing that and scaring the daylights out of me.

My gun came out of its holster before I finished
my turn, and I aimed it at the doorway. I could shoot
the ticks off a dog, sober. I could damn well hit a
body, dead or alive, no more than ten feet away no
matter how drunk I was.

"Easy, Cali." Arlene held her palms out in a pla-
cating gesture. The half grin had returned. "That's
the second time this week you've pointed a gun at
my chest." She batted those long lashes. "I'm starting to think you don't like me."

Her amusement faded when I went to holster the
S&W and missed. Got it on the second try, though.

"Cali? You been drinkin' again?" Her look of
sincere concern almost undid me, and I couldn't afford to come apart right now.

"You standing in for my ma again?" I returned,
slamming the weapon the rest of the way home and
managing the safety strap on the first attempt. Hoo-
ray for me. Anger at myself warred with my anger
at her.

Arlene closed the distance between us, skirts
and petticoats swirling around her shapely legs. Cup-
ping my cheek with one hand, she turned my face to
hers. Inches apart, her alcohol-blurry image blurred
further. "This isn't what your ma *or* pa would have
wanted from you."

I jerked my head away. "I can hold my liquor.
I drink with the boys all the time." The argument
fell flat when my head twist sent the room, and me,

tumbling. I landed on my ass a couple of steps up and reached back to rub my bruised rear end.

"Not like this," Arlene said. "I ain't seen you this drunk since the night…."

She didn't need to finish. I already knew she meant the night my parents died.

MY FATHER had been a U.S. Marshal, transporting prisoners from small towns like Oblivion to the big cities where they could stand proper trials and rot in proper prisons. On a rare journey home, he'd run across a lone gunman robbing a wagon full of new settlers. They'd gotten into a gunfight, and Pa won, shooting the robber in the head.

Once back in Oblivion, he got word that a group of outlaws were preying on some of the more isolated settlements like Oblivion. Not any of the real famous ones like Billy the Kid or the Dalton gang, but a bunch to take seriously nonetheless. The unnamed band of criminals had robbed a few banks in the area, stolen some horses from a handful of ranches, hit some supply wagons, including ones headed for Oblivion, and taken the shipments meant for the saloon and the store. But the most important piece of information he received was that they'd recently lost one of their own to a traveling U.S. Marshal, and they were right crazy about getting revenge. Everyone thought Pa's reputation and his authority would keep them out of the town proper. If the outlaws were going to strike, they'd go after Pa when he headed back out, so he'd have to be extra careful.

They'd been wrong.

The gang rode into town, much bigger than anyone had suspected, fifteen or more rough young men, drunk, angry, and well-armed.

Over a dozen citizens died that night. A bunch of us had taken shelter in the schoolhouse—my mother's schoolhouse, smart with its fresh coat of red paint and white trim. Somehow the outlaws had figured out Pa was with us, and they surrounded it. Ma was one of the first to die, a lucky shot through a window and through the heart. Even at twenty-six years of age, her loss hit me hard. I might have been a grown woman, but I'd always be her little girl.

In the midst of the attack, all I wanted was to throw myself into a corner and sob my heart out, but Pa wouldn't have it.

"The living have to fight for the privilege," he said to me, though his eyes told a different story of guilt, pain, and loss. "We'll mourn when we're safe." All for my benefit, but I let him believe he'd convinced me.

More followed Ma into death while we waited for help that never came. The sheriff and his deputy (his son) had ridden to the next town over to get more men, but it took over an hour to get there through the mesas on horseback, and as that hour passed and dragged into two, then four, it became more and more likely they'd fled for good. Pa and I and a few other townsmen kept the screaming, shouting gunmen at bay with our own pistols and rifles, but the outlaws had stolen ammunition to spare.

When Pa went down, a bullet in his gut and blood pooling beneath him, I knew he wouldn't survive. Doc knew, too, shaking his head at me with a grim tightness to his lips. Really, though, he'd died with Ma. In body, he'd stayed at the window, carrying out his duty to the town. In spirit, he'd crossed over with her, his face expressionless and his eyes vacant until he got hit too. In his last moments, Pa passed me his Marshal's badge, not that it carried any power once he died, but it meant something to him. And to me. His grip, always so strong, clung weakly to my hand.

"You're a survivor," he told me. "Don't make a liar out of me."

"I won't," I promised, with no idea how I'd keep my own word. "I love you." At least with Pa, I had the chance to say goodbye. I could only pray that in death, Ma could see into my heart.

He passed with a final wheezing breath, and I went to the back of the schoolroom and grasped the ladder leading up to the big old bell Ma rang every school day to let the town kids know class was about to begin.

A hand caught my arm.

"What the hell do you think you're doing?" Arlene.

I stared into her sweat-streaked face, barely aware of tears streaming down my own. "Whatever I have to," I told her, jerking free of her grip.

"Let them handle it." She gestured to the few men at the window. "They're picking them off."

Back then, Arlene hadn't yet learned to shoot. But she learned in the days following.

"Not fast enough. Can't you smell the smoke? Something's on fire." I pointed to the small patches of night sky I could make out around the bell. "We need someone up top. I'm the only one who can handle a gun who'll fit."

"Cali—"

"Don't. You want me to be more open to your opinions, run away with me."

In the bit of moonlight coming through the windows, I could swear she blushed. "I just wanted to say be careful."

I didn't know what to say to that, so I muttered something incoherent and climbed.

I had to suck in a breath and squeeze past the metal bell to make it onto the roof. One false move and I'd ring the dang thing and announce my presence to the entire attacking gang, but I managed it and crawled to the edge of the black slanted rooftop.

The outlaws on their horses rode circles around the building, forcing me to freeze each time they passed. Even in those days, before becoming sheriff, I dressed like a male, favoring dark colors. It made me just another shadow amongst shadows. Our enemies were easy enough to spot, though. While we'd kept the schoolhouse in darkness, between the noise of thunderous hoofbeats, the raucous drunken shouting and cursing, and the torches some carried, no one could miss seeing the robbers. We'd taken down a few. I could make out large mounds of fallen horses and smaller ones of men. But they knew to keep riding, moving too fast for good aim, firing at anything that moved behind our windows while gripping their mounts with their legs alone. The flames flickered over their faces, turning them into something out of Dante's *Inferno*.

I flashed back on nights by our hearth, Ma teaching me the classics, ensuring my education would serve me, regardless of the path I chose. There'd be no more such nights. I forced a breath through a suddenly tight chest.

And speaking of infernos, the outlaws had indeed set fire to several parts of the schoolhouse.

The front porch had caught, and the trellis up the east side with Ma's climbing roses, all burnt now, all ash. If we didn't drive the gang off soon, we'd be roasted alive.

I stretched out flat on my belly, hesitating when the structure creaked and groaned beneath me. I prayed none of the townsfolk inside would get the notion I was one of the attackers and fire a gun straight up. Hopefully, Arlene had warned them of my intentions. They needed to give me a few minutes to do what I'd come out here to do.

I lay still at an uncomfortable angle, head lower than my feet, squinting into the night while the cool air chilled my face. The breeze carried scents of sagebrush and smoke. Peace and war.

At last I spotted what I'd searched for—their leader, sitting atop his horse just beyond the circle of riders. His pride, his complete assurance, infuriated me to the point of seeing red beyond the flames.

I accounted for the passing riders coming between me and my target. Eight outlaws left in total, two near their leader for protection, five of them crossing my line of sight at almost even intervals, but not quite even enough for a definite count of the seconds. I judged the way the leader's horse shifted uneasily amidst all the noise and smoke. Hell, I even took the breeze into consideration as I held my breath and my finger tightened on the trigger of the pistol Pa had given me for my birthday.

The gun's report, so close to my ears, would have deafened me, but I'd been down in the school with all the other guns firing and every sound had already seemed muffled. Arlene and I had practically been shouting at each other to be heard above the racket. Besides, I didn't need to hear to know I'd hit what I'd aimed for—the leader's heart. He slid from the horse's back in slow motion to land in the dirt—an undignified lump of dead flesh. The riderless horse reared, flinging its head back in its distress.

"One," I whispered, hoping Pa would hear me somehow.

Keep count, Cali. Be sure to keep count.

We're only practicing.

Don't matter. You always keep count, you hear me?

Yeah, I could hear him in my head even now. I suspected he'd always be in there.

The outlaws' shouts and screams of fury carried even over the residual ringing in my ears, horrific, hideous sounds like banshees in the night. One paused to hurl another torch at our refuge, flinging it onto the roof to land a foot from where I lay. I grabbed it before it could catch, used my hat to beat out the flames so it wouldn't be seen when I dropped it, and deposited it directly over the edge into a horse trough in front of the school, just to be safe.

None of them saw me. All their attention focused on their leader, gathering him up and draping his body across his pawing horse. They must have assumed the shot had come from within the building, not atop it. Otherwise, faced with one young woman, they'd have killed me and finished murdering the rest of us. They rode away amidst a rain of howls and shouts, the chilling sounds promising future destruction, though they never returned after that horrible night, and later we heard that a posse had been sent out and caught them three towns over.

The next afternoon, with our dead buried and the damages under repair, the mayor took me aside for a private chat. Afterward, he held a special council.

"We need someone braver than that lily-livered Richards in the position of sheriff. Someone who won't light out of town the minute there's real trouble. Someone we can count on to do what needs to be done."

Mutterings echoed through the town hall. People had liked Sheriff Richards, but he'd never needed to show much bravery, never been tested the way he'd been the night before. And he'd failed, miserably.

"Now, we know troublin' times are ahead," the mayor continued. "Them bandits won't be the only ones. With the recent droughts and food shortages, outlaw gangs are forming all across the territories. We need a new lawman, but I'm not seeing any of our menfolk rushing to volunteer for the job." This earned a smattering of nervous chuckles. A few of the older boys and young men shuffled their feet or lifted a hand, but mothers and wives held them in check. Didn't blame them. No one wanted to lose a loved one. Or two.

I stood in the rear, side by side with Arlene, the backs of our hands brushing as our arms hung by our sides, me breathing in the scent of her favorite perfume and trying not to tear up. My head pounded from a tremendous hangover. The rush of the previous night had worn off, but the effects of the post-rush drinking hadn't. The loss of both parents had definitely sunk in. Arlene had found me wandering aimlessly through town the next morning. I hadn't slept. I couldn't go home. Oblivion's tiny hotel had offered me a room, free of charge out of gratitude, so I wouldn't have to return to that too-big-for-me-now house on the edge of town, and I'd crashed there for a couple of hours prior to the meeting.

I should have gussied up a bit, put on a better appearance for what I knew would be a momentous announcement from the mayor, but I couldn't work up the energy.

The hotel wouldn't let me freeload forever. If today's town meeting didn't go the way I hoped, I'd be heading for the poorhouse. No way I could afford to keep the family home. I made some money working at the stables, but it wasn't anything regular. Pa and Ma had let me live with them, Ma holding out some hope I might meet a nice young man who'd ask me to marry him, Pa knowing I wasn't the settling down type and likely knowing more than that about me.

So much to do, so much to take care of. I didn't know where to begin, and I'd pretty much lost myself in thought when Mayor Jones started talking again.

"I'm proposing something, well, rather radical, I must say," he said. "With her acceptance, the council and I have discussed it, and we're instating California McCade in the position of sheriff." He glanced meaningfully at the men in the room. "Assuming no one else wants to challenge her for the job."

Several people gasped in surprise at the mayor's announcement, but I didn't so much as blink an eye. He wasn't taking any chances on me refusing and embarrassing him. We'd discussed the whole thing earlier, from accommodations to salary, and I'd already agreed to take the job, assuming the town would have me.

"Are you crazy? Would you have your wife run the mayor's office?" shouted one of the cattlemen.

Which was, by no means, a foregone conclusion.

The mayor reddened at the outburst but didn't argue.

I snickered. If rumors were to be believed, his wife did, actually, run the office. Her husband made a good public figure, personable and well-spoken, but he had too much of a fondness for drink to be counted on to make the tough decisions. I let the gathered audience argue and waited to see which way the cards fell.

To be honest, I didn't much care either way. I should have been proud, honored, but all I felt was numb. I was mourning and hungover, and I really hadn't done anything to earn the position. I'd gone where no one else would have fit. I was a natural shot. Any man with those qualifications would have done the same.

I glanced around, noting some of our leaner men and boys, folks I hadn't paid much attention to the night before, what with everything going on, but I knew they'd been in the schoolhouse with me. Folks I knew could handle a gun.

So, maybe not.

A female sheriff. To my knowledge, it had never been done. The slow burn of determination built in my belly, a reason to keep going.

"Yeah?" came the voice of the mayor's wife when more dissenters got vocal. "And where were all of you while Cali was crawlin' across the school-house roof? Looking for a skirt to hide behind, no doubt."

"You calling us cowards?" a man shouted.

"You volunteering?" she hollered back.

The man shut up and shuffled his way toward the front doors.

Arlene's hand came down on my shoulder. "Don't even think about it, Cali." Her voice rasped against my ear.

"Why not?" I whispered without turning my head. It solved my employment problem and gave me a place to live, to boot.

"You can argue all you want." Mayor Jones turned away from the crowd. His smile beamed at me from across the room. "But I haven't seen any volunteers." He winked.

"Just, well, just because," Arlene stammered, at an unusual loss for words.

Now I did turn to face her. "Because you're worried about me takin' on a man's role in public rather than exclusive to your bedroom?" I whispered. Searching her eyes, I asked, "You makin' me a better offer?"

Arlene flushed red from the tops of her barely corset-covered breasts to her forehead. "You know we can't. Where would we go? What would we do?"

I had answers, but I kept them to myself. I'd sworn to protect Paradise Found's secrets unless I intended to join them. Arlene hadn't said yes, and I wasn't breaking that trust now. "We'd figure something out."

She shook her head, crossed her arms over her chest, and turned away from me.

It was the second time in as many days I'd cornered her on the topic. My emotions were raw, and I needed someone permanent to replace the ones I'd lost. I pivoted back to the podium. "Didn't think so," I muttered, anger boiling just beneath the surface of my calm exterior. In all my thoughts of the future, Arlene alone came to mind as an acceptable partner, someone I might be able to tolerate over the long haul. We both kept odd hours and liked a little whiskey now and then. We'd known each other since our teen years, understood each other's oddities. Compatibility at its finest.

All around us, clusters of folks muttered amongst themselves, shuffled their feet, or made for the exits. But I barely saw any of them through my haze of rage and hurt.

Dammit. After all I'd been through the last twenty-four hours, if she'd agreed, I would have packed our gear, saddled our horses, ridden with her out of Oblivion, and never looked back.

A single tear escaped and tumbled down my cheek, and I whisked it away with my shirtsleeve before anyone could see. Shows of emotion now wouldn't help people accept me as sheriff. And if Arlene didn't intend to fill the new void in my life, I'd take the whole damn town.

In the end, there were no other candidates. Mayor Jones had timed it perfectly. I was a bona fide hero, and he'd played on the town's fears. Besides, if anything happened to me, at least my death wouldn't make another family suffer the way I was.

I hired Jake Baylor as my deputy a week later. He didn't have leadership potential, but he took orders well enough. He had that "I'm going to save the world" glint in his eye—just what deputies, and sheriffs, needed.

Otherwise, I was alone in Oblivion and apparently going to stay that way.

CHAPTER 6

"CALI?"

Not as alone as I thought. Someone was calling me.

"Cali? Hey, Cali!"

And shaking me by the shoulder.

I blinked and stared into Arlene's concerned eyes. The sheriff's office reformed around me, blotting out the memories of how it had come to be mine. Arlene smiled, and it warmed something deep inside. We might not be "together," and we might indulge in other partners from time to time (okay, *she* might), but some piece of us would always be connected.

"You drifted away there," she said. "I thought you'd passed out. Too much whiskey and not enough sleep." Scrunching her body between me and the stairway wall, she slipped her arms beneath mine and hefted me up to my feet. "Let's get you to bed."

Any protests I might have made got lost in a jaw-cracking yawn. My muscles ached like I'd been in the saddle for a week. Losing folks under my protection had placed a heaviness in my chest I couldn't shake.

What the hell had I been thinking, getting myself drunk when I had killers to stop?

Another yawn put my conscience to rest. Alcohol or not, I needed sleep. Couldn't remember the last time I'd had a good, restful night, what with all the running around, searching for murderers and such. Nothing I could have done tonight—at least not well—drunk or not drunk.

Up the creaking stairs and into my solitary room. I blushed at the mess I'd left, not having planned on visitors. The old oak wardrobe stood open. My clothes poked out of drawers or dangled off-center from crooked hangers. The double-wide bed sat unmade against the far wall, beneath the solitary and very dirty window overlooking Oblivion's main street. I wasn't a good housekeeper on my best days, but this was particularly bad, even for me.

If Arlene ever needed more convincing I wasn't good romantic partner material, this was it.

To my relief, she made no comment, just plunked me down on the edge of the bed. The springs creaked beneath my weight. I groaned as I bent to remove my boots, but she stopped me with an uplifted hand and then pulled them off herself.

Had I washed up this morning? Couldn't remember. Must have used the water pitcher and sponging bowl on my dresser, since my plan had been to visit Robert at Paradise Found. One didn't meet with their leader while smelling like graveyard dirt, blood, and horses. Hopefully, my feet didn't stink.

Arlene unfastened my gun belt next, sliding the heavy weapon and holster from around my narrow waist. She draped the assembly over the chair across from the bed and hung hers beside it. Up until that moment, I hadn't even noticed she was wearing a gun belt around her tiny waist.

"Can't be too careful with things as they are," she murmured at my raised brow.

I managed to slip my vest off and toss it at the chair, missing the seat by a foot at least. It joined a variety of other discarded laundry on the floor. My hat had no better luck.

Arlene set both aright on top of my gun and belt and crossed to me.

"Slide over," she commanded.

I remained where I was, though the room rocked around me. I'd lost count of the number of shots I'd drunk, but I'd bet the bottle on my desk was down to a finger's worth or two.

"Lucinda, remember?" I slurred.

"Truth be told, in bed she wasn't very memorable. Probably why I get more business than she does." She squeezed her way to sit on the bed beside me, pulled off her own shoes, and tucked them under the bed. Taking my hand in hers, she drew it onto her skirt-covered knee. "You, however, are impossible to forget." Her tone sobered me a little, and I peered up at her. "I worried about you today when you took off."

I yanked my hand away. "Thought I was runnin' like our last sheriff?"

Arlene shook her head, eyebrows raised. "Never. I knew you were goin' to try to find answers, answers that maybe don't want findin'."

I drew in a breath to speak, but she cut me off.

"I worry about you. Haven't I earned that right?"

She had. Since she'd ridden up to the stables some ten years back on a horse who'd thrown a shoe, we'd had our ups and downs, but we'd always been there for each other. My folks hadn't approved of our "friendship" at first, her being in the profession she was, and they never found out exactly what that friendship entailed, though I suspected Pa knew, but her persistent charm had won them over.

Through the years, I'd wondered what kept a beautiful, intelligent woman like Arlene in a town like Oblivion doing the job she did. Now, in my drunken state, I thought I might be starting to see.

She leaned her head toward me, and this time I didn't pull away. When our lips met, hers caressed mine with gentle teasing. At least until I yawned again.

She laughed, tapping the tip of my nose with one delicate finger. "Till morning, then." Reaching down, she pulled my legs up on the bed and crawled around to lie between me and the wall. The window stood open, but New Mexico wasn't offering up any breezes tonight. Heat stifled my little room.

Sweat gathered on my neck and chest, but it couldn't keep me awake. Before I knew it, I'd fallen sound asleep, spooned up against Arlene, breathing in perfume—heather mixed with lavender and that pleasant fresh scent that could be no one's but hers.

THE HAIRS on my neck and arms stood up. I blinked into the darkness, waiting for my eyes to focus. The moon cast rays across the wood-planked floor and my little round woven carpet. Somewhere in the distance, a coyote howled. Another answered it, and then silence.

Arlene slept beside me, lips slightly parted, dead to the world, her curves in shadowed outline as tempting as always. It never ceased to amaze me how peaceful she looked when she slept. I ran one finger over her soft cheek, drawing my hand away when she stirred. She mumbled something, rolled, and returned to deeper sleep.

I stood and padded to the window in stockinged feet. From the moon's height, I could tell I'd rested a few hours, no more. The sleep had cleared my head, and my vision no longer blurred, but a headache thrummed just behind my eyes.

My first instinct told me to sleep more, but something had woken me up, and if it hadn't been Arlene....

A stair creaked.

A quick glance told me Arlene had locked the door to my room from the inside, but in my earlier drunkenness, I couldn't remember if she'd done the same with the one downstairs... couldn't even remember if she'd shut it.

Creak.

I scanned the rest of the room for my gun but didn't spot it. Damn, where had Arlene put my pistol and holster?

I moved to the door and held my breath, pressing my ear against it, straining for any other sounds.

I heard one—a faint whimper, almost like the mewling of a kitten, but not quite.

Creak.

Whatever it was didn't wear shoes. I couldn't hear footfalls. Just….

Something whimpered outside my bedroom door.

The squeak of bed springs almost stopped my heart in my chest, and I whirled to see Arlene sitting up, running a hand through her mussed hair. She blinked at me in confusion.

"Cali, what are you doing?" she whispered.

I opened my mouth to respond, when whatever was outside threw itself at the entry. I yelped at the impact, jumping away while the door shook in its frame and rattled the rusty hinges.

"What the hell?" Arlene demanded.

"Who's there?" I called at the same time.

Another crash against the door. In the center of the wood, I spotted a dark jagged line, a crack forming. It lengthened by inches as I watched. The whimpering increased in pitch and volume, rising to a whine and then an all-out howl of frustrated despair.

I backed away until my legs hit the bed, but Arlene was clambering off the end, stumbling in the darkness to the chair and tossing my vest and hat on the floor to reveal our weapons hanging in their holsters. She tossed mine onto the mattress beside me, and I snatched it up and hauled the pistol from the leather and aimed it at the door.

"Don't shoot until we know what we're dealing with," I cautioned, watching her point her own weapon. "I'm the sheriff. It might be someone searching for help."

"While trying to break your door in?" Another slam punctuated Arlene's words, and a hole formed in the center of the wood, splinters flying into the room.

A pale hand reached through the opening, moonlight glinting off white skin and a couple of gaudy rings—a woman's hand. It fumbled for the inner knob. At the same moment, several screams carried from outside the window, and I thought I detected smoke on the night air.

"Just hold on there!" I yelled to the unseen figure. The half moan/half howl rose again, sending chills skittering along my spine. Keeping my gun trained on the hand, I sidestepped around the bed until my butt connected with the window frame and I could turn for a quick look outside. What I saw made my heart drop. "Dammit! The general store's burning." Must've started quick. The white adobe exterior wouldn't have caught fire easily, but with all the grains and other combustibles inside and the wood flooring, one knocked-over lamp would have spread flames fast. The building glowed like an oven, orange-red at the doors and windows, fire licking through broken panes and the outside walls beginning to blacken but not burn.

Eye Killers got distracted by fire, or so Robert had said, but I figured someone fighting an Eye Killer could have started the blaze. Assuming Robert's explanation was true. Assuming I believed any of this.

The glow lit the night sky, clearly visible even at the far end of the main street. Dark figures raced around the store's exterior, some carrying lamps, others throwing buckets of water at the flames, but they didn't all look to be assisting. A few lurched about like the miners had when coming into town. As I watched, one attacked a man holding a lamp, sending the light flying and starting a new fire on the porch of the post office. The lurcher threw a hand across its face, trying to ward off the brightness while its potential victim got away.

"It's insanity out there." I pointed out the window.

The arm we couldn't see bashed against my bedroom door, and the whole thing caved inward to dump the woman on the floor.

"It's insanity in *here*," Arlene muttered.

I didn't dare take my eyes off the woman while she struggled to rise. Fumbling came from the corner, the clank of glass on metal, and a light flooded the room as Arlene lit the lamp I kept on my bedside table.

"Lucinda?" she asked, incredulous.

I stared. The woman's face jerked up, wide, glassy eyes meeting my own before I could turn away, raven-black hair framing a ghostly white face. Something gripped me from within, holding me in place, forcing me not to blink. It soaked up my thoughts like rainwater into dry earth.

"Lucinda, we can help you," Arlene said, stepping forward and letting her gun drop to her side. She reached out a hand.

Her motion partially across my line of sight jarred my brain loose. "No!" I commanded. Arlene froze where she stood. "The light." I couldn't make more words form. My teeth clenched around them like a vise.

I must have gotten something across to her, though, because she swung the lantern completely between us and Lucinda, the flickering flame causing Lucinda to blink and allowing me to break eye contact with her. Staggering to the side, I gripped the bedpost for support and drew short rapid breaths into my lungs. I hadn't been breathing. If Arlene hadn't intervened, I would've suffocated.

"You all right?" she asked, aiming her gun once more. Lucinda had made it to her knees. Some part of her mind still understood firearms because she hesitated at the sight of Arlene's pistol. Lucinda's mouth hung agape, but no coherent speech came out, only that mewling sound. I wouldn't make the mistake of meeting her eyes again.

"I think so," I answered, still panting. The wound in my back ached as each intake of air stretched the bandages and healing skin. "We need to lock her in one of the cells. Maybe Doc can figure some way to fix her." Even as I said it, I had big doubts. She looked as dead as the miners had, just still moving. But I'd have Doc try. She might have slept with my girl, but no one deserved this fate.

From outside, I heard folks shouting my name and cries and pleas for help. The fire must have been spreading. My head swiveled from Lucinda to the window, my soul torn between two sources of need.

"Go," Arlene told me. "I'll handle her."

"How?"

"Don't worry, darlin'. I roped a few calves before my saloon days. Born and raised on a ranch." She reached out and yanked the sheet off my bed, holding it out in front of her like a net. "Go on, shoo!"

For once I didn't argue with the "darlin'" or her orders. Lucinda had the doorway blocked, so I swung a leg over the windowsill in preparation to drop down onto the metal awning over the porch.

"Don't look in her eyes," I called as an afterthought.

Arlene threw the sheet, which fell over Lucinda's head and blotted out her gaze. She shrieked and clawed at it with broken red fingernails, tangling it further. "Got it covered." Arlene grinned, wide and unrepentant.

I focused on the heavens. God save me from smartass saloon girls. Then I dropped over the sill into the smokey night air.

CHAPTER 7

I HIT the metal awning in my stockinged feet, slipping and sliding on the smooth surface before I remembered my boots lay upstairs. Thank the good Lord the sun had been down for hours, letting the metal cool some. Regardless, I'd gone off half-cocked.

I skidded to the edge, catching my toes on the lip and pinwheeling my arms while trying to maintain my grip on the gun. Overbalanced, I toppled backward and clanged onto the overhang butt-first. Not the most auspicious of arrivals on the scene, that was for sure.

I flipped over onto my stomach, ignoring the heat seeping through my shirt, and scooted down until most of my body hung over the edge. Dangling by my fingertips, I released and dropped to the street.

From upstairs came the sounds of a scuffle, and I hesitated but had to trust Arlene to handle Lucinda. The glow in the sky had brightened, and bits of ash rained down to catch in my hair.

No hat, no boots, no gun belt. I must've been quite the sight as I trudged my way toward the fiery post office and general store. Drawing closer, I saw the saloon had caught as well, flames racing along the boardwalks between buildings and across wood floors. Al wouldn't have to replace that front window after all.

It had become pretty apparent that the fire had doomed the east end of town. My town. A town I'd sworn to protect and failed. My sight blurred for a moment as tears threatened, but I willed them away. This wasn't the time for that.

I hoped there'd be time later.

I drew closer to the chaos. Panic-stricken citizens darted past me with buckets, filling them from horse troughs, or running from those afflicted with whatever had gotten Lucinda and the miners. I still couldn't accept Robert's Eye Killers story as fact. My parents had raised me to use my head, to reason things out, and not give in to fanciful ideas. It had to be some disease like pox or polio, something new and deadly.

And unstoppable.

My cheeks burned from facing into the roaring flames and from a rage too intense to tamp down. My fingers tightened around the grip of my pistol, still fully loaded. It didn't take long to find a target. I aimed at Hank, the saloon's piano player. He'd tackled Al, and the two rolled across the ground, Al shouting obscenities and Hank making a noise like an injured horse screaming in the night. The two had always been best friends, like brothers. They'd never argue, let alone get into an all-out brawl. When Hank raised his head and howled, I caught sight of his glazed eyes and knew for certain.

I waited until their struggle paused for a moment with Hank still on top, then fired, the bullet piercing him beneath the chin.

"One." The syllable growled from my throat.

Beside me, the roof of the store caved in, crashing into the interior and drowning out whatever thanks Al might have offered.

Three steps brought me to another target, and I put a bullet through the forehead of Annabelle, the schoolteacher. She'd had one of her students transfixed, the Callahan boy. His lips had turned blue and his throat distended before I broke her gaze with my gunfire.

"Two." I watched the kid race screaming and panting into the darkness. Bending, I shut Annabelle's eyes. At least this time they didn't pop open. No blood, no surprise. Head shots seemed safer than heart. After all, it had worked for the miner who'd attacked me.

"Be gone! Be gone! I banish thee!"

The Sunday morning pulpit voice carried a full block from the church at the end of the street to where I stood beside the crumbling general store. Smoke and smells of burning corn and rye dizzied me, and I half imagined apparitions within the curling clouds, driven from their host bodies. Few sinners could resist the preacher's booming command.

Icy fingers reached from behind to grab my face and pull, attempting to turn me around. I swung an elbow back, driving it hard into a soft abdomen while biting the flesh of the hand down to the bone. Only the slightest of coppery-iron tastes met my tongue rather than the flood I'd expect from a normal human being. No scream of protest came from my attacker, but the fingers released, and I whirled and fired.

"Three," I whispered. Mayor Jones lay at my feet, unmoving. I'd never been a huge supporter of his politics, beyond his appointment of me as sheriff, of course, but he hadn't been a bad man. Now he was dead. By my hand. One thing to kill strangers. Quite another to kill folks I'd known all my life.

I shivered hard despite the heat of the flames in the buildings around me.

Men shouted and women shrieked as the post office collapsed in on itself. Sparks flew like fireflies, igniting the adjoining stables. I heard the panicked shrieks of the horses within, Chessie's unmistakable high-pitched whinny carrying above them all.

I didn't spot any more immediate threats to the townsfolk. Maybe the spreading fires had driven the attackers into the shadows. Some determined citizens had formed a bucket brigade, hopeless as it now seemed.

Considering, I wasn't entirely sure I wanted all those flames put out.

Instead of jumping into the line, I raced for the stables, threw open the door, and darted inside. Already it had filled with smoke, and I could see glowing spots in the wood of the walls and ceiling where the flames were eating their way through.

I released each trapped horse in succession, swinging open the stall gates and flinging myself to the side to avoid the stampeding animals. They disappeared through the open stable's doors, hopefully for us to recapture another day, if any of us survived this. But they wouldn't burn.

My Chessie pawed at the last gate, her hoof cracking sharp against the wood. "Easy, girl," I called over the roar of flames. "Easy, Chessie." She calmed at the sound of my voice, but her wide, too bright eyes told me she could bolt at any moment.

I released the crossbar and stood back, letting her do as she would. Even as frightened as she was, she hesitated, head tossing and nostrils flaring. She danced to the side, then returned to me, unwilling to leave me alone in the burning building.

"I'm right behind you, girl. Go on. Yah!" Reaching out, I slapped her gently on the flank, and she took off, neighing, into the night. Unlike the other horses, I knew she wouldn't go far. I'd raised her from a foal, been present at her birth, and she'd probably make straight for the sheriff's office and wait for me beside the hitching post there.

Eyes streaming and chest tight from smoke, I coughed my way outside into the marginally cooler air. My jaw clamped shut on a scream as a figure loomed up before me, all darkness and shadows.

Then I spotted the bird on the shadow's forearm.

"Dammit, Preacher, don't do that, not tonight."

Pandora squawked, cocking her head from side to side. Then she cooed at me, a soft little warble I'd never heard the creature produce before. Leaving

Xanthis's arm, she fluttered to my shoulder and settled her wings against her sides.

I'm not sure which of us was more surprised by
her actions, me or Xanthis.

"Not possible," the preacher murmured.

"What, that your pet might like me? You always
said she did." I turned on my heel and stalked away,
looking for something else to shoot, ignoring Pandora's scramble to balance herself. The schoolhouse
burned in the distance, one more casualty of the
flames. Maybe that damned building was just destined to burn to the ground sooner or later. I wondered how many lives we'd lost.

"Pandora and I have fought evil for centuries.
She can't choose another. Not now. Not when I'm so
close." Xanthis reached for the bird, but she swung
out a talon at his questing fingers. "You need me,"
he admonished the critter. "Without my help, you'll
never regain favor amongst the gods. They'll never
turn you back."

Pandora let out a long shriek, almost as if she
were trying to drown him out, shut him up. I couldn't
rightly blame her. This ranting was asylum-worthy.

"What the hell are you talking about?" I continued walking, not looking at him but keeping him in
the corner of my eye. His raving had risen to a whole
new level. Centuries, my ass. Fighting evil with a
glorified chicken on his arm. And the rest of it? God
only knew.

"Hell is exactly what I'm talking about. Demons
arisen, infesting those who've trespassed against

them and anyone else within their grasp, and me this
close to ending them."

I caught the glint of his cross as he waved it
about.

"You're *this close* to ending up dead," I snapped.

He kept ranting like he hadn't heard me. "No different from others I've vanquished: Medusa, harpies,
sirens, Apep in Egypt, Loki in the Norselands."

"You're mixing your cultures, Preacher. And
calling out other gods—isn't that pagan talk?" If
I humored him, let him ramble, it might calm him
down.

"All related, all related. Different names for the
same beings, different ways to deal with things but
interconnected just the same. And I've earned my re-
ward, my immortality. You can't take that from me!"

Was he shouting at me or the bird?

"You're out of your mind." No real surprise,
given the circumstances. My sanity hung by its own
fragile thread. As if reading my thoughts, Pandora
cooed into my ear and nuzzled my cheek. I could
actually grow to like this bird. Maybe.

Standing in the center of the main street, I turned
in a slow circle. Building after building was aflame,
the entire town crumbling around me. The roof of
my office shot brilliant orange-and-red fire into the
sky, and I could only hope Arlene had gotten herself
out in time. No sign of Chessie, thank God. Loyal
she might be, but not stupid. She'd find her way back
to me in the morning, if I was still around.

The bucket brigade had abandoned its efforts. People rushed into the doomed homes and

businesses, attempting to save whatever they could. At the open end of the street, more movement caught my attention—a horde of shambling figures: men, women, and children.

"Saints preserve us," Xanthis breathed beside me.

My thoughts exactly.

I scanned the buildings, watching unaffected people running to and fro, bundles of treasured possessions clutched to their chests or tossed into anything they could use to carry them. My eyes fell upon the church, its imposing structure with its tall steeple piercing the sky and dominating the town. Standing apart from the other buildings, it remained untouched by fire and, with the exception of some outlying farms and ranches, would likely be the only structure in Oblivion to survive the night.

"The church!" I shouted. "Get to the church!" I broke into a run, Pandora flapping on my shoulder, and grabbed every person I passed, screaming and pointing first at the approaching danger and then the religious sanctuary.

Many folks ignored me, so caught up in retrieval of their precious valuables, but a fair number followed me and the preacher as we led the way to the church steps.

The demon-possessed, or Eye Killers, or whatever they were had become clearly visible now, wide white eyes reflecting flames and moonlight, though apparently too far away to hypnotize anyone with their gazes. Yet.

Xanthis and I flanked the double church doors, hurrying folks through to the inside and shouting for them to move all the way forward to make room for as many as we could squeeze into the space. Given that our preacher expected everyone in church on Sunday, it had been designed to hold the entire population of Oblivion, so really, I just wanted people as far from the front doors as possible.

The mayor's wife, probably unaware that I'd shot her husband earlier in the evening, tripped on the front steps and dumped an armload of clothing and jewelry at our feet. She scrambled about on all fours, clutching and grasping at whatever she could salvage.

"Leave it," I ordered. The walking dead had gotten close enough for me to shoot. I pulled the trigger, catching one of the stable hands between the eyes. "Four," I whispered, and with my gun belt buried under the remains of my burned-out office, that left me two shots.

The scrabbling woman glared up at me. "This is all I have left. No home, and that good-for-nothing husband of mine off trying to get votes in the next election by playing hero."

Something inside me snapped. I seized the mayor's wife by the starched collar of her gingham dress and hauled her to her feet, holding her to face me full-on. "He's not 'playing hero.' He's dead. And unless you and everyone you're blocking behind you want to join him, you'll get your tail end in the church and get the hell out of the way!" With that, I shoved her hard through the double doors, and watched with satisfaction as the remaining townsfolk poured through after her.

"Back! Back!" Xanthis yelled, waving his cross high and wide. A few of the demon horde hesitated, gazes turning toward the glittering metal of the religious emblem, but most seemed unaffected.

"Get inside, Preacher." I laid a hand on his shoulder, all my anger gone in a rush of sudden exhaustion.

Two bullets, twenty or more possessed friends to hold off, and a breeze had kicked up, carrying ash and glowing embers ever closer to the church roof.

No hope, a voice murmured inside my head. *No hope.*

But I had to try.

When the town council swore me into office, none of this had been in my job description, but protecting Oblivion's citizens had, and I'd failed miserably at that.

"Preacher," I said again, raising my voice above the moans and wails of the risen dead, "inside, now. And take your bird with you." I nudged Pandora down my arm from my shoulder, but her talons dug into the fabric of my shirtsleeve.

Xanthis looked at me as if seeing me for the first time, then turned to Pandora. "She won't come to me. My time has ended. You've been chosen. I don't know why, but you've been chosen, and when the odds are better, she'll bring you forth to rise up and fight again." And with that lunatic pronouncement, he turned and marched into his church, abandoning me to the coming onslaught.

I scanned the shambling mass before me, wondering where I should place bullet number five.

Bullet six had a special purpose, a personal one, if the evening's proceedings went where I expected they would. I didn't know if it made a difference whether they killed me or I killed myself, but I'd do everything in my power to avoid becoming possessed or infected or whatever the hell was going on here.

On my arm, Pandora went still as stone. That's when I spotted Arlene.

Off to the side, but ahead of the others, she staggered toward me, Lucinda right behind her, and both covered in grievous blackened and blistered skin, but I knew them. I knew everyone in this crowd. I'd grown up with them, gone to school with them, built this town with them.

All gone. All gone.

A vicious trembling took up in my limbs, shock at what I'd had to do tonight finally catching up with me. It startled the bird, causing her to take flight in circles around me, but I blocked her out. My breath came in rapid gasps. My hand shook so badly I could barely sight my pistol.

Shot number five made the loudest sound I'd ever heard.

I watched Arlene's body tumble backward, falling at Lucinda's feet, though Lucinda didn't hesitate to go around Arlene's now truly lifeless form.

Choking down a sob, I turned and ran into the church, following Pandora and slamming and barring the doors behind me.

God, please let Arlene have found peace.

Let me find it too.

CHAPTER 8

WITH MY back against the inside of the church doors, I slid down them to land with a thump on the wooden floor. The first arrivals had lit the lamps, casting everything in eerie shadows. Pandora flapped toward the peak of the angled ceiling, then settled on one of the rafters to stare upon us all with solemn eyes.

Preacher Xanthis had made his way to the pulpit, where he held rapt most of the remaining townsfolk with his rousing speech of hell on earth and the glories of heaven. Yeah, I figured he knew we weren't leaving this building alive, any of us. We'd best all prepare ourselves.

A handful of people were standing pews on their ends to block the windows. However, a few folks crouched around me, Doc amongst them, handing me a cup of water, patting me on the shoulder, and generally watching for what I planned to do about all this.

Too bad I didn't have any plans in mind.

"What's our next move, Sheriff?" Sam had his daughter with him, one arm around her thin frame. The girl had never been quite the same after those cattle rustlers tried having their way with her, and now she looked how I felt—half catatonic and scared out of her wits. I searched the small crowd for Sam's wife but didn't see her. Didn't want to think much about her beyond that.

I opened my mouth to answer Sam's question, but before I could disappoint him, the wood behind me gave a mighty jolt, flinging me forward into Doc's arms. As I struggled to right myself, Xanthis came to a pause in his sermon, and a low moan carried through the closed doors—a moan that shifted to a word.

"Caaaliiii."

I turned to stare at the door, glad I couldn't see beyond it. I knew the voice. Heard it every damn day. Guess he was still looking to me for guidance, even in demon-possessed death. And hearing him told me something else as well. The Eye Killers were learning how to better manipulate their hosts.

"Aw hell, I'm sorry, Jake," I breathed. One more soul I'd let down. One more person I couldn't save.

"Not your fault, Sheriff," Doc assured me. "No mortal being could have foreseen this." He ran a hand through his scraggly beard. "Heard back from my pal in Chicago. 'Cording to him, ain't nothing could have produced those results in those miners' bodies short of witchcraft or voodoo." The physician gave me a half grin. "'Course, he also suggested I'd been hitting the sauce too hard again. Wish I had me a bottle now."

Me too.

The banging on the doors grew more insistent, bringing up images of Lucinda and by association, Arlene. I forced them into a box in the corner of my mind and closed the lid tight. No doubt they'd escape later if given opportunity, but not now. Dammit, not now.

Pressing my palms flat against the floor, I shoved to my feet, only swaying a little when I got there. Doc steadied me, then studied my face with a professional eye. "You should sit a bit longer, Cali. You're not altogether there yet. May not be for a while, and no shame in it, considerin'." His gaze turned to the doors trembling in their frame.

"Haven't got a while. Not gonna sit down and die, either. Get some folks to shore up the doors," I ordered, not waiting around to see those orders carried out. My vision blurry with tears, I stormed in torn and bloody socks to the pulpit. I caught Xanthis in mid-tirade as I reached across the polished wood surface, grabbed and shook him. "You're this great fighter of evil? This destroyer of monsters?"

The preacher's head bobbled up and down like a child's toy.

"Then how, dammit! How?"

His eyes darted to the side, toward the tiny door of the storage room where he kept the prayer books and hymnals, before he glanced quickly away.

"What? What's in there?" As a child, I'd helped put away those books any number of times and never seen anything in the closet beyond shelves and some dust and spiderwebs, maybe a few candles for dark, rainy Sundays.

Above us, Pandora screeched, the sound piercing and terrified. I followed the noise, spotting several glowing places in the church's ceiling, places where the fire had reached us at last. So much for that faint hope. Children screamed and parents clutched them, knowing they could do nothing to protect them further.

But maybe I could.

I pushed through the cluster of frightened people to the closet just as the damn bird settled once more on my shoulder. Throwing open the door, I scanned the interior and found exactly what I'd expected— dusty shelves of tattered hymnals. Behind me in the sanctuary, the roof creaked and cracked, and I turned back to see one of the crossbeams sagging in the center while everyone beneath hastened to reach the sides of the building. The pounding on the entry became a staccato of drums as more and more fists joined Jake's.

I wanted to smash something too, and I lashed out with my empty palm, slamming it on the bookshelves in front of me.

The shelves moved.

They swung inward on hidden hinges buried behind layers of dirt and mold to reveal a set of crude steps carved first into the earth beneath the church, then into what looked like stone in the flickering lamplight.

I felt someone behind me and knew it was Xanthis.

"Where does this lead?" I demanded, whirling on him. Was there a way out? A place of safety for the last remaining citizens of Oblivion? Had he kept it from us all?

Xanthis spread his hands in surrender. "It's more storage," he admitted. Then, after a pause, "And a tunnel."

"A tunnel," I said evenly, counting to ten in my head and taking a deep breath—anything I could do to keep from throttling him. "A tunnel to where?" Some sort of secret, safe escape route for the crazy avenger, no doubt.

"It leads into the gold mine."

Okay, maybe not so safe. A howl that might have been wind or might have been something far more harmful carried from the closet, raising the hairs on my arms and neck.

I turned to stare back down the steps as realization struck. All those miners. Going to church. They might have been seeking salvation, but they'd been doing something else too. Digging. For Xanthis.

This was what had kept the miners going, even when the mine had stopped producing gold.

"How did you pay them?" The collection basket never got *that* full.

For all his craziness, Xanthis had followed my train of thought. "I have my resources."

"In the basement?"

He nodded.

"And how did you keep it a secret?" Maybe not the best time for questions, but when something like this went on under my nose, I needed to know how.

"Pay desperate people enough, promise to keep paying them, and they'll keep quiet as—" Xanthis smiled without much humor. "—church mice."

"Let's see these resources." I took a quick step back into the church and checked the ceiling. The center beam had dropped a few more inches, and I could see stars past the smoke in a few places where the fire had made holes in the roof. The front doors had cracks running down their lengths as well, but the crossbar held. So far. Our sanctuary was rapidly becoming a deathtrap. I was no architect, but I hoped we had a few minutes to check the tunnel for more of the possessed. Wouldn't do to lead folks out of the frying pan, into the fire. Or, in this case, the other way around.

In the end, Pandora made the decision for me, squawking and taking off for the stairs, then disappearing into the depths of the stairwell. Grabbing a lamp from Doc, I followed, Xanthis right behind me.

I aimed my pistol with its single bullet straight ahead, the fingers of my other hand white-knuckled around the metal loop at the top of the lamp. The dirt, then stone steps sapped the warmth from my stockinged feet, sending new shivers up my calves and thighs.

We'd no sooner hit the bottom when I heard Doc's shouted curse from upstairs, followed by a tremendous crash and panicked screams that cut off midshriek. I turned and tried to race back up, pushing past a startled Xanthis, but a cloud of smoke and debris met me halfway.

Ash and dust filled my lungs, sending me into a fit of coughing that doubled me over where I stood. I hacked and heaved, eyes streaming from the irritation, lungs straining to draw a clear breath. The cave walls trembled with the impact of something heavy, and I heard a muffled clang from above. A piece of my mind identified it as the church bell falling, sounding its own death knell. Unable to see a damn thing, I let Xanthis grab my arm and tug me to the basement floor. In my haze, I heard Pandora screeching and felt wings flutter by my face, her feathers softer than rose petals.

Xanthis took the lamp from my suddenly limp fingers. A moment later, the space at the base of the stairs flooded with light as he lit a series of additional lamps hung along the walls at odd intervals.

I blinked to clear my vision, gaze going to the preacher as he remounted the stairs. He cast a sorrowful look in my direction. "Blocked, though I can hear some scratching and moaning from past the collapse. Evil never gives up."

So, the walking dead had invaded whatever remained of the church, no doubt finishing off the rest of Oblivion's inhabitants, while I sat down here, neat and pretty.

I wanted to throw up.

Instead, I stood and examined the room we were in, searching for the tunnel Xanthis had promised. I could follow it, get out through the gold mine, and circle back into Oblivion. If anyone had survived, I intended to find them. If not, Chessie was out there somewhere, and she'd find me. I could ride her to the next town, form a posse, get some TNT, and close that damn mine but good.

But if I didn't make an offering, would that stop this madness?

The stairwell ended in a large space, bigger than the church proper above us. Various odd furnishings lay scattered about: a perch for Pandora where she now sat, preening her feathers, a wardrobe with its door ajar, and some open chests of what appeared to be coins and jewelry—enough for an offering, perhaps? If only I knew where to put it. Robert had said it had to be placed at the heart of the damage, which to me meant wherever gold had been struck first, wherever man had first offended the earth demons by taking from their rocks, their home. I had absolutely no idea where in the mines that would be.

I went to the wardrobe, thinking it might hide the tunnel entrance, and jerked it farther open to find everything from togas to armor, kilts to flowing robes made of Orient silk. Some were styles and fabrics I'd never seen before.

"I had to blend in," Xanthis explained from behind me. I heard the shrug in his voice. "If I liked the look, I kept it. Hid it, came back for it later, and took it along."

None of his words made sense. I turned to face him. "You're insane."

He plucked at the sleeves of his black preacher's coat, ignoring my words. "This is quite possibly the most uncomfortable disguise I've ever had the displeasure of wearing."

My empty fist clenched, and I half raised it before forcing it down to my side. "Everyone I know is dead, and you're complaining about wardrobe?"

This time I saw his shrug. "After a while, you get hardened. In the war between good and evil, people die. It's inevitable."

I stared at this stranger, a man I'd known for almost but not quite a year. Or thought I'd known. He'd appeared after the death of our previous religious leader—a quiet, elderly gentleman who spoke softly when offering words of comfort. Unlike Xanthis with his fire and brimstone, his calls to rise against the Devil. Xanthis had baptized Oblivion's children, stood by their grandparents' graves, performed wedding rites. All as if he'd cared. All an act?

"And how had you planned to fight this 'war'?" I demanded. "You show up out of nowhere, settle in, settle down. Months pass and nothing happens, and then the dead walk and everyone dies. What have you done to stop any of it?"

I threw open another cabinet, this one black wood with intricate carvings, taller than me and four times as wide. My mouth dropped open at the sight of what it held.

Weapons. Dozens of them. Knives, spears, swords, arrows and bows, shotguns, pistols, even some foreign ones like throwing stars and a katana. Even before becoming a U.S. Marshal, Pa had been fascinated with weapons, and I'd inherited that love, plowing through book after book on the subject.

Xanthis reached over my shoulder and closed the weapons storage in my face, like he was afraid I might damage them. "As you can see for yourself," he said, "it's not like I've been idle." His voice echoed in the open area, bouncing off the natural stone walls. "In my first months here, I took care of some nasty spirits in the Indian tribes that had invaded the bodies of mountain lions and black bears." He waved a hand at the clothing cabinet. "There's Indian garb in there somewhere, and stage makeup. An impressive job, impersonating a wandering shaman, even for me." As he spoke, Xanthis's voice took on an accent I'd never heard before, not quite European but close, lilting and exotic, as if his true nature had begun to seep through the more agitated he became. "When Pandora didn't do her part, I knew I had more work here. These demons are new. I haven't encountered their like before. And sometimes the physical approach isn't the right one to take. Demons require a religious faith for banishment, one I've been building in our little community for just this sort of eventuality."

Our little community. We meant nothing to this man, other than a means to defeat one more of his foes.

"Eventuality? You knew all along, the minute you knelt by that first dead miner in the street. You knew it was coming before that thing staggered into town. You knew what we were dealing with and didn't tell me?" More of his "women shouldn't be sheriffs" horseshit, no doubt.

"I knew something was coming, otherwise Pandora would have sent me elsewhen. I didn't know what. And when I figured out the demon part, I needed you to come to it yourselves, all of you, to believe. Only belief in evil, and by default, good, can vanquish demons." He paced the length of the basement cavern, running a hand through his hair, staring down at his polished black shoes. "It should have worked," he muttered.

My mind raced. Pandora the bird sent him? Else*when*? More images of Xanthis in an asylum came to my head. And *what* should have worked?

All the cross-waving on the church steps, the pleading to the people upstairs to have faith. All for nothing.

But it had been Christian faith.

"The Eye Killers aren't out of Christianity."

The pretend preacher's head shot up. "What? What did you call them?"

"The Eye Killers," I repeated. "At least that's how my… contact… referred to them. They aren't part of Indian lore, either. She said they predate the tribes here, though with rumors and legends, she might have been mistaken."

Xanthis had gone stock-still, eyes so round and large I could see the whites all around the pupils. Even as I watched, the blood drained from his complexion, leaving him pasty in the lamplight.

"That's what these are? I know that legend… had to know all of them to pass as a shaman. What they call the Eye Killers are Elemental demons,

demons of earth, air, fire, water." He paused. "And
you're correct. They are not of Christian origins."

"In this case, they're earth Elementals," I spec-
ified, resuming my search for the elusive tunnel.
Time was a-wasting, if anyone was to be saved. I
prayed there would be.

"Earth…." The preacher's voice trailed off. He
sank down on his haunches, as if his legs could no
longer hold him up.

In front of the weapons cabinet, I spotted deep
grooves in the stone floor. The wooden container had
been swung outward repeatedly. I gripped it by its
side and shoved, hearing more hidden hinges creak
as the thing moved. It revealed a dark passage leading into unknown depths.

From somewhere in the inky blackness came an
inhuman howl of despair.

Wind, I told myself. Only the wind.

But thinking back on the crowd of possessed
people outside the church and the former survivors
inside, I knew a lot of folks were unaccounted for.

"Dear gods," Xanthis said, switching faiths
again, "it's my fault. My fault they're still here."

I opened the cabinet and dug through its contents, tossing daggers and arrowheads to clatter
on the floor of the cavern. "What're you babbling
about now?" He'd worn my patience thin. Scanning
a stack of boxed ammunition, I found the correct
caliber and loaded my pistol. Then I yanked out a
holster and gun belt I thought might fit and wrapped
it around my waist—a little big, it hung on my hips,
but it wouldn't fall off so long as I didn't have to run

anywhere. Too bad there weren't any boots or hats likely to fit me in his wardrobe.

The howl came again, a conglomeration of multiple pitches, multiple voices. Running was looking more and more probable, if I could find some way past them.

I stared into the dark, straining my eyes, sensing no movement, but I could only see a few dozen feet into the tunnel.

The man-made tunnel. The man-made tunnel that Xanthis had ordered built.

I turned to focus on where he sat, no longer the great avenger but an old man, crouched and trembling, white with the knowledge of his ultimate failure.

"You *are* responsible. The mine had run dry. The diggers would have left. *You* kept them here to dig your escape route, paying out of those spoils of war," I said, gesturing at the chests of valuables, "and by doing that, you kept offending these earth Elementals, these demons, destroying their sacred mountain, or whatever it is they hold dear."

Pandora chose that moment to leave her perch, flapping between the two of us. I thought she'd settle on Xanthis to console him, but instead she came to rest once more on my shoulder, head held high and proud.

"Yes, yes," Xanthis said, his tone a thin whine. He stared at the bird. "This… this must be why she's chosen you. I'm no longer worthy, even less worthy than a mere woman."

I gave him my fiercest glare. No matter how in-adequate I felt in the face of this threat, at least I hadn't caused it. The muscles in my neck and shoulders tightened. I spoke through gritted teeth. "Look, Preacher, I've asked you before, just what the hell do you mean by—"

A new sound from the tunnel cut me off, the sound of shoes scraping on stone, sliding in uneven steps and growing ever closer.

That's when the damn bird bit me.

CHAPTER 9

"SHIT, BIRD!" I screamed, even as Xanthis winced in sympathy to my pain, or maybe at my unladylike language. Ladies could go to hell. That bite hurt like the Devil himself. I peered into Pandora's beady black eyes. "And you and I were just gettin' to be friends." Actually, I was more than a little hurt, considering the bird might be my last living friend on the planet. I sure wasn't counting Xanthis. I swatted Pandora away from where she'd sunk her razor-sharp beak into the side of my neck, but she avoided my swing and flew off to return to her perch. "I thought that critter never bit anyone," I accused, pointing a trembling finger at Xanthis.

"I said she'd never do it without a very good reason. Before tonight, she's never bitten anyone... except for me."

I rubbed at the spot, the skin below my jawline swelling and an uncomfortable tingling lurking beneath the surface. My fingers came away stained with blood. Holding them out for Pandora to see, I asked, "So, what'd I do to deserve this, huh, bird?"

Scraping and shuffling from the tunnel suddenly got a whole lot louder. The first dead man shambled into the room—a rancher I recognized from some of the town meetings. Distracted by Pandora's attack, I hadn't seen him approach from the tunnel's mouth, but now he stood before me in all his horrific glory, tattered clothing hanging from tattered flesh.

Maybe Pandora had been trying to warn me. I shot her a quick tight-lipped smile of apology before drawing my gun from the holster I'd borrowed.

More bodies followed the first, women with bonnets hanging from their necks and bloodstained petticoats swirling about bruised and battered legs, men in nightshirts, children....

Six shots, and more walking dead were still filing in from the passageway. I reholstered the pistol.

There was no way we were getting out of here alive.

Forgiven, Pandora fluttered to my shoulder while Xanthis and I backed away from the horde, toward the far wall of the cavern. The tingling in my neck had grown in intensity, and I pressed my fingers harder to the spot, willing the pins-and-needles sensation away. Instead, it spread outward, flooding beneath my skin like a swarm of ants crawling through my bloodstream.

The basement cave had grown warmer, too, and sweat prickled on the back of my neck and on my face. I glanced over at Xanthis, who was grabbing a spear from the cabinet, but he seemed unaffected. The dead weren't sweating, either, but somehow, I doubted they would.

While the preacher swung the spear back and forth and stabbed a few ineffectual times, I searched for the source of heat. The ceiling was stone, so little would have carried down from the burning church above.

I rubbed both hands over my arms, then up and down my pant legs, Pandora flapping to keep her balance, but the ants kept crawling, and I came to the horrible realization that the heat was within me as well.

"Quit fighting it, Sheriff. It's not pleasant by any means, but it's worse if you fight."

"Fight what?" And he'd called me Sheriff. For the first time. Whatever was happening to me was going to be bad.

"Don't worry. You'll return. When you're needed, when you have a fighting chance, you'll return."

I wanted to shout at him to make some sense, but my mouth no longer seemed to work well enough to form words. Things got fuzzy as my temperature rose, the recesses of the cave blurring in my sight. My back hit the stone wall, and I used it for support, trying to soak up the coolness from the rock without success.

Xanthis waved his hands and the spear in the air, shouting and taunting, drawing the possessed souls away from me. "Here! Here! I'm the one you want. I'm the reason you're here."

His voice rose and fell in my hearing. I couldn't concentrate.

A bright light flared in my peripheral vision, and when I turned my head, I jerked away from a burst of flame inches from my face.

My God, Pandora!

What remained of her red-and-gold brilliance drifted to the cave floor, almost lost in the fire consuming her.

Phoenix, whispered my mother's voice, wrapped up in one of her Greek mythology lessons. Phoenix….

Impossible.

Right, and Eye Killers went around killing and possessing people on a daily basis. If I could believe that, I had to believe it all.

Behind the flames I could see Pandora's eyes, still watching me, always searching. Throwing her head up and back, she opened her beak in one final heart-wrenching screech before her feathers blackened and her body turned to a pile of smoldering ash.

Nauseous from the smell of her burnt body and dizzy with fever, I panted, sucking as much air as I could into scalded lungs. Heat roiled through me. Red tinged my sight. I was vaguely aware as the crowd of Eye Killers swarmed Xanthis at last, overwhelming him and burying him in a mound of walking dead flesh.

My consciousness detached from my body, and I saw rather than felt the skin of my neck ignite. Flames licked at my cheek, but I sensed only the vaguest awareness of pain, enough to make me scream, yes, but nothing compared to what it should have been.

I shrieked until my throat went raw, more from the horror of seeing my skin blister, smelling my burning hair and clothing, then flesh, watching the fire work its way down my collapsed body.

The possessed townsfolk finished with Xanthis, leaving him a bloody pulp on the floor, and turned to me, but the fire distracted them, forcing them to blink over and over. They couldn't mesmerize me with their gaze, not that it would have mattered by then. I had little left to hypnotize.

Surprised my eyes still functioned, I watched their unsteady approach. Even in the midst of burning to death, I didn't want it to be them who took me, and I tried to drag my arm to my side and grasp my pistol.

None of my muscles worked. I glanced to my right to see why, head lolling more than turning.

I never knew skin could melt.

Lord Almighty…. Lord Almighty…. Lord Almighty….

Muttering the phrase, losing consciousness, I could only hope God might hear me. The pain receded, and I floated upward, above the horde and what was left of my body. I didn't want to look upon the blackened mass, but I had no eyelids to close. Then everything faded away.

CHAPTER 10

Somewhere, Sometime

I FLOATED, bodiless, a shade detached from anything tangible. Mists and shadows, darkness broken by sprinklings of light. The world as I knew it no longer existed in a way I could fathom. No muscles to tense, no heart to race, no voice to scream.

No idea how long I drifted, a night haunt with nothing to scare.

Consciousness returned slowly, a gradual re-awakening that never fully took hold. I could see, to some extent, though I no longer possessed eyes. And I could manipulate my "body," which, at a glance down at myself, resembled more of a vaguely woman-shaped glowing light than a corporeal figure.

Was this what death felt like?

Ma, Pa, Arlene, all the others I'd lost, were they wandering this place in forms like mine?

As more awareness filtered through, I took in my surroundings.

Heaven certainly was a disappointment.

Plain white stone walls broken by a few columns and alcoves carved at intervals, each containing something metal I couldn't quite make out from my current position. Torches in much more ornate holders than the cave I'd left glowed and flickered.

I tried to take a step and failed. No feet.

Willing myself forward worked better, and I managed a cross of the open space in a series of sporadic lurches of light to the nearest alcove. Within the alcove, a cage sat on a pedestal, a cage containing....

Pandora?

The red-and-gold bird shook itself, ruffling feathers and blinking tiny black eyes in a very negative response.

No, not Pandora. The pattern of colors looked wrong. Too much gold, not enough red. Much shorter tailfeathers. Then again, the last time I'd seen Pandora, she'd been... and I'd been....

Better not to think about that.

A marble bust stood to the right of the gilded cage, the carved chest and head of an attractive man with sharp cheekbones and deep-set intelligent eyes. Letters at the base likely spelled his name, but I couldn't read the Greek.

And then I could.

Adonis.

The bird preened and strutted side to side on its narrow perch, and I realized something else besides its name.

It could hear my thoughts.

I floated from alcove to alcove, each with its own marble bust and cage, some empty, others containing more of the red/gold avians. *Attis, Ikaros, Silenos, Helene, Tisiphone…. Pandora.*

The bust depicted a beautiful woman with long, flowing hair and sad eyes.

I'd swear the bird in the cage had the same eyes. I had to have lost my mind entirely.

A pop sounded behind me, not so much noise as the feel of air displacement, and another column of light joined mine. I couldn't make out features, but I got the sense of masculinity—strength, confidence, and all-around male *presence.*

What is this place?

Not heaven, that was for damn sure. Hell maybe. And if so, I wouldn't argue whether or not I deserved it, considering what I'd done tonight.

I caught the sense of humor, a fluttering in the glowing figure as if the entity were laughing at me.

Newcomer, eh? Which one wore out his welcome this time?

Um… Xanthis? I thought back, taking a guess at his meaning.

Bah. Xanthis. Never could abide that chap. More ego than brains. More interested in his own good than the good of mankind. You're bound to be an improvement.

Cackling, hoots, and caws erupted around me, echoing off the stone walls and the high ceiling as the birds voiced their agreement. Xanthis apparently hadn't been a real popular guy.

Color me unsurprised.

Something tugged at me from the inside out, an uncomfortable sensation, though nowhere near as horrific as the initial burning had been. Particles of light like a swarm of fireflies floated before me, drifting from my being and dissipating into nothingness.

Good luck to you, the other figure called.

Wait! Good luck with what? What's happening to me? I willed myself to hold together, but it was like trying to catch rainwater in a sieve. Before me, Pandora faded to transparent, then vanished. More bits of me sparked off and burned out in the heavy air of the chamber—embers from a dying campfire.

You've been chosen to fight the darkness, vanquish evil and all that rot.

And if I don't want to be chosen? My thoughts weakened as the last of me disassembled itself.

The other figure chuckled, throaty and low. *Being chosen isn't a "choice." Just be glad you never offended the gods enough to get yourself turned into a bird. For them, this* is *hell....*

CHAPTER II

State of New Mexico, Oblivion, 2019

I SPUTTERED and coughed, spitting out a foul powdery substance that filled my mouth and covered my lips.

Where was I? Where had I been?

The odd sensation that I'd been somewhere else, someplace far away, gnawed at me, but for the life of me, I couldn't remember. Just a vague sense of columns and stone that faded from memory even as I tried to piece it together and… gone.

Darkness pressed in on me; I could see nothing, and the knowledge that Eye Killers had surrounded me before I'd lost consciousness in Xanthis's underground chamber sent me flinging myself against the closest wall, frantically feeling along the cold stone for one of the lamps that had to be there.

My head bumped one of the metal holders, and I yanked the lamp from its base, hauling it in to clutch it to my chest. All my nerves seemed hypersensitive, from the chill of the iron to the lump forming at the top of my skull.

Matches, matches…. My fingers fumbled in my pants pocket where I kept them and withdrew the mostly empty box. I dropped two before I managed to extricate one and strike it on the rough strip.

Light flared, firelight, and all the previous events flooded back to me, making me drop the match, but thank God not the lamp, on the cavern floor. The tiny flame extinguished itself.

"Damn it to hell," I muttered, taking three more attempts before succeeding in lighting another one.

I stared for a long moment, dumbfounded, at my fingers, amazed I had them. Amazed I had matches, or pants for that matter.

The light didn't cast very far, but I couldn't see any walking dead. Xanthis's body had fallen beyond my range of vision, so I couldn't spot that, either.

Could it all have been some sort of hallucination?

I blinked and shook my head, snapping myself out of my daze, and lit the lamp. The glow spread outward, revealing the disturbed pile of black ash to my right, from where I'd come. From—at least by my best calculation—right where I'd awakened.

No, it couldn't be.

Something else had burned there. Something else. It couldn't have been me. I was right here, fully whole and fully clothed, right down to my borrowed holster, my pistol, and my dirty socks. Those weren't my ashes. I hadn't had that in my mouth.

Bile rose quickly and I gagged, then vomited, spewing clear liquid sprinkled with black flecks on the stone at my feet.

I hit the floor hard on my knees, shaking bad enough I had to set the lamp aside or shatter it. My stomach tightened for round two....

Farther to my right, a second pile of ashes shifted.

I gave a yelp, scrambling backward on my rear like a crab, pressing my spine against the wall. My hand found the butt of my pistol, and I yanked it free of the holster, watching my arm shake when I aimed it at the movement. The dim light cast by the lamp I'd left behind glinted off bits of red and gold within the fine black powder.

My mind raced as I tried to organize events in my head, place where each one had occurred.

"Pandora?" I whispered, my voice sounding loud in the empty space even at low volume.

A soft coo answered me.

I breathed a sigh of relief and holstered my gun. "Pandora! You scared me half out of my wits. Come here, girl." No way I was alienating the one other living creature down here. Besides, she was the solitary link I had to whatever had happened to me.

The bird reared its fine-feathered head, shaking off the rest of the ash as it stood, then flew to my outstretched arm. We studied each other in the flickering light.

Not quite the same Pandora I remembered. Her feathers looked fluffier, downier. She looked...

younger. Not newborn as the legends said, but certainly more youthful.

For a split second, the oddest image of a lovely long-haired woman blurred my vision, then vanished, though I had no idea where that thought had come from.

While I held her, she preened, spreading her wings to show off their glorious colors.

So, phoenixes got youth, and I got dirty socks. At least I hadn't come back as an infant.

But if all that "consumed in fire" had actually happened, where had everyone else gone?

Pandora refolded her wings and sidestepped up my arm to my shoulder, where she nuzzled my cheek. The softness of her feathers tickled me, and I rubbed at the spot, then let my fingers wander down to the beak bite on my neck.

Gone.

Made sense, I guess. New skin, no wounds. Wished the mystical hoodoo had provided some clean clothes and some boots, though.

After retrieving the lamp, I made a circuit of the cavern, lighting all the other lamps I could find intact. A few had fallen and broken on the stone, making them unusable. When I examined their holders, I found they'd rusted through.

Xanthis had lit the lamps when we'd come down. Had they been that way, or—?

I didn't want to think about the "or" possibility.

With more light, I could make a better search of the room, and I literally stumbled upon Xanthis's remains—white bones in a crouched position, not a trace of flesh on them, though a few bits of tattered clothing clung to the skeleton. Fractures crisscrossed the skull, and I prayed he'd died before most of those wounds had been inflicted. The metal cross lay nearby, along with the spear, both also rusted.

That didn't happen overnight, or over a fortnight.

How long? How long? The question rambled about in my head like an Indian chant.

I filled a pocket with ammunition from the weapons cabinet that had caved in on itself and scattered its contents across the floor. Bullets were valuable resources no matter how much time had passed.

Hesitating over the chest of gems and coins, I decided to leave Xanthis's treasure. Even if I could carry it all, I still had no idea where to put it to appease the Eye Killers, and I doubted anyone would find it easily down here.

I'd gone two steps up the staircase before remembering the blockage above. "Guess we're using the escape route after all," I told Pandora.

She bobbed her head and cooed her agreement. Her intense black eyes glittered in the lamplight.

Gun in one hand, lamp in the other, and bird on my shoulder, I stepped into the dark, scary tunnel.

Shadows on the walls and stone ceiling had me jumping every five feet. I expected one of the Eye Killers to appear at each turn, and my twitching must have finally gotten to Pandora because she launched from my shoulder to fly ahead. We passed a number of other tunnels branching off to the left and right, but the phoenix flew straight, and I had nothing to lose by following her.

After walking (and flying) almost an hour, I spotted a pinprick of daylight and nearly tumbled into a chasm in my haste to reach it.

Pandora circled my head as I waved my arms, trying to both retain the lamp and gun and maintain my balance on the pit's rough edge. I managed the gun, but the lamp fared less well. It slipped from my grasp to disappear into the pitch-black chasm, its light growing ever fainter as it plummeted into the depths. The shatter when it hit bottom barely reached my ears.

I stood, panting on the edge, afraid to take a step in the dark for fear of following the lamp down. Then my eyes adjusted and I saw the spot of light I'd noticed, even brighter now that the lamp was no more. I skirted the rim of the pit, envying Pandora's wings.

Together, we reached a small cave-in blocking the majority of the passage, and on my side of it, I found what I believed to be the bones of some of Oblivion's possessed citizens. No way to be sure, but it made sense.

So, Elementals might be immortal, but corporeal bodies disintegrated regardless.

Good to know.

It took some effort to dig my way past the rockfall. I hated myself for doing it but ended up using a couple of the longer, thicker bones to pry loose the heavier boulders. There just weren't any other tools.

Once the spot of daylight grew wide enough for me to squeeze through, I did so and found myself in more familiar territory. I'd been down to the gold mine a few times to settle disputes, bring in a debt welcher, and once to find a couple of kids who'd wandered in too far… and never came out. Had the demons been taking their revenge even then? Despite familiarity, I hated the place. It had felt eerie to me long before Robert told me the tale of the Eye Killers.

I followed the wheel ruts made by the miners' carts in silence, noting with discomfort the rot and cracks in the support beams they'd placed along the walls. Not a sound could be heard save for my breathing and the occasional flap of Pandora's wings when she flew close to me, so when I rounded a curve and spotted the three men, I nearly died a second time.

It took several moments for me to regain control of my heart rate. When I did so, I realized the men hadn't moved.

"Um, hello?"

Nothing. Not a twitch. Not a peep. Could the demons freeze people as well as control them?

I crossed to the closest man, a miner in overalls, checkered shirt, and wide-brimmed hat, his hands clutching a pickax, which he held poised to bring down on a rock pile. Waving my hand in front of his face did no good. I tapped him on the arm. My tap resonated.

Hollow. Like the fancy mannequins in big-city shop windows.

The other two were the same, one positioned in midstride, a sack of rocks slung over one shoulder, the second raising his right hand in permanent greeting while the left had a grated-bottom pan dangling from its fingers.

What the hell?

I headed for the mine entrance, following the glare of sunlight and shielding my eyes against the brightness. Once more I wished for my damn hat. The pain in my newly bruised and sliced feet had receded to a dull ache, but I didn't look forward to the long hike back to Oblivion. Or what remained of it.

Outside, I turned to study the gold mine. Same, but different. Someone had cleared the area around the opening, removing rocks and shrubs that might trip a person. A big sign painted in bright yellow read "New Mexico Historical Society—Gold Mining" in large print with a detailed explanation of the process in much smaller lettering underneath. Another more freshly painted sign read, "New Attraction—Try Your Hand at Gold Mining. $10.00. Keep Whatever You Find!"

Ten dollars? To swing a pick and sift through stone? For that, I'd better be guaranteed to strike a vein. Or two. Maybe they'd meant ten cents?

Judging from the sun's position, it was just after sunrise. I made my way to where the mining camp should have been and found it, rebuilt after the rampage of the Eye Killers and peppered with more hollow dummies depicting various everyday miner activities: cooking, laundry, rock sorting, sleeping, banjo picking. Signs stuck out of the ground beside each one, explaining their actions. One described the odd circumstances surrounding the massacre of the miners who'd lived here. They blamed the local Indian tribes, except they referred to them as… "Native

American" tribes? Yeah, I supposed one could call them that.

Whatever title folks used, I knew damn well Indians hadn't murdered the miners.

So, in the time I'd been gone, the mine had become… a tourist attraction? An *historical* tourist attraction?

How goddamn long?

Pandora inched closer to my neck, snugging her head behind my ear. The surreal scene set the tiny hairs on my arms rising. Despite my discomfort, I read every sign and label, hoping maybe one might mention where the miners had first struck gold, but found nothing. Figured.

"Time to go," I told the bird. Then I paused and went back to the closest mannequin, studying his feet.

Might work.

With little regard for the dummy's creator—and I had to admit, these were some damn realistic creations—I knocked the statue on its side and yanked off his boots. The material felt odd in my hands—not leather but some flimsier substance. They fit. A little big, but workable.

Too bad the historians hadn't seen their way clear to include any of the miners' wives in the display. Just more of my luck.

I stole a hat, too, though I had to tear two holes in it where it had been stapled on.

Pandora and I headed out of the camp, down a wood-planked path to a wide cleared space covered in gravel.

That's when I spotted the contraption.

A big tan metal contraption off to the side, the farthest of its four doors open and hanging askew from the rest of the frame. The thing had windows, and someone had broken all of them, leaving bits of glass all around it and quelling any guilt I'd worked up over taking the boots as I crunched my way to its side.

"Like a tiny steam train," I muttered, kicking one of its wheels and feeling my foot bounce back from whatever covered it. "A steam train without steam. And without rails." What I took to be the backside had a horse depicted on it and the word "Ford" engraved beneath the horse. The side said "Mustang."

Ford must have been the horse's name.

A pang of longing for my sweet Chessie, no doubt long gone, tightened the muscles in my chest. I took comfort in the fact she hadn't burned to death. Like I had.

I rounded the corner of the vehicle and came face-to-face with the contraption's engineer—or what was left of her.

Invisible from my direction of approach, the body lay sprawled beside the miniature train, hanging out of the damaged door. She had long red hair pulled back into one gathering like a horse's tail, wide, staring brown eyes, and she looked a helluva lot like… me.

Hat, shirt, black vest (which I missed), dungarees, and boots, though her boots had heels completely inappropriate for walking or riding, but otherwise, we might have shopped at the same general store. I

checked her neck for a pulse and found none. She'd
been beaten badly, bruises covering her face, and a
trickle of blood ran from a gash on her forehead and
stained the gray rocks and pebbles—fresh blood.

I ducked down, then raised my head just above
the side of the mini-train, scanning the area for
whomever might have done this, though I had a pretty good idea. A trail of shuffling footprints, one foot
clearly dragging a line across the gravel behind the
other, led away from the gruesome murder. That and
the fact that the woman didn't seem to have put up a
fight led me to one suspect. An Eye Killer. And there
was no trace of it now, save the footprints.

Gun in hand, I followed the trail on a circuitous
route, skirting the edge of the miners' camp and finally leading into the mine. The killer had paused in
several places, prints turning and facing toward the
tents, then continuing on.

Whatever it was, whoever it was, it had been
watching me. Those prints were fresh. Despite
the rising sun and the increasing heat of the day, I
shivered.

I returned to the vehicle, thinking I should do
something for this woman before heading into town.
No matter how much time had passed, New Mexico still had plenty of buzzards, and they circled
overhead, just waiting for me to leave. Nobody deserved to be buzzard food, especially somebody who
resembled me so closely. Besides, if an Eye Killer
had murdered her, I supposed there was a very real
chance she might become possessed. The miners I'd
found hadn't all gotten up and walked around, just

the three, but I didn't want to take chances. I had no idea just how many of the Elementals were still left. They'd controlled half the town before my... demise. And they could choose hosts as they saw fit. Nothing said they couldn't choose this woman now or later.

I crouched beside her, noting a scattering of discarded pamphlets and a folder of papers on one of the interior seats, a brochure grasped in her hand. I pried that loose first, noting a photograph on the front, one *in color*, of the "Oblivion Gold Mine" and listing tours beginning at 10:00 a.m. I glanced at the sun and guessed the time around eight or so, so she'd been very early and waiting in the little train for some kind of guide or group.

Which meant I wouldn't be alone for too much longer. And I had no idea what people would make of me, in this age of color photos, miniature trains, and tourist attractions, except that they'd find me with a dead woman and no way to account for being here.

A tour guide might be able to answer my questions about the gold strike, but I was a sheriff. I knew exactly what they'd think, and that settled my decision.

Whispering a prayer of apology, I grabbed the stranger by the shoulders and dragged her across the gravel area, around the opposite side of the camp from the path the Eye Killer had chosen, and then into the mine itself, ever vigilant for her murderer. Past the mannequins and into the tunnel, I returned with the body to the rockfall and shoved her through the opening I'd made, then hesitated on the edge of the pit.

Pandora chose that moment to let loose an alarmed squawk, right in my ear. Red wing feathers thwapped me on the chin. She hopped from my shoulder and used her beak to pluck at the woman's vest pocket until I slipped its contents into my hand. Some sort of identification holder, complete with a number of durable cards, one with the victim's picture, again in color, imprinted on it.

"Sandra Meadows," I said to the woman, "from Arizona. We could have been sisters." In the photograph, without the bruises, the resemblance was even more striking. I shoved the card into my pants pocket. A number of other cards with numbers and names like Visa and Discover—that one with Sandra's picture and a dog on it—I tossed into the pit. Another said "insurance." I had no idea what a Blue Shield was, beyond the obvious, but I figured everyone could use a little insurance, especially me right now, so I put it with the keepers. I also kept the money I found, staring in disbelief at the dates on the bills, the latest of which read "2019."

Oh, dear Lord.

The cavern rocked, and I put a trembling hand to my forehead, then wrapped my arms around myself. Over one hundred and twenty-five years had passed.

One hundred and twenty-five years!

My throat closed up, cutting off my air, and I had to count in my head to drown out the internal screaming, mine and the remembered voices of the entire town. Pandora shoved her soft feathered head beneath my arm, cooing and clucking softly, but I pushed her away. She cocked her head to one side, watching me force breath into my lungs.

"I never wanted to be some evil-fighting hero," I snarled, crumpling the bills I still clutched in my fist and shoving them in with the photo identification I'd taken.

Yes, you did, the voice in my head whispered. *That's why you became a sheriff.*

I told the voice to shut up and finished searching Sandra Meadows's clothes. What I discovered in her other vest pocket almost stunned me more than the year.

A badge.

Sandra Meadows had been a sheriff too.

CHAPTER 12

I WAS wearing a dead woman's vest. God forgive me. My folks raised me with a "waste not, want not" mentality, and if I didn't find shelter before nightfall, well, desert nights got pretty cold. I sure wasn't spending tonight in one of the flimsy fake miners' tents. Or the mine itself.

Picking my way back to Sheriff Meadows's vehicle, I tried not to think about her body in the cold, dark pit or the satisfied sigh that seemed to rise from the blackness after I pushed her in. I tried not to think about closing up the hole I'd made in the rockfall so no one would ever find her. I tried not to think about color photographs or miniature trains or still-wandering Eye Killers or the year 2019.

Not thinking was impossible.

Why now? Why now? Surely there'd been other, earlier opportunities to bring me back so I could settle things. I glanced at Pandora on my shoulder, but she wasn't answering any questions.

I scuffed my boots over the blood spots beside the "Mustang" until I'd erased them from sight, then searched the metal contraption for anything else I might find useful. At least I hadn't discovered any pictures of friends or family in her pockets. That would have been too much to bear.

Part of me wondered at my emotional reactions to her death. Maybe it was the resemblance. Or maybe the culmination of so many losses was getting to me. Whatever the cause, I felt almost glad for it. I never wanted to become hardened like Xanthis had been, no matter what the emotional cost.

The folder of papers on one of the seats drew my attention. The last thing I expected to find inside was a photograph of me. While I waited for my heart to start beating again, I sank onto the leather seat to give it all a good read.

I remembered the day the mayor had a slew of black-and-white photographs taken with that new-fangled Kodak camera. A professional photographer up from New Orleans had passed through town, and Mayor Jones had this burning need to "commemorate" everything and everyone in Oblivion. "For posterity," he'd said. If he only knew how right he'd been. I'd just been voted in for my third term as sheriff, and I stood tall and proud—and stock-still, arms and legs aching while the picture was taken—in front of my office, my star polished and shining on my chest.

I flipped the picture over, searching for the words I'd written on the back, but found blank whiteness. Indeed, this paper was much too thin for a photograph. Somehow, someone had… copied?… my picture onto this flimsy sheet. If it had been the original, it would have read, in my cursive scrawl, Sheriff Cali McCade, April 8th, 1891, by my reckoning, four months ago.

Four months and a hundred and twenty-five-odd years. I didn't even know what month it was now. Sometime in spring, judging from the budding yellow-and-orange poppies around the mining camp.

I'd stored the picture in my journal, not egotistical enough to frame it and hang it on the office wall. Part of me wondered what else had survived that fiery night. Last night. God.

My fingers turned to the next sheet, a typed letter:

Dear Ms. Meadows,

It is our pleasure to inform you that you have been selected out of hundreds of applicants to portray Sheriff Cali McCade in our upcoming season of *Harsh Reality: Living in Oblivion.* Please report to Oblivion, New Mexico, by 3:00 p.m. on Friday, April 13, 2019, to meet the director, Erick Taz, and the rest of the cast and crew. You'll need to leave your car in the Oblivion Gold Mine parking lot and walk in. (Driving and walking directions are enclosed.)

I strongly recommend reading the *New York Times* bestseller *Women's Lib in the 1890s, the Recovered Journals of Sheriff Cali McCade* prior to your arrival, in order to better understand the woman whose life you'll be living as part of our series. You are

not to bring anything with you. Everything
you'll need will be provided in order to preserve the authenticity of the experience for
the cast and our viewers. Further details re-
garding your payment, and insurance waivers are enclosed for your signature. Please
fax them at your earliest convenience.

Looking forward,

Ryan Nichols (Casting Director)

I didn't understand a lot of the individual words,
but the gist of the letter came across. The dead woman hadn't just been here to tour the mine and search
for gold. This was a "parking lot," and I was sitting
in her "car." What a ridiculous name for the mini-
train. But more interesting, she was supposed to portray *me* in a theatrical performance.

Heat crept into my face as my mind flitted
through the contents of my journals, my hopes and
dreams, my thoughts about Arlene and any other
women who'd wandered into and out of my day-
dream fantasies. I knew of the *New York Times*, the
most widely read newspaper in America. In a hundred and twenty-five years, I'd become some sort of
historical celebrity.

Jesus, Mary, and Joseph, what had that damn
bird gotten me into?

Except maybe I had an answer to my question—
why now?

Now because people were digging in the mine
again. Now because that would have stirred up the
Eye Killers. Now because Sandra Meadows's job

offer to portray me gave me a reason to be here and, maybe, access to some allies.

Xanthis had said I'd return when the time was right, when I had half a fighting chance.

Maybe the earliest time for that was now.

My shoulders stiffened at the sound of crunching gravel and the roar of machinery approaching. I slid from the, what was it again? Car. Right. I slid out just as another car pulled up beside Sandra Meadows's. This one featured a bright blue exterior that shimmered in sunlight. It rode low to the ground, a sleek vehicle despite the noise and smell of the smoke it produced from its rear.

But when its driver turned off the sound and got out, she captured my full attention.

Oh, dear God, she looked like Arlene.

Well, not exactly like Arlene. Maybe even a little better-looking. More polished. But it could have been Arlene's sister or cousin. The resemblance was uncanny.

The blood drained from my face. My legs went weak. I heard a roaring in my ears, almost drowning out her words.

"Hey there, darlin', you all right?"

No, no, no. She even sounded like Arlene. Except Arlene was dead. I'd killed her. Me. And I was forced to admit now, I'd loved her.

The stranger-who-could-not-be-Arlene took one look at my expression and practically hurdled the front of her blue car. Warm, gentle arms caught me just before I would have hit the glass-strewn ground.

I was dimly aware of Pandora squawking and whirling away into the sky.

Traitor, I thought as it all faded.

"I'M FINE. Fine," I mumbled as not-Arlene stopped her mini-train at what looked like a tiny shed and talked with a man in a blue uniform.

The vehicle rumbled around me, but with all I'd gone through today, it did little more than draw forth a passing moment of wonder. I'd come to mere minutes after passing out, but the fog remained, everything outside the windows of the mini-train blurred, and my savior's voice was an underlying yet soothing murmur.

The … guard? … pointed toward some buildings up ahead, indistinct in my haze and the glare of the sun. Not-Arlene slid behind the wheel and we moved forward, my head lolling against the seat. "Just too much heat," I said.

And dying and traveling one-hundred-plus years forward.

My head swam, and I closed my eyes, not opening them even when we stopped for the second time.

"Security told me where I can put you for a rest," Not-Arlene explained. She sounded worried. I didn't blame her. I felt like shit and likely looked worse.

Her door slammed. Mine opened, and she hooked an arm around my waist, drawing me upright. Leaning on her, I just managed to stay standing.

With my eyes squeezed shut against the dizziness, I could almost imagine this *was* Arlene, helping me to bed after a full night of whiskey and cards at the saloon.

Except there was no saloon, no cards, no whiskey, no Arlene.

My boots scuffed dirt, then hit a step and landed on wood planks. A door creaked open, then more stairs and the undeniable sense of familiarity, but I would not, could not bring myself to open my eyes. Dreams within dreams, and I wasn't ready to wake up and face whatever my reality might be.

Another door creaked, and then my knees bumped a low-lying bed. Soft, gentle hands eased me onto a mattress, and I slept as soon as my head hit the pillow.

I SHIFTED as I woke, a cold, wet cloth slipping from my forehead. The bed springs creaked. Smells of wood and fresh paint I hadn't noticed before assailed my nostrils. A spring breeze shifted the hair on my forehead. Somewhere along the line, I'd lost my stolen hat.

One eye cracked open. What I saw made me sit bolt upright, heart thudding and every muscle taut.

My room. My little room above the sheriff's office.

But not my room. Not quite.

For half a moment, I'd basked in the desperate wishful thinking that I'd dreamed it all. One long, terrible nightmare. God knew I'd had plenty of those over the years. What difference did a few new bad dreams make? But as my head cleared and my vision focused, I noticed subtle differences about my living quarters, and a few major ones.

The bed, the nightstand, the chair, the wardrobe all would have belonged in any number of Oblivion's homes, just not mine. The decorators had placed it all correctly, but the colors didn't quite match, nor did the styles. It was as if someone had collected the town's furnishings and then chosen items at random—oak for the nightstand, chestnut for the wardrobe, and the overstuffed down mattress was too soft and expensive to belong to a sheriff.

I wondered how they'd even gotten the positioning right, then remembered my sketches. I'd filled the pages of my journals with pictures of everything and everyone in Oblivion while passing long, hot hours on the porch, waiting for some problem to arise so I'd have work to do.

Standing, I went to each piece of furniture, running my hands over deep cracks in surfaces, the de-silvering of the mirror, the chipped and faded paint. After so much time, this was likely the best they could do.

It then occurred to me that the building itself shouldn't even be standing, nor the entire town for that matter, and I rushed to the window to peer out.

Like the room, Oblivion was not quite Oblivion.

They'd rebuilt the town, and recently, judging from the way my fingertips came off the windowsill tacky with white paint, but they'd gotten a few things wrong. The saloon stood on the right instead of the left side of the street. The general store had a tan facade where it should have been clean, white adobe.

The church looked perfect in every detail.

A chill swept through me as I studied it, precisely placed, dominating the end of the street like an angry father towering over his children. So exact was it, I wondered if, somehow, it had survived the fire. The stone foundations might have stood, at the very least, and the rebuilders could have guessed from there. Then again, there was no structure in town I'd drawn in my journal with such painstaking accuracy as that church. How couldn't I? It drew the eye and the soul.

Thinking of the church brought unpleasant images of Xanthis, and I discovered another problem with the scene. Pandora. I saw no sign of her.

A soft tapping on the door jolted me from my thoughts, and out of habit I called, "Come on in!"

Half expecting the fake Arlene, I stared at the stranger in my doorway, a small, wiry man with neatly trimmed brown hair, round-rimmed glasses, pressed pants, and button-down shirt like he'd dressed for Sunday services. He'd even polished his boots. Nobody polished boots in Oblivion. What was the point? One walk down dusty Main Street would unpolish them right quick.

He held out a hand for me to shake, and I noted the long red scratch across the palm, and several other nicks and cuts on his fingers. Cuts and scratches like a bird's talons might make.

"Good to see you again, Sheriff. Glad to see you up and about. I'm not sure you remember me. I'm Ryan Nichols."

The casting director mentioned in Sandra Meadows's letter. Right. I guess it had been a while since they met. Otherwise, he might have figured out I wasn't who he thought I was. I took the outstretched hand, suppressing a smirk when he grimaced at my grip. Roping, riding, and the occasional arm wrestling at the saloon didn't make for flabby muscles. His, on the other hand, felt pretty weak. And I'd gone easy on him, what with the cuts and all.

I released him and gestured around my... the room. "How did I get here?"

Ryan frowned. "You don't remember? You fainted."

Shaking my head, I said, "I don't faint."

That got a laugh that started the anger boiling deep in my gut. Western women weren't delicate flowers, especially this one.

"Well," he went on, oblivious, "between the heat, the excitement of today, and whatever happened to your car, you lost consciousness out in that parking lot. Alliso—I mean, Arlene—" He winked. "—brought you in. She said you came around, then conked out like you were exhausted. You've been sleeping ever since. You drive all night or something?"

Nope. Burned to death. Takes a lot out of a body. "Something like that," I muttered.

The little man took up pacing the length of the bedroom. I refused to think of it as mine, no matter how similar it looked.

"Fuck," he continued, "I hate working reality shows."

I blinked. Despite my profession, most gentlemen didn't feel comfortable enough around me to use profanity in my presence, not until they got to know me, and though I hadn't heard the word "fuck" used quite that way before, I got the intent.

"Come on. I'll take you to the others."

I had a million questions, half of which I discarded because they'd give me away, but I followed him out the door and down the no-longer-creaking stairs. We passed through my not-quite-right office, and I shot the chair behind the desk a longing look. It had been a long day. In my timeline, I'd been up all night, too, and the short nap I'd taken after whatever happened to me in the "parking lot" (I refused to admit I'd fainted, even to myself) hadn't been nearly sufficient to catch up. A loud growl from my stomach reminded me I hadn't eaten since yesterday, or in one hundred and twenty-five years, either.

Ryan laughed at the gurgling and rumbling issuing from my abdomen. "We'll take care of that. Filming starts tonight, and we're opening the series with an old-fashioned town barbecue."

I glanced at the sky, surprised to see the sun just past its zenith. More lost time. I'd rested most of the day. Guess dying and being reborn really did take a lot out of a person. But I had yet another victim, Eye Killers to stop, and apparently, a whole new town to save.

The pit had seemed pleased with the offering of Sandra Meadows's body, though that hadn't been my intention. Maybe that would at least hold the Elementals off for a while. I didn't dare hope it had been enough.

Another thought occurred. "Say, um, you haven't seen my, um, pet, have you? A red-and-gold bird?" I tried not to glance at his damaged hands.

"Yeah, we've met," he growled, then stopped in the street and faced me, turning with such speed he kicked up a cloud of dust. "You and Arlene sure are breaking the rules. We made an allowance for her car, considering your collapse and all…."

I glared. He ignored me.

"But we said not to bring anything, including—" And he punctuated his anger by pointing a sliced finger at me. "—obnoxious pets."

"She wouldn't leave my side." Truth.

"Well, now she won't leave our preacher's side. Damn near tore up the parrot we'd got him. Had to send it back to the city in one cage, and its feathers in a separate bag. Humane Society is gonna rake us over the coals."

"So she's safe, then."

"Yeah, safe and hired."

I could tell it killed him to say that.

"You'll find a little more in your direct deposit, so long as you're willing to let us use her. Too late to get another damn bird. And the director loves her. She even responds to the name, Pandora."

Well, of course she did. I wondered if she really liked their version of Xanthis or if she'd been smart enough to realize this was the only way they'd let her stick around. Secretly, I suspected the latter.

Ryan took off again, huffing down the street toward the wrong-color general store, and I followed. Looked like Pandora wasn't leaving Oblivion.

And neither was I.

CHAPTER 13

WE ENTERED the store to a level of noise and
activity its predecessor had never known. People
crammed the small space in front of the ordering
counter—many of whom I recognized, or sort of
recognized. I could pick out the new doc, Preacher
Xanthis with *my* bird on his arm, and a Deputy Jake
much more handsome than the scrawny, bad-com-
plexioned partner I'd left in the past. Still, my heart
twisted, and I swallowed a sudden lump in my throat
at the sight of them all.

There was our mayor, and Sam standing next to
his daughter, though the eighteen-year-old looked
awkward and uncomfortable, swatting flies away
from her face, and I doubted the pair had any real
blood relationship. Sam, however, was the spitting
image of my Sam, the one I remembered. That one,
the directors had cast well.

"How…?" My voice broke, and I coughed to
cover it. "How did you get so many lookalikes?" I
asked Ryan. They weren't all perfect copies. Not by
a long shot. More like spit-polished recreations of

the rougher real thing, and some were way off, from what I could tell. The closer ones made my insides squirm.

The casting director preened at my compliment. "Used a few old black-and-white photos from the vault at Town Hall and the sketches and descriptions Cali McCade had in her journals, mostly. Some of the surviving ranches had a photo or two. I did my research." He raised his eyebrows and cocked his head at me. "You must have too."

Right. Because Sandra Meadows wouldn't realize these *were* lookalikes. She would never have met the first citizens of Oblivion. I nodded, putting on my I'm-so-studious face.

"Of course, I needed them a little better-looking than their originals, but you get thousands of people to show up at coast-to-coast audition sites. You're bound to find what you're looking for. At least for this kind of gig, they don't have to be able to act worth a damn."

I picked out Hank and Al, too, among a couple dozen others, all of whom had more flash and flair than the folks I remembered but bore startling resemblances nonetheless. Then my eyes settled on Arlene.

She'd been leaning against the side wall beside a pile of flour sacks, but when she saw me, she straightened and came right over, a concerned frown on her pretty face. "Hey there, Sheriff. You had me pretty scared out at the mine. You all right? What the hell happened to your car?"

I glanced around for Ryan, hoping for some sort of excuse not to answer the interrogation, but the casting director had vanished into the crowd.

Pasting on my best smile, I took the hand she extended and shook it, surprised when the strength of her grip matched mine. My Arlene had always possessed strength of personality, but physical strength, not so much. This one had beauty *and* a right firm handshake. Interesting. "Not sure what happened to my... car," I said, dredging up the word she'd used for the miniature train. "I, um, went for a walk up to the mine, and when I got back, it was as you saw it."

Close enough.

"Damn hoodlums," she said, shaking her head. "I got in yesterday. Was talking with the park ranger up there."

Park ranger? Hope surged through me. Maybe this ranger could answer my gold mine questions.

"He said there'd been some vandalism," Arlene continued. "Figures it was kids from Los Alamos way, though that's a helluva long drive just to commit some mischief. Your car was in the wrong place at the wrong time."

That was for sure.

Not-Arlene leaned in closer, close enough I could smell her perfume, and it wasn't the brand the real Arlene used, thank God. If it had been, I might have swooned again. "Listen," she said low enough for no one else to hear, "I gotta confess. I didn't read the dang book. I skimmed it. We're not supposed to use our real names, but do I call you Sheriff, Cali, or what? Do you know?"

I swallowed hard, tears pricking my eyes, and checked the safety strap on my borrowed holster to avoid looking at her. "Either one, depending on whether I'm working or off duty."

Arlene bumped my shoulder with her own. "You sure it's not 'darlin'"? I definitely got the impression we're secret sweethearts from some of those journal entries your predecessor wrote." She leaned in closer, warm breath tickling my ear, and whispered, "I didn't skim those." And it didn't seem to bother her one bit.

Interesting.

A man behind the store's counter thumped the polished wood surface for attention, and the conversation dropped to low mutterings.

"Yeah, sometimes you would call me darlin'," I whispered, and begged the tears not to fall.

Arlene gave me a strange look and opened her mouth to say more, but the store's "owner" started making announcements.

"Welcome, folks!"

I appreciated his jovial smile, though he looked nothing like the store's former owner. In fact, I couldn't place this man's origins—dark-skinned and angular features, maybe India?

"I'm Malek, wardrobe and props manager for *Harsh Reality*. I see some of you came in costume, but you'll be discarding everything here, especially any real weapons you might be carrying, licensed or not." His gaze fell on me and my holstered pistol. "That's a fine piece you've got there, Sheriff, but I'll be taking care of it for you."

Man had a good eye to spot it so fast, and I nodded my acknowledgment while mentally kicking myself for not hiding the gun in my room. Then again, I hadn't known when I might be needing it.

"My team has done extensive research." He gestured at two women and a man behind him. "And we'll provide you with the appropriate attire and accessories. Everyone in this room was mentioned by name in Cali McCade's journals at one point or another, so you're the premier players."

The swell of pride in the room was almost tangible. The few who'd continued their private conversations stopped and gave the shopkeeper their full attention. Nothing like playing on a man's ego to get him to cooperate.

"Most important to address is the weapons you will be allowed to handle. You've all signed the insurance waivers, right?"

More laughter.

"Well, not to worry. There are no real guns on *Harsh Reality*, only very realistic-looking paintball shooters." Malek held up a sample, a pistol that could easily have been my S&W. "They load just like regular revolvers, and for those of you not familiar with guns, we'll show you how. My own design," he added, laying it on the counter with a gentle fondness. "The director will tell you more about your roles, the pistols and rifles, and how to keep from getting booted off the show, when you all get to the barbecue. For now, when you hear your name, come on up and get your clothes and equipment. There's a few small curtained-off areas in the back for you to change. Then

drop your own belongings off here. I'll lock up any
valuables in the storeroom safe. You'll get them back
when you leave the show...." He grinned. "Some of
you sooner than others. If you need any additional supplies over the next week, I'm the one you see. I'll be
right here. Oh, and at the end of the week, everything
not used up gets returned, you hear? We're packing up
and moving overseas. *Harsh Reality: Castle Life and
Death* starts filming next Thursday."

A week? Was that all the time we had? How was
I supposed to defeat evil in a week?

Apparently I wasn't the only one surprised by
the short time frame. One of the men to my left
muttered to his wife, or at least she was the woman
pretending to be his wife, "How they gonna shoot
twelve episodes in a week?"

"Split days. They'll film for seven but chop it up
to make it look like twelve or fourteen or whatever.
So long as they get enough hours of footage, they
can break it into as many parts as they want. They've
got hidden cameras everywhere. They'll get hours
and hours of stuff they can't even use."

Most of what I overheard only served to confuse
me further, but the point was made. I had a week,
and that was it.

I shuffled with the crowd, using them to separate
myself from Arlene, and collected the gear provided
for me. Safe in my little curtained booth in the back,
I examined everything.

The clothing seemed fine, if a little better made
than my own. Hat, boots, pants, shirt, vest, straight
out of the photograph. Didn't much care what they

dressed me in. The undergarments made me chuckle, though. Little lacy, frilly things no respectable woman in my day would have worn, but I guess research didn't matter about things no one would see. At least, I hoped no one would see these. And I sincerely hoped I could figure out how to put some of them on. I peered into the corners of the back room. Still no sign of these hidden cameras of theirs or their operators.

It was the gun that concerned me. A lot. The pistol might resemble mine on the outside, but that's where the similarities ended. Weight and balance were all off, and the paint pellets, tiny round things that fit into the ends of bullet-shaped carriers, wouldn't do more than decorate an Eye Killer in a nice, pretty shade of red.

"Just what the hell am I supposed to do with this?"

"Not kill your costars," said a voice from over my shoulder.

I jumped. I hadn't even realized I'd asked the question out loud, but the man strolling in through the rear door of the store had clearly heard me. He looked me up and down, nodded, and extended a hand, which I shook.

"Erick Taz, director, at your service. Damn, woman, you're the spitting image of Cali McCade. Ryan did his job well casting you."

"Um, thanks."

He spent another minute studying me, and I took the opportunity to examine him as well. Tall, fit, dressed in Western wear to blend in, but he had some dark glasses covering his eyes. I wondered if those protected him from the sun and where I could get a pair. Would the Eye Killers be able to penetrate those dark lenses? I filed that away for now and finished my assessment. Erick's brown hair was cut short and neat, like he'd just had it trimmed, but a day's growth of stubble covered a square jaw. A city-slicker posing as a cowboy, but not hard on the eyes.

"And a real sheriff too," the director continued. "Just remember," he said with a kind smile, "you're not on duty here. Any crimes you see being committed are just stage-play, for the cameras. I read your dossier. I know you're pretty good with hand-to-hand. If someone starts a fight with you, you don't have to pull your punches, but try not to rough anyone up *too* much." Taz winked. "If you read the book, you know McCade's sanity was in question toward the end of her life. We don't expect you to act out that part."

My sanity? I stared at him, mind racing to the last entries in the journal. Walking dead men, Eye Killers, demons. Yeah, I guess that did sound pretty crazy.

"And we definitely don't want you shooting your cheating lover in the head and burning down the town. History does *not* need to repeat itself here for us to get good ratings."

"Wait. What?" I felt my eyes narrow.

Taz gave me a sympathetic look. "Sorry. I'd forgotten how much those follow-up investigations sucked for the women in law enforcement. Must have been tough finding out the country's first female sheriff lost her mind over her secret female lover and destroyed the city she'd sworn to protect. Hard losing your hero to modern forensics."

He turned and headed out the way he'd come in.

"I didn't, she didn't…." But he'd already gone.

I wasn't some sort of historical celebrity. I was an historical outlaw. If that's how I was being remembered, history needed to change.

CHAPTER 14

I PASSED the next few hours alternating between staring down Main Street in a dazed stupor and peeking into corners looking for these alleged cameras the director referred to. Never did find any, so either they'd gotten a lot smaller over time or my distraction cut down on my attention to detail. And I didn't understand what the cameras were for, anyway. What good were a bunch of photographs going to be in a theater show? Maybe for the marquee?

Until the barbeque, I avoided talking at length with anyone. Not that I disliked these folks, but it felt too strange. I imagined the conversation. "Oh hi, Mayor. I shot you in the head. Don't remember? Well, that's okay. Apparently I was crazy at the time."

Yep, nice, friendly chat.

As the sun set, we all gathered in the center of Main Street, where someone had set up some cooking fires and long tables laden with bowls of potato salad, rolls, baked beans, and pitchers of lemonade. Women with aprons over their dresses turned slabs

of meat over the fires. It all smelled wonderful, and I
grabbed a plate and took two yeast rolls, a fork, and a
scoop of potato salad, then stood to the side, munching and watching the proceedings. In the history of
Oblivion, I couldn't remember a similar gathering.
When we got together as a community, it took place
in the town hall or the church. Main Street was for
horses and wagons. Speaking of which, I didn't see
any. Did they think we all traveled around on foot?

The other performers milled about, plates in
hand, mostly alone. We weren't a town. We were a
gathering of strangers. And no one knew what to say
to each other.

The number of sort-of familiar faces continued
to haunt me. Maybe there were only so many physical types amongst humanity, but the constant flash-
backs they were causing didn't help my precarious
state of mind any.

After some uncomfortable silence, Erick Taz
strolled out of the general store and stepped up on
the boardwalk lining the street. He clapped his hands
for attention. "Welcome to Oblivion!" he shouted.

Several people applauded. Others cheered. The
rest of us just waited. I set my fork and now empty
plate with some others on a side table and crossed
my arms over my chest.

"You're about to participate in the most unusual reality show the *Harsh Reality* team has ever
produced."

I listened, glad for the explanation for myself
but wondering why he needed to clarify things for
people who should have already known how this

worked. Following his gaze, I saw he directed most of his words to a small group of men I hadn't previously noticed, standing in the shadows of the saloon's front awning. City folks for sure, they wore suits and carried small black or gray boxes they tapped on fast and furiously—some kind of portable typewriters, maybe. I figured them for newsmen.

"Instead of the standard 'fish out of water' approach where we dump people into unfamiliar environs and say 'go,' in some cases we've actually managed to cast people who currently hold similar jobs to their counterparts from the Old West." He swung a hand out toward Arlene, caught by surprise and gnawing on a rib bone. "Our saloon girl is a Vegas showgirl." He pointed again. "Our preacher is a pastor from Albuquerque."

Xanthis nodded in response, while on his arm, Pandora gave a little squawk and bobbed her head. Everyone laughed. Even some of the newsmen smiled.

"Our sheriff is an actual sheriff from a very small town in Arizona." He tilted his chin toward me. "And so forth. We're not asking them to become the former citizens of Oblivion, nor are we asking them to drop all references to modern day, but we've asked them to do some research and see if they can live in the lifestyle of those harsh times. The Old West was full of dangers—outlaws, unfriendly Native American tribes, droughts and fires." He paused for effect. "Outdoor plumbing."

That got a good laugh. Did everyone have indoor plumbing these days? What a luxury.

"And we'll be throwing a few surprises their way. Only our main players are regular folks. Our extras are paid actors, and they have some tricks up their sleeves. If anyone gets tired of oil lamps and no AC, they can leave at any time. And of course, if anyone gets himself shot up by our specially designed weaponry—" He held up one of the paint-shooters. "—he is pronounced officially dead and is sent home."

I scanned the rest of the gathered assembly. Not too many had guns. I did, and Deputy Baylor. Arlene had one, because of course I'd written about it in my journal, and it was strapped around her waist over her red-and-black-striped satin skirt with black petticoats beneath. A few of the other menfolk had rifles.

"Now that doesn't mean you all should get trigger happy. This isn't *Survivor* or one of those other 'last man wins' shows. The final way you can be sent home, and stop getting a nice paycheck, is to do something completely out of character. If you 'kill' someone, you'd better have a good reason." Taz focused on me again. "No insanity pleas."

More laughter, but not from me.

"Well." He clapped again. "The hidden cameras are already rolling, microphones are on. Only places you're safe are inside the bathrooms so no one will see you washing up, and in the outhouses, so think about what you want the world to see and hear. Now, let's"—Taz lowered his voice and wiggled his fingers in the air, backing into the general store as he spoke—"go back in time for some *Harsh Reality.*"

He disappeared inside.

To take his place, a trio of musicians arrived, one with a fiddle, another with a banjo, and a third with a washboard. They set to playing a rousing square dance number that helped break the ice. People paired up, and soon we had a regular hoedown going, though I suspected the decent dancers were the paid "extras" the director had mentioned. The few main players I saw attempting the steps managed to stumble all over themselves and their partners.

The newspapermen had vanished as well, and I still couldn't spot the dang cameras, or the audience for that matter. When a hand tapped me on the shoulder, I jumped.

Really, I needed these future folks to stop surprising me.

I turned to give the culprit a piece of my mind and looked down into the face of an overeager fourteen- or fifteen-year-old kid. He bowed, sweeping off his hat in a dramatically gallant gesture.

"Dance, Sheriff?"

It took everything I had to maintain a straight face, but *he* was so serious, I didn't want to hurt the young man's feelings. I cocked my head to one side, sizing him up. "You any good?"

"Regional square dance champion for my freshman year."

They had competitions for these things? Oookay. "Well, let's go, then."

He took my arm and twirled me into the already positioned dancers, and damn me if he wasn't as good as he'd boasted. "What's your name?" I shouted over the music and the steps-caller.

"For this week, it's Adam."

"Well," I said as everyone bowed to their partners, "I'm pleased to make the acquaintance of such a fine dancer." Beside me, a woman yelped as her man tromped on her toes. "My feet are pleased too."

The song ended, and before Adam could suggest another turn, a warm hand grasped one of mine. I turned and focused on a shiny gold star like the one pinned to my own vest. The new Deputy Baylor.

Though he obviously wanted my immediate attention, I held up my free hand and smiled back at Adam. "Thank you for the dance," I told him.

"My pleasure, Sheriff." He took off his hat and bowed once more, then wandered off to the side of the makeshift dance area where several girls his own age waited.

Now for my new admirer.

"Jake," I said, inclining my head politely. Not just more handsome but older too, closer to my own age. In fact, glancing around, I realized none of the main players were hideous or grossly overweight. Some things about the theater hadn't changed.

"How about a dance, Sheriff?" Jake tipped his hat.

"You can call me Cali. I'm not on duty."

Tucking his thumbs into his own vest, the deputy puffed out his chest. "Aren't we always on duty?"

"No," I told him with a firm shake of my head. I pointed at the sky. "Sun's down. We're off. Lawmen have personal lives, too, even out here. But if there's any trouble…."

"We're always on call," he finished for me. "Got it." He leaned in closer. "You really memorized that book of hers, didn't you?"

I smiled and let him lead me into the cluster of bumbling dancers. "You could say that."

We swirled and twirled. I breathed in the aroma of roasting meat, wildflowers, and male. Would've much rather been dancing with Arlene, but that wouldn't happen in public. Jake stepped on my foot. Twice. That hadn't changed. The real Jake Baylor couldn't dance worth spit either. When the music slowed, he caught me in his arms, pulling me in so our vests brushed. I didn't release him but took a step back. "This is polite space." Though judging from the other couples, that space had narrowed over time.

A tug brought me back in close. "Maybe I don't want to be so polite."

I raised my eyebrows.

"Come on, Cali. You gotta believe those two had something going. A woman sheriff and a male deputy? No way they weren't lovers, even if she did keep a woman on the side. Bisexual and ahead of her time. Let me tell you, your character might have been the star of the past, but I intend to get a real acting gig out of this deal. If we work it right, we'll never have to put our lives on the line for shit pay again."

I stopped dancing, not caring when the next couple bumped us. The man cursed—something foul a gentleman would never use in public. The woman muttered an apology.

"Let me make this plain. We aren't lovers. We never were." Heat rose to my face. Bad enough I had

to put up with this farce if I wanted to track down
the remaining Eye Killers. But I'd had my fill of
horseshit being said about me. "You were my friend.
I trained you. You looked up to me. You were polite
and respectful. At all times."

"To a woman? I doubt that. I'm betting Cali Mc-
Cade slept her way into office. Nothing else explains
the only female sheriff in those times."

Cameras be damned, Eye Killers be damned, I
slugged him.

People might have made up a lot of things about
California McCade, but no one would ever say I
couldn't throw a punch. Or call me a whore to my
face.

Bright red blood flowed from Jake's nose as
he staggered to the side, covering it with one hand.
It ran down his chin and spattered the collar of his
spanking-new white shirt. I saw his free hand twitch
toward his holster, then clench and unclench instead,
going to smooth the outside of his pants leg.

Really? This was no killing offense. Just a little disagreement between partners. Not that I much
wanted to partner with him, but I'd do what I had to.
I'd have to keep my eye on this man if he was that
quick to think about pulling a gun, even a fake one.

Placing a hand on my hip, I smirked at him.
"You gonna decorate me with red paint? Hey," I added, waving at his stained shirt, "we can match."

My new deputy growled, low and fierce,
and I braced my feet apart for a full-on brawl. All
around us, couples stopped dancing. Even the musicians ceased playing. I lowered my voice. "Really,

Deputy, is this how you handle the law where you come from? We're supposed to stop this kind of bullshit, not start it. You started it, I stopped it. Let it be done with."

The tension never left his shoulders, but he broke eye contact with me, turning to where Doc stood nearby, medical bag at the ready. The gathering breathed a collective sigh of relief when Jake let himself be seated on the boardwalk step to have his nose tended. I didn't *think* I'd broken it.

"Come on, let's get you fixed up," Doc said to him. His slow southwestern drawl rumbled across the gathering. Gentle, uncallused hands got straight to work.

I turned away and came nose to nose with big brown eyes and long dark lashes.

"You all right?"

I faced the present-day Arlene. In her fitted black boddice and flouncy skirt, she had curves like an hourglass. "Long as you don't call me darlin'."

One side of her mouth quirked upward. "Wouldn't dream of it. That's a damn fine right cross you got there. Wanna dance?"

My eyebrows shot up. She had to be joking. To my surprise, the musicians had started up again, but I'd lost myself in Arlene's brown eyes. "I'm thinkin' these folks might object to that kind of fraternizing."

"Right. Stay in character." She pouted her full red lips. "Pity."

Could they have found a "showgirl" who also preferred the company of women? How would they have figured out such a thing? Come out and asked? Had times changed that much?

I wondered if she was also an "upstairs girl" in Vegas, wherever that was.

"I'd rather stroll, check out the town," I said, hoping to figure where these folks had put everything, 'cause half of it was wrong.

"Fair enough." She crooked an elbow, inviting me to take her arm.

I stepped away faster than a horse shying from a rattler. No. No, no, no. This wasn't my Arlene. I'd lost my Arlene, left her to get possessed by the Eye Killers and been forced to put her out of her misery with my own damn gun. I wouldn't let that happen again. And besides, even the act of linking arms would send the wrong message to the townsfolk. Neither of us needed that kind of trouble.

If the Eye Killers came and I lost her again, I was damn determined not to have gotten close to her.

Arlene held up both hands, palms out. "Whoa, okay, Cali. I won't crowd you. Maybe a stroll will let you clear your head. I'll be around when you get back." With a smile to show she held no hard feelings, the Vegas showgirl drifted away into the milling townspeople.

Clear my head. Right. My head was so twisted and turned, I wondered if I'd ever see clear again.

CHAPTER 15

MY FEET carried me from building to building, the wrongness of each one muddling me further. Someone had gone through and lit the kerosene lanterns hanging from the lampposts set at uneven intervals, and I imagined things hovering in the darkness, waiting to get me alone and strike. It was like being in a dream I couldn't control, or a nightmare I couldn't wake from.

Before I knew what had happened, I found myself trudging up the church steps. The door creaked when I pushed it, and fresh paint assailed my nostrils. Otherwise, not much had changed. The sanctuary stood silent, dark, and empty, moonlight casting odd shadows through the windows. No stained glass here. The town couldn't afford it. Just natural light, "pure like God intended," Xanthis used to say.

I removed my hat and left it on a shelf by the door. Then I took a match and candle from a bin at the entrance, lit the wick, and moved from lamp to lamp to brighten the gloom. Out of curiosity, I opened the storage closet and shoved on the shelves.

Nothing. No secret staircase. But the closet seemed larger, longer from front to back. So they had rebuilt the church along with everything else. And when they did, they hadn't included a hidden space behind a moving bookcase. They'd simply built the storage room and placed the bookcase against the true back wall. Which meant the stairs were probably right beneath the floor at the rear of the closet. And getting to them and clearing the cave-in would take nothing short of an explosion. I'd have to go in through the main mine entrance, the same way I came out, if I was to retrieve the treasure. Then I had to know where to put it. Too much. Too damn much. The weight of the world rested on my shoulders.

I returned to the worship area of the church. Still pressing the smooth wax candle between both palms, I knelt before the heavy wooden cross suspended above the simple lectern.

I hesitated for a long moment before speaking. Then the words tumbled out like water over river stones. "God, I'm not much for prayin'. Haven't been since you took my ma and pa in the same night. And maybe I deserve punishin' for my absence. They say you have a purpose for everything, and I couldn't see it then. Not quite sure 'bout it now, either, 'cept that night led me to become Oblivion's sheriff, and being the sheriff led me here.

"If I've been chosen, like Preacher Xanthis said, then please, God, please give me the strength I need to defeat this evil. Please…." My voice broke, and a tear fell upon the candle, not enough to extinguish it, but making it flutter and flicker. "Please don't let me lose them all again," I finished in a whisper. Whether I knew them or not, this was my town. Anyone in it was my responsibility. I had to do a better job.

The sobs tore through me, doubling me over where I knelt and echoing in the empty space, but I didn't try to hold them in anymore. I'd given myself permission at last to mourn my friends, my acquaintances, my lover, and my town, and the floodgates weren't closing anytime soon.

I don't know how long I cried, but by the time I'd wrung myself out, my collar was soaked and my throat had gone raw. Hitching in an uneven breath, I stood on trembling limbs, put out the lamps and the candle, and returned what remained of the stick of wax to the bin. I retrieved my hat, put it on, and tipped it to the cross, then made sure to shut the heavy doors behind me.

The moon hung high when I reached the main street, the musicians long gone and all signs of the barbeque cleared away. I headed for "home," feet and eyelids growing heavier with every step. A party was in full swing at the saloon, piano music carrying on a spring breeze, and a need to be around people almost pulled me in to join them, but a jaw-splitting yawn convinced me otherwise.

I made a quick stop in the outhouse behind my office, hoping against hope the director told the truth about the absence of cameras there. Nothing wrong with my backside, but I sure as hell didn't want pictures taken of it.

Then up the stairs to my bedroom, where I threw myself on the bed fully clothed and stared at the ceiling for at least an hour. Not my bed. Not my room. Everything felt wrong.

Maybe if I stuck to my normal routines, I could fool myself into getting some sleep. After all, I couldn't very well fight evil while exhausted. That in mind, I went back downstairs and settled in at my desk.

My first thought had me going for the gun safe. No one had set the combination, probably because I'd never written it down and they wanted to make sure I could get into it, so I set it now—Pa's birthday like I'd always had it. I drew out the leather-bound journal, expecting blank pages and surprised to see my own handwriting within. Not my original, but our director had tucked a copy of *Women's Lib in the 1890s—The Recovered Journals of Sheriff Cali McCade* inside, and I spent a few minutes reading the author's commentary on my journal entries before the false assumptions began turning my stomach.

Snatching up a pencil, I flipped to the end where some clean sheets of paper had been added and scribbled furiously:

I was not and am not a whore. Every success I had, including becoming sheriff, I earned.

I was not and will not become a murderer. When I kill, I do it out of necessity and with much regret. Anyone who says otherwise can damn well go to hell.

Slamming the journal shut, I returned it to the safe.

A quick rummaging in my desk revealed my key ring, which I clipped on my belt, and when I went to close the drawer, I heard a rolling thunk in the back. Holding my breath, almost afraid to hope, I reached far in and closed my fingers around a bottle. I pulled it toward me with a grateful sigh.

"Dear God and props manager, for that which I am about to receive, I am eternally grateful. Amen."

Malek had failed to provide a glass, but that didn't stop me from uncorking the whiskey and taking a healthy draught. Good liquor. Not my usual brand, according to the label, but rich and smooth with a heady aroma that made me prop my feet up on the desk, close my eyes, lean back, and inhale.

I AWOKE with my head pillowed on crossed arms atop my desk. The sun burned too bright against closed eyelids, and my mouth tasted like something had died in there while I slept. When I sat up, every bone in my spine popped and cracked.

"Mornin', Sheriff!" Too friendly and too chipper to be heartfelt, my deputy leaned in the doorway, took one look at me, and frowned. "You look like hell."

Since I couldn't deny it, I chose a glare for my response instead.

"Look, Cali, we got off on the wrong foot. And while my nose isn't happy about it, our little argument at the barbeque certainly got plenty of attention."

Yep, black-and-blue bruises decorated the bridge of his nose, and it had swelled. Not nearly as handsome as the day before.

"How about we let bygones be bygones and start over." Jake crossed the office, one hand extended.

I didn't take it. "Listen," I said, rising to my feet, "if you want attention, go run for mayor. Otherwise, we have jobs to do, and I intend to do mine, real or not." I brushed past him, snagging my hat off the desk where it had fallen sometime during the night. "In my real life, I'd be headed for the stables right now, so that's where I'm going. Come find me if there's any trouble."

I managed not to slam the door on my way out, but only just.

I'd have stomped all the way, but my overfull bladder had other plans, and I detoured back to the jail's outhouse. The door stuck, and I'd sweet-talked it into opening by kicking it a few times when someone came up behind me and slammed me face-first into the wood, knocking it shut once more.

One hand held my cheek against the splintery door. Another gripped my right wrist, trying to prevent me from reaching my ridiculous paint-shooter. It wasn't much of a grip, and I could have broken it at any time, but the attack was too coordinated to be an Eye Killer, and my curious side wanted to know what the hell this person wanted.

"Just what do you think you're up to, bitch?" A woman's voice, though not one I recognized.

I hadn't met many women other than not-Arlene since I'd been here. In fact, I'd met none, though I'd seen plenty strolling around with names I knew and faces I didn't. I tried to give a response, but it came out garbled. She let up on the pressure a little.

"I said I'm about to go take a shit. If you'd like specifics—"

Slam. A few wood chips fell from the door to land at my feet as my face connected again, hard. Okay, this wasn't amusing me anymore. Soon I'd be as bruised as Jake.

Gauging my attacker's position, I lifted one booted foot and stomped backward, bringing it down in the middle of the other woman's shoe. When it comes to boots and ladies' shoes, I'll take boots every time. The woman yelped, releasing me and hopping away on her one good foot.

"You fucking bitch!"

I hid my shock at the language. Hanging with the boys at the saloon, I'd certainly heard, and used, plenty of harsh words, but I wasn't used to hearing them from actual ladies. Turning, I studied my opponent, and a lot of things fell into place.

Flowing skirt, too tight bodice, gaudy jewelry. "Let me guess," I ventured. "You're Lucinda."

"Damn straight," she snarled, reaching to rub her injured foot through the little black velvet shoe. "And Arlene is mine. The history books say so, and so do I. So back off."

I frowned, and my bladder gave another uncomfortable twinge. Sure, I scribbled a few unrepeatable phrases in my journal about Arlene and Lucinda when I'd caught them together. Didn't make it a permanent thing. Didn't mean I wanted to be reminded of it, either. Reaching out, I grabbed the front of her silk bodice and drew her in until our noses practically touched. "I've had too little sleep and no coffee.

And I'm betting," I said, low and even, "this is another power play for the hidden cameras. You start a fight with me, you get more attention. Only I don't want attention. I couldn't give a horse's ass for attention. And I will finish any fight you start the same way I finished with Deputy Baylor last night 'cept with a lot more blood involved."

Lucinda's throat shifted as she swallowed hard.

"However, if you're really serious about wanting Arlene for yourself, you should know this. Arlene belongs to whomever she wants to belong to. She always has. And neither you nor I have anything to say about it." With that, I thrust her away from me. She stumbled, then fell, landing in a small puddle of who-knew-what just outside the outhouse and dirtying her pretty skirts. "Now, if you don't mind, I'm going to piss."

I yanked open the door and slammed it behind me, waiting to lower my breeches just long enough to hear her limp away.

Holy hell. And *I* was the one everyone thought was crazy.

CHAPTER 16

ASIDE FROM the occasional bite, kick, or getting thrown, horses are safer than people. Safer, more loyal, more trustworthy, and oftentimes smarter.

I shoved open the stable door, stirring up dust and shaking down hay from the second level loft. At the sight of the four horses leaning their curious heads out of the stalls to stare at me, my chest tightened. Beautiful animals, all of them—an Appaloosa, an Arabian, a Morgan mare, and a gray stallion of indeterminate breed. Again, I hadn't expected any broken-down nags, since they were here for their theatrical performance, but these specimens surpassed even my expectations. I cooed to them as I passed, pausing to rub the white blaze on the Arabian's nose and getting an appreciative nicker in response. Gentle too. No snorting or hoof-pawing at the gates. Probably trained to tolerate even small children. I wished I had some sugar cubes and resolved to get some the next time I went to the general store.

Something small and brightly colored winged through the door I'd left open and settled on my shoulder. I reached up to rub the soft, feathered head. "Hey there, Pandora. Thought you'd forgotten about me."

She shook herself, head waggling from side to side—a negative answer if ever I'd seen one, and I laughed.

"Won't Xanthis be missing you?"

Another headshake.

"Well, don't get yourself in trouble. I might need you around here."

Pandora bobbed up and down in response. Just how smart was this dang bird, anyway? Her answer didn't do much for my state of mind. I tried to ignore the implications as I continued along the row, reading off the names of the horses scrawled on their stalls' chest-high doors: Flyflicker, Miss Ellie, Barnaby, Grace.

When I reached my usual stall, I stopped dead still, eyebrows rising as I took in the creature waiting for me with affectionate brown eyes. Someone had carved "Chessie" into the crossbeam on her stall's gate, and indeed, she was the right coloring, height, and apparent age to have been my Chessie, but I knew with the deepest sadness my Chessie was long gone.

I didn't even attempt to stop or wipe away the tears that ran down my cheeks as I threw my arms around the horse's neck and sobbed. The motion sent Pandora squawking to the rafters, but I didn't care. Stroking the horse's mane, I drew in breath after breath of her sweet scent—hay, oats, and the distinctive yet comforting smell of *horse*. She stood patiently through it all, finally nuzzling my braid to get me to stop.

Damn, I thought, swiping away the wetness on my face. I could count on one hand the number of times I'd cried in the last year, and here I was, coming apart at the seams twice in less than a day.

You're just tired, I told myself.

Either that, a little voice inside me whispered, *or you really are going crazy.*

The horse shifted in her stall and gave me her second surprise beyond her beauty. She wasn't a she. She was a he.

"Well," I said aloud, "that does change things." Not my opinion of him, not in the least, and I reassured him with a quick pat of his flank. But he'd need a more appropriate name. Chessie would no longer do.

I scanned the ground, picked up the first sharp rock I could find, and drew a big X over Chessie's name carved in the wood. Hadn't seemed right, anyway. No animal could replace my Chessie.

Tapping the stone against my chin, I pondered over names. Chessie and I had lost one another. Sandra Meadows, my modern-day counterpart, had been taken from her equine companion as well. At least I assumed she'd named the horse depicted on her vehicle after an actual animal. I hoped someone was taking care of that horse, somewhere.

In big block letters, I scrawled the name "Ford" next to the crossed-out "Chessie." Least I could do to honor the poor woman whose body I'd dropped in a mine pit.

Which reminded me. Sooner or later I needed to get myself back to the gold mine. I'd gone a whole day without seeing any evidence of the Eye Killers. If they hadn't yet made their way into the rebuilt Oblivion, maybe I had a chance to stop them before they could. But first, I had to come up with a plan.

Resettling on my shoulder, Pandora studied Ford, and he returned the stare. She cooed at the horse. He wuffled back. No, I was not believing the two could communicate. Not for one damn minute.

Somewhere in the distance I heard a male voice calling Pandora's name—Xanthis, no doubt. The bird nuzzled my chin once more, then winged off through the stable door. Fickle critter.

Ford bumped my chest with his nose, snuffling softly at me, and his insistence broke into my thoughts. "Sorry, boy, no apples."

The general store would have them, though, and a rumbling in my stomach told me I needed breakfast as well.

I gave Ford one last rub under the chin and headed out, getting about halfway to the store before I realized I had no money. Well, the bank sat to my left. I wondered if my account with them was historically accurate.

Inside, the establishment bustled with activity, more than it had in my day. Much more. Seemed as if half the town needed to make a withdrawal, which made sense, I supposed. Arlene bobbed a pert curtsy at me and winked as I entered, then returned to counting some bills at one of the counters. I guessed she'd just made a withdrawal.

There were quite a few bills, and she placed each one down almost reverently, then picked them up and counted them into her palm once more.

Saloon girls. Every dollar accounted for, always, and Lord help those who tried to short-change them.

I got in a line of folks waiting for the single teller—a decent enough recreation of Miss Clara, her glasses balanced precariously on the tip of her nose and her hair pulled back in a severe bun as it always had been. She saw me step into line and her upper lip curled in a snarl. No one in town, not even Lucinda, had hated me as much as Miss Clara. To her I was improper, and that's all it took for some folks.

And of course, I complained about her in my journal. Frequently. So that's how she'd play her role. Payback, I supposed, for all my written whining.

"So we've already lost two." The teenager behind me gave a harsh laugh. "Hard to believe anyone would wimp out so fast."

I turned and recognized her as Sam's temporary daughter, with Sam standing next to her.

"And the Lansing family. Don't forget them. No guarantee they're gone, though. Malek said they never collected their day's pay. Maybe they're off planning something for the ratings. The son, Adam, he looked pretty devious."

Adam. Hmm. I knew that name. Couldn't quite place it, though.

Sam glanced at me and nodded a hello, then turned to his daughter.

"You're probably right about them plotting," the girl agreed. "Or maybe," she said, all seriousness, "the Eye Killers got them."

My shoulders stiffened. Had everyone read my damn journal?

"Now, don't you worry about that none. We should all assume those were just the ramblings of a sad, jealous, lonely woman." Sam flinched and shot me an apologetic smile. "Sorry, Sheriff. No offense meant."

"None taken," I managed through gritted teeth. Hell, if I hadn't seen them myself, I'd think it was crazy.

I started to turn back around, but something at the girl's neckline caught my eye, and I focused on a five-pointed star hanging from a silver chain around her neck. She followed my gaze and wrapped her fist around it, tucking it down her dress. "I'm Wiccan," she said, her tone challenging me to fault her.

I just stared.

"Good witch," the girl explained, "top point of the pentagram pointing up." Then she sighed and rolled her eyes.

Maybe everyone in this time period knew all about witches, but I didn't. Good or not, I wondered if the Eye Killers weren't the only problem I was supposed to take care of in this town. I scanned her from head to shoes. Didn't look like much of a threat, despite her mouth, and her announcement hadn't fazed any of the other folks waiting. I decided to let it go.

"What? They didn't have witches in the Old West?" she asked, misinterpreting my scrutiny.

"They didn't advertise themselves," I said dryly. I returned my attention to the line.

My turn came at the window, and I asked to see an accounting of my balance. Miss Clara sighed as if I'd requested the most toilsome task imaginable. She pulled out the ledger, letting it thump onto the wood surface, and flipped to the appropriate page, then turned it around so I could read.

I skipped to the bottom, and my eyes almost popped out of their sockets.

"How… how did it come to be so much?" I had almost fourteen dollars in what must have started as an empty account. My usual rate was $1.50 a day. Somehow I'd struck gold, and I hadn't even been back to the mine. Maybe I got extra for putting up with bullshit. What was the going rate for that?

With the bank's high ceilings, my voice had carried, and the conversation around me ceased, several people in line behind me, including Jake Baylor, crowding closer to see. I shooed them back with a glare.

"Let me guess. You didn't read your contract." Miss Clara peered at me over the rims of her glasses. How they stayed on her nose, I had no idea.

If there'd been a contract, Sandra Meadows had signed it, not me. "Refresh my memory. Please," I added as an afterthought.

She pointed a sharp-nailed finger at the listing of deposits I'd skimmed over and read them aloud, even while upside down, to me. "Bonus for barbecue

fight—$3.00. Bonus for church visit—$4.00. Bonus
for diary entry—$2.00." She tapped on the final one.
"This came in while you were standing in line. Bonus for horse chat—$3.00. All that plus your regular
daily rate comes out to about $14.00. Congratula-
tions," Miss Clara added in a tone that spoke of anything but happiness for me. "You're rich."

A woman standing behind me gave a low whistle. "And don't forget, when you leave the show,
they give you a matching balance with two extra ze-
ros added. Fourteen hundred dollars for a day's work
ain't nothing to sneeze at."

Fourteen hundred dollars. My hands closed on
the edge of the counter to steady myself. Indoor
plumbing, hidden cameras, fine horses, and now this.
What wealth our country had in this future!

"That's pretty fantastic," Sam said from where
he'd moved aside for me. He smiled a genuine smile,
but his daughter didn't look so pleased. She popped
something in her mouth she'd been chewing on like
a cow since I'd noticed them.

I held up a hand to silence her smacking and
popping. "Wait. You're telling me they have cameras in the church? I'd think a church would be, well,
sacred." And my journal. They'd gotten in my safe
and read my journal? How? Or was there a peephole
over my desk and someone hiding upstairs? Had
they watched me enter the new combination on the
safe and then taken the journal? Was that even possible? Holy hell. A throbbing took up behind my eyes
and settled in, threatening to become a full-blown

whopper of a headache. After the bank, I might have to go see Doc if this kept up.

"No place sacred around here except the out-house," Sam reminded me with another smile and a shake of his head. I'd always liked the Sam of the past, and I was beginning to like this one too.

Well, this explained a lot. People weren't just trying to start acting careers. They had money at stake. And clearly folks did a lot of foolhardy things for money, past and present.

"You know," Jake sneered, "for a woman who claims she doesn't want attention, you sure are get-ting a lot of it. That sob-fest at the church was in-spired. You almost had me believing it."

"How would you know? Did you follow me?" He couldn't have. Last I'd seen of him, Doc was fix-ing up his bloody nose. I supposed he might have trailed me after that—I wasn't sure how long I'd wandered before heading for the church—but I'd gotten pretty good over the years at noticing when someone tracked me.

"Oh, can the bullshit, Sheriff." Jake closed what little space remained between us, forcing me to look up if I wanted to meet his eyes. "I went to the second floor of the courthouse like everyone else."

Huh?

Jake leaned down until I could smell his tobac-co-laden breath. "You can quit the eloquent perfor-mance. Crying in the church, crying over your horse. Pulling the directors' heartstrings."

"Yeah," Sam's daughter piped in. "Stealing all the limelight for yourself. Hogging up the cameras.

Nobody even noticed when I pretended to be bitten by a snake."

"That's just it. I don't think she *is* pretending." Arlene. So much for my tracking senses. I hadn't even heard the woman move up behind me, but I welcomed her presence at my back now. "Step away, Deputy. You're crowding the sheriff."

The two faced off, Jake's right hand twitching toward his holster, Arlene's resting on her hip right above her own, which she still wore with her skirts, and I wondered if I'd have to stop a gunfight right here in the bank. Then Jake surprised us all by bursting into laughter.

"Nope, sorry, Sheriff… and Arlene." He tipped his hat to me in a mock salute. "Not giving you the satisfaction of getting more bonus money by having two folks fight over you." He fixed me with a glare. "At least not today. You might end up fooling the idiots who make up middle-class America, and you might be fooling this one." Jake jerked his thumb at Arlene. "But you aren't fooling me. You're in it for the cash like everyone else."

"Aren't you a little afraid of pissing off your future fans with comments like that?" Arlene asked.

Jake waved if off. "Nah. The director said he didn't care how we talked, just whether or not we could live in this environment. You know how these reality shows work. The more obnoxious we are, the more the audience eats it up. And besides, he can edit out anything he really hates." Then he strode out of the bank without finishing whatever business he'd had.

I watched him go until the door swung shut behind him, then glanced down in surprise at my own
fingers wrapped around the grip of my paint-shooter.
Lot of good it would have done me. Needed to re-
train my reflexes. In a real fight, I didn't want to be
reaching for a useless weapon.

Flexing my hand, I turned to face Arlene.
"Thanks. I think."

She frowned at the qualifier, but now I had to
question everyone's motivations. Arlene had seemed
genuine just now, and at the barbeque for that matter,
but maybe she'd done some vaudeville melodrama
before becoming a, what had the director said? Vegas
showgirl. If Jake were to be believed, who knew how
much money the three of us had just made for our little spat? So far, the one person I felt I could trust in
this time was Sam, who headed for the exit, guiding
his daughter with a light grip on her arm. Well, no
more sarcastic comments from her, at least.

She threw me a nasty look over her shoulder.

For now.

CHAPTER 17

SINCE I didn't know if prices were what I remembered, I withdrew a couple of dollars and got out of the bank, where I ran straight into three young men wearing kerchiefs over their faces. They pointed real-enough looking guns at me, and though I'd bet my newly earned pay they fired paint pellets, I wasn't willing to take that gamble. That, I'd leave to the saloon poker players.

Hands in the air, I leaned against the bank entrance. "Can I help you boys with something?"

One raised his eyebrows in surprise, and his kerchief slipped, revealing a pock-marked teenager. "We're robbing the bank," he informed me, tugging the face mask back into place. His voice cracked on the word "bank." His two buddies snickered.

"No, you're not." I'd spotted a bit of red paint on the leader's fingers. Seemed some of the pellets leaked. Least I knew what I was dealing with. The three boys exchanged confused looks.

"You're not gonna draw your gun?" a second one asked.

This would-be robber sported dirty-blond hair and blue eyes and spoke in a higher pitch. I reassessed the trio. Two boys. One girl. Ah, the Davidson siblings. I'd written in my journal about catching them stealing candy from the back room of the general store. Looked like they'd decided to up the ante a bit.

"Nope," I said, answering the gun question. I lowered my hands. My stomach growled. The sun hung straight overhead. Coming on high noon and I still hadn't had any breakfast. I swallowed a yawn. Or my dang coffee. Another damn power play. Let's all get into a shoot-out at the bank and rake in the dollars. Only just like Jake inside, I wasn't playing.

"Why the hell not?" The leader poked me with the barrel of his pistol.

It was all the opportunity I needed. My hand flashed out and I grabbed the end of the gun, twisting it from his grasp and twirling it neatly to point at his chest. I smiled. "Because I have yours."

Some of the townsfolk had noticed the doings outside the bank, and Jake approached with his pistol drawn. Beside him came Al toting the saloon's shotgun. None of the trio noticed.

"We can still shoot you!" the other brother chimed in, resting his free hand on the girl's shoulder. He was shortest and youngest, and his bangs fell in his eyes, almost obscuring his vision completely.

"Not before I fill your pal here full of holes… erm, paint." I gave a minute nod to Deputy Jake and Al, in position with their guns trained on the teenagers' backs.

The younger boy glanced at the girl, his sister. "It'll be great!" he enthused. "There'll be a funeral for Alex and the sheriff, and the two of us could still rob the bank."

"But I'll be off the show!" the leader complained.

"You snooze, you lose, bro."

A small pit of worry formed in my stomach. If I'd misjudged the situation, I could end up sent "home" too. One, I had no home. Two, I needed to be here to stop the Eye Killers.

Thank goodness, Jake had heard enough, and his lust to be a hero overruled his desire to see me "dead." "Then I guess you all lose." He fired the pistol at the kids' feet. The bang didn't resound quite as much as real gunfire, but it made all of them jump. A red splotch marked where the pellet hit the ground.

The last two armed robbers threw down their guns and raised their hands high.

"You want me to arrest them, Sheriff?" Jake asked, picking up the discarded weapons.

"Nah, just send them home to their folks. In my time, they'd get the tarnation beaten out of them." Not sure how folks dealt out discipline now.

"In your—?" Al laughed. "Right, Sheriff Mc-Cade. Right. Say, this was kinda fun. You need to deputize me again, you just holler, all right?"

"Sure thing, Al." A crash resounded from the saloon across the street. I waved him in that direction. "Better get yourself back to your own problems."

The larger man took off running, probably sensing another opportunity to earn "attention points."

I turned to the kids. "Just one more thing before you all git. Where'd you get the guns?"

The girl lowered her hands a fraction, thought better of it, and raised them high again before answering me. "Malek at the general store sold them to us. Anyone who wants one can buy them, so long as they have money."

Oh, that was just dandy. Lots more trouble for me to deal with.

My stomach growled. Loudly.

But not right now. I turned and started walking in the opposite direction from the one Al had taken.

"Hey, aren't you going to do something about the bar fight?" Deputy Baylor indicated the sounds of breaking glass and men shouting.

"Nope." I kept walking. He took up pace beside me. I stopped and faced him. "I'm getting breakfast." I took another glance at the sun. "Or lunch. Go make yourself a couple of dollars breaking that up. Then meet me at Miss Josephine's and bring the mayor."

Jake's eyebrows shot up.

"That's an order," I told him.

For the first time in two days, I saw a genuine smile from my deputy, a genuine greedy smile, like a dog sizing up a cat dinner. "Thanks, Sheriff. Maybe you're all right, after all." He ran off after Al.

WITH A plate of fried chicken polished off and a piece of Miss Josephine's apple pie in front of me, I at last had a chance to catch my breath. I sat in the tiny front-parlor-turned-restaurant in Miss Josephine's resurrected house and stared out the window at the goings-on. Two other diners occupied a table against the wall, but otherwise, the place was empty. Over the course of an hour and a half I'd witnessed a fist-fight, an attempted horse theft, and a man with a sack over his shoulder claiming he'd struck gold at the old mine. Of course, when folks made him dump it, turned out he'd filled the bag with nothing but rocks. Attention. They all wanted attention. Oblivion was reminding me more of a schoolhouse than a town.

Miss Josephine herself, or a reasonable facsimile thereof, stood beside me, clucking disdainfully and wiping her hands on her apron. "Silly folks gonna get themselves shot. Me? I'll play my role and have something to leave my grandchildren when I pass on." She ran a hand through her graying hair, smoothing a few strands into place. "If you have any sense, you'll take my advice and do the same, Sheriff. When you serve vittles to folks, you hear a lot of talk. They're gunning for you, the lot of them."

"Don't I know it," I said, not taking my eyes off the window. "But apparently being their target *is* my new role." After placing a few coins on the table, I stood and retrieved my hat from the hat stand.

"Only if you let it be," she called after me as I strode back into the chaos. "Only if you let it be."

I ran into Jake and the mayor coming in as I walked out and set a few ground rules about what to do with all the folks getting themselves arrested, then hit the boardwalk at a fast pace with half a mind to set up a chair in front of the office and continue to view the show, but the thought reminded me of what

Jake had mentioned at the bank, something about seeing me from the second floor of the courthouse. Which didn't make sense. The windows up there faced away from the church.

I took the courthouse stairs two at a time, then slowed as I neared the top. Voices carried from the open doorway leading into the upper floor, and one of them was mine.

You're not gonna draw your gun?

Nope.

Why the hell not?

Sounds of scuffling followed my prior conversation with the young bank robbers.

Because I have yours.

Several people laughed uproariously at my witty banter, and I heard Director Taz say, "Priceless. Just priceless. I couldn't *write* dialogue that good. And you say she has no acting background? The woman's a natural."

How the hell had they gotten my voice? Was this a product of these "microphones" they'd mentioned? We had dictaphones and gramophones, sure, but the sound never came out so crystal clear.

"She's not a natural. She's delusional."

I vaguely recognized that voice. Doc. The new Doc. His slow, steady drawl when he'd fixed up Jake's nose came back to me. And I didn't like what the doc was saying. Not one bit.

"Go ahead and replay that church scene," he suggested. I heard some shifting and clicking.

My sneaking skills had always been better than my tracking. Slipping through the open door, I sidled up behind the gathered assembly.

Three men and a woman sat in big comfy chairs in front of glowing rectangles, with Doc standing behind them. I could name Erick, Ryan, and Malek, but the woman, I didn't know. While I tried to figure out where the glow came from, I nearly gave myself away with my sharp intake of breath. Good thing the moving figures on the rectangles had them all transfixed. Yep, moving figures. People. People who talked. Moving, talking photographs.

And one of them was of me.

"There! Right there!" Doc shouted, pointing a finger at the image of my tear-stained face. "That's real emotion, not acting. I might be a family practitioner, but I have a secondary degree in psychiatry, and I'm telling you, our sheriff is taking this thing too seriously to be healthy."

Watching myself kneel in the church and ask God for strength shocked me almost as much, if not more, than coming face-to-face with my looka-like, Sandra Meadows. Or meeting the new Arlene. I forced myself to take slow, even breaths while I fought the urge to drop like a stone in a well.

Or a body in a pit.

"Serious doesn't make her crazy, Doc," Ryan put in a little defensively. Maybe he felt guilty about casting a "delusional" woman to play my role. "It's just for the television." He gestured at one of the boxes.

Time to break up this little party. I tore my eyes from the "television." Interesting term, and it made sense. If telephones could reproduce sound, then I guess televisions could reproduce, well, visions. "Ahem!"

All five turned to face me, the seated ones' chairs rotating. Doc's lips curled downward into a scowl.

"If y'all have something to say about my state of mind, maybe you'll be kind enough to say it to my face."

Erick jumped up quick to offer me a smile and his seat. "Cali! Glad you stopped in. Let me introduce Danielle Vasquez, the assistant director."

I shook the hand she extended and nodded a greeting to the others. So, a female director. She dressed smartly in tailored pants, a button-down shirt, and high heels completely impractical for Oblivion. I'd never seen such a combination, but it suited her.

"Don't pay any attention to Doc. He's just playing his part," Danielle assured me, running a hand through shoulder-length dark hair.

"Right. And that part appears to involve locking me in an asylum." I pasted on a smile and took the offered chair, my aching body sinking into leather cushions. "Might have to rethink sticking around if that's the case."

A look of true horror passed over the directors' faces. "Oh no, you can't leave," Ryan stated, tapping on what looked like typewriter keys in front of yet another television, or something similar. A bar graph appeared on its glass surface. When I peered closer,

I saw the names of all the major Oblivion cast members, with mine sporting the tallest bar. Tallest by a lot. "These are projected audience reaction ratings. You're gonna be a hit, Cali. An overnight sensation. The next *Xena: Warrior Princess* maybe. When this thing airs, we're predicting women, particularly women in primarily male-dominated professions like law enforcement, and of course lesbians, will be the highest percentage of our viewers. And that's a first for *Harsh Reality*. Unlike some other reality shows, we haven't had the best success with female viewers in any of the fifty states."

My mind raced to catch up. *Fifty* states? And people in all those states would somehow be watching… me? Maybe like a telegram, these moving pictures could be sent out. And I wasn't even ready to think about how easily he tossed "lesbian" about like it was no big deal, like no one cared about it at all. I was starting to think I might need that asylum.

"I'm betting that's been Cali's goal all along," Erick said, reseating himself and putting an arm around my shoulders. Somehow I managed not to flinch. I'd never cared for contact from strangers.

"What do you mean?" asked Doc. Even no longer facing him, I could still hear the glare in his voice.

"Law enforcement. Women. Cali McCade was their hero until the historians dug up old Arlene and had the bullet in her head tested against the ones recovered from the old tree behind the sheriff's office where she took target practice. Then, of course, they had to dig up a few more bodies and match the bullets that killed them as well. They all came from the same gun. Not conclusive proof, but…." The director let us draw the same conclusions everyone else apparently had.

More futuristic wonders, testing bullets. Lucky me. All I cared about was someone had given Arlene a proper burial, even if investigators had gone and unearthed her later. I wondered who'd done the burying. Certainly not the walking dead, but if anyone had survived that awful night, they'd have seen to it. I hoped they'd put her back.

"Now she's making up for it. Doing what she can to reinstate Cali's good name." From the corner of my eye, I saw Erick nod with satisfaction at his conclusions, and if it kept me out of the nuthouse, I was perfectly willing to accept them.

"Cali might not be a good name, but it is an odd one." Doc had to ruin it, heading off on a tangent. "Especially with that spelling. Not common of the time period. I wonder if it's short for something."

"California," I told them out of habit. Lots of people asked about my name, but I was more focused on the "television" and an image of myself in the stables talking to Ford. And Pandora. Wow, I did look pretty crazy. "My folks were headed there when their wagon broke down in Oblivion, and Ma gave birth earlier than expected. Rather than risk traveling with a newborn, they settled."

"Of course," Doc stated with far more meaning that the two words should have allowed.

Shit. I'd never written about my name in my journal. I hadn't started keeping one until I turned thirteen, and from then on, I'd focused on the day-to-day.

Ryan laughed, but it sounded forced. "Some imagination, eh, Doc?"

"Yes, quite the imagination." He turned and stomped down the stairs in his heavy boots.

"Careful," Malek warned, lowering his voice to be certain the departing doctor didn't overhear. He leaned down to speak in my ear. "Doc's earning extra pay acting as our on-site physician as well as a cast member. That gives him some authority. He's on the physicians' board at a New York hospital. Lots of pull. And he's just come under investigation in a malpractice suit. News broke right after we signed him. I'm guessing he's short on funds or he wouldn't be here at all. He's not a psychiatrist, but he dabbles in it, and if he can make more 'attention money' proving you're crazy on national TV, well, negative attention creates as many viewers as positive."

I nodded my understanding, stood, and paced to the window to watch Doc march across the street. A man with a purpose, and I was it. Miss Josephine's words about being a target came fluttering back to mind.

Hellfire.

Erick Taz came to look with me, and together we witnessed another pair of robbers, kerchiefs and all, come riding up to the bank. At the same moment, a second duo approached on foot from the opposite direction, and the foursome stood staring at each other in the street, gesturing and shouting for the competing pair to leave.

I wanted to pull all my hair out but satisfied my frustration by pinching the bridge of my nose and counting to ten.

"You know," I told him, "Oblivion's bank was never robbed. Not once in all the time I—California McCade lived there. Gold mine or not, it wasn't big enough to attract that kind of—" I almost said "attention," but that was rapidly becoming a dirty word in my vocabulary. "—notice."

The director grinned, showing perfect white, even teeth. Nobody had teeth like that unless he got them out of a jar. He gestured out the window. "That's reality TV for you."

I spun on my heel and headed for the stairs while calls for the sheriff carried through the open window on the evening breeze. "This isn't reality," I growled. "This is ridiculous."

CHAPTER 18

THE CLOSER I got to the bank, the more insistent the cries for my intervention in the current robbery became. One woman right out front was even running around in tiny circles pleading, "Help me, help me, save me, save me!" as if any of the robbers had the slightest interest in involving her in their little melodrama.

I tilted the brim of my hat down to block the setting sun's glare and stopped, staring. "Miss Clara?" I called in disbelief.

The bank teller stopped her bad acting and cries for help and looked me straight in the eye. "I've gotta eat too," she told me and returned to her frantic darting back and forth. The two pairs of would-be thieves continued their argument without so much as a glance in my direction.

"Where the hell is Deputy Baylor?" I snapped, searching the gathered onlookers for him.

Al stepped forward from the crowd. "At the jail, lockin' up Arlene for propositioning someone outside the saloon."

My heart made a traitorous drop into my stomach. I shook it off. It was all theater play, right? So what if she was sweet-talking someone else?

For money.

Of course, I only had Deputy Baylor's word for any of it. If he saw Arlene as competition for my affections and *attention*, I wouldn't put it past him to lock her away on false charges.

I blew out a breath. Wishful thinking. Which still left me to deal with four more bank robbers.

Well, dammit, I'd had enough for one very, very long day.

I didn't know who was behind the red-checkered kerchiefs, and I didn't care. Drawing my pistol, I took careful aim.

One, two, three, four.

Each of the men stared in disbelief at the red splotches decorating the fronts of their shirts and vests. Then, in the worst display I'd seen yet, they slid from their horses or crumpled to the ground respectively, rolling around and moaning, crawling about on all fours, dragging themselves across the dusty, manure-strewn street, until, at long last, they had all "died." I gave half a thought to shooting Miss Clara as well, then explaining it away as a stray shot, but she'd fallen on her knees beside the closest dead man, ripped off his kerchief, and was keening, "Oh, he was my brother! My brother!"

Miss Clara never had a brother.

I rolled my eyes heavenward. "God, why me?"

Doc strode forward, kicking the bodies over—nothing like the care the real Doc would have

shown, criminals or not, fake bullets or not—and
pronounced each one departed. Then he cast a wary
eye my way. "Four out of four chest shots. Each one
right over the heart. Impressive. You're a dangerous
woman, Sheriff McCade."

A woman who should be locked up went unspoken.

I chose to ignore him and raised my voice. "That's
what anyone else who tries to rob the bank tonight will
get, dammit. In fact, I swear by all that's holy, I'd best
not hear about any more trouble until morning. And I
mean well after sunrise." A fly buzzed into my face, and
I took off my hat and swatted at it, then threw the hat on
the ground and stomped on it. Hell, I was rich. I could
always get another one. "God knows, I need some goddamn sleep! Y'all hear me?"

Mutterings and nods from the crowd.

I snatched the hat off the ground and slapped it
against my thigh to shake off the dust. "Spread the
word. I'm going to bed!" Turning, I marched off, but
not before overhearing Doc's parting shot.

"Probably the best thing for you, Sheriff. You
sound like you need plenty of rest."

For once, I couldn't argue with him.

I STOPPED off at the general store long enough to
buy some apples and sugar cubes and leave standing
orders for no more guns to be sold between now and
the end of the week. Malek, ever in character while
tending the shop, agreed. After all, I was the sheriff,
and unless the mayor overruled me—which he might,
but I didn't intend to tell him about it—my word was

law. However, Malek admitted he'd sold quite a few weapons before I'd issued the command.

My day kept getting better and better.

Half-eaten apple in hand—my dinner—I gave a second one to Ford at the stables, making sure he got a good brushing from the stable hand and had plenty of oats. Then I treated him and the other horses to a few cubes of sugar for dessert. I wondered, if I earned enough money on this job, if I might be able to buy Ford from his true owners. I could tell we'd already developed a bond, Ford and I, and I didn't think I could bear to part with another animal companion so soon, even if it wasn't due to death—mine or his.

Back in the office, I spared a quick glance for Arlene, sound asleep and lips slightly parted (God, so much like the real woman I'd lost) on the first cell's cot. The lamps were lit, and the flickering light cast the whole scene in a romantic glow… with the exception of the bars, of course. I looked quickly away.

The other cell remained empty. As I'd laid out for my deputy and the mayor after my lunch, Jake and I wouldn't be locking up folks for their pranks and money-grabbing attempts, first because none of it was real, and second because Oblivion didn't have nearly the number of cells we'd need. Instead, I'd decided to fine them, much to Jake and the mayor's approval, since the money we collected would go to the town and indirectly, to our salaries, along with those of the schoolteacher and the postmaster and anyone else paid out of town funds. Not much when divided all those ways, but better than the town paying to feed and bed down twenty or more folks in a tiny jail. Hadn't occurred to me until

later that I was treating all this like Oblivion would continue on after this farce theater show ended, but at least
I was remaining "in character" for them.

Regardless, if Jake had still locked Arlene up, it
meant this thing between Arlene and Jake was personal. And probably about me. Again. Damn that phoenix
for choosing me. Why couldn't I have died like everyone else? Then I wouldn't feel so damn alone even
while caught in the middle of darn near everything. If
Pandora flew in that instant, I might have plucked her
and roasted her over a cooking fire.

Trying to keep quiet and not sure why I cared
about waking the saloon girl, I eased myself into
the desk chair and slipped my journal from the safe.
Lessons didn't always come easy to me, but when I
learned them, I learned them well. I hunched over
the leather book, hiding it from any cameras I hadn't
found and keeping my thoughts on this crazy future,
Arlene, and Jake between me and the paper. And
then there were the Eye Killers.

Tomorrow was Sunday. Surely the shenanigans
would be fewer on a Sunday. First I'd get some
sleep. Then, come hell or high water, I'd find a way
to get up to the mine and find that park ranger and
see what he knew about the first gold strike up there.
And maybe, just maybe, I could put a stop to this
once and for all.

I kept the dials covered while I changed the lock
on the safe, from Pa's birthday to Ma's, and closed
the journal inside. The empty whiskey bottle lay
in the wastebasket where I'd dropped it the night
before, and it didn't look like the prop elves had

replaced it. Guess I had to get more from the general store, which, according to the loudly ticking clock on the wall, would be closed at this hour. Sighing, I let my head thunk onto the desktop.

"You all right?"

I sat up straight. I'd forgotten all about Arlene in the cell across from me. She stood at the bars, watching my face, hers full of concern. Somewhere along the line she'd removed her heels, gun belt, and corset dress, leaving her in her white lacy cotton drawers and a nearly see-through chemise.

"Forgive me for sayin' so, Sheriff, but you look like shit."

Despite myself, I laughed. "You certainly are quite the sweet talker. You say those things to all the other ladies and gents?" I batted my eyelashes.

She responded with an all-too-familiar grin. Dammit, did she have to grin like my Arlene too? "Not much interested in gents, to be honest. Not seeing any ladies around here, either. I'm more interested in women with beauty, brains, and a fine right cross."

And damn if she couldn't pull off that outrageous line.

I retrieved my hat from the back of the chair, smoothed out my hair and the hat (it hadn't survived my stomping unscathed), and plopped it atop my head. Then I leaned backward and put my feet up on the desk. Not my desk. My desk was oak. This one was pine. But a fair replacement, newer and in better condition than the one that had burned to ashes.

"So," I said matter-of-factly, "I thought you told me you never got caught working outside the saloon."

Arlene's brows turned down in consternation. "I never said—"

"Never mind, never mind." I waved a hand to shut her up. Dammit. *This* Arlene hadn't said that. *Mine* had. Malek had warned me to be careful, and I was making a royal mess of the whole "look, I'm sane" thing. "I was thinking of someone else."

"Some other attractive saloon girl in your life?" One side of her mouth quirked, threatening to grin again.

"Yes, actually," I said with complete seriousness.

Arlene frowned instead and changed the subject. "So, regardless of what I didn't say, I wasn't working, just making friendly conversation. Honest!" she added at my raised brow. "I made sure it was part of my contract. I'd play the part of one of Oblivion's 'upstairs girls,' but there was no way I was sleeping with anyone I didn't want to. I hate to accuse a lawman of lying, but—"

"But Jake made it up. Not surprised," I finished for her. "He's as moneygrubbing as everyone else."

"Not everyone."

I took my feet down, crossed my arms on the desk, and rested my chin on them, watching her from beneath the brim of my hat. From experience, I knew this meant I could read her expressions but she couldn't really see mine. A useful advantage sometimes. "Really? Then why are you here?"

"Why are you?" Arlene countered. She turned around and leaned against the bars with her back to me. Well, so much for the hat idea.

I'd never been much for lying. Wasn't planning to start now. For a moment, the desire to tell her everything almost got to me, the utter, lonely need to have anyone else *know*. Luckily, reason prevailed, and I settled for, "I'm trying to fix something that went wrong a long time ago."

Her head bobbed up and down once. "You mean that whole 'Sheriff McCade losing her shit and shooting me in the head, then burning down the town and ruining her reputation' thing, right?"

"Something like that, yeah."

A long silence settled over the office, exterior sounds of creaky wagon wheels, horses' hooves, and people talking as they passed carrying through the quiet.

"Cali?"

"Yeah?"

"You know that wasn't you, right?"

Aw hell. "Really? You too? I'm not crazy!" I shoved myself away from the desk so hard I knocked off the lamp, shattering the protective glass. Scrambling around the front, I managed to stomp out the flames before they did more than leave a couple of black streaks on the wood floor.

Arlene had turned to watch me, maybe worried she'd get caught in a history-repeats-itself blaze. When I'd dance-stepped on the last glowing embers, she spoke. "I'm sorry. Really. You just… you seem so real, like you believe every word you say. When I saw your face at the church, well, when that airs, I think everyone in America will want to reach out and hold you. Including me." She extended a hand through the bars, and like a drowning swimmer grabbing a lifeline, I took it.

She felt warm and soft and safe. Not the same as holding the hand of the former Arlene, but I needed the human contact. It grounded me. A little.

I snatched my keys off my belt and used my free hand to unlock the cell. "If I'm not holding bank robbers, I'm not holding you."

"But you *are* holding me."

Looking down, I laughed. Yep, I still had her hand, through the bars, and it prevented her from exiting. I let go, and a flutter of disappointment trickled through me.

"Hey," I said while she sat down on the cot to lace up her shoes. "You never answered my question."

Arlene shrugged. "I always loved the Old West. Read tons of Westerns as a kid. Watched reruns of *Bonanza* and *Little House on the Prairie* until I'd memorized every episode. I grew up in Vegas, but I'd never experienced the West, you know?"

I didn't, but I kept that to myself.

"Anyway, when I saw auditions for *Harsh Reality* advertised at the Vegas Hilton, well, I went. I was between jobs and about to lose my apartment 'cause I couldn't afford the rent. Had no idea what I was going to do. And damn if they didn't cast me on the spot. Said I was a dead ringer for that Arlene girl, and I saw the old photos. Pretty uncanny." She yanked the second shoe on and grabbed the rest of her clothes, skipping the corset and pulling the dress over her head while I hung the keys back on the wall.

"Yeah, uncanny," I managed through a suddenly tight throat.

Oblivious to my discomfort, Arlene lifted her empty gun belt from the foot of the cot, tightened it around her tiny waist, draped the unused corset over one bare shoulder, then nodded to me. "Well, Sheriff, thanks for showing a gal a real good time. I'll get my gun back from the deputy later." She strode through the cell door, then paused to take both my hands. "I'll just be heading over to my room above the saloon." She locked my gaze with hers. "Unless, maybe, you'd like to offer up a cup of coffee or have a game of cards?" Arlene's eyes smoldered with desire. She leaned in close, so close I could have sworn I heard her heart beating.

My hands clenched in her grasp while I fought the heat that surged within me. "I don't have a stove," I told her, "and I can't play poker worth a damn."

"Then how about this instead?"

Before I could pull away, she'd pressed her mouth to mine. Applying just a hint of pressure, she hesitated, and I felt her breath still while she waited for my response. My lips parted of their own accord, and I tasted sweet Kentucky bourbon mingled with just a hint of fresh mint. Her tongue teased mine gently, testing my resistance and finding none while my hands released hers and found their way around her waist.

How ironic was it that the last person to hold me this way had also been Arlene?

An image of shot number five filled my memory, and I sucked in a gasp, jerking away from her like I'd taken a bullet myself.

"What? What's wrong?" The saloon girl didn't try to touch me again, seeming to sense my need to remain free, but her brown eyes had filled with concern, and I knew she wanted to hold me. Instead, she wrapped her fingers around one of the cell bars, the other hand dropping to her side. The cell door squeaked on hinges that needed oiling.

"Nothing," I tried to tell her, but it came out choked. "I… I lost someone. Not long ago." Good God, had it only been a couple of days?

And one hundred and twenty-five years, I reminded myself.

"I'm sorry," she said, sincerity in her tone. "Someone like me?"

I nodded, unable to say more.

"I understand." Arlene turned to go, then stopped at the office door. "But get to know me a little better, will you?" She smiled that maddening grin, softer than before but equally endearing. "I'm a pretty unique individual." Then she was gone.

I was left wondering if that had been a genuine display of attraction or another play for the cameras I only then remembered had to be in my office somewhere. And what was the world going to think about that kiss between two women? Arlene acted like it meant nothing to this modern age, but I wasn't that confident.

Ah well, I could always say it was my own touch of attention-seeking behavior.

Even if my heart and the rest of my body said it had been a lot more than that.

CHAPTER 19

"SHERIFF! SHERIFF Meadows!"

No. No, no, and no. I'd had maybe four hours of sleep, and darkness filled the room. I rolled over, pulled the goose down pillow over my head, and pressed it to my ears. Someone was absolutely *not* shouting outside my window in the middle of the night.

Besides, they wanted somebody else.

"Sheriff Meadows!"

If I tried hard enough, I might get back to that dream I'd been having, the one about Arlene and a moonlit swim and—

"Sheriff Meadows!"

Meadows, Meadows. It sounded familiar.

I sat straight up in the bed. Right. Meadows. I was supposed to be Meadows. Or rather, she was supposed to be me. I ran my hands through my disheveled hair. God help me, I was losing track.

"Try 'Sheriff McCade.'" Doc's voice, snide and obnoxious. And what the hell was Doc doing standing around outside my office in the middle of the night?

The sound of a muffled slap carried through the window, and I wondered who had hit whom. "Knock it off, Doc. I don't have time for that crap. Sheriff Meadows? Sheriff Meadows, wake up."

I recognized the first voice now—Director Taz.

Fully awake and still confused, I threw my legs over the side of my bed and froze.

What if…? I lit a lamp and hesitated before stripping off my nightgown, the one I'd found in my chest of drawers along with some undergarments and socks. I struggled with the thing that support-ed my breasts, wrangling the hooks and straps into place like a horse's saddle that needed to be cinched up. Still didn't understand the presence of modern underwear when everything else fit my time. Maybe they knew I wasn't the corset type. Or they'd just made a mistake. Either way I was glad for clean clothes.

I snapped one strap sharp against my bare skin, while I continued to worry. What if I *was* this Sandra Meadows and I'd had some kind of mental break-down and now I couldn't remember any of my old life?

No. No, I told myself, tossing the gown aside and buttoning on a clean shirt from the wardrobe. I'd seen Sandra's body, disposed of it. A shudder passed through me at the recollection.

Unless that had been a hallucination.

I swiped a hand across my eyes, drawing in a deep breath. Hallucination or not, right now the world wanted me to be Sandra Meadows.

Decently covered, I strode to the window and peered out, spotting Doc and the director standing just beyond the porch overhang. Outside of their presence, I didn't notice anything else amiss, though the lamps in Miss Josephine's place were lit, which seemed a little odd.

"What?" I demanded, in no mood for reality show games.

The expression on Erick Taz's face in the moonlight wiped the scowl from mine. "Sheriff, I know you're on an official leave of absence, but we have need of your services. We've got a dead body. A real one," he added, knowing that under the circumstances, the distinction mattered.

"I'll be right down."

"JAKE'S ALREADY on the scene, and we've called in the Los Alamos police, but they're a pretty far haul, so it'll be a while before they get here," Taz said.

"Called in?" I asked him, still half asleep and not thinking such a question might make me look stupid.

The director frowned and pulled a small black rectangle from his pocket, waving it at me before he put it away. "You're on camera. For the most part, I'm not. The crew have cell phones for emergencies, thank God, although with the lousy reception, it almost proved pointless, but I finally got through. We never bothered reconnecting the phone in the store."

"Cell" phone. I knew what a "telephone" was. The general store had one, and in my time, it worked... occasionally. Apparently these newfangled "cell phones" were equally unreliable, but it was some kind of miniature communication device, like the mini-train was a car. Okay. Got it.

"I convinced Jake to wait for you," Erick Taz went on, "since he's a deputy and you're a sheriff. Not an easy task, I might add, and an agreement I'm not sure he'll stick to." He smiled without looking at me. "He doesn't seem to care for you very much." The smile vanished as the director set a brisk pace toward wherever this body lay, and Doc and I flanked him, hurrying to match his stride.

My eyebrows lifted. "He's really just a deputy?" I'd had him figured for a sheriff himself in real life, what with the way he swaggered about and talked so big. Thought maybe that taking orders from an equal, coupled with me being a woman, was why he had a bone stuck in his craw about me. But after two days in these modern times, I'd seen that women regularly occupied positions only held by men in my own era. So either it boiled down to the difference in our ranks or he was an aberration. Or just an ass.

Erick Taz nodded. "Small town in Tennessee."

Small town, huh? And *that* was the "dangerous job for shit pay" he needed an acting deal to get out of? Well, I guess some folks had low thresholds for danger. Then again, Oblivion had to be smaller than wherever Jake came from, and look what dangers that had brought me. I suppressed a laugh no one would understand, not wanting to add more credence to Doc's "crazy" accusations. The urge vanished when I saw where we headed.

"Oh no," I breathed. Not that poor, sweet old lady. Not again. Natural causes. Dear God, please let it have been natural causes.

"'Fraid so," Doc acknowledged my fears with as much emotion as a frozen pond.

"Aw hell."

We stopped at the back door to Miss Josephine's place, the entire house lit up like a Christmas tree from within. I would have reached for the handle, but Taz blocked me. "Just remember, Sheriff, you have no real jurisdiction here. I want your impressions, that's all. Don't go moving the body, or anything else, for that matter. Leave that to the local law."

"Right," I agreed, resisting the urge to tell him just how much jurisdiction I really had, and pushed my way through the unlocked door. Unlocked, of course, meant nothing. I'd taken to locking the office door after the Lucinda confrontation at the outhouse, and any number of other unfriendly encounters I'd had since folks found out how much money I'd accumulated at the bank. Not to mention the ever-present possibility the Eye Killers would return to town, which I hoped against hope they had not. But as a rule, no one locked doors in the middle of nowhere. Better to leave them open so folks could get in if you needed help.

A blast of warm cinnamon smell greeted us upon our entry. Even as we proceeded through the back sunroom, I held out hope the victim might be someone other than the home's owner. Stepping into the kitchen dashed those hopes.

Poor Miss Josephine lay sprawled across the floor, a thin layer of spilled flour covering her clothes and all the surrounding furniture. The dropped bag rested beside her, still open. So were her eyes, and a shiver ran the length of my spine. Besides her eyes and a slight bluish tinge around the lips, she looked peaceful.

I tore my gaze from hers to scan the rest of the room. Whatever had happened, it happened mid-cinnamon buns. A tray of the unbaked treats waited by the oven in preparation for tomorrow's rush of Sunday breakfast customers. Another full tray sat cooling. My deputy stood off to the side, leaning against the counter with his arms crossed over his chest, the picture of impatience.

"'Bout time." Jake pushed himself away from the counter to stand straight, the same pose he'd always assumed when making a report, back when I'd known the real Jake. "No sign of foul play. No indication anyone else was here except the kid who found her."

"Kid?" I asked, keeping my position at the door. Walking in from this direction would mean tracking through the flour. Jake must have come through the front.

"One of the Davidson siblings. The girl. She was prowling around town, probably looking for a new way to rob the bank. I shooed her off and she came over here. Said she smelled the rolls and wanted the recipe. More likely she wanted to steal one. She spotted the body on the floor and ran screaming for me."

"Any sign anyone else was involved?" I asked.

Which translated to: Did she die of natural causes, or did someone help her along?

Jake shook his head, which surprised me. I'd expected someone else. A dead someone else, though he might not have recognized it right off. "There's footprints outside the side window, but they're a mess. The girl's most likely. And a bunch of people have tromped through the side and backyard. Tons of prints there."

That figured. Miss Josephine's home had boasted beautiful gardens, and she invited folks to stroll after a meal or while they waited for an available table in her parlor restaurant. The directors had done a good job of recreating those gardens, and the flowers kept the whole area smelling of yucca, lavender, and campanula overlaid with whatever delectable meal Miss Josephine was currently preparing.

Erick started to reach for a roll, then caught himself, blushed, and pulled his hand back. "Besides, we've got the whole thing on video," he put in.

Video? Oh, he must have meant the cameras. Of course. With the technological advancements, it would amaze me if anyone ever got away with murder anymore.

"Unless we're looking at poison, there's no way anybody else was responsible."

Doc turned to the director. "Try to shut down your melodramatic mind for a bit, will you? Without any modern-day equipment, I can't be sure, but to me it looks like an old-fashioned heart attack or stroke. No foul play."

And nothing disturbed. No footprints in the flour, no knocked-over furniture, though that in itself felt off. People having heart attacks had a tendency to thrash around, didn't they? "I'd like to see that... video."

THE THREE of us—me, Doc, and Taz—made a grim parade heading over to the courthouse. Jake stayed behind to meet the local lawmen and fill them in on what we knew. Or thought we knew. I must admit, if I hadn't had a need to see the video myself, I would have enjoyed watching today's law enforcement carry out their duties with all the marvels this future offered. Then again, maybe I didn't want to see how obsolete we'd become. Crimes should practically solve themselves. And for now, I had a job of my own.

The assistant director, Danielle, already had the scene on the television in front of her, and after exchanging solemn greetings, she set the pictures in motion.

"You have the cameras working in the middle of the night?" I asked. "How much is actually happening at this hour?"

Taz pressed his lips together, but Danielle reached over to slap him on the arm. "Forget 'trade secrets,' Erick. A nice old woman is dead."

The director shook himself. "Right. Of course." He met my gaze. "The cameras and microphones respond to light and sound, respectively, turning on automatically. That way we don't miss anything. Good thing too," he added. "I'm sure the police will want a copy of this."

"Shh," Doc ordered, and we turned our attention to the images.

Miss Josephine stood in the center of her spotless kitchen, whistling "Clementine" and rolling dough into long snakes to wrap into buns. She moved to the wood-burning oven, checking the heat for her baking, and pulled the finished tray of rolls out to set on the counter. God, I'd always loved Miss Josephine's treats. In my time, the old lady could barely keep up with the town's demand for her baked goods, served with a few words of wisdom. She'd be sorely missed, then and now.

Something caught the attention of the woman in the television. Miss Josephine frowned, strode to her window on one side of her home, and peered out.

"This is when we think whatever hit her, well, hit her," Danielle said, keeping her voice low so we could hear any sounds from the video.

There were none. Miss Josephine backed away from the open window, eyes wide, mouth frowning. She stopped in the center of the room, remained stock-still for a long few minutes, then seemed to struggle for breath. Not struggle in the sense of clutching her throat or waving her arms, but her eyes bulged farther, and her lips turned blue. She sank to the floor, toppling onto her back to assume the position in which we'd found her. A rustling carried from the window, like an animal escaping through brush.

Or an Eye Killer heading back to the mine. And that was all.

I didn't like the implications. Not one bit. If there *had* been an Elemental-possessed person back there, it meant the Eye Killers were getting smarter with their human hosts, learning when they would be discovered or be outnumbered.

"Nothing from the outside of the house?" I asked.

Taz shook his head. "No cameras activated outside, since there were no lamps lit out there at this time of night. She wouldn't have seen the need. In fact, she only had the kitchen lights going when Jake got there. He lit the rest of the house for us and the police and paramedics."

A few seconds later the Davidson girl's face appeared at a different window in the television, one the cameras could actually view in Miss Josephine's place, along the rear wall. She took in the scene and started screaming for Deputy Baylor, just like he'd described. Danielle pressed a button, stopping the pictures from moving, and we stood in silence absorbing everything we'd seen.

"Stroke," Doc pronounced. "Or a quick series of them. She never cried out, never called for help. Like her brain functions were failing her. And then the choking." He frowned. "Though that's usually an aftereffect, not a cause of death. Maybe she had something in her mouth when it happened, like a piece of one of her cinnamon rolls or some gum." He shook his head. "Paramedics will figure it out. If they ever get here."

I strode to look out the window, the sounds of that rustling in the bushes playing over and over in my brain. With the exception of Miss Josephine's house, the town of Oblivion lay dark, but I knew the killer hid out there somewhere.

"What do you think, Sheriff?" Erick, looking for my confirmation.

I gave it to him. "I agree with Doc." They'd never believe my true thoughts.

Doc snorted in response. "First time for everything."

A loud wailing like ancient Irish tales of banshees made my heart leap, and I dug my fingers into the windowsill to keep from showing my fear. Not the same sort of screaming I'd heard from the Eye Killers before, but equally terrifying. In the distance I spotted red-and-blue flickering lights, harbingers of more evil to come.

Erick peered over my shoulder. "Gotta show off and wake the whole damn town coming in. Rile everyone up." He glanced at his watch. "Took their sweet time too. Cops always drag their feet when shit happens on unincorporated land." He looked at me for my agreement, then flushed. "Present company excluded, of course."

These were the police. I uncurled my fingers, taking a few chips of wood with them. "If y'all are finished with me, I think I'll head down and see if they need any help."

The director nodded. "We'll be right behind you, soon as we get a copy of that video for them and lock up the courthouse."

I left, knowing I had no intention of mixing with the arriving lawmen. Police by nature were an inquisitive bunch, and the last thing I needed right now was that curiosity turned toward me.

Instead, I veered off the main street, pushing my way through folks emerging from their homes in nightclothes and hastily thrown on pants and shirts, the entire town drawn out by the noise and lights. Lots of worried mumbling, some remaining in character, talking about demon flashes and witchcraft, others suggesting a player had gone off the deep end and really hurt or killed a member of the cast.

I thought I detected a general note of relief when people saw me, strolling along and uninvolved. Guess I was everyone's first choice when it came to a person losing control. For the moment, I was happy not to fit in with their assumptions.

CHAPTER 20

BEFORE THE doctors and lawmen could climb out of their arriving cars, I darted around back of Miss Josephine's house. The footprints Jake had mentioned lay outside both kitchen windows, but it was impossible to tell one set from another or how old they all might be.

Moving around to the side of the house, I put my back to the clapboard and traced with my eye the pattern of destruction of the surrounding plants and thin grasses. With the waning moon and the lamps shining from the building as my only sources of light, I couldn't see as well as I would've liked, but it turned out not to matter. A few feet away, the dirt turned to loose stones and harder packed earth where feet wouldn't have left prints.

Remembering the rustling I'd heard on the… video, I scanned for the closest brush—straight ahead and extending into the desert, toward the mine. Well, I didn't have any other options. I plunged into the bushes. Some scattered clouds obscured the moon, and the darkness closed over me.

About thirty feet in I decided Doc could lock me away now. Going after an Eye Killer in the dark, unarmed? I had to be insane.

Fire. I should have brought a lamp or a torch. No, that would have sent out my location like a beacon, drawing both the modern-day lawmen and the Eye Killer right to me.

Turning back would do me no good. The general store would not be open for hours and wouldn't sell me a real weapon even then. Malek had my S&W locked up tight in the store safe. I'd seen him put it in there myself, muttering how it was a "beautiful heirloom," a real "museum piece."

Suddenly I felt old.

I could have enlisted the aid of the police. Yeah, and ended up locked away for sure.

I kept walking. Low-lying brush and brambles caught at my pant legs, scraping the denim with audible scratching sounds, the dry plants shedding leaves as I passed. Well, no one would have any trouble following *me*. A coyote howled in the distance, raising the hairs on my skin with its eerie sadness. All around, the night seemed to be waiting.

Here and there I found evidence someone else had come this way, but whoever it was, he was small. When breaks in the clouds let the moonlight through and where the ground was soft enough, I saw footprints two-thirds the size of my own.

In my head I tried to catalog every Oblivion resident I'd met so far, searching mental images for the possible culprit/victim. I stepped into a clearing, tall weeds and dry grass waving under the night sky, and in a sudden burst of clarity, even before I spotted the small shadow on the far side of the open space, I knew.

The Eye Killers had taken a child.

"Shit," I breathed, heart thudding. I don't know if he could hear the thunderous beating or if my curse had carried farther than I intended, but the shadow's head shot up, and the light glinted off too bright eyes. Not close enough to mesmerize me. Not yet.

Never taking my eyes off the figure moving slowly toward me, I crouched, feeling around for a rock or stick. My hand closed on a fist-sized stone, and my nails clawed at the dirt until I'd dug it out of the ground. Hefting it in my palm, I stood.

The boy—and now I could tell for certain it was a boy of about fourteen—closed the distance between us. About fifteen feet remained, and I struggled to fix my gaze on his chest, his legs, anywhere but the face. The grass rustled with each of his steps, that and my harsh breathing the only sounds.

You're going to kill a child, a voice inside me whispered. Not a question, a statement of fact.

"He's already dead," I reminded myself out loud, where I could hear it. The boy moaned.

I thought hard, trying to recall... yes, Adam. In the bank, Sam said the missing boy's name was Adam. He'd disappeared along with his family. And then I made the connection. Adam. From the square dance. The nice young man. Oh dear God. My eyes darted around the open space, trying to penetrate the deepening shadows. Where was his family now? No sign of them.

"Adam," I called, hoping to stall him, hoping to delay the inevitable. Now that he'd come closer, I could see the twisted arm hanging loose at his side, the caved-in ribs and caked blood on his torn shirt. I didn't dare look higher. "Adam, if you're still in there, try to make them leave. I don't want to cause you more pain, son."

Nothing. No response. And when he fell upon me, we both went down in a tangle of limbs.

Turning, twisting, I fought to keep my head to the side, my face away from his. My free hand clawed and ripped at his shirt, shredding already shredded clothing. He had the hand that held the rock pinned. I couldn't bring it up. Child or not, the demon inside gifted him with unnatural strength.

Over and over we rolled, my skull thudding along the ground and my grunts of pain punctuating the night. At some point, the back of my head encountered another rock, bigger and harder than the one I held, and the edges of my vision grayed at the impact.

I drew my knees between us and into my chest, then thrust outward, hurling the smaller body away from mine. I panted where I lay, eyelids squeezed shut, but nearby movement sent me clambering to my feet. My legs barely managed to support my weight, and when I opened my eyes, the clearing spun and wavered.

Don't look at him. Don't look at his face.

Never before had I noticed how much hand-to-hand fighting relied on watching an opponent's eyes, gauging his next move by a flicker here, a glance there. Now all I had were shifts in his stance, an adjustment of balance.

He launched again, no sluggish moves, not like the other Eye Killers I'd encountered, and I wondered if they'd learned how to control the dead better over time. Had they gone dormant when Oblivion burned, just waiting for foolish men to reopen the mine, the town? Surely if they'd been preying on people in the area for the last one hundred twenty-five years, everyone would know of their existence by now and be avoiding this place, not holding theatrical performances here.

Our bodies met with a rib-shattering crunch—his, not mine, thank God. We fell to the ground again. The boy might not have had any formal training, but the demon inside fought like a professional. Moans suggested he felt the pain of his new injuries, and a piece of rib bone protruded through the skin of this chest and the fabric of his shirt, but it didn't slow him down one bit.

No more time. My head pounded like a sonofabitch, and I knew I'd black out soon. Putting behind it all the strength I had left, I swung my right arm blind—and missed. The rock and my hand passed through empty air. He'd drawn back and I'd swung short.

If I was going to succeed in making contact, I had no other choice but to look at him and hope to get in one more shot before he had me.

Fast, McCade, fast. One quick glance. That's all. Just….

Time stopped. My mouth dropped open. My throat closed. A tunnel formed between my eyes and the boy's, and all I could do was stare down it, fall into it, the Eye Killer's pupils pulling me in, sucking away my breath, my soul.

Run! Run!

But I couldn't move, couldn't breathe.

Precious seconds passed. My lungs burned. The rock slipped from my limp fingers, and what seemed like minutes later, I heard it hit the ground with a distant *thunk*. But it couldn't have been minutes. If it had, I'd be dead.

Maybe I was dead already.

Something small and fast-moving flailed in my face, beating at my cheeks and nose with feathered ferocity.

Feathers, red and gold.

Pandora!

Concentration broken, I heaved breath after wheezing breath into my lungs, then hit the ground on hands and knees just as the boy made a grab for me. This time, he was the one who clutched at empty air, but that wouldn't last long. Vision still sparkling, I kicked out and swept his legs from beneath him, then scrabbled about in the dirt until I came up with the rock.

The phoenix whirled in rapid circles over the Eye Killer's face, preventing him from getting another lock on me. Pandora's intervention had renewed my strength and hope. I crawled to the Eye Killer's side, checked for the bird's position to be sure I didn't hurt her, and brought the rock down. Again. And again.

Even after the skull caved and I sensed no more resistance, even after I heard squishing sounds that filled my mouth with bile, I continued to pound, not looking at him but focusing on the pinks and golds of the sunrise lightening the New Mexico sky.

Back in Oblivion, church bells rang, calling all the good Christians to Sunday service. They'd be wearing their Sunday best, smiling and chatting, expressing their sadness over Miss Josephine.

I turned and spat the foul taste from my mouth. Good Christians. Now I was even less certain I could count myself among them.

CHAPTER 21

IN MIDDLE-OF-NOWHERE New Mexico, disposing of a body wasn't that hard. Unfortunately, middle-of-nowhere had shrunk a bit in one hundred and twenty-five years.

A river ran not too far from Oblivion, maybe a mile and a half out past the mine, and in spring it flowed high and fast. But reaching it while carrying a teenager, even one small for his age, turned out to be pretty rough. Then factor in the pounding headache and any number of cuts, scrapes, and bruises, not to mention lack of sleep.

I had to avoid all signs of civilization as well, crouching with the body in ditches next to a couple of impressive roads, waiting for dozens of cars to pass at speeds I'd have thought impossible, then hobbling across as quickly as my battered legs would carry me. At least Pandora knew when to hide as well. She kept low and out of sight whenever we neared anything man-made.

At long last, the sound of distant roaring water reached my ears, and I parted brush to find myself on the mesa's edge overlooking the rushing river far below. This much had not changed. In my younger days, I'd come out here to think, much to Ma's disapproval. Indians, snakes, and any number of other dangerous critters roamed the area, and a young girl, no matter how good a shot, wouldn't have stood a chance against many of them. But I'd survived.

I'd survive this.

Pulling the body off my shoulder, I forced myself to study it for the first time, hogtying my emotions and analyzing what I saw. No obvious signs I'd involved myself in his death. No finger-shaped bruises or scratches that couldn't be explained by brush or rocks as easily as fingernails. And since Eye Killer-possessed bodies didn't bleed much, his blood hadn't gotten on my clothing, either. Just my own. Anything else, the river water should wash away in a matter of minutes.

I leaned out over the edge and judged which way would be the roughest one down, then, with one last prayer for forgiveness, rolled the body over the cliff. I couldn't bring myself to watch it bounce off the rocks in its fall, but the thuds echoed up to me, diminishing in volume as the corpse got farther away.

I did, however, check to make sure it had hit the water. If it hadn't, I would have needed to find a way to the bottom and put it in the river. But I saw no sign of it, so the water had already taken the body. With any luck, no human would find it. And if they did, they'd attribute the death to an accidental fall. Truly, I would have preferred to bury him. He deserved a proper burial. None of this was his fault. But I had no tools to dig a grave, and I couldn't have risked leaving the body long enough to find some.

No, this was the only way. I couldn't afford to think otherwise. Doing so might be the unbalancing point in my tightrope walk with sanity.

I kept telling myself that during the entire walk back to Oblivion while Pandora cooed on my shoulder and nuzzled my cheek for comfort.

When I got there, the lawmen's vehicles had left, Miss Josephine's house sat quiet, and strips of bright yellow paper crisscrossed both entrances to her place suggesting they didn't want anyone else going in there. In fact, the entire town was silent, the one sound being voices singing hymns coming from the church.

As usual, I'd show up late.

I slipped in through the doors during a high point in the singing, the loud tones drowning out my entry. Pandora took off from my arm and made a direct line for the preacher, coming to rest on the podium's edge. Everyone focused on Xanthis, who, true to form, sang louder than anyone else. Arlene, seated in the rearmost row, noticed my entrance, however. She took one look at me, frowned, and waved me over, shooing the folks next to her so they'd slide and make room.

I squeezed on the end, closest to the aisle by the wall, and let the exhaustion soak me to the bone.

"You all right?"

The family to Arlene's left shushed her, but her glare sent them back to their singing.

"Fine."

"You don't look fine. What happened to you?"

I shrugged, reaching for a hymnal and flipping to the correct page. "Took a walk to think, got lost, tripped in the dark, don't want to talk about it." I finished with a glare of my own.

The saloon girl pressed her lips together but said nothing more.

Xanthis spoke of the peace of death and the gates of heaven. I prayed for Adam. Xanthis pronounced us all sinners and urged us to repent before our own times came. I prayed for Adam's parents, wherever they had gotten off to, and anyone else who'd disappeared from Oblivion. Xanthis roused the congregation to their feet in a resounding chorus of "Holy, Holy, Holy." I prayed for those I'd left behind, one hundred and twenty odd years in the past. Xanthis lowered his head to give the benediction and say a final word for Miss Josephine. I prayed for her soul and my own.

AFTER CHURCH I wanted nothing more than breakfast and bed, not necessarily in that order, but as usual with my eating and sleeping habits of late, neither was meant to be.

Folks tended to linger when the service ended. Some of the ladies served juice and homemade treats in the little churchyard between the building and Oblivion's cemetery, and my eyes misted at the absence of Miss Josephine. I heard her name mentioned in every cluster of conversation. Even if Preacher Xanthis hadn't said prayers for her,

everyone would have known by now. Word spread
fast in a small town.

I also heard my own name, said with sniffs and
disdain from the womenfolk. Didn't know if they
were playing their parts or expressing their true opinions. Either way, their reactions fit. I did look like
hell—wearing yesterday's clothes, hadn't cleaned up
for church. A washcloth and a pitcher of water could
work wonders. Still, I'd felt God might prefer me
to attend services dirty rather than not go at all, and
I'd had a lot of need of him of late. The washcloth
could wait.

Arlene followed me as I got a cup of coffee and
a cornbread muffin, taking one for herself. "Lips are
flapping. You've got a black eye coming on, and
your cheek is bruised. People are wondering who
took you down. I've heard Jake, Lucinda, and even
my name come up in this crowd."

I stiffened. My eyes roved the gathered assembly, meeting a few others who turned quickly away.
If I heard a rumor like *that* about Arlene, I'd put a
stop to it right quick. She didn't deserve a reputation
of being a person who bodily injured her friends.

"You gonna tell me what really happened?"
she asked around a mouthful. A couple of crumbs
dropped to the front of her clean blue-and-white
gingham dress, much more appropriate church wear
than her flouncy dresses with their tight bodices, and
I resisted the urge to brush them off for her. She'd
worn no makeup, her beauty pure and natural, and
smelled like sunshine and soap, like she'd bathed in
the stream. Beside her, I looked even worse.

"Nope."

One side of her mouth quirked up. "You're a stubborn mule, you know that?"

I tried to keep from grinning and failed. "Yep." Turning to leave, I almost collided with Erick Taz, dressed in full Western garb and blending so well with Oblivion's residents I hadn't noticed him in the congregation.

His eyes widened when he took a good look at me, but he shook his head as if he'd decided to let it go. Instead he warned, "You might want to stick around, Sheriff." Erick had a definite glint of mischief in his eye. "I'm here to make an announcement that affects you."

The Eye Killers, I thought. Or the body... bodies. Had they found Adam already, or Sandra Meadows in the pit?

Part of me wanted to make a run for it, disappear into this modern-day world and never look back. But duty and a morbid sense of curiosity made me follow Arlene and the rest of the crowd to the front of the church, where our director positioned himself at the top of the steps.

"Well, folks," he began, spreading his arms wide, "you've made it through two days."

Not all of us, I thought, but I kept my mouth shut.

As if he'd read my mind, Taz frowned. "Well, not everyone. Most of you know that the lovely woman playing our Miss Josephine passed away early this morning from a stroke. The paramedics and police agree after seeing the body and viewing the footage that even if she'd been home in a modern city with modern medicine close at hand, the attack came on so swiftly it wouldn't have mattered."

Well, he had the attack part right.

"We have cast a new Miss Josephine, who'll be arriving by wagon sometime this afternoon. Not that we think a person can be so easily replaced," he hurried to add when the mutterings turned a bit more angry, "but she had the only restaurant in town aside from the saloon, and most of you don't have the means to cook for yourselves, or the skills. We don't want anyone to starve or live off the general store's apples for the next five days."

That comment he directed at me. I didn't return his good-natured smile. Besides, I liked apples, and I could cook in a pinch. Maybe no one could stand to eat it but me, but that was beside the point.

I raised my voice. "So, what are you planning on doing for her family?" All heads turned to stare at me.

Taz blinked. Clearly this had not been part of his plan. He cast a glance off to the side, where I spotted his assistants, Danielle and Malek. They shrugged.

"We, um—"

"She came here to leave something for her grandchildren," I told him and the assembled audience. "Didn't have much, I'm guessing. A donation of whatever you'd contracted to pay her for the week would be a nice gesture. She certainly hadn't planned on leaving." This time I smiled, though with more sadness than humor. He didn't.

Making this a pissing contest between us might not have been a smart move. He could have me kicked out of town at his whim, and then how would I protect any of them or get the information I needed to stop the Eye Killers?

Not like you've done such a great job of that so far, guilt whispered. I told it to shut up.

Practicality, then. Right now I had a roof and a bed and a ready supply of food. I had Pandora and Ford. I could live off the land if I had to, but it would make things a whole lot harder.

But Miss Josephine wouldn't have been here if not for him and this whole crazy production. "No matter what the law and the medical men told you," I said, making certain my voice carried to the edges of the crowd, "she worked for you."

She was your responsibility, my words said. *You owe her.*

Taz opened his mouth to argue, then clamped it shut. A muscle in his jaw twitched. At last he nodded, once. "Done."

The crowd released a collective breath, then started a spontaneous round of cheers and applause. Our director had to shout to regain their attention. "All right, all right, settle down. I'm a damn hero, I get it." But the smile had returned, and he didn't appear all that angry at my manipulation to make him one. "Now for the real reason I'm out here."

The audience quieted.

"Some of you have done pretty well for yourselves the last couple of days." His gaze roved over me, Arlene, Jake, even Lucinda. "And others have

been, as one of our cast put it, 'ridiculous.'" He focused on the remaining clusters of would-be bank
robbers and Miss Clara. The four I'd "killed" had
already gone home. "So, we've come up with some
more organized ways for you to prove your worth.
I promised you surprises, and here's the first—an
old-fashioned barrel-racing competition, behind
the courthouse, in two hours. And anyone who put
'horsemanship experience' on their résumé is signed
up. If you lied, you had better bring some liniment.
Check the list on the courthouse doors. Find your
mounts in the stables. And—" He paused to give us
all a wink. "—good luck."

CHAPTER 22

IN MY day, folks didn't barrel race as a random pastime. You did it if you wanted to win a prize at the state or county fair, you did it if you worked for the rodeo, and you did it if you joined a traveling show like Buffalo Bill's Wild West. Otherwise, you got in the saddle for work, travel, and necessity, not to show off.

I don't know why I even bothered to check the list on the courthouse doors—of course they'd put my name there, whether Sandra Meadows attested to any riding skills or not, more than likely. But I checked it anyway and found it, scrawled in the first slot.

Heaving a sigh, then stifling a jaw-cracking yawn, I tromped down the steps and headed for the stables.

Two hours later, roughing it in the woods looked better and better.

Seated on Chessie, with friends and neighbors cheering me on, I would have felt a lot more confidence. But as I eyed the course from Ford's back, surrounded by virtual strangers, nerves tied my stomach in knots.

Not to say Ford wasn't a dream to ride. He had a smooth gait, an easy nature, and a humorous tendency to glance over his shoulder at me when he wanted another sugar cube or piece of apple. But he handled differently from Chessie. I knew her. I didn't know him.

And I had more important things to do, dammit. As soon as this nonsense ended, I was riding out to the mine, sleep or no sleep. At least two people had died, likely more, and I needed answers.

We drew lots for the riding order, me ending up toward the end of the bunch. Nonparticipants lined up along temporary fencing, the children climbing to sit on the top rails. The riders gathered in a cluster of eager horses, working to keep their mounts from kicking or biting one another.

As Taz had suspected, it became apparent that few of Oblivion's citizens had real riding skills. While Ford and I waited off to one side, others got too close, one ending up almost getting trampled when his mare threw him.

The mayor handed out numbers on colored sheets of paper with string tied through holes at the top that we could put around our necks. I got number thirteen. Beside me, on a gray stallion, Jake snickered.

"Not your lucky day, eh, Sheriff?"

"You have no idea."

Of the fifteen competitors, I noted three women: myself, the Davidson girl from the attempted bank robbery, and one more I didn't recognize in a wide-brimmed hat with her hair tucked up beneath, hiding the color. Not Arlene, though in my day, the original could ride just fine. The men included Jake, Al, and Sam, among others, but not Doc. Doc, I understood. Regardless of ability, he needed to be ready to deal with injuries, and he had a little tarp-covered booth set up with chairs, water, and his medical bag on a small wooden table.

I caught Arlene's eye, raising my eyebrows, and she gave me a sheepish smile. Guess reading Westerns and wanting to be a cowgirl didn't make you one.

Of the men, Sam appeared the most ill at ease. White-faced and sweating, he sat his mount like a child on his first pony. Under no circumstances did he belong up there, and I reminded myself that this wasn't the real Sam, a ranch owner who'd had experience with horses. His daughter stood nearby, and I could overhear bits of an argument between them.

"Forget this. We'll earn the money another way," she was saying.

"We need this bonus," he told her, setting his jaw.

The contest began, and after the first few riders swerved, staggered, and stumbled their horses through the course, knocking over the barrels and earning penalty points that put their times into negative numbers, I thought I might have a chance at winning this thing. Not that I cared one way or another. I had already vowed to donate any winnings to Miss Josephine's memorial fund (I'd overheard talk of an additional collection being taken up), and I'd enjoy wiping the smug grin off Jake's face, but really, I wanted the game to be done and over with.

Jake managed to finish the course without knocking anything down, as did the Davidson girl, but with unimpressive times in exchange for their careful riding.

The unknown woman in the wide-brimmed hat rode next. From the moment the start gun sounded, the crowd could sense this rider's talent. She and her horse moved like one being, weaving between barrels as easily as if they had gone on a Sunday trail ride, but at blurring speeds. When she came to a dirt-churning halt, without so much as brushing a single barrel, the townsfolk set up a rousing cheer, which rose to a roar when the mayor announced her time—a good ten seconds faster than any of the previous riders. Instead of exuding overconfidence, she accepted the applause with good grace, nodding and swinging out of the saddle to lead her tired horse to the water trough. I noticed she walked with a slight limp.

Tough act to follow, and Mayor Jones called my number next. Ford and I gave it a good run. We bumped two barrels but didn't knock any down. Still, the contact cost us, and we came in five seconds behind the leader.

"It's okay, boy. I know you did your best," I whispered in Ford's ear, passing him the last of an apple from my vest pocket and patting his flank. "If anyone's to blame, it's me. We'll do better next time." Of course, that depended on me living to see a next time. We moved aside to watch the rest of the competition.

No one else managed to knock the leader off her game, and Sam as the last rider pretty much wrapped things up for her. I studied Sam as he got into the starting position, with much maneuvering and side-stepping on the horse's part and shifting about in the saddle on Sam's. "He's got no business being out there, with his skills, at his age," I muttered. Ford flicked his ears back at me and whinnied in agreement. One throw and he could break a hip. Or his neck.

On the sidelines, I spotted Sam's daughter, both hands pressed to her lips, eyes wide and concerned, and my estimation of their closeness shifted. I'd thought they couldn't be blood related, but they had some connection between them, a grudging friendship or dependency if nothing else.

I pulled the reins, preparing to guide Ford to the mayor and tell him to pull Sam out. Even our illustrious director looked ready to put a stop to this, but Mayor Jones fired the starting gun and Sam's horse leaped forward.

That's all it took.

Without someone experienced at the reins, Sam's horse tossed the older man over its head. Sam flew headfirst into one of the barrels, then lay sprawled across it, unmoving, while the horse continued bucking and running about like a wild thing. Women screamed, and parents hauled their children off the fencing to avoid the madly flying hooves of the panicked animal.

Without thinking, I kicked Ford into motion, racing toward the crazed beast. Manes and tails,

hooves and forelegs flew around me as I held my
reins with one hand and clutched at the other horse's
reins with the other. I missed on the first three tries,
then nearly got yanked from the saddle myself as I
caught them up in my right fist.

Ford held steady while the other horse pulled
and twisted me from side to side. Sam chose that inopportune moment to groan and roll, right into the
path of his horse's hooves.

"Stop!" I shouted. "Sam, don't move!" I winced
as the leather strips dug into my palm, wishing I'd
worn gloves.

The older man blinked up at me, likely delirious
from a head wound sending a thin stream of blood
down the side of his face, but something registered
because he quit moving. By now, several others had
reached us, including Arlene, who waved her arms in
the air, whooping and howling to draw the spooked
horse away from Sam. The Appaloosa pawed the
ground, coming gut-wrenchingly close to crushing
Sam's hand. Then it took notice of Arlene's antics.

As soon as she had the spotted Appaloosa's
focus, Arlene changed her tone, speaking in low,
soothing words. I thought about telling her to clear
out, but it seemed to be working.

"Do you have any idea what you're doing?" I
asked her in the same soft tones.

"None whatsoever. But it worked on *Bonanza.*"
She grinned.

I gave a mental shrug. "That's it," I said, joining
Arlene, keeping my voice low. I spoke as much for
Sam's horse as for Ford, whose eyes stared wildly

at the folks gathering around us. But he held steady, and if I hadn't been mounted and still gripping two pairs of reins, I would have hugged him.

Ford and I led the other horse to the stable boys on the sidelines. Arlene walked beside us, her hand on the horse's halter, just to be safe. Doc passed us, heading for Sam, who'd sat up and didn't look too worse for wear except for the cut on his head. After another couple of minutes, Doc nodded, and two of the other menfolk helped Sam walk to the physician's tent.

Taz met me and Arlene at the edge of the clearing.

I swung out of the saddle, landing on both feet, fury-heat rising to my face. "What the hell were you thinking, putting him out there like that? You want two deaths in two days?"

Three, my conscience whispered. I ignored it.

The director met my glare with one of his own. "He knew what he was in for. He signed off on horsemanship. He signed the waivers. He could've walked."

"And lost his pride along with the income? Not likely."

"That was quite a dramatic moment. He'll get his bonus."

"That doesn't make it right!" It took everything I had not to hit him.

"Cali...." Arlene laid a hand on my shoulder, but I shook her off.

Before I could continue my tirade, Taz lowered his voice. "Listen, Sheriff," he said, "let's get something clear between us. Sam's not the only one who has finances at stake, here." He gestured around at the buildings—the buildings *Harsh Reality* had paid to rebuild from the ground up. "I'm out on a limb and in the red. I did *not* care for that little stunt you pulled to get Miss Josephine a memorial fund, but I let it go because it will be good for the ratings. It will make *me* look good. And I do not especially care for *you*, either. But again, you've been good for the ratings. Until now. This little argument is *not* good for ratings because I will never let it make it to the airwaves." He turned to leave, then whirled for one last shot. "A lot of people are depending on the success of this show. The minute I feel you're more of a hindrance than a help, I'll have your little ass out of here faster than you can say 'yeehaw.'" Taz stormed away, moving into the shade where his assistants waited with cold glasses of lemonade.

I watched him paste on a smile for them, like nothing had gone wrong between us, but the glare he cast in my direction told me our conversation would not be forgotten.

"Always knew Hollywood was full of assholes," Arlene said.

We handed the horses over to their caretakers, me giving them an order to be extra generous with Ford's oats and passing them a few coins to make sure. Then I headed for Doc's tent to check on Sam.

His daughter had beaten me there, and she sat beside her pa, one hand on his arm, the other holding a bandage in place so Doc could secure it. Sam, for his part, kept trying to shoo everyone away. His expression held frustration and embarrassment.

Doc saw me coming. "No broken bones. No concussion so far as I can tell, though he should take it easy the next day or two."

I wanted to tell Sam how stupid he'd been, but I held my tongue. He knew.

His daughter pursed her lips like she'd swallowed something sour, but she stuck out her hand. "Thank you," she said. "Thanks for saving my dad."

That sounded honest. I shook her hand. "You're welcome."

"We haven't been properly introduced," she told me. "I'm Beth." She must've seen my raised eyebrows because she continued, "Yeah, that's my real name."

It had been my Sam's daughter's name too.

"And he's my real dad," she added, jerking a thumb at Sam. "Well, he adopted me, anyway, and that's how I see him. And he's the only thing that stood between me and going into foster care when Mom lit out after some younger guy. We don't always see eye to eye, but…." She shrugged.

I got it. They had each other, and that was it.

"Anyway, you ever need anything, just ask," she finished.

"Same goes for me," Sam said, standing beside her. He wavered for just a moment but covered it well by putting an arm around his daughter's shoulders.

"Oh no you don't," Doc jumped in, shoving the stool under him and pushing him firmly back onto it.

Guess he hadn't covered the dizziness as well as he and I had thought.

Sam gave me a grin that said he knew he'd been caught. "I owe you one, Sheriff." He paused, gestured for Beth to lean down, and whispered in her ear. She nodded with a genuine smile. "How about you joining us for Sunday dinner? You too, Arlene. I saw you put yourself out in front of that crazy horse. Beth cooks like a dream, and I *know* you both haven't been eatin' regular the past few days."

Behind him, Doc shot me a jealous glare. I couldn't have cared less.

"I'll bake a pie. Apple," Beth put in, already planning. "And I practiced with the ice cream churn. I think I've got it right."

Arlene beamed and licked her lips in anticipation. I tried not to focus on the quick motion of her tongue and failed. "I could use a home-cooked meal, that's for certain," she said. Then more quietly, "Whatever the behind-the-scenes cafeteria is serving out of the saloon tastes like hospital food, and the new Miss Josephine, God rest the first one's soul, hasn't arrived yet. How about it, Cali?"

There'd be three Miss Josephines once the newest rode in, but I didn't correct Arlene. I glanced at the sun overhead. Early afternoon. Still enough time to ride up to the mine, see what I could figure, and get back for a late supper. Of course, it meant foregoing a proper lunch and a nap. I studied Sam and Beth, saw the eagerness there to pay me back. I didn't want to disappoint two of the only friends I'd made here, even if one of them might be a witch in training. Looked like lunch would be another apple meal for me. "I've got a few things I need to take care of, but if you can hold supper until, say, seven, I suppose that'd be all right."

"Great!" Beth chirped, no longer the sullen, jealous teenager I'd met at the bank, but a young woman enthusiastic about showing off her skills.

And speaking of skills…. The mayor walked to the center of the barrel-racing course and held up a hand for silence. "Ladies and gentlemen, it is my pleasure to announce the winner of today's competition—Number six, Miss Lucinda Juarez."

I could have smacked myself in the forehead for being so dense. Of course. That's why the woman limped. I'd stomped on Lucinda's foot outside the outhouse. I suppressed a smirk. Guess I stomped harder than I'd thought.

Lucinda swept off her hat, letting the long dark hair fall down her back in a stream that reached her waist. With grace, she accepted the trophy and an envelope I assumed contained the promised cash prize from Mayor Jones.

"And in second place, Number Thirteen, Sheriff Cali McCade!"

That caught me by surprise. I hadn't realized there'd be a prize for second, but I went on out to shake the mayor's hand and get my award. "Nice riding," I said, passing Lucinda on my way. I meant it too. Not many could handle an unfamiliar horse the way she had.

"Thanks," she said. "I might be playing a whore, but I raise horses in the real world."

It took me a moment to process her words. The real world. Right. These people had other lives, lives they'd return to at the end of the week. And I'd made some unfair assumptions about this Lucinda based on the previous one. Granted, her behavior at the outhouse hadn't helped her case any, but still, I'd prejudged her.

I took the second-place envelope, sought out the church ladies in the crowd taking up a collection for Miss Josephine, and handed the money over to them. The little silver-colored trophy I kept for myself. An indulgence, but one my conscience could afford. A moment later, Lucinda joined us, placing her envelope in the collection box as well. I watched for any hesitation and spotted none.

Yep, I'd definitely misjudged this Lucinda. Maybe she thought she'd get it all back in attention bonuses, but I didn't think that was her reasoning. Death affected people so close to home, even if you barely knew a person.

CHAPTER 23

I RODE Ford out of town while the rest of Oblivion packed picnic lunches and planned Sunday outings. A pair of teenage boys tossed a ball back and forth. (At least they weren't robbing the dang bank.) I overheard some women talking about a knitting circle and some men gathering fishing gear to take to the pond; I suppressed a pang of jealousy. All right, I didn't knit, couldn't even sew on a button, but I'd caught some whopper fish in that pond.

One in particular had always eluded me, a big old catfish, smart and wily. He broke line after line, stole lure after lure after I spent hours on the porch making them by hand. I made it my personal goal to catch that fish, even if I ended up releasing him out of respect afterward. But I never did snag him. And now, like every other living thing in my first lifetime, he was long dead.

A pall of sadness and loneliness fell heavily on my shoulders. Surrounded by people, I still rode through this life alone. Ghosts and shadows shrouded every individual. I couldn't even consider forming new bonds with the folks I'd met. At the end of the week, we'd all go our separate ways.

I wondered where the hell I'd be going.

As if she could read my emotions (and I wasn't entirely sure she couldn't), Pandora winged out of the bright blue sky and landed on the pommel of my saddle, beak pointed straight ahead to face head-on whatever we found.

"Xanthis is going to miss you," I warned her, grasping the reins in one hand so I could stroke her beautiful feathers with the other.

She turned her head to stare at me, then shook it from side to side.

"Okay, guess not."

And I was talking to a bird. Again. Well, now I had an answer as to where I'd be going at the end of the week—the asylum looked more and more likely, especially if Doc happened to be looking out his office window while Pandora and I conversed.

Any other time, I'd love a mile ride in this kind of weather. The sun produced a pleasant heat without making me sweat. The spring flowers bloomed, their bright colors accenting the rough trail we followed, and the steady clip-clop of Ford's hooves beat out a hypnotic rhythm, but knowing my destination filled me with dread.

At least this trip out, I'd armed myself. A quick run to the general store provided me with a pair of good sharp knives in two sizes and a belt sheath to carry one in, once I made up the explanation that I planned on doing some whittling. Woefully insufficient against Eye Killers but better than shooting paint. I'd hidden the second one in my desk drawer. Always good to have a spare stashed away.

Before me loomed the mining-camp-turned-tourist-attraction, and I slowed Ford's pace further so that I might scan the area before riding into a potential trap. What I wouldn't have given for a posse I could trust right about now. Despite being independently minded, I worked well with others in a pinch. Okay, that's assuming they could follow my orders. But who could I tell this crazy story to?

In the empty parking lot, I swung out of the saddle and tied the reins to one of the many wooden posts designating the "spaces." The knot I made hung loose—tight enough so that Ford couldn't pull free but easy to undo if I had to make a quick escape. Pandora hopped off the pommel to land in her usual spot on my shoulder.

I noticed the absence of Sandra Meadows's car. I circled the place where I'd discovered it, and broken glass and bits of metal littered the ground, but someone had removed the vehicle. Other grooves cut into the gravel, and I guessed a second car had dragged the other away, perhaps to someplace where it could be repaired.

What I didn't understand was the absence of all other signs of life. If this was a tourist attraction, an historical site, where were the tourists?

Maybe they shut down on Sundays?

With all the flagrant cursing and overly forward behavior in this time, I hadn't figured folks for heavy churchgoers.

Pandora and I headed for the mock campsite, me all the while keeping a sharp lookout for either the Eye Killers or the elusive park ranger several people had mentioned. Plenty of footprints covered the ground, some of them uneven with one foot dragging, but I couldn't tell which were old and which might be new. It hadn't rained since I'd arrived, and who knew how many folks had tramped through this area in the past couple of days?

When Pandora and I reached the tents, I saw that someone had taken away all the statues, including the one whose boots and hat I'd stolen. That meant some sort of staff worked here, and I wasn't finding the workers by standing around staring at empty tents. I eased the knife from its sheath and let my arm hang down at my side. No need scaring harmless folks with a great big blade, but I wanted to be prepared. "Hello?" I called.

Yep, Doc could go ahead and lock me in the nuthouse right now. If any Eye Killers lurked in the area, I'd be drawing them right to me.

But nothing happened and no one responded. Well, might as well go whole-hog. I turned to Pandora. "Anyone around? Do you know?"

She cocked her head, listening intently, then launched herself, her talons scratching me through my shirt as she propelled into the air.

"Thanks," I muttered, examining the small tear she'd left in the fabric. I watched her soar over the camp, fly through a couple of tents, and flap her way up to the mine itself. She disappeared into its dark mouth as if a beast had swallowed her whole, and I held my breath, then released it as her reds and golds hurtled from within its interior.

Holding out my arm, I grimaced while her claws found purchase. "Anything?" I asked her.

She shook her head.

Okay then, time to go check out the mine myself.

I trudged my way through the camp, careful to give a wide berth to every tent flap, even with Pandora's assurances, but no walking dead staggered out to greet me.

At the mine's entrance, I stopped, noticing a bright yellow sign on a worn wooden stake that hadn't been there on my previous visit.

CLOSED FOR REALITY TV (with a simplistic smiling face drawn next to it)

NO TRESPASSING

IN CASE OF EMERGENCY, CONTACT PARK RANGER SAM ELLERTON IV AT (505) 555-5720.

I didn't know what the string of numbers meant, but the name sure had some impact. Ellerton. Ellerton was Sam's last name. My Sam. From my time. And the sign referred to Sam the fourth and reality TV. No wonder *Harsh Reality*'s Sam looked so much like the one I'd known. He'd descended directly from the original. He was my Sam's great-grandson. Even that distant connection shooed away a little of my loneliness.

A surge of hope swept through me. If Sam was the park ranger and a direct descendant, he might very well have the answers I was searching for. I knew for a fact he'd dabbled in a little gold mining when his ranch was doing poorly. Heck, I was even invited to dinner—the perfect opportunity to ask my questions.

I spun on my heel, exhaustion driven away by the first joy I'd felt in days.

A low moan echoed from the depths of the mine.

Well, shit.

Every fiber of my being demanded that I get the hell out of there, make tracks to Sam's place, get my answers, and finish this fight, but I'd taken an oath. Maybe it didn't matter anymore. I wasn't a real sheriff here. My badge meant nothing in this place and time. Maybe my duty lay with the greater good. But if even the slightest chance existed that the moaning had come from some poor, innocent, dying victim of the Eye Killers, I had to go in and check it out. Xanthis had become hardened to the suffering of the individual, focusing so much on the big picture that he lost all empathy for the folks he strove to protect. I refused to let that happen to me.

Pandora caught my sleeve with her beak, trying to pull me away from the cave mouth, but a two-pound bird had little effect on a grown woman of, well, a lot more pounds than two. "Come or stay," I told her, "but I'm going in."

She squawked, shaking herself and ruffling every one of her glorious feathers.

"Come or stay," I repeated with more force and stepped into the colder, darker interior. The chill passing through me wasn't just the temperature dropping.

For the first few feet, I could see clearly, the bright sunshine streaming through the opening to light my way. Of course, I noted as the moan came again, the sound emanated from the farthest depths of the mine.

I passed the abandoned equipment and the explanatory signs, the statues having been taken from this part of the exhibit as well, and tried to trace the voice to its origin. But the rock walls distorted the moaning each time, making it echo and seem to come from all directions at once.

I brandished the knife before me, more concerned with my immediate survival than about scaring any innocents. With every step the mine grew darker and darker, the shadows longer and longer, and each corner more likely to hide an enemy. Pandora, who'd decided to stick with me after all, kept up a constant litany of chirps, squawks, and screeches, whether to chastise me or comfort herself, I didn't know. They echoed, setting off a cacophony worthy of a dozen phoenixes.

"Hey," I whispered to her, "you know you're telling anyone who might be listening that we're here, right?"

Pandora fell silent.

It got too dark for me to see more than a few feet ahead of me. I'd avoided grabbing one of the lamps off the wall and lighting it because I didn't want to give away our exact location. The sound might be distorted, but the light would act as a guiding beacon. However, the positives outweighed the negatives at this point, and I turned to detach the nearest lamp from its holder. Of course, it stuck in place, these bolts being new, not rusted. Guess the park staff didn't want folks making off with their expensive lamps. Hats and boots were bad enough.

Something heavy and metal clonked me in the back of the head.

Pandora launched, and I went to my knees, barely avoiding cracking my forehead on the cave wall in front of me and adding another injury. The clang of the hit resounded while my vision shifted and spun. Instinct sent me rolling to my right. My feathered protector screeched and hissed, the motion of her wings so close I could feel the breeze they made. Then she was gone from my side.

I ended up on my backside, blinking and staring, trying to make out anything between the blurred eyesight and the darkness. All I could detect were shadows, one small and darting about, making a lot of noise, the other large and clunky, swinging what might have been a shovel at the fluttering annoyance.

My fingers clenched around the handle of my knife, but I feared throwing it. Accurate with guns was one thing. Knife-throwing was quite another. I knew I'd have to hit the thing in the head to do any good—an almost impossible shot with my injuries in the dark.

A dull ache pounded in my skull. I reached back with my free hand and felt the wet stickiness of blood. Head wounds bled a lot, even small ones. I knew that much without being a doc, but the headache and dizziness probably meant a concussion, or worse.

"Come on, Pandora," I urged her. "Go for the eyes. The eyes!"

I had no idea who my attacker was or had been. The mine was too dark. From the size, at least it wasn't another child I'd have to put down, though that would have been physically easier. One major advantage of the deep shadows, the Eye Killer couldn't mesmerize me. And if the phoenix could claw its eyes out, I wouldn't have to worry about getting closer to it.

The Eye Killer swung the shovel, missing Pandora but almost clipping me with the tip.

Okay, getting closer wasn't a good idea, regardless.

Pandora put up a good fight, but I could tell she was tiring. Her motions grew more sluggish, and the shovel got closer and closer to making contact. I'd have to do something or risk losing the one living being I could count on in this time.

Just as I raised the knife, I heard a sickening clang and a pained cry from the phoenix.

"No!" I screamed, wincing as it echoed.

Pandora fell, and I dropped my weapon and dove to catch her before she could hit the rock floor, then shielded her when the shovel struck me in the back.

The air whoofed out of me, but I kept her curled in the crook of one arm, unable to see the extent of her injuries, unable to tell if she breathed at all. The little body felt fragile and broken.

White-hot rage flooded me. I waited until I heard the grunt preceding the Eye Killer's next swing, whirled around to face my attacker, and grabbed the metal end of the shovel in my free hand. The sharp edge bit deep into my palm, but I ignored the pain and sudden flow of warmth, instead gripping harder. With all my strength, I thrust upward, driving the shovel's wooden end into the Eye Killer's gut.

Ribs cracked, surprising me, and I had to figure they'd already been damaged in whatever fight had killed this poor lost soul and left him open to being turned into an Eye Killer in the first place. The creature howled, releasing the handle and stumbling backward. I surged to my feet, wavering as the mine's interior spun around me, then steadied. I flipped the shovel around, caught it in my hand, and brought it down on the Eye Killer's head. It connected with a tremendous ringing like the sound of the church bell.

Not enough.

Weakened by my wound and having only one arm to work with, I hadn't possessed enough force to crush the skull. But I'd done damage. The monster fled, moaning and gasping, into the darker caverns that branched off the main cave. "Puuut iiiit baaack," it groaned.

I knew what it meant. I didn't pursue him. I had other things to worry about.

Using the distant daylight as my focus, I staggered, then crawled on my knees and one hand until I reached the cave mouth. With the sunlight warming my body and drying the blood on my hand and head, I gently placed Pandora on the ground before me.

"Hey," I said, probing her with a careful finger. I smoothed the ruffled feathers away from her little black eyes, which were closed. "Come on, don't leave me alone." My voice rasped from my throat. Tears welled in my eyes. Her breast wasn't moving. "I'm sorry," I sobbed. "I'm so sorry." She'd tried to warn me. She'd saved my life twice. And I'd let her die.

I lifted her again into my arms, feeling the shattered bones beneath the soft red and gold, cradling and rocking her for I don't know how long until the blood loss took away my consciousness.

CHAPTER 24

"WE SHOULD get Doc," a man's voice whispered.

Bodies shifted in the room, boots sliding over a wood floor. I wanted to open my eyes, but the lids weighed down like rocks.

"No, we absolutely shouldn't," a woman argued back. "Not until we get the whole story or make up a better one. Unless you want the nice boys in white coats to show up and cart her off."

Arlene. Now I knew her. And the first was Sam. The sound of a creaking chair carried to me as one of them sat.

"Damn good thing I got to her first," Arlene went on. "Nearly broke my neck doing it too. Thank God my horse knew how to handle a rider better than I knew how to handle him. And it's just luck you came out to check the mine and were there to help me with her."

The comforting scents of good home cooking threatened to make my stomach rumble. I thought I could smell a pot roast, gravy, yeast rolls, and apple pie.

Sam's house. Somehow, Arlene and Sam had gotten me to his ranch house. It wasn't far from the mine. I remembered Beth planning an apple pie for tonight's dessert.

"Look," Sam said, "I owe the sheriff. I'll do what I can. But I don't know how we can protect her. I mean, you said they got the whole thing on audio and she sounded nuts."

"Just audio, and *I* never said anything about nuts." Arlene blew out a breath. "Don't care what Deputy Baylor and that quack Doc say. They've been out to get her since the get-go. And since their little argument at the barrel racing, our illustrious director isn't too thrilled with her, either. But I'm telling you, someone else was in that mine. Cali might be taking this all a little too seriously, but she didn't make all those moans and groans herself, didn't injure herself, either. And she damn well didn't kill her own pet bird."

My chest tightened. Pandora. They'd found her. She was truly gone. I swallowed the sudden lump in my throat.

Then the rest of the conversation sank in. They'd captured the sounds of my fight with the Eye Killer, but only the sounds. Taz must have set up microphones in the cavern, maybe planning on having us do some gold mining for *Harsh Reality.* Probably had cameras in there too, but with the lamps out, they wouldn't have come on.

The Eye Killer had escaped, which left me looking like a lunatic.

I managed to crack open an eye, taking in Beth's bedroom—frilly white curtains, pink quilt covering me, whitewashed furniture weathered with age. I knew this room. I'd carried Beth in here myself when those cattle rustlers had tried raping her. Well, the Beth of my time. This room hadn't changed with the passage of years except for the aging furnishings. My Sam had made this furniture. Nice to see it had lasted so well.

Groaning, I tried raising myself on my elbows and fell back when the room spun and my stomach turned over. Two pairs of hands immediately grabbed my shoulders and legs, holding me down.

"Easy, Cali," Arlene warned. "We don't think you're concussed, but neither of us have medical degrees, even though Sam here knows a little first aid, so take things nice and slow and let us help." She got me sitting up while Sam shoved a couple more pillows behind me.

I blinked, clearing my vision on the third try, and felt my head. One of them, Sam probably, or maybe Beth, had bandaged me up. Holding my hand out in front of me, I saw they'd fixed that as well.

Arlene passed me a glass of water from the nightstand, and I spotted a deck of well-worn tarot cards and some clear pyramid-shaped crystals beside it, resting atop a copy of *Wicca for Beginners: Fundamentals of Philosophy and Practice* by Thea Sabin. Interesting, but not immediately important.

The water went down cold and refreshing, and I cleared my throat, passing back the glass. "Ford?" I asked.

The two exchanged confused looks, and Sam turned to Arlene. "Your real last name's Ford?"

Arlene shook her head. "No, it's—"

"Ford's my horse," I interrupted, not wanting to hear Arlene's real name. To me, she'd always be Arlene Candler. I needed her to be.

"Ah," Sam said, the clouds clearing. He scratched at the bandage on his own head and smiled. "Your horse is fine, stabled out back with Arlene's Appaloosa and Beth's mare. Arlene led him in behind her own. We're not an operating ranch. Not since the old days." He smiled sheepishly. "Which is why I'm rather lacking in riding skills. That and a back injury in my younger years keep me off the wild ones, well, most of the time." He blushed, probably thinking about his earlier barrel-racing folly. "But my daughter likes to ride for fun, so we've got the facilities."

"Not since...." I trailed off, fitting pieces together. "This is the original house, isn't it? It hasn't changed at all." Made sense, really. The fire wouldn't have spread far outside Oblivion. Surrounding farms and ranches might have survived all these years, and adobe aged well.

Sam nodded, dragging his chair to the side of the bed. "It is," he said slowly, brow furrowing, "but how would you know that?" Cocking his head to the side, he studied my face. "Did you come through on one of my tours? I rarely forget a face."

"Tours?"

He spread his arms wide, encompassing the room and the entire house in one gesture. "We're on the *National Register of Historic Places*," Sam said with pride evident in his voice. "I give tours of the house as well as the old gold mine. It's a family tradition."

I shook my head and winced at the pain it caused me. "No, I've never taken a tour."

"Then how—?"

"Look," I said. "Is there someplace where we can sit and talk? I've got a helluva yarn to tell, and I don't think lying in bed is going to add any credence to it." I swung my legs over the side, closing my eyes while the next wave of dizziness passed.

Arlene plunked down beside me, sinking the mattress so I slid toward her. Her soft curves felt safe, so I stayed put. Hadn't had enough "safe" lately. "You need to stay in bed, and this room is one of the safest for talking in the house. Sam says they've got cameras out here too. Part of the conditions of employment for the show."

"But I negotiated not to have them in the bedrooms and, of course, the bathrooms and kitchen, which we modernized, in exchange for their use of the rest of the house. We actually passed you through that open window to keep you off their recording devices." Sam waved at the white lace curtains fluttering in an evening breeze, stronger than earlier and a possible precursor to a spring storm. "They might have caught you on one of the exterior cameras, though, despite it getting dark. Either way, it won't be long before they figure out where you are. I'm sure the cameras outside the mine picked up you and Arlene leaving."

"Well, we'll have to come up with something, then," I stated. "In the meantime—" I broke off as the door swung open and Beth entered with a rolling cart laden with food and dishware.

"Thought I heard voices in here. Glad to see you up, Sheriff. You had us all worried." She frowned. "Really sorry about Pandora. She was cute."

"Yeah, me too." Though I could just imagine the bird's reaction to being called "cute." I blinked to avoid crying in front of my rescuers.

Beth served up the meal, heaping plates high and passing them around with napkins and silverware. Then she took one for herself and sat cross-legged on the woven carpet of pink-and-yellow pastels.

I hesitated before speaking, studying the girl on the floor. Telling my story to grown men would be hard enough, but a skeptical teenager.... I eyed the tarot cards and crystals again and took a chance. "You're willing to accept things that seem rather far-fetched?" I asked her. "Things most folks aren't?"

She returned my stare without blinking, a forkful of meatloaf halfway to her lips. "I practice the Wiccan religion, well, except for the vegetarian thing, although meat isn't actually forbidden." She blushed, then ate the meatloaf. "I believe there's life on other planets," she continued without further pause, "and I believe in life after death. I also think some people have extrasensory perception."

Well. I didn't get all of that, but I understood enough. If I'd been wearing my hat, the raising of my eyebrows would have knocked it clean off. Arlene covered her mouth with one hand, suppressing a grin, but Beth's father took her answer in stride. So, Arlene would be the hard sell. Got it.

Steeling myself, I took a deep breath, let it out, and launched into my tale. "I'm… not exactly who you all think I am. I'm the real Cali McCade." I waited for the inevitable laughter and teasing, but it didn't come. Instead, the three of them watched me, listening with mixed expressions to what I had to say.

"The fire that wiped out the original Oblivion was started in a fight between the town and the Eye Killers," I continued, pausing for some mashed potatoes. Damn, the girl could cook, and I nodded my approval at her. She beamed. "I'm assuming you all read, or skimmed," I added, glancing at Arlene, "my journals."

Three nods.

"Well, it's all true. Every impossible word. I didn't go crazy. I didn't kill the Arlene of my time in a jealous rage." Looking down, I focused on my hands gripping my plate. "She was possessed. Putting her out of her misery was the hardest thing I've ever done." The memories flooded me, and my appetite vanished, but out of respect for the young and talented chef, I continued eating. "Those Eye Killers, those demons or Elementals, or whatever the hell they are, they're back. Maybe they never left, but I'm thinking the new gold mining thing you've got going on for the tourists up at the mine may have sent them into a frenzy, reminded them of what they originally lost. They're responsible for Miss Josephine's death and the disappearances of a bunch of other folks who've left the show without their final pay. And one of them attacked me in the mine today."

I stopped there, gauging their reactions. Beth's eyes were wide. She'd stopped eating, and her food sat cooling on her plate. Sam held fork and knife, one in each hand, his gaze fixed on me, mouth grim, but he nodded once. I could hardly believe his affirmation, and I wondered what he knew that I didn't.

Arlene, as predicted, put her plate on the dressing table and paced the length of the room. She shot glances at me from the corner of her eye, some amused, some concerned. At last she threw both hands in the air. "Seriously? Sam, seriously, you're buying any of this? I figured you for the levelheaded sort, even if your daughter admits to being some kind of New Age hippie. And you!" she accused, whirling on me to point a finger down at my chest. "When you said you meant to restore California Mc-Cade's good name, I wasn't thinking you meant this! It's the money, isn't it? Taz got to you, right? This is some crazy play for the mother of all bonuses and you're all playing me for a laugh, right, Sam? Where are the cameras? Here?" She peered into a space between the armoire and the wall, then opened the cabinet and shoved the hanging dresses from side to side along with some dungarees and pants in a variety of colors. "Taz gonna jump out and yell 'Boo'?"

Beth set her plate on the rug and got to her feet, walked to Arlene, and shut the armoire doors loudly and firmly in her face. "We're not hiding anything or anyone," she said.

Sam pursed his lips, then spoke. "Beth and I aren't playing you, Arlene. But that *would* make a good excuse to give Taz, Deputy Baylor, and Doc when they come calling." He glanced at the darkening sky outside the open window. "Storm's probably got them staying put in town, but they'll be out here soon as it passes."

Arlene ignored him. "Right. Not playing." She returned to the bed, sitting down next to me and taking the plate from my lap. She set it aside, then grasped my hands in hers. "I really like you. Could grow to like you a whole lot more. But I can't deal with this. Look me in the eye, Cali. No, *Sandra.* Look me in the eye, Sandra, and tell me you really believe what you're saying."

I looked her in the eye. "The name's Cali, and I believe every single syllable."

Arlene released my hands. "Fuck," she muttered, turning away, then standing to pace some more.

"Listen," Sam interjected before I could let my anger get the better of my mouth, "I've worked at the mine site for a lotta years. And while nothing ever happened to me, thank God, there've been a good number of unexplainable accidents up there. Only one or two at a time up until last month, then a whole slew of them. State almost shut us down. We've got more missing persons in this county than any other in New Mexico, most centered around here. And folks have seen and heard things, including me."

"Howling, moaning," Beth put in. "Drove off most of the tourism at the mine. That's why we started giving tours here at the house. They cut Dad's hours, and we needed to pay the bills."

"Which is why I agreed to do this stupid reality show," Sam finished. "Beth's got dreams of going to culinary school, and we're scraping together the funds to get her there."

"Well," I said, reclaiming a fluffy yeast roll from my discarded plate, "you're off to a great start, school or no school."

Beth opened her mouth to thank me, but Arlene interrupted.

"Are you listening to yourselves?" she practically shouted. "Even if you want to believe in demons, which, I guess, is your religions' prerogative, how exactly do you explain the one-hundred-and-twenty-something-year-old woman sitting here telling us all this? And what is supposed to have happened to Sandra Meadows, huh?" She glared at me. "You just, what? Took over her body? Gee, I hope she didn't have any friends or family or anything. You stole her life?"

"Something like that," I murmured, focusing on my fingernails, rough and broken. "Not my choice." I didn't want to think about Sandra Meadows, down in that pit. And I sure didn't want to explain it to them. I needed to change the subject. I needed a distraction.

Outside the open window, lightning flashed, and a crack of thunder made us all jump. A fiery ball of red and yellow hurtled through the curtains, landing in my lap in a screeching, trembling mass of feathers.

"Oh my God," I whispered, trying to pry the phoenix from my vest. "Oh my God, Pandora." The tears flowed, matting her feathers to her shivering body, but neither of us seemed to care. Tucking her up under my chin, I rubbed my face against her soft, downy head. I ran my hands over her, feeling for broken bones and finding none. I should have known, should have realized she'd come back, or at least suspected. But she hadn't been dead the last time she... transformed. It must take longer when she's dead.

Or she was waiting until the coast was clear.

Regardless, here she was, alive and whole, and I vowed never to risk her again. An empty promise, perhaps, but one I'd try to keep.

Lifting my head, I turned to my companions. "This," I said, continuing to stroke the frightened animal, "is the reason I'm alive today. Pandora is a phoenix." My lips quirked upward a little. "And she bites."

CHAPTER 25

"A PHOENIX. Like the Greek mythology phoenix?" Beth asked, crawling over to pet Pandora. The bird allowed it, much to my relief. I think she was too terrified to mind.

"Apparently. And the bite of one gives a person the power of rebirth, to come back whenever that person is, well, needed, I guess." I let Pandora lie in my lap, spreading my hands helplessly. "Really, I have no idea how it works. She bit me. I burned. I woke up here, healed and whole. Not the most pleasant experience, going or coming." I risked a glance at Arlene, who'd gone pale. "Maybe you should sit down," I suggested.

She didn't budge, instead pointing an unsteady finger at the animal in my lap. "That... that's impossible."

"Which part?" Sam asked dryly.

"I... she was dead. I buried her." Arlene ran both hands through her hair, completely disheveling it. "I didn't have much time," she babbled, picking up speed as she spoke. "I saw Sam headed toward us. We needed to get you out of there. But the shovel was right there, so I covered her over with a few shovelfuls of dirt. I thought you'd want that."

I smiled. "I would have. Thank you."

"You're missing my point!" she shouted, making me wince and Beth jump. "The bird was dead. Stone dead."

"I don't doubt it. I watched her die. And I didn't know for sure she could come back from that. But here she is."

"No. It's a trick. She wasn't really dead. She was stunned or something. Or… or it's another bird. That's it." The sudden hiss of the arriving downpour softened her panicky tones but could do nothing for her white face and wide eyes.

I still had half a yeast roll, and I fed bits of it to the phoenix, hoping to calm her, though she continued to tremble. "She's the same bird," I said, watching her with concern. "Admit it, Arlene, you've never seen one like her before. I doubt highly you'll see two of them in your lifetime. In a dozen lifetimes." Although I had the strangest feeling *I* had seen more than one of these birds… somewhere. I shook the odd half-formed memory away.

Running my hands over her again, I double-checked for injuries, thinking maybe that's what had her so upset, but all I found were some bits of debris between her talons. I held them up for Arlene and the others to see—some dirt and some ash.

"Oh… wow," Beth breathed.

Sam grinned. Arlene huffed and turned away.

"So, what's got her so frantic?" Sam wondered aloud. "The storm?" To punctuate his words, another streak of lightning crackled across the night sky, and thunder rolled, causing even the sturdy adobe ranch house to vibrate on its foundation.

I stood, keeping Pandora cuddled with one arm and gripping the closest post of the bed with the other to steady myself. Sam reached out to help, but I shook my head, which of course made the dizziness worse. "It'll be gone in a minute," I told him, closing my eyes and counting to ten, then saying a quick prayer when counting didn't work. The sense of unbalance faded.

"I don't think it's the storm," I said, answering Sam's earlier question. "She's hundreds of years old. I wouldn't think a little lightning and thunder would bother her. In fact, the only time I can recall seeing her this worked up was—" My voice broke off as a horrible thought occurred. "Oh… fuck," I whispered, borrowing this time period's favorite obscenity.

Hurrying to the window, I peered into the darkness but could make out nothing beyond a few feet from the sill: some browning grass that could use this rain, a wilting flowerbed, maybe a tree stump, but I couldn't be sure.

The lightning flashed, revealing the entire side yard, and two shambling figures headed toward the house, straight for the window in which I stood silhouetted.

I turned to the other occupants of the room. "Put out the lamps," I ordered. "Fast!"

"Why? What's wrong?" Arlene stood at my shoulder, trying to see past me as the thunder rumbled again, but without the lightning, she had no hope of spotting the approaching Eye Killers.

"Stay here and wait," I told her, pulling down on her arm with my free hand, "but do it on your knees."

She let me drag her to the floor, and I reached over to set Pandora on the bed. She cooed at me, gripping the wooden frame with her claws.

"While you're down there, you might consider a prayer," I told her.

Arlene snorted in disbelief, but she stayed down, turning to face the window and peer out. "Can't see a damn thing in this storm."

Beth and Sam had put out the bedroom's two lamps, and I sensed them crawling across the floor to us, then made out their shadows as my eyes adjusted to the minimal light coming from outside and under the door to the rest of the interior of the house. "Do you have any guns? Real ones, I mean."

"We've got a few." The darkness hid Beth's expression, but I could hear the smile in her tone. "What do you need?"

"Whatever doesn't shoot paint."

She scrambled across the wood floor and the throw rug. The door to the hallway opened and closed, casting a brief beam of light through the room, and running footsteps faded into the house.

"Now hang on a minute," Arlene warned. "Let's not do something stupid."

The lightning lit up the sky, and she got a look at the Eye Killers moving toward us. Instead of the apology I expected, she laughed.

"That's it?" She had to shout over the thunderclap, and Sam and I both shushed her. "Oooh, sorry." Arlene lowered her voice to a dramatic whisper. "Is that it?" she repeated. "A couple of extras made up to look like zombies?"

"Zombies?" I figured she meant my walking dead, so I didn't wait for an explanation. "They're not made up. They're—"

"Look, darlin', I hail from Vegas. We specialize in theatrics there. Makeup, special effects, the works. So, before you get crazier than you already are and do something really stupid, let me just put a stop to this right now or some poor actors are gonna end up dead."

Before I could grab her, Arlene stood and swung her legs over the windowsill, then dropped onto the muddy ground beyond.

"Arlene!" I hissed, throwing myself after her, but Sam caught me around the waist.

"The guns, Cali. Wait for the guns. Besides, she might be right. Taz said he would be throwin' a few tricks our way."

I studied the approach of our new arrivals and shook my head, tensing to break Sam's hold on me when the door to the bedroom swung open again. The figure in the doorway turned her head from one side to the other, long hair flying, then shut the door behind her. "Um, where's Arlene?"

"Gone. You got the guns?" I asked.

Metal scraped on wood. The historical society wouldn't care for the gouges in the floor, I thought, mind wandering as my head pounded. "Here," Beth said, pressing a pistol into my hand. "Try to be careful with this. It's an antique." Then she stopped and chuckled softly. "Well, maybe not to you." She passed something much longer to her pa and kept another pistol for herself. Then she yanked a couple of boxes of bullets out of her dress pockets and dropped them on the floor beside the window.

Despite the seriousness of the situation, a grin tugged at my lips. "A woman who cooks and shoots. You're gonna make some cowboy real happy someday."

Beth laughed softly in the darkness. "I haven't fired one of these since I converted to Wicca, but I used to be pretty good. Won ribbons and everything. And under the circumstances…."

My fingers loaded the S&W by memory, and I knelt up to look out the window again. Another flash of light showed Arlene had made it halfway to the approaching couple, and it was indeed a couple, a man and woman, the female's dress torn to strips and blowing wildly in the storm's wind. Arlene slowed as she drew closer, and I credited her with *some* sense, but I didn't see how I could reach her before she got to them.

When I swung my legs over the sill, Sam didn't try to stop me again. However, his hand closed on my forearm. "Be *sure*, Cali. For God's sake, be sure."

I nodded, knowing he could make out that much. "Stay put. If they get close, whatever you do, don't look in their eyes. You'll need to shoot for the heads, but get them on the ground first, if you can. That way, you can avoid the eyes and still not miss." But it wouldn't come to that, if I could help it.

Two heads bobbed in the darkness, both of them having read my journal and knowing the Eye Killers' power. I thought I heard an audible swallow from Sam. "Maybe I should come with you," he managed.

"No, Sam. You're protecting your home and your family. That's where you belong." I pointed out the window. "And I belong out there." Besides, his injury would slow the both of us down. He had no more business fighting Eye Killers than he did riding horses. "You know," I said, risking one more minute and focusing on the blob that was Beth, "while I hesitate to add any more magic to this situation, good or bad, if you're a witch, this would be a helluva good time for a spell."

The dark blob on the right shrugged. "It's more of a lifestyle choice. I haven't gotten to actual spells yet."

Figured.

Releasing the windowsill, I dropped to the squishy ground and went straight to my knees when a fresh wave of dizziness hit. Not the most auspicious of beginnings, or the most heroic. I had my gun in one hand, so I had to use the other to push myself up and wore plenty of mud before reaching my feet.

The rain soaked me in seconds, and I regretted leaving my hat inside, but it might have cut my limited field of vision even further. Strands of stray hair hung loose from my braid and dripped into my face.

My filthy clothing stuck to me, and my boots made sucking noises in the muck as I crossed the yard.

Thank God Arlene had halted, letting the couple approach her, and that bought me time to close the distance between us. A brilliant streak of lightning went from clouds to ground, striking in an empty corral to my left.

If we didn't deal with this soon, the Eye Killers wouldn't need to get us. Mother Nature would take care of it for them.

I had a brief hysterical thought that maybe Mother Nature and the Eye Killers were related, like mother and children, them being Elementals protecting the earth and all, and I had to clap my hand over my mouth to stifle a nervous laugh. This, of course, succeeded in smearing mud across my face. Sighing, I wiped it away with my sopping sleeve.

The lightning had done more than hit the corral. It had revealed the identities of the Eye Killers to Arlene. I heard her laughter roll under the responding thunder.

"Hey, Cali," she shouted, "look here! The Lansings have come calling." She had her paint pistol in her grip and waved it at the Eye Killers. "We should invite them in for pie. What do you think?"

Lansing. My mind raced, then crossed the finish line. Right. Adam's parents. Well, now I knew where they'd gotten to. I also knew they hadn't been the only folks to vanish from Oblivion's recreation, and I searched the shadows. "I think you should come on back here and get behind me," I answered. Two of them and we might have a chance. More, and history would definitely repeat itself.

"Why? So you can claim all the credit? We may not all be sharpshooters like you, Sheriff, but even I can hit a target this close. And if you really believe this is real, I'm aiming to prove to you otherwise." She turned to face the Lansings, or what remained of them, oblivious to the grievous wounds they bore or wishfully thinking them to be stage makeup. Her voice lowered to a dramatic pitch. "Now, you hold it right there and no one has to get hurt."

"Arlene, they're dead. Look at them." I picked up my pace, then staggered to a halt when the world around me rocked and swam. Placing my hands and the pistol on my knees, I lowered my head, closed my eyes, and took deep, even breaths, willing the nausea to pass.

"Ah yes, they're dead. They're zombies. That means I'll just have to shoot them."

I heard the double pop as Arlene fired off two shots.

"Not good enough, eh? Guess head shots are in order. This is gonna hurt, you know." The walking dead apparently didn't take the warning, and I heard her pull the trigger twice more.

Then came Arlene's shout of surprise, which didn't surprise me at all.

No, dammit, no. Not again. Please, God, not again. Sick or not, I made myself walk, then run toward the ensuing struggle, keeping my eyes closed as much as possible and guiding my way by grunts, curses, and the pounding of fists. Twice I slipped and skidded in the mud and almost went down but somehow kept my footing.

I risked cracking my eyes open when I got close and was relieved to find the vertigo had lessened, though everything still looked blurred. I stared, disbelieving, at the scene before me.

Under any other circumstances, it would have been comical, a middle-aged couple, heads and clothing covered in runny red paint, beating the tar out of a well-built much younger woman. Taz would have kissed a chicken to get it on his cameras. But this wasn't the stage, and I was through playing.

I raised my real S&W, using the limited visibility to risk focusing on Mrs. Lansing's head so I could find my target. I fired.

And missed.

"One," I said under my breath. "And shit."

The crack of the weapon registered, though, and the woman stopped her assault on Arlene to turn on me. That gave Arlene the chance to break Mr. Lansing's grip and shove the man away. Lansing stumbled but didn't fall and rallied himself to come back for more.

Arlene's wide eyes fixed on my face. "That's a real gun. Are you crazy? No, wait. We already know that. Put it away before someone gets killed." She panted the words, winded by the fight.

In the next flash of lightning, I studied her. Her face was a mass of bleeding scratches, and she had a black eye coming. "I told you. They're already dead. Think, Arlene. Really. You're hurt. This isn't a game."

Her laugh came forced. "They just got carried away. They didn't mean to—" Arlene's words broke off as Mr. Lansing succeeded in straightening and facing her head-on. Inches apart, the Eye Killer caught her in its deadly gaze.

"No!" My scream carried over the next clap of thunder and rolled with it across the yard. Though I'd almost been a victim myself, I'd never watched the killing process from the outside, not in person anyway. Lightning flooded the yard with its blinding light, and the blood drained from Arlene's face. Her lips worked, but no sound came out. The paint-shooter dropped from her hand and she froze, her throat muscles distending while she silently fought to breathe.

I aimed my pistol at Mr. Lansing, but his wife got in my way, and instead of risking another stray shot and the possibility of hitting Arlene, I swung wild and struck Mrs. Lansing across the face with the gun. Her head snapped back, jaw cracking, but she didn't go down. Wrapping both arms around my shoulders, she dug in her nails and tried to force me to look in her eyes, but I closed mine. I wrenched my upper body from side to side and kicked her shins, knowing every second that passed brought Arlene closer to suffocation.

Once again boots proved superior to women's shoes, as my pointed toe caught her midcalf. Her hold broke, and I hooked my leg around hers to throw her to the ground, opened my eyes, and found my target. I couldn't trust my wavering vision for a head shot, but my second bullet went clean through Mr. Lansing's chest.

"Two," I said, gasping for air while Arlene did the same.

It was enough. The Eye Killer flailed backward, and I followed through with a high kick to his left temple that shattered his lock on Arlene.

Thanks, Pa, for the fighting lessons to go with the target practice.

Even if you find yourself without a gun, you always have weapons. You've got hands and feet. Use them.

To my utter surprise, the dead couple faded into the darkness, one shambling, one crawling away on all fours, then rising to hobble off. I had half a mind to follow and finish them, but Arlene's wheezing concerned me, and my recurring dizziness could easily make me the victim rather than the victor.

They were learning—a terrifying thought—and I knew they'd be back, in greater numbers next time, but by then I'd hopefully be healthier with some better-armed believers at my side.

I made it to Arlene, grimacing as her grip closed on the deep claw marks in my shoulder. I ran my hands over her face, her neck, checking for any serious wounds, making sure air moved in and out.

"That… they…."

"Just breathe," I told her. "Be glad you still can." Shifting, I embraced her, pressing her body against mine and listening to the beat of her heart. I'd saved her. This time, I'd saved her.

We stood like that for several long minutes, letting the rain wash over us, before heading to the house.

CHAPTER 26

"YOU LOOK like a woman who could use a drink," Sam said, coming into Beth's room with a bottle and three glasses. After setting them on the dressing table, he uncorked and tried to pour the whiskey, but his own hand shook so badly, I reached over and took it from him. He smiled his thanks.

Not that I was any too steady myself. It had been one helluva night, and my headache had risen to an internal roar, but the dizziness had passed for now. "Never waste good whiskey," I said, filling the glasses halfway, then shrugging and pouring to the brims. I waved the bottle at Beth, white-faced and cross-legged on the floor. "You want one? Tell me where the glasses are kept and I'll fetch one for you, cameras be damned."

"I'm underage," she told me, though the misery and tremor in her voice suggested she wished otherwise.

"Underage? Like you have to be...." I trailed off. In my time, if you could shave or shoot, you could drink. "How old do you have to be?"

"Twenty-one," Sam said, passing his glass to Beth with a nod for her to take a sip. "And I don't care. You're not gonna arrest me, are you, Sheriff?" He winked at me.

"Hell no." I gave a firm shake of my head and promptly regretted it when pain lanced through my skull.

We drank in silence, gathering our thoughts or simply piecing together our fractured sanity. I picked at the drying mud on my pants. We'd certainly made a mess of Beth's room, not to mention ourselves. Arlene and I had crawled back in through the window, leaving a path of dirt, water, paint, and blood across the floor. Some had transferred to Sam and Beth when they helped us and fixed up new injuries with their first aid kit, so we were four sorry-looking folks in one sorry-looking bedroom.

Even Pandora showed wear. She clung to the rounded top of one of Beth's bedposts, eyes closed, sound asleep, her little chest distending and retracting as she took even breaths. Well, she'd had a hard couple of days.

Outside, the rain had abated, but the clock on the wall read almost midnight, so I doubted anyone would come searching for me tonight. I also doubted I could ride Ford to Oblivion in my current condition.

"You got a place for me and Arlene to bunk for the night?" I asked. "Don't worry about the cameras. They have to know I'm here by now."

"One guest room, two twin beds. I'm afraid you'll have to share the space," Sam said. "Three

doors down the hall on the right. And guest bathroom across from it."

I glanced at Arlene, who'd recovered a little.
She returned the look I gave her. "Not a problem.
Thanks," I said, though my nerves twinged a bit at
the thought. The two of us, alone in a room? A rush
of heat flooded me, and it wasn't from the desert
temperatures.

"Ditto," she said.

Whatever that meant, but I got the gist.

"There's some old clothes of my ex-wife's that
should fit you both," Sam told us, nodding to Beth
to find them. She stood and left. "I can run all your
discards through the laundry machines out back."

"I suggest you close and lock the windows and
keep the guns handy," I told them, pushing myself to
my feet. My muscles did not want to comply, and I
groaned the whole way. "I don't think they'll come
back tonight, but I'd rather be as safe as possible."
I gestured at the gun on the table where I'd left it.
"Mind if I keep that?"

He grabbed a couple of boxes of bullets from a
pile by the window and passed them to me. "Consider it a gift. Don't let any gun experts get a good
look at it, though," Sam warned. "And Malek, our
props manager, is something of an enthusiast. He's
been drooling over the piece you showed up with
and talking about it to anyone who'd listen."

I traded him my paint-shooter for the real weapon
and slipped the S&W into my holster. Unless someone
examined it *very* closely, he wouldn't be able to tell the

difference. Armed and dangerous—well, dangerously
exhausted—I headed for the door, then stopped.

"You mind if Pandora stays in here tonight?" I
asked Sam.

He shrugged. "She alerted us to the zombies before. I'd feel better with her in here, actually. I doubt
Beth will mind, so long as the bird doesn't poop on
her bed."

I glanced at the sleeping phoenix, imagining the
centuries she'd lived, the horrors she'd seen, and
the intelligence she'd demonstrated. "She won't.
Thanks."

I walked down the hall to the guest bathroom.

Now, maybe I'd been raised in the middle of nowhere, but as a Marshal, Pa had traveled a lot, and
he'd brought home stories of the marvels of modern
plumbing—indoor running water you didn't have to
pump, toilets that whisked away your business at the
pull of a chain, and tubs you could soak a body in
without losing the heat or carrying up bucket after
bucket of water warmed over a fire. A person could
find such wonders in high-class mansions and fancy
big-city hotels out west, or in most homes on the east
coast, but not out here.

I never expected to find them in Sam's ranch
house.

It took some doing to get things flowing in the
shower, but once I did, I thought I'd gone to heav-
en—a sharp contrast to the past week of hell.

No amount of water could get me clean, but I
scrubbed at the mud, paint, and blood until my skin
glowed red. Then I stood there longer, letting the hot

deluge beat upon my shoulders and loosen the tightened muscles.

I have to admit it. I screamed when Arlene turned
on the bathroom lights. Same as showers, electric
lights were common to bigger cities and wealthy
homes, and some places even had streetlights run off
of electricity, but we'd never gotten that far in Oblivion. I'd carried my kerosene lamp into the bathroom
with me and bypassed the tempting switch on the
wall, suspecting what it might be but not wanting to
risk it.

So I stood there, butt naked, half-blind, and
screaming, when the room flooded with light.

"Woah, Cali!" Arlene shouted. She yanked a
towel from the rack, fumbling until she had the
shower door open, then shoved the towel through
the opening.

I took a deep breath, shut off the water, and
wrapped the thick, fuzzy cloth around my body before I stepped out.

"Jesus," Arlene whispered. "Jesus, you had me
thinking we had Eye Killers in here for a second." We
were both shaking, and I let myself be pulled against her.
"Sorry! I didn't mean to startle you." Her heart pounded. I could hear it through the nightgown she must have
found among Sam's late wife's things. "Calm down.
Easy, now. You'll wake everyone back up."

Considering she was as rattled as I was, I
couldn't resist a half smile.

Sam's house must have had a second bathroom
somewhere, because Arlene had found a place to
clean up as well. She smelled fresh, like a spring

afternoon overlaid with whiskey, and when I could lift my gaze to hers, I saw her damp hair plastered to her forehead. One strand dangled in front of her eye. I tucked it behind her ear.

"Arlene," I said, breath hitching a little, "I'm naked."

"I can tell," she murmured back.

Yeah, she certainly could. When I glanced down, I saw the buds of her nipples poking through the damp fabric—my fault—of the nightdress made of some white glossy material that clung to her curves and left little to the imagination.

"Um." I swallowed. "If that's modern women's bedroom fashion, I could get used to it," I told her, my bold streak resurfacing.

Arlene blushed very endearingly, released me, and crossed her arms over her breasts. "Sorry."

"Not a problem."

"So what *is* the problem?"

I stepped away, wrapping the towel more firmly around myself and reaching for a pile of clothes someone had placed beside the basin. No nightgowns for me, apparently, and that suited me fine. The loose-fitting shorts and sleeveless shirt would do, though they revealed far more than I would have preferred. Not as much as Arlene's attire, however.

"It's the lights," I admitted. "We didn't have electric lights in Oblivion." I couldn't remember if I'd seen the light switches elsewhere in the house, but they definitely hadn't been on, probably to maintain the realism for the show and fulfill the contract Sam had with our director.

Arlene swept a shaky hand across her eyes. "Right. Lights. Look, Cali, I gotta admit, I'm still having a rough time taking in all that happened tonight."

"Even after everything you saw? Even after what that Eye Killer did to you?" Anger curled in my belly, waiting for an excuse to release.

"I don't know *what* happened to me tonight. Sam swears you had real bullets in a real gun, but the Lansings could've been wearing bulletproof vests, I guess."

Bulletproof vests. Once more, I envied modern law enforcement. "That would mean you think I'm still 'playing' you, Arlene. Why would they wear such things, otherwise?" I took her hands in mine. "I know it's a lot to swallow. Hell, I didn't want to believe it, either. But I've seen too much evidence to doubt anymore. Will you help me stop them?" Holding my breath, I waited for her answer.

"*Can* you stop them? I mean, assuming all this is real."

"You want to believe me or you wouldn't ask that."

Arlene's mouth twisted in a humorless smile. "I want to believe *in* you. As far as those *things* are concerned, I'd prefer for them not to be real."

Wouldn't we all?

"I think I can stop them. I know a way, but I'll need information from Sam." I yawned, and my jaw cracked. "In the morning. Over breakfast. Right now I need sleep more."

She showed no signs of leaving the bathroom, so I dropped the towel and pulled on the shorts and shirt. To my surprise, she didn't turn away. That was all right with me. The more she looked, the more I had her on my side.

We crossed the hall to the guest bedroom, fully aware we had stepped into the "recording zone." The rest of the house lay dark and quiet, though Sam had left lamps lit at our bedsides and I had the one I'd carried from Beth's room. They'd shut the windows and locked them, which pleased me despite the increased temperatures. Eye Killers could break glass, but we'd have some warning.

"I asked if we could turn on the AC, but Sam said the compressor makes noise and the microphones would pick it up, so we're going to have to sweat," Arlene said, wiping her brow.

"AC?"

"Never mind."

She took my dirty clothes from my hand and left with them while I hung my holster and borrowed weapon on a chair placed before a small writing desk. Damn, I wished I had my journal. These events needed to be recorded. If I failed, maybe someone else could use my notes to succeed. But there'd be no writing tonight. I didn't think I had the energy to lift a pencil or form coherent words at this point, anyway.

The room wasn't too stifling after all. The rain had cooled things down, and even with the windows locked, the temperature would do for sleeping.

I never heard Arlene return, but somewhere in the wee hours of the morning, I awoke to her soft, even breathing in a dark room.

Cooler had turned to cold. I shivered in the thin clothing, rattling the bed springs. Sam's guest bedding consisted of a sheet and coverlet, and I pulled both over me but couldn't drive away the chill. I sneezed.

"Come here," Arlene murmured from the adjacent bed.

I thought about it. For all of ten seconds. Then I slid from between the sheets and crawled in beside her warm figure, curling myself against her back. We fit in the twin bed, barely, if we stayed pressed together. It made a good excuse.

When she rolled to face me, she nearly knocked me off and had to grab me around the waist to keep me from hitting the floor. That forced our full lengths to touch, and any sense of cold left me in that moment.

Her hands roved over my back, and I found a great advantage in the thin clothing. Every touch raised goose bumps that flowed across my skin. She slid her fingers beneath the shirt and conscious thought fled.

I sucked in a gasp when she traced my ribs. How long had it been since I'd been touched this way? I stifled a giggle.

About one hundred and twenty-five years.

That, unfortunately, reminded me of whom I'd been with at the time, and I sighed and rested my head on her shoulder, wishing… wishing… not to be with the real Arlene, a woman who'd never commit to me, but that I hadn't had to lose one to find the other.

"Too fast?" my companion whispered in the darkness.

"Too many memories," I answered.

"You want me to stop?"

"No, just… understand if I need some pauses."

She nodded, her head moving against mine. We lay still for several moments, and I realized she was waiting for me to take the next step. My lips found their way to the base of her neck, and I entertained myself, nibbling at the sensitive skin there, then tugging on her earlobe with my teeth. Arlene growled in response and resumed her explorations.

I couldn't help it. I moaned and stifled the sound by pressing my mouth more firmly against her skin.

"Microphones," she reminded me, laughing softly.

"Not in the bedrooms."

"In the hall, though. Probably right outside the door."

"Shit." I stiffened in her arms, and she shifted her hands to rub my back and shoulders until I relaxed. I doubted I'd get loud enough to be heard from the hall, but some things I just didn't want to test.

"You can't be quiet?" Arlene teased.

"Is that a challenge?"

"Sounds like one on both sides." Without warning, she rolled, placing me beneath her, her legs spread to either side of mine. She found the hem of my borrowed shirt, raising it so the slick material hissed up past my rib cage. "You seem cold," she commented, the grin evident in her tone. "Let me warm you up."

I expected her fingers, so when she lowered her head and her mouth closed over my right nipple, I shrieked, then clamped my jaw shut, remembering her warning.

Arlene tsked. While she licked one, she massaged the other, then switched, heightening the tension further and turning me to pure liquid between my thighs.

She paused, lifting her head to look at me, though I couldn't make out her expression in the dark. "You're making noise," she accused.

Was I? Had that been coming from me?

Ah hell. Taz wanted a show. If the microphones could really pick us up from the hallway, we'd give him one helluva performance.

I reached between us, sliding my callused hands down the sides of the slippery white material of the nightdress Arlene wore. Satin? Very nice, and cool to the touch. She sucked in a quick intake of breath. Yep, definitely could see the advantages here.

"Cali," she breathed.

Thank God she hadn't called me Sandra.

I massaged her heavy breasts through the fabric until she pushed my hands away, pulling back long enough to draw the gown slowly and teasingly over her head. I raised my hips to slip off the shorts and then the top, tossing both somewhere on the floor. Both of us naked, I pressed my body to hers. My fingers traced her abdomen in meandering circles and indistinguishable patterns. Her breath caught again.

"I'm the 'upstairs girl,' remember? How about you let me lead for a bit? Otherwise, this is going to be over very soon," Arlene said with a lopsided grin.

I looked into her eyes and nodded once, speechless. I was used to my Arlene wanting control, but this was different, sensual, like she was giving something to my body rather than taking from it. Arlene's lips trailed from my breastbone down across my stomach. I clawed her back in response, certain I left marks while she tickled and teased me.

"Arlene," I begged her, voice hoarse and ragged. No, I didn't call her by her real name. I wasn't sure she'd ever told it to me, and if she had, I couldn't remember it. Maybe hypocritical of me, but right then I needed her to *be* Arlene, different but the same, and mine, all mine.

And she didn't seem to care.

She raised her head, pulling from my grip. "You want me to keep going?" she asked, tracing my face with her fingertips. "I don't want to push you if you aren't ready."

"You can't tell?" I panted, heart racing, pulse beating in my temples. I was hot and so aroused I thought I might die from it.

"Consent is important with me," Arlene said, a shadow of fear passing through her eyes before it vanished. "In Vegas, people don't always ask before they take."

Oh hell.

Yes, this Arlene was definitely different. And I needed to remember that and treat her accordingly. "I'm sure. Are you?" Dear Lord, please say yes.

"Oh yeah." She leaned down, rubbing taut nipples over my own. I moaned in response. "Now," she whispered, sliding a finger inside me without warning and making my hips buck, "where were we?" In one smooth move, she'd straddled me. I closed my eyes and let everything go.

LATER, WE lay wrapped in one another's arms, warm and content. I stroked her shoulder with my fingers, then slid a hand down to rest on her abdomen. "And you said you weren't a good rider," I teased.

"Helps to have a willing mount," she returned.

I laughed, then grew serious. "You never did answer my question."

In the first rays of morning light coming through the window, I saw her raise an eyebrow.

"About helping me," I clarified.

Now it was her turn to get serious. She thought it over for a full minute before responding. "I can't promise that. I want to, but I'm not shooting real guns at real people, no matter how they moan and groan."

I opened my mouth to remind her these people weren't real. Not anymore. But she cut me off.

"I promise not to stop you. Will that do? I don't want to lose you, in any way. Girls in Vegas come and go. I haven't had many people I valued in my life. But you're asking for too much."

Swallowing the sudden lump in my throat, I nodded. It would have to do. For now.

CHAPTER 27

AT THE front of Sam's house, someone pounded on the door.

I rolled off one side of the bed, Arlene rolling off the other, and grabbed my holster and gun from where it hung on the chair. A split second later I remembered clothing and gave Arlene a sheepish grin.

"I don't know," she said, quirking an eyebrow. "Holster and nothing else would be damn sexy."

"I guess you can dream," I told her.

"Oh, you can count on it."

I pulled on shorts and shirt, then strapped the holster over top and caught a reflection of the ridiculous image in the room's full-length mirror. "I'm out of character," I said, hauling on my boots to complete the silliness.

"Do you really need the gun? I doubt zombies knock."

"I need the gun. And you need pants or a skirt and a shirt or something."

She'd put on the nightdress again, but she couldn't go to the front door that way.

About that time, Beth stuck her head around the corner of the guest room door. She caught sight of Arlene, then glanced at me and blushed, averting her gaze. "Sheriff, you, um—" She cleared her throat. "There's a couple of cops from the Los Alamos police here to see you."

My heart jumped into my throat. Not what I'd expected at all. Taz or Doc, yes. Modern law enforcement? No. Had they come to take me away? Put me in a place for crazy people? My feet felt like I'd stored weights in my boots, but I nodded and headed for the door.

Arlene touched my shoulder. "You want company?"

"Not if that company's wearing what you're wearing," I told her. "I'm in enough trouble already. Don't need that kind of distraction."

Her blush matched Beth's. "I'll go find my clothes, and yours, and join you." We parted in the hallway, her turning right toward the rear of the house and me following Beth to the front hall.

I thought we'd go into the parlor, but she made another turn and stepped into the kitchen, where Sam was handing cups to two uniformed officers sitting at the circular wooden table. While they stood to greet me, I glanced around the familiar and yet not-quite-right room I remembered. Pandora perched on the counter, plucking scraps of toast and bacon from a plate. She cooed a greeting but didn't leave her breakfast. Time had replaced the old stove and refrigerator with metal contraptions covered in buttons, knobs, and intriguing levers. The wood-and-glass

cupboards looked the same, one coat of white paint
covered over with another and another and still chip-
ping in places, but the counters bore more machines,
including a carafe that bubbled and sent the smell
of wonderful coffee swirling through the room.
Now there was a modern advancement I could truly
appreciate.

When I turned back to the table, I saw the policemen studying me from head to toe, one open-
mouthed, the other grinning. "Sheriff Meadows?"
the older one asked. His slight paunch extended
above the waistline of his uniform. He had a warm
smile and a shock of graying hair that gave him a
fatherly appearance.

I nodded.

The younger man snapped his mouth closed,
then opened it again. "That's not a real piece, is it?"
he said, gesturing at the holster at my side.

"They shoot paint," Arlene said, stepping in behind me. The woman had to be a quick-change artist
to get into dungarees so fast, and not just any dungarees but ones that fit her like a second skin. I hadn't
noticed the night before, but I was paying more attention now that my head didn't hurt quite as much.
She had her own gun at her side, and she pulled and
passed it, grip first, to the officer who'd asked. "Besides, she's licensed," she added.

"Of course she is," the older cop hurried to in-
terject. "My partner was just curious. I'm Willows.
This is Finkelstein. We'd just like to ask you a few
questions, Sheriff."

Finkelstein finished turning Arlene's gun over in his hands, giving a whistle of appreciation. "Damn thing looks real. Yours too," he added with another glance at my own, very real pistol. His eyebrows lowered, and he pointed at Arlene. "Don't let these things out of the filming areas. Except for television and film purposes, toy guns have to have bright orange tips on them to identify them as toys. Wouldn't want a kid pointing one of these at a cop and getting shot by mistake." He handed Arlene the prop. Ever the showgirl, she twirled it with a flourish and returned it to her holster to secure it with the rawhide strip.

"Oh, don't worry, Officer. I'll be glad to return it to the crew. Darn thing's heavy." Playing the weak card seemed to work for her, though I knew her to be anything but. And it kept the attention off me, which had to be her plan. Smart woman.

The policemen chuckled in sympathy.

"What did you need, officers?" I asked, dragging a chair across the tile floor and seating myself. Arlene stood behind me, hands resting lightly on my shoulders. I watched the cops' eyes go from me to Arlene and back again, a knowing smile appearing on Finkelstein's face, and wondered again at the accepting nature of this future time.

The jovial Willows sobered. "Last night, the body of a young boy washed up on the riverbank a few miles from here. We've identified him as Adam Lansing. You know him?" He watched carefully for my reaction.

I gave him shock and surprise, which came naturally under the circumstances. Not about Adam's death, which would have been false, but at the fact that that's what they'd come for and that they'd found the body so quickly. The river ran high and fast in the spring, unless things had changed over time. It should have taken longer for the body to hit the shore. Just a continuation of my bad luck, I guess. Sam looked equally startled. I'd never mentioned the teenager-turned-Eye Killer, and Arlene's grip tightened. She had to be remembering me coming into church bruised and bloodied, had to be wondering if the woman she'd slept with had murdered a kid.

Well, no point in hiding anything, since the cameras would tell all. "I danced with Adam the first night," I admitted.

Willows's smile broadened. "You're the fifth female to tell us that. Of course, all the rest were about fifteen years old."

"I danced with him too," Beth put in from the stove where she'd resumed cooking.

Finkelstein nodded, pulled a small machine from his pocket, and tapped on it, making notes, I assumed. "Right. We'll need a sample from you too."

"A sample?" Beth and I asked almost in unison.

Sam placed a mug of coffee in front of me, and I wrapped suddenly chilled palms around the steaming cup, then brought it to my lips and took a careful sip. I sighed as the strong liquid burned down my throat. Not as effective as whiskey for calming nerves, but I needed my wits about me right now.

"The river washed away most of the evidence," Willows explained while I drank. "No one saw him after the little social y'all had. It looks like he wandered away from town and fell off the cliff in the dark and landed in the water, which carried away the body. It's covered in cuts and bruises, likely from the fall and river rocks, but with his parents gone missing around the same time and still not turned up, we're taking a closer look. The one thing we found were strands of hair wrapped around a button on the boy's shirt, a variety of hair types and colors. We'd like to rule out anyone who was dancing with the boy, since that's how the hair transfer probably occurred. If we find a strand we can't identify, then we might have someone to pursue."

Sam turned a chair backward and straddled it, sitting with us. "So, my daughter's not a suspect."

I braced myself for the answer, resisting the urge to grip the edge of the table and reveal my tension. If she was a suspect, so was I, and a much more probable one, given what Doc, Jake, and Taz already thought of me. I couldn't afford a trip to a real jail. There'd be no hiding I wasn't who I claimed I was, and it would take precious time, regardless. And if somehow they decided to charge Beth.... I swallowed hard, masking it with a sip of coffee.

I'd take the blame before I let that happen.

Willows laughed, his belly shaking. "No, sir. And neither are you, Sheriff," he said to me.

Arlene's hands stopped clutching so hard.

"Coroner puts the time of death sometime on Friday night. She can't pinpoint it exactly, thanks to the water damage to the body, but we can rule out pretty much all the women in the reality show from the camera footage we've seen. Particularly you, Sheriff," Willows added. "You were up late, and we can account for your whereabouts all the way into the early hours of Saturday morning." He gave me another warm smile. "That was some scene in the church, ma'am." He tipped his hat. "Well done. My own daughter's with the force. She's gonna love that when it airs."

I managed a small grin, the pieces falling into place for me. Adam had gone missing after the bar-beque. He must have run afoul of the Eye Killers and died that night. Then I killed him again on Saturday night/early Sunday morning. Which nobody but me needed to know right now.

"So you need some hair, then?" Sooner we got this over with, sooner they'd leave. I had my own business to conduct this morning.

Finkelstein retrieved a bag from beneath the table and removed some tweezers and some white gloves made of a resilient, stretchy material. He donned the gloves and came around to me. "Just a couple of strands. Won't hurt a bit." He plucked four or five hairs from various points on my head and held them up to check and make sure he had the roots attached. Then he did the same to Beth.

"Just one more question before we go," Willows said, studying me with a critical eye. "How'd you all get so banged up? The director mentioned some funny business up at the mine."

I put a hand to my cheek, remembering the bruises and the black eye from my various fights with the
Eye Killers. The others looked just as bad, with Sam's
head bandage and Arlene's scratches. Beth didn't
have any noticeable injuries, but the strain of the past
twenty-four hours showed in her young face.

"Reality TV isn't all it's cracked up to be," Sam
said, then laughed at his own words. "Or maybe it
is. I got thrown off a horse. Arlene got caught up in
a brawl at the saloon over a game of cards, and the
sheriff here broke up that brawl, along with a number
of others. We signed insurance waivers. Guess they
had a reason for those."

"As for the mine," Arlene put in, "that was a stunt
gone bad. Sometimes when you try for too much attention, you fall flat on your face. Literally," she added, poking a teasing finger into my upper arm.

I managed not to slap her hand, but only just.

"Huh," Finkelstein muttered, putting away his
equipment. "Didn't get to see any of that footage.
Your director would only show us stuff from the relevant hours. Claimed everything else was protected
by his right to trade secrets and we'd need a warrant
to view it."

"Guess you'll just have to watch the show!"
Sam boomed, escorting them to the front door.

"We'll do that," Willows said, tipping his hat
one more time. "Say," he said, pausing with one foot
on the porch, "could I have your autographs, um, for
my daughter?"

Finkelstein reached over and smacked the older
man on the back of the head, but it didn't stop Beth

from running to the kitchen to grab a paper napkin and a pen. We all scribbled our signatures, and I was careful to write "Sandra Meadows aka California McCade." I avoided looking at Arlene's real name, not that I would have been able to decipher her chicken-scratch handwriting, but I wanted to cling to the illusion, at least a little longer, no matter how unhealthy I knew that to be. Beth wrote "Beth" and Sam wrote "Sam," since he'd been named after his ancestor, but I raised an eyebrow at his daughter.

"Had it legally changed after the adoption, with Dad's help. I like the historical significance. It's cool." She jutted out her chin like she was daring me to argue with her.

I just nodded my approval. Names were important. They held power. I was glad she'd had power over hers.

I presented the napkin to Willows, following with a firm handshake, and the two officers left. Sam shut the door behind them.

Four relieved sighs echoed down the front hall.

CHAPTER 28

WHILE BETH made a breakfast big enough to feed the entire town of Oblivion, Sam, Arlene, and I settled back at the kitchen table. We'd closed the swinging doors to the room, hopefully cutting our conversation off from the hallway microphones. I propped my elbows on the smooth wooden surface and rested my chin in my hands. "How much do you know about the first gold strike up at the mine?" I asked.

Sam fiddled with his fork and knife while he considered my question. "More than you might think, actually. When gold got found, folks filed claims, and sometimes even before finding anything, if they had a good hunch. That way, no one could legally mine in exactly the same place. Those claims got recorded in the clerk's office, which was in Oblivion's town hall, and then a letter was sent to the state government to file there, as well."

I nodded, knowing some of that. The records clerk had been a young man who often played cards at the saloon, though I couldn't recall his name.

Sam laughed as he added more cream to his coffee. "Heck, let me know if I'm boring you. It feels like I'm giving one of my tours. I had to memorize all this to get my job with Parks and Recreation."

"No, go on," I told him, shifting on the chair's thin cushion. Some of the previous night's bruises were starting to really hurt. Beth must have noticed my discomfort because she opened a cabinet, pulled out a small bottle, and dumped a couple of orange tablets into her palm, then handed them off to me.

When I looked at her in confusion, she said, "Painkillers."

I nodded and swallowed them dry.

"Anyway," Sam said loudly, like he didn't appreciate being interrupted, "those claim records were kept in the town vault, a metal vault," he stressed. "And it survived the fire."

Just like my gun safe.

"Some of the documents are on display in a museum in Los Alamos. Real shame we don't have more. It was a fascinating time period."

A wave of emotion speared me like a blade, and my eyes misted. Sam's pleasant tone shifted to one of concern.

"I'm sorry, Cali," he said, patting my hand with his big callused one. "This is all pretty fresh for you, isn't it? How long have you actually been, well, in the here and now?"

"What day is it?"

"Monday," Beth supplied, placing eggs, bacon, and toast in front of me so I had to move my elbows.

"Three days," I told them.

Arlene paused in her chewing. "You mean, when I found you in the parking lot, you'd just gotten here?"

"Something like that," I said. "I came out of the mine. There's a tunnel running from there all the way to a room buried beneath the church where I… died, burned, however you want to describe it. I'd rather not go into detail. The access stairs through the church closet are gone, but the room's still there. The mine seems to be the focus of everything. That's why I need information. I need to know exactly where the first gold was found, and I need to put it back. According to an old friend who dealt with these Eye Killers once, that's the only way to stop this—pay back what was taken, or the equivalent thereof, then stop tromping around in there like it's mankind's personal playground."

At that, Sam brightened. "Well, you're in luck. The first of everything is always so important to people. The historians dug into that records vault and organized each claim by date, tracing back to the initial gold strike. Took them weeks to get it all in chronological order." He paused, thinking back. "You know, my great-granddad had the gold fever too? He got in late, never found a damn thing. If he had, things might be different today for me and Beth." Sam stared off into the corner of the room, lost in the past.

I looked around too. Didn't seem to me like they were doing so badly. They had a comfortable home, food on their table, clothes on their backs, and I couldn't help thinking of the bathroom fixtures. Of course, with wages like the reality show folks were receiving, this might feel like poverty in comparison, but coming from the harsh living conditions of my time, well, this was luxury.

A sudden thought occurred to me. "You know, Sam, if we're successful, you're out of a job. The mine will need to close and stay closed, that is unless you want to put in regular offerings of less-major things like grain and corn to make up for the tourist invasions."

"I could do that," Beth put in. "Sounds almost like something out of one of the Wiccan teachings."

Well, at least it would stop people from getting killed and possessed.

"One problem at a time," Sam interrupted, regaining everyone's attention. I nodded for him to continue. "There's a pit. A real deep pit. At the bottom, I'm told there's a small side cave. Real small. Never seen it myself. I'm not much of a climber. But that's where the first gold was found. The pit's in one of the branch tunnels. I used to include an actual visit to it in the tour, but a cave-in blocked most of the passage leading there, and instead of risking another one, I went ahead and closed it off pretty much completely."

A real deep pit. Of course. Lucky me.

"I know the one. Nearly fell in it on my way out."

"It's a doozy," Sam agreed. "Goes about forty or fifty feet down. If you're thinking of exploring it, you're gonna need a long rope."

"And good climbing gear," Beth said. "I've got some friends who do some spelunking around here.

I could borrow their equipment, maybe trade some baked goods for the use." She flipped some more bacon in a pan and watched it sizzle.

I took a bite from the strips on my plate—perfect and crunchy. "Much obliged, for the help and the bacon."

"But putting the gold back.... How are you planning to accomplish that? We don't keep a lot of gold bars lying around." Sam sipped his coffee.

I studied the three of them. Yeah, I had faith. Arlene might be in Vegas show business between jobs and hard up for cash, but she'd proven herself to me, even if she didn't fully accept what I'd told her. After what we'd been through already, I could count on these folks.

"There's a treasure." I briefly described the chests of gold and gems Xanthis had hidden beneath the church.

Three sets of eyes bugged out. Arlene practically drooled.

"Don't get excited," I continued. "It's going in the pit. That is, assuming I can first get back to it and second carry it to where it needs to go. I'd prefer not to go through the mine tunnels any more than I have to, which means finding a way into the old staircase. Maybe with some dynamite...."

"Now, *this* would make a great TV show," Beth said.

Arlene snapped her fingers, startling everyone, including Pandora, who squawked indignantly. "Sorry," she said, reaching over to stroke the bird's head. To my surprise, she allowed it, rubbing herself more firmly against Arlene's hand. She had a real way with animals, whether she'd had training or not. Or maybe Pandora was mellowing a little. She'd let Beth pet her the night before. "Anyway, I was shooting the bull with some of the guys over a card game." She winked at me. "And one helluva game it was. I won almost ten dollars."

A lot of money in my time, but it was the rest of the statement that had my attention. "You shot a bull? With red paint? Where were you playing cards?"

Sam spit a mouthful of coffee on the table, laughed, and wiped his chin. Beth almost dropped a plate of eggs. Even Pandora seemed amused, cackling and flapping her wings. Okay, more vernacular I didn't understand. It suddenly occurred to me that I'd assumed the phoenix only traveled forward in time, but if she understood modern sayings, maybe she could move in both directions. Which meant Xanthis had too.

But there had to be a catch somewhere. A "one shot at each evil" kind of deal. Otherwise, Xanthis would never have failed. He could have just kept going backward again and again after each mistake, correcting whatever he did wrong to stop the evil. The rest of us would have been oblivious to his doings. So there had to be limits.

And what *would* happen to me if I accomplished my mission here and appeased the Elementals? I'd made some friends and formed attachments against my better judgment. Was I now destined to keep losing people I cared about as Pandora transported me from century to century? A little bit of sympathy for Xanthis crept into my heart. What an incredibly lonely life to live, and one I hadn't asked for. But that was a consideration for a different day.

When it didn't look like my breakfast companions would stop laughing anytime soon, I held up my hands in defeat. "Okay, I get it. I'm behind the times. So shooting the bull means…?"

"Talking," Beth supplied. "It means talking." She giggled.

"Right," Arlene continued as if nothing had happened. "We were in the saloon. The guy who runs the place is ex-military."

"You mean Al?" I asked Arlene. The Al of my time could barely handle the bar's shotgun, and I happened to know he'd been turned down for the army because of poor eyesight. But we weren't talking about my Al.

"Right, Al. That was his name. Malek isn't going to let anyone have TNT. The risks are too great, and the show's insurance is too high. But I'm betting Al, or whatever his real name is, could show us how to make something explosive from what we've got on hand."

I fixed her gaze with mine. "Thought you weren't going to help me."

"Consider it an investment. They catch this on film and it'll get the biggest ratings ever, and that's how I'll sell it to Al too. He might serve good drinks, but he isn't the brightest." Her tone and expression said she was teasing. At least that's what I hoped, and that she really had decided to help.

"Yeah, we'll make a fortune, right before they lock us away for blowing stuff up," Sam said, rubbing his face with his hands. "This is nuts." He held up a palm to forestall my retort. "I believe you, but it's still nuts."

"I've thought that since the first three Eye Killers strolled into Oblivion."

"Well, we've got four days to do whatever we're going to do," Beth told us, clearing plates away. "After that, the set gets closed down and everyone goes home. I heard they're thinking about opening Oblivion up as a tourist attraction next fall."

"Yeah," Sam muttered, "I can give the tours." He spread his arms wide in a welcoming gesture and raised his voice. "Come see the Old West town. Don't mind the zombies. They just want to make you permanent residents." He paused, looking at each of us in turn. "Well? What do you think?"

WE SPLIT up after the meal. After I changed into my now clean clothes, Arlene and I rode to town to talk to Al, and Sam and Beth stayed at the house to contact her cave explorer friends. It surprised me that Taz and Doc hadn't come calling, but maybe the police had told them the whole mine thing was a stunt.

We'd barely gotten onto Main Street, Pandora riding on my shoulder, before Jake came running up, almost startling Ford into throwing me.

"Easy, boy," I told the horse. I patted his neck and stroked his mane. "Learn some sense, Deputy."

Jake scowled but muttered, "Yes, ma'am."

"That's 'Sheriff.'" Yeah, I had a tenuous hold on my temper, knowing Jake had joined the "Let's Lock Cali McCade Away" club. My headache had faded completely after the full meal and painkillers, so that helped, but I was still in a foul mood. "What's the trouble?" We continued riding toward my office at a slower pace, forcing Jake to jog beside us.

"Well," he stammered, "you see, I was over at the saloon, uh, making sure the upstairs ladies were being treated right…."

"You mean partaking of their services," Arlene muttered, loud enough for us both to hear.

I turned to her. "They aren't actually selling themselves, are they? I mean, it's one thing to play a whore in a show and quite another to actually be one. You said your contract didn't include that." And I'd wanted to think this time period's Lucinda had a decent sense of morality, well, with the notable exception of all her swearing.

Jake shook his head so fast his hat almost fell off. "The director's not forcing anyone. And the girls aren't accepting money. Abigail and I hit it off, and if two consenting adults happen to like each other, well…."

I exchanged a look with Arlene. "Well, we can't stop that, now can we?"

"No, we can't," Arlene agreed, shooting me a wink.

Damn if I didn't blush. I tried to hide it by shifting Pandora from my arm to the saddle, but Arlene's snicker told me she saw it anyway.

We reached my office, and I dismounted, waving Arlene on to the saloon. "Go ahead and see to our business," I told her, then followed Jake inside.

Things appeared much as I'd left them. The jail stood empty, the cot made up, the keys hanging on the nail. My gun safe was locked and secure. Someone had replaced my bottle of whiskey and set it at the edge of my desk. I eyed it but discarded the idea of a drink this early in the day. Besides, I needed my wits about me with Jake around, since he'd decided I had none.

"All right, then," I said, sliding into my chair and feeling every bruise and scrape.

You're getting old, Cali, I told myself, then smiled at the truth of that thought.

"So, you were busting your britches at the saloon, ignoring your duties even though you knew I was checking on something up at the mine. And don't say you didn't know, because Arlene and Sam told me you heard the goings-on up there."

"Yeah, we heard you. What the hell were you doing, anyway? Cops said it was a publicity stunt, but I'm not buying it. Not with the dead bird and all."

So the cameras outside the mine had picked up the death of the phoenix in my arms. Well, that was an easy fix. I waved at Pandora, who'd followed us inside. "What dead bird?"

Jake flushed. "Oh. Right. Anyway, well, while I was otherwise engaged, um, the Roberston siblings finally managed to rob the bank."

I couldn't help it. I laughed. I laughed until my sides hurt and tears streamed down my face, and then I laughed some more.

Jake stared at me like I truly had lost my mind, and I kept laughing. In a world filled with Eye Killers, phoenixes, and dead kids, a bank robbery was the most normal thing I had to deal with. How sad was that?

CHAPTER 29

"HOW MUCH did they get?" I asked, wiping my eyes on my shirtsleeve that smelled of lilacs and lavender. And thank you, Arlene, for washing my clothes.

"Three hundred and eighty-seven dollars and fifty-two cents. They cleaned out the vault."

My eyebrows rose before I remembered times had changed. That amount wouldn't go far today, judging from what they intended to pay all the performers in this show if we made it to the end of the week. Of course, under the circumstances, that could be a very big "if." Which reminded me that I had much more important things to worry about than a bunch of amateur bank robbers.

"Let them have it," I said, folding my arms over my chest.

Jake blinked at me. "I'm sorry?"

"You heard me. Let them have it. If there's nothing in the bank, maybe they'll stop trying to rob it. And if they do keep on, we don't need to get involved, since there's nothing to steal. Close the place down. Give the bankers and tellers a vacation. Hang a sign on the door."

"But... but what about wages? How are folks gonna get paid? How will they pay for what they need?"

I sighed. "They'll do what we—they—did back in the... old days. They'll barter goods and services. Should make things interesting and keep folks busy, which means less trouble for us and more time for us to pursue... other interests."

Jake thought it over. A slow grin spread across his face. "You know, Sheriff, you got a real conniving streak in you."

"Really?" I said, putting on my poker face. I couldn't play worth a damn, but I had the face. "I hadn't heard."

I DIDN'T see Arlene, Sam, or Beth for the rest of the day, but the mayor came by to tell me a stable hand and the stock boy from the store had gone missing, along with the chambermaid at the hotel. According to the rumors, some ten people all told had vanished, and I doubted any of them had left due to harsh living conditions. They'd gone without their money and without their cars, which had been left somewhere outside of town and out of view of the cameras.

I didn't count the bank robbers, either. They'd fled Oblivion, but word had it they'd made camp at the lake where the men went fishing. I hoped that was true. The lake lay in the opposite direction from

the mine, but the robbers were around Beth's age.
Old enough to call adults in my time, but not old
enough to drink in this one. Maybe I'd send Jake out
to check on them in the morning.

After trading a lesson in antique gun maintenance to Malek for a couple of the general store's
sandwiches, I decided to turn in early. Pandora had
abandoned me for Preacher Xanthis, I'd dropped
Ford off at the stables, and I had no idea how long
it would take my companions to gather their equipment and information.

Despite being alone, I made my evening rounds
around the town in better spirits than I'd been in days.
Because I wasn't really alone anymore. I had help,
and folks who believed me and believed *in* me.

Which got me to thinking about the ones I'd left
behind. Taz had mentioned bodies buried after the
great fire. I assumed he meant in the cemetery behind the church, and my footsteps turned that way
before I realized I'd changed direction.

That's when I heard the moan.

Drawing my very real pistol, I circled the dark
place of worship, checking corners and behind bushes for anything that might leap or shamble out at me.
The night was still, and back here, the streetlamps
cast no light, making vision by moonlight sketchy
at best. I wanted to kick myself for not bringing a
lantern, but I hadn't planned on leaving Main Street
when I'd set out. I gripped the S&W tightly, knowing I had to be sure before firing it. A mistake could
cost someone his life.

When the sound refused to repeat itself, I wondered if it could have been wind. But there'd been
no breeze since the previous night's mad storm. A
coyote, maybe?

I hadn't been behind the church since I'd made
my leap forward in time, but it hadn't changed much.
Aside from the semi-orderly rows of overgrown
wooden markers, two things contradicted my memory. The number of graves had increased by a dozen
or so, and a stone crypt like you might see in a big-
city cemetery stood at the rear of the property. The
crypt had a lantern hanging beside its entrance, and it
stood out like a lighthouse in a sea filled with rotting
crosses.

Straining my ears, I listened but heard nothing
out of place: some crickets, some quiet rustling as
lizards chased each other through the brush. I holstered my gun and wandered along the path that
weaved between the graves. When I came to my
parents, I said a quick internal prayer, thankful that
they'd remained undisturbed but unwilling to share
my private moment with the microphones that Taz
had no doubt placed out here.

I moved on, scanning the markers each time the
moon peeked from behind the clouds. They leaned
at all angles, some missing their cross beams, most
illegible from weathering. The new graves, I soon
discovered, weren't much newer than the old ones,
except to me. All the dates I could make out read the
same—the night of the Oblivion fire. I swallowed
hard and searched out names as I walked the row:
Hank the piano player, Annabelle the schoolteacher,

Mayor Jones, Joseph the stable hand, and Arlene—
everyone I'd shot that awful night and many more
erased by time. At my side, my gun hand trembled.
Well, at least they'd put the bodies back in the ground
after determining my weapon had killed them and
deciding I'd gone crazy. I still wondered who'd buried them in the first place. Robert, maybe. Or maybe
some other folks who survived the massacre, living
on the outer farms and ranches, had found the bodies
and honored the dead.

I came to the crypt—a rectangular stone structure about the size of a few stable stalls put together, maybe six or so, making it considerably longer
than it was wide. The lantern flickered, illuminating
a plaque embedded in the door.

In Memory of Those Who Lost Their Lives
10/5/1892. Here lie the remains of the

unidentified citizens of Oblivion, New Mexico,
recovered from the burned-out ruins, and

those found in a mass grave outside the Oblivion
gold mine.

New Mexico Historical Society
Established 1/13/2019

Huh. The bodies from the town I understood.
But a mass burial in one unmarked grave? Had the
Eye Killers returned to the mine and abandoned their
hosts? I remembered the insufficient number of bones
I'd come across *inside* the caves. This would account
for the missing. With no one in the immediate vicinity to torment, I supposed it made sense, but who
could comprehend the whims of Elementals? And
how had they come to be mass-buried? Over time,

the growth and desert might have covered them, or another group of miners might have stumbled upon the remains and done the right thing. My head hurt from all the conjecture.

While I appreciated the gesture on the part of the state of New Mexico, these folks deserved more. There should be names for each and every one of them. Good, hardworking, churchgoing people lived here, and they should be remembered. Maybe when all this ended, I'd put together a list and have another plaque made.

I turned to leave, already composing the memorial's wording in my head, when something scraped on the stone.

Whirling, I drew my pistol and closed the distance to the crypt's door. Upon closer examination, I found it stood ajar. Pressing my ear to the crack, I made out definite movement inside, and another groan.

Not an animal that somehow managed to trap itself inside. I'd chased any number of rabbits, coyotes, and even rattlers out of barns and back storerooms. This voice sounded human, and in distress, but whether that was a dying distress or an already-dead-I'm-going-to-kill-you distress, I had no way of knowing without further investigation.

I closed my cold hand around the colder metal door handle and pulled slowly. It creaked, but not a lot. Someone had maintained this memorial, oiling the hinges. If Sam ran the tours of the mine and his house, he may have been in charge of this site as well, and I would have expected no less from him.

The gap grew wider, and a narrow beam of light streamed out. Whoever lurked inside had a second lamp.

Eye Killers' powers of control and suffocation were weakened by fire, so I doubted they'd carry lanterns. However, a victim might have brought one out here.

When the opening stood wide enough for me to slip through, I did so and stood at the end of a short, narrow corridor running between rows of handles on the walls on either side. I could only assume the handles opened drawers containing whatever the Historical Society had managed to recover of the bodies from Oblivion.

The second lantern, a more modern variety with a "bulb" instead of a flame, sat on the floor just inside the door. How it ran without an electricity source, I had no idea, but I added it to my already long list of modern things I did not understand. The lamp cast a long shadow down the passage where I could make out two dark figures grappling at the far end.

I crept along the corridor, keeping to one side and out of the lantern's beam so that I had as much light as possible. The closer I came to the end, the more details I could make out, and I could now discern a man wearing dungarees, hat, and boots with his back to me, and a woman in a short skirt pressed against the rear wall.

They had their heads together, and the man's hands roved up and down the woman's sides, then disappeared between them. She moaned.

Ooookay. I'd heard of some bizarre courtship rituals and sexual fetishes, feathers and such. Hell, the Arlene of my time had enjoyed me locking her up in handcuffs, not that I'd ever told anyone except....

Shit. I'd written it in my journal, so I supposed everyone in the United States of America knew by now. Wonderful.

But I'd never heard of anyone pursuing romance in a crypt. Private, yes, but dust, mold, and dead bodies didn't make for great atmosphere, not to mention the sacrilegious nature of the whole thing. Maybe they figured this would avoid cameras and microphones.

Bemused more than anything else, I holstered my gun for the second time this evening and watched for a few minutes, assuming they'd notice me sooner or later. Not that I'd turned voyeur, but this couldn't be allowed to continue. Not in here.

They didn't notice me. Their actions grew more heated, though, and the woman's moans got louder. I couldn't see what the man's hands were up to, but apparently he was very effective with them. Clothing rustled, a button popped and clattered to the floor by their feet, and I watched the short skirt slide up the girl's thigh. Before they could embarrass themselves, and me, any further, I cleared my throat. Loudly.

"Ahem!"

Two people never separated from one another so fast. The woman banged her head against the wall, then set to cursing up a storm, while the man spun on his heel to face me, at which point I got my second shock of the evening.

The man wasn't a man. It was another woman. Lucinda, to be precise.

She wore the riding gear I'd seen her in at the barrel race, hair tucked up under her hat, but there was no mistaking her now that I knew her better. And the one wearing a skirt happened to be Danielle Vasquez, the show's assistant director.

Which left three very startled women staring at one another in a crypt full of dead people.

Well, I'll be damned.

Certainly I, of all folks, wasn't judging, except this was a crypt and should be treated with respect. I'd stumbled upon some pretty surprising scenes as the town sheriff, including an incident between a wandering stranger and a bull that I preferred not to think about too closely. Beyond that, though, I believed folks should do what made them happy and take that happiness wherever they could find it in a hard world, but I also believed some things should stay in the bedroom behind closed doors and windows, all of them locked, for those private things. The crypt door did not count, in my estimation.

I'm ashamed to say I wasn't the first to recover from the shock. That would have been Danielle, who swept a hand through her hair, massaged her bruised head, and smoothed her skirt down so it covered a more respectable length of thigh.

"Well," she said, offering a grin. "Seems you're a little too good at your job, Sheriff. You gonna arrest us for trespassing?"

The walls seemed too close, and I hadn't found my voice yet, so Lucinda jumped in with, "Of course, you could just join us." Her eyes traveled from my hat to my boots, lingering in the areas of my chest and hips.

That got me choking on whatever I'd been about to say, to the point where the assistant director had to run over and rap me on the back to get me to stop. I coughed and cleared my throat again, studying their faces with their utterly unrepentant smiles. Surprised, yes. Embarrassed, hell yes. Ashamed, not one bit.

Which reminded me once more that one hundred and twenty-five years had passed. Times had changed. For all I knew, sex groups of three or four or, hell, maybe ten, were completely acceptable in polite society, though I doubted that included the sex-in-a-crypt part.

I put on my best no-more-nonsense face. "Well, um, ladies," I said, "the churchyard's open to all of Oblivion's citizens. I'm assuming you're both here just paying your respects."

Two heads nodded, but the mischievous grins remained.

"And now that you've finished doing so, you'll be taking your respectful selves elsewhere."

The grins faded at last. "Aw, come on, Sheriff. This is one of the only places in a half-mile radius besides the great outdoors and the outhouses that doesn't have cameras." Danielle pouted.

I sympathized. Really, I did. Before making my rounds, I'd considered finding Arlene and spending the night with her. But I'd grown tired of being watched and listened to, so I didn't pursue it.

So I understood. But these remains, these *people* buried here were *my* people. I couldn't tell these women that, but I couldn't let them continue such actions here.

"You're overlooking the most obvious option," I told them.

Two sets of eyebrows rose.

"The room above Town Hall. With all that equipment, you wouldn't want to film there. Where do Taz and Malek sleep?" I didn't recall any cots or sleeping bags when I'd gone to the second floor.

"They stay at the Oblivion Hotel." Danielle's smile returned, growing broader by the moment.

The hotel wasn't really called that. Old man Humphries, who ran the place had, in a moment of delusional grandeur, named it the New Mexico Rose, but I supposed the sign had been lost in the fire like so many other things, and I didn't think I'd mentioned it by name in my journals.

Danielle took Lucinda's hand, then leaned over and kissed me on the cheek before I could think to move away. "Great idea, Sheriff. Here I am missing what's right under my nose. I even have a key. Thanks!"

They scampered to the exit. Well, Danielle scampered, hauling Lucinda behind her, and I followed them, first to make sure they left the cemetery, and second to not get left alone in the dark, scary crypt when they took the lantern with them.

I stepped out, shook my head, and let the heavy door shut with a resounding clang.

CHAPTER 30

TUESDAY MORNING brought bank robbers to my door.

They showed up, battered and bedraggled, two carrying torn sleeping bags and camping gear, the third hauling the bag of loot over his shoulder. Before I could so much as get out of my chair, young Alex Davidson plunked the sack on my desk, the coins rattling inside.

"It's all there, Sheriff. Three hundred and eighty-seven dollars and fifty-two cents." His voice wavered, and not from puberty. "Can you lock us up, please?"

My eyebrows rose. "'Scuse me?" I studied the three of them. None looked like they'd slept a wink all night. The girl, Katherine I think her name was, visibly shook where she stood in her riding boots. The other boy, Patrick, had the skin tone of snow in winter.

I stood and came around the front of the desk. "Before you fall down, why don't you all have a seat and tell me what the hell happened to you?"

They crumpled as a group, plopping on the floor like bags of flour and propping themselves against the interior walls of my office. Really, I needed to get more chairs.

"We don't know!" Katherine cried, lower lip trembling.

"We aren't really related," Alex said. "All our parents are here, doing different jobs in town, but they've got us playing these Davidson kids, so we hang out together and talk a lot. We've all been camping before, so we figured hiding out by the lake would work, but none of us had ever seen the shit we saw last night."

"Hey, they warned us about cursing on camera," Patrick put in, though he didn't sound very adamant. "Do you want to get kicked off the show?"

"I don't give a flying fuck what they told us," Alex shot back. "And at this point, I'd *love* to get kicked out. Except my *parents* think this is the easiest money they've ever made. Look, Sheriff, we know you're real law enforcement in the real world, and we're telling you, there's something really weird out there." He waved a hand in the general direction of the door.

"Can you be a little more specific?" I had a feeling I knew what had scared them, but I wanted to be sure.

"Zombies," Katherine whispered, not looking at me. "I know it sounds crazy, but that's what we saw. We saw Mr. and Mrs. Lansing. They were bloody and beaten up, and they had gunshot wounds."

"We were fishing at the lake, but we heard them come into our camp. They tore through everything, then came after us. We lost them in the rocks, then doubled back, grabbed whatever we could carry, and rode back here." Alex pointed out my front door. "Our horses are tied to the post outside."

"I'll get someone to feed and stable them after we're done," I assured him, then fell silent, steepling my fingers in thought.

Well, this presented a problem. If I took them seriously, here, on camera, I'd have Doc and Taz in my office in a heartbeat. But the Lansings were missing, and the police were still searching for them, so far as I knew, which meant the teenagers' announcement about seeing them would draw attention either way. Damn, being the sheriff had never been so complicated in 1891.

I glanced at the two empty jail cells and made my decision. "Your camping gear still up to use?"

Three heads nodded.

"All right, then. If it will make you feel safer, Katherine can take one cell and you boys can have the other. Use your gear to make yourselves more comfortable. I don't make a habit of catering to kids in my jail. I'm also not saying I believe in zombies," I said extra loud for the microphones to catch, "and I'm not promising how long you can stay, but I can justify locking you three up for a day or two as punishment. Your real folks know where you are?"

Alex said, "We caught my dad outside the post office when we rode into town. He thinks we're nuts but figures it'll be good for a few bucks. He said he'd pass it on to the other parents."

"Good enough." I walked to the cells and let the kids inside, then made certain the locks would hold. They collapsed in relieved heaps onto their cots and torn sleeping bags.

The Lansings needed to be taken care of once and for all, and I supposed that job fell to me, but before I could go find Ford and head out, the sounds of dozens of hoofbeats carried like a thunderstorm down Main Street.

"What the hell?" Alex asked, hopping up to stand on his cot and peer through the tiny barred window above the narrow bed. "Indians? Seriously? We just went from reality TV to reruns of *Bonanza* on Nick at Night."

"Better than *Night of the Living Dead*," Katherine murmured.

I swallowed a groan. Last thing I needed now was tribe trouble on top of the Eye Killers. I checked my S&W, still fully loaded, and stepped onto the porch. Sure enough, four Indians in full warpaint rode up and down Main Street, hollering and howling and destroying anything they could knock over with their long spears, including streetlamps and storefront signs. One wore an elaborate headdress. I supposed he was the chief, though local tribes didn't go in for headdresses. That was a plains Indians thing, at least in my day. So who the hell were these guys?

The "chief" had a shotgun he fired repeatedly into the air. Oblivion's citizens scattered in all directions, some screaming, others throwing rocks and sticks at the warriors.

Idiots. Didn't they realize they could be killed?

I froze with my gun in hand. Maybe I was the idiot.

I hadn't thought much about Indians since I'd come forward in time. Hadn't thought much about them before then, either. The ones living near Oblivion had been peaceful farmers, and for the most part, we left each other alone except for some trade goods. Oh, there had been trouble between the settlers and the natives in other areas, plenty of it, but we'd been lucky, and I'd encouraged folks to treat our local tribal members with respect and courtesy. In these modern times, I hadn't spotted any native settlements on my sojourns to the mine or the river. Didn't mean they weren't around, though.

So were these real warriors or more of Taz's surprises? If they were real, they were the stupidest Indians I'd ever seen, riding into the heart of town in such small numbers.

Shit. I had to find out one way or the other, and taking chances with these peoples' lives didn't satisfy my conscience.

If I was going to take one of the riders down, I needed higher ground.

I turned and raced back inside, holstering my gun, then took the stairs up to my room two at a time. Below, I could hear the three kids chanting, "Go, Sheriff, go!" but I tuned them out.

Climbing through windows had become something of a habit of late, one I could do without, and

I settled myself outside on the porch overhang in a precarious squat. The sun bore down, and the brightness almost blinded me, but I could see when one of the Indian riders turned his horse and kicked it into a full gallop along Main Street—and right past the sheriff's office.

When he rode beneath me, I sprang, going from a crouch to a full launch and tackling the warrior off his horse. We both hit the ground hard, rolling over and over in the dirt, grappled together until we slammed full force into a trough of water at the side of the street. I wound up on top, and the tribesman blinked up at me, the one eye I could see streaming from the dust, and his wig—his wig!—turned sideways and half obscuring his face. He yanked off the black hair revealing red underneath.

The "Indian" was a white man.

"More goddamn playacting." I shoved him away from me and pushed to my feet to loom over him.

He scrambled backward like a crab, tossing his wig to the side. "What the *fucking* hell!" the actor growled. I supposed the performance ended once I knocked him off his horse. "Are you out of your goddamn mind? Throwing yourself at me like that could have broken both our necks. They aren't paying me enough for this shit. I'm calling my union rep." He stood and dusted himself off.

Behind him, I spotted the other two warrior riders plus their "chief" reining in their horses and proceeding toward us at a much more sedate pace. Taz chose that moment to emerge from the saloon, and he stalked along the boardwalk, face creased in a deep scowl. His gait swayed a little, and I wondered how many whiskeys he'd had while he'd been in there.

"You really are a crazy motherfucking bitch, aren't you?" Taz snapped when he got within earshot, then closer until his nose nearly touched my forehead. "Do you have any idea how much these stuntmen cost? They're getting paid by the hour! And the insurance! We're gonna have to scrap half the footage and reshoot the end of the raid, and I'll never get the same spontaneity out of the townspeople again. Dammit!"

The hired warrior shoved his way in between us. "Oh no. I'm done. You can get someone else. You said they'd shoot some red paint, maybe throw a few rocks we could dodge on the horses. I don't do unplanned stunts, especially without the proper pads and gear."

I wanted to knock both their heads together. "I don't know what you're so all-fired angry about," I said to Taz. I pointed at the roof I'd leaped from. "You wanted spontaneity, you got it. Besides, this is your fault. How was I supposed to know they weren't really on the warpath?"

"How were you—?" Taz stopped, staring at me, red creeping from his face to his hairline and down his neck. "Oh, that's rich. That's really rich. I'll have to add that to the list Doc is making for your competency hearing."

That did it. I reached out and shoved Taz until he fell on his directorial ass. He glared up at me, eyebrows lowered, and I got the distinct impression no one had ever dared treat him that way before. Well, it was about damn time.

The other three fake Indians arrived then, and I had further reason for my anger.

"This!" I said, pointing at the lead Indian. "This is why white men never could make true peace with the Indian tribes." I had no idea if the United States government had succeeded over the intervening years, but considering all this nonsense, I rather doubted it. "You don't understand them," I ranted. "You don't even try. And then you blame them for everything." I thought about the sign at the gold mine describing the "Native Americans" who'd wiped out the miners and how very wrong the historians had been.

The chief had gotten off his horse, and I grabbed him by the buckskin sleeve and hauled the befuddled man over to where Taz still lay on the ground. "In my journals, I wrote that our local tribe consisted of *peaceful* people who *didn't wear headdresses.* And for the most part, we honored each others' customs. But here in your little *reality* show you're making them out to be bloodthirsty morons who'd send four lone warriors to ride into a town full of white men *with guns.* If this were reality, they'd have been dead in seconds, or they'd have had guns of their own, and there'd be a real war starting up." My train of rage was jumping the tracks, switching from one source to another so fast I could barely keep up with how many different things made me furious about this scene.

"You don't fake an Indian raid! It's not funny. It's not entertainment. In towns not far from Oblivion, people died on both sides of the conflict. People who didn't deserve a shotgun blast or an arrow through the heart. You're mocking them. Laughing at their expense."

Before the chief could move away from my ranting self, I grabbed at his headdress and pulled, coming away with both the adornments and his black-haired wig. This actor was a blond. "Then you've got white men playing the Indians, like you're trying to set them up and make them look warlike and stupid. I'm betting you couldn't have gotten real Indians to participate in this time-wasting farce."

And there was the heart of my rage. Wasted time. Wasted time playing these stupid games while kids got scared camping out at the lake and more good people died like the Lansings and Miss Josephine and everyone I'd left behind in my Oblivion. I needed to get those explosives, get the climbing gear from Beth's friends, get to Xanthis's hidden treasure, and somehow carry it all to the mine pit before—

"You're fired."

The list faded from my mind. The tirade died unfinished in my throat. Dread washed over me in a wave. I needed to be here. Right here. This job was hard enough without having to get in from the outside. Maybe I'd misunderstood him.

"What?" I whispered through clenched teeth.

Taz stood. "You heard me. Fired. I don't give a damn how good you'll be for the ratings. You're more trouble than you're worth." He stomped to the Indian with the shotgun, yanked it from the startled man's grip, aimed it at my chest, and shot me.

The impact of the paint bullets staggered me back several steps, hitting with enough force that I knew I'd have bruises. Dang, I never realized getting hit with a fake weapon would hurt so much. I stared down at my splattered shirt front. Red streaks tracked over my breasts and stomach and made dark splotches on my black vest.

"Congratulations," Taz said. "You're dead. We'll edit the film and make it look like one of the Indians shot you." He gazed around at the crowd of citizens who'd gathered on the boardwalks. Arlene stood amongst them, shaking her head, one hand covering her eyes. She had Al, saloon owner and ex-soldier, with her, the large man watching for what I'd do next. The director found the individual he was looking for. "Deputy Baylor," he called, waving him over.

Like a well-trained hound, Baylor trotted to the director's side.

"You're the sheriff now, Jake. Don't fuck it up the way McCade did." Taz turned to me. "Get your stuff from Malek at the general store and get out. Your car's fixed and parked at the lake with everyone else's. We took the cost out of your earnings. Accounting will direct-deposit your final check in a week or so. Get lost. And take your damn bird with you. She keeps disappearing from Xanthis's place anyway." He spun on his heel and stormed off. The Indians followed, leading their horses.

Jake and I stared at each other while the onlookers dispersed. He took off his hat and ran a hand through his hair. "You know, this isn't how I really

wanted this to go, Cali… Sandra," he corrected himself. "After that first day, we made a decent team."

I wasn't in the mood. Besides, I could see him
scanning the building exteriors for the hidden cameras and half posing with one hand on the butt of his
gun while he talked. "You've got what you wanted,
Jake. Drop it." Trying to ignore the paint smell on
my clothes, I stalked toward the store.

Holy hell, what had I just done?

CHAPTER 31

TAR, FEATHERS, and horseshit, I'd really messed up this time. Here I'd been concerned about getting through with Taz's games so I could accomplish my goals, and now I'd made getting anywhere near my goals ten times harder.

Halfway to the general store I changed directions, going to my room above the sheriff's office instead and ignoring the sympathetic comments of the teenagers in the cells. Thin walls in Oblivion, even in the jail, and they'd heard the whole shouted exchange.

Malek didn't have anything of mine that I needed to retrieve, save my personal S&W, and getting that would mean turning in my current weapon, which would raise all sorts of questions about how I'd acquired a real gun and why I'd brought it to the "set." Jake had gone to the saloon, probably to celebrate his promotion before moving into the jail, which bought me an hour or so of peace.

I used the time to take a sponge bath from the washbasin and change into a clean shirt and vest from my wardrobe. They could charge me for the clothes for all I cared. Even if I did manage to survive my final showdown with the Eye Killers, I doubted I'd be able to fool real bankers into handing me money from Sandra Meadows's account.

So, where to go. That was the real question.

I couldn't stay in town, not with the cameras everywhere, unless I wanted to sleep in the outhouse or the crypt. I couldn't return to Sam's house for the same reason.

I went downstairs and paced in front of my desk, hoping for the strike of inspiration, when my eyes fell on the teens' discarded camping gear. "Can I borrow some of that?" I asked, pointing at the pile. "All I need is a tent, a ground cloth, and some cooking supplies." They'd spread their bedrolls over the floor and the cots, and I couldn't bring myself to ask for one of those. Besides, the weather had turned warm enough to sleep without one.

"Sure, Sheriff!" Alex piped up. "I mean, urm, ex-sheriff?"

"She's still a sheriff, dumbass," Patrick said, smacking him in the back of the head. "She's a real officer of the law."

"No offense taken, boys," I assured them.

I opened the cell and pulled out a tent and poles, a piece of tarp to lie on so moisture from the dirt wouldn't seep into my clothing, a box of matches, some fishing gear, and a couple of cook pots, then wrapped the items in the tarp. When I stood with my bundle, I glanced around, wondering what else I needed. I'd transferred the bullets Sam gave me to my vest and jeans pockets. My journal was likely safer in the gun safe, since no one else knew the combination, and I could come back for it later. Maybe.

"You know, I'm thinking I might want to go into police work when I graduate."

Katherine's words stopped me halfway to the door. I spun to face her. The two boys snickered in their cell.

"No, you don't," I said with enough venom that she took a step back from the bars. "You want to grow up, keep your family around you, have friends and suitors and pets and a life that's wonderfully predictable." I reached for the doorknob, then added, "And that means getting out of show business too." Then I left.

Halfway down Main Street, Pandora settled on my shoulder.

Well, at least one thing in my life could be counted on as routine.

TWO HOURS later found me at the lake, little more than a pond, really, with Ford tied to a nearby tree. Yes, I'd stolen a horse. I was a horse thief—a crime punishable by hanging in my time. But I'd left a note tacked to his stall telling Taz he could keep my payment, and if that didn't amount to enough, he could sell my S&W too. Judging from Malek's constant drooling over my gun, I had to think it would fetch a hefty price. I'd lost one trusted mount. I wouldn't lose another.

I'd also written a quick message to Arlene and given it to the hotel desk clerk for delivery so she could find me. If she hadn't given me up for foolishness.

I set up my tent well away from the churned-up ground where the kids had obviously camped and far from the rows and rows of smelly cars in the half-dust, half-grass clearing beside the lake. Pandora liked the water, and while I worked, she spent the time at the lake's edge, flapping her wings and spraying droplets everywhere until I had to stop and watch her and laugh.

So long as she showed no distress, that probably meant an absence of Eye Killers. Damn good thing too. The late-afternoon sun and not enough sleep had me dozing. That, and the fact I hadn't eaten all day.

I forced myself to stay awake long enough to make a fishing pole from the branch of a nearby tree, tie some line and a hook from the kids' supplies to it, and hang a worm on the end. Then I attached the pole itself to my wrist and leaned back on the grass to wait for a bite.

When the yank on the line awoke me in the late evening, I hauled in my dinner, a nice-sized catfish, but nothing like that old-timer I'd hunted in my earlier days. I hoped he'd lived a long, happy life and died of old age.

I hoped I'd get the opportunity to do the same.

With no breeze and plenty of dry wood at hand, the fire started without much fuss, and soon I had the fish cleaned and cooking. Okay, burning might be a better description, but I was no Beth. I could catch 'em, I couldn't cook to save my own life, and if I had to sleep out at the lake more than a day or two, I'd starve. Even Pandora wouldn't touch the bits I tried to give her, preferring the leftover worms I had caught for bait instead.

Boots moving through brush had me up on my feet, tin plate in one hand, gun in the other, but I relaxed when Arlene appeared, approaching from the direction of Oblivion. She raised a hand in greeting, and I seated myself to wait for her. When she got to my campsite, she plopped down on the opposite side of the fire and dropped the bag she'd been carrying next to her.

"Fish?" I offered, extending the plate.

She eyed my half-burnt, half-raw dinner. "No thanks." Reaching in the sack, she hauled out a small picnic basket, opened it, and proceeded to spread out what looked like chicken salad sandwiches, a couple of bottles of a brown, bubbly liquid labeled Coca-Cola and looking slightly like sarsaparilla, and three apples.

"Three?" I said, raising an eyebrow.

She stood and offered the odd apple to Ford, who munched it eagerly. Guess the thin grass was no substitute for the oats and hay he'd been getting at the stable. I stood and scraped my plate into the lake where predators wouldn't come looking for fish parts and snagged myself a sandwich. The chicken salad had grapes mixed in—one of my favorite combinations.

"You know," I said, munching and gesturing at the discarded fishing gear, "if you'd been here a little sooner, you could have saved a poor catfish's life."

"I'm more interested in saving *you* from a food poisoning death." She bit into her apple, the juice running down her chin before she wiped it on her sleeve. "Besides," Arlene said, turning serious, "you have no idea how hard it was to get to you. Taz kept sending the fake Native Americans through, hoping to recapture his 'spontaneity' and failing every time. Eventually, he gave up and sent them home. Then I had to get the food. Malek was under strict orders not to give me anything extra, but he slipped it to me anyway. And that assistant director...."

"Danielle," I supplied.

"Right. She arranged for one of the exterior cameras to blank out long enough for me to sneak away." Arlene cocked her head and looked at me sideways. "What'd you do to get on her good side?"

Given Danielle's sexual preferences, that question could have meant a lot of things, but I took it at face value and shrugged. "I never got on her bad side. She and Malek seemed to like me from the start. Of course, Taz did too—"

"Only so long as you were making him money. Different sort of 'like.'" She took a swig of cola. "Anyway, Taz and Doc are watching me and Sam every minute. It's not that we're prisoners or anything, but they don't want us seeing you."

I raised my eyebrows. "They know where I'm at?" So far as I knew, they hadn't installed cameras this distance from Oblivion, with the exceptions of the mine and Sam's house.

"They're not sure, but they're guessing. They know you took Ford, so you didn't drive off. There's no law against camping here, so they can't make you leave, but they may give you a hard time. Al said he'd stop by later tonight. They aren't watching him, and he always goes out for a smoke after dark but leaves the camera zone 'cause Taz doesn't want any smokers onscreen. Oh, and a security guard comes through that clearing every night to check on the vehicles, so be aware of him and don't accidentally shoot him as an Eye Killer or something."

"Unless he is one," I said darkly.

Arlene nodded slowly, eyes fixed on mine, considering me. "You know, Doc's back on the 'Crazy Girl' kick. He's been drinkin' it up at the saloon, talking about how he's gonna get all kinds of publicity when this show airs and he has you brought in for a psych eval. Maybe even write a book about the experience. The Baker Act lets him declare you a danger to yourself, and he's got the credentials to make people believe it, malpractice suit or no malpractice suit. Beyond that, he's got some reality show ideas of his own to film at the psychiatric hospital, of all things. He says it's gonna pay off his debts, and from what I can tell, he has plenty of them."

I shook my head. "I've had quite enough television for this lifetime or any other."

Arlene laughed, and the sound warmed my insides. I took another sip of Coca-Cola. "You know, they'd just come out with this back in my time," I said, holding up the bottle. "But you could only get it in the cities at drug store soda fountains. Taz is a little off."

"He's probably making money off the advertising." Arlene took a minute to explain the concept of using brand-name products in television shows and getting kickbacks from the companies who made them. When she finished, she reached out and brushed a strand of hair behind my ear, suddenly serious. I went to tuck it into my braid, but she caught my wrist in her fingers. "Cali," she said, voice low and sultry.

The evening crickets roared like thunder in my ears, or maybe that was my heartbeat speeding up. Somewhere out on the lake, a frog croaked and a fish jumped and plunked back into the water. I took her fingers in my free hand and pried them away.

"Arlene," I whispered, "I can't take a roll in the hay with a woman who doesn't believe me one hundred percent. Not again," I amended, thinking of the night in Sam's guest room and surprising myself with the heat that flooded me at the memory. "And I certainly can't give my heart to that woman. You're here. You're not just staying out of my way, you're helping me. Does that mean you trust me?"

"I… It's a lot, Cali. A helluva lot. My mind keeps wanting to explain away what happened with the Lansings Sunday night. Bulletproof vests for them, a panic attack for me. That would cause symptoms like hyperventilating and choking. Maybe."

"You could always ask Doc," I spat.

I turned, placing my back to her so I could stare out across the lake. The surface lay dusky gray and looking-glass smooth under the dwindling light. Calm and peaceful. Nothing like my current mood. I took a deep breath and let it go, knowing I couldn't afford to alienate anyone else today. Trusting or not, I needed Arlene and the assistance she could provide.

"My Arlene never doubted the Eye Killers were real." It slipped out, just tumbled from my lips with my exhalation. So I kept going. "She didn't live long enough to get the details, the demon part, but I warned her and she believed me and did what I said. I never found out what went wrong that night, how she ended up one of them."

A flash of Arlene throwing a sheet over Lucinda came to my mind's eye. Had Lucinda wriggled loose? Had another Eye Killer come along? Or had Arlene doubted me after all and released Lucinda?

It killed me to think I'd never know.

Arlene was silent a long moment. Then, "Tell me more about your Arlene."

"She was…." My throat threatened to close, but she'd asked, and I wanted to tell her. "She was a lot like you. A lot." I kept facing the lake. No way could I discuss this and look at her. "She once told me she went sweet on me the same day she came into town. Took me a spell to figure that out. I had my folks, and horses, and dreams of going to the city to study art."

Arlene snorted behind me. "Art? Really?"

"Well, it certainly wasn't going to be cooking."

She laughed, and I smiled a bit, some of the icy anger cracking from around my heart. The memories hurt, but not so much now that I'd accepted the time that had passed. Days for me but decades for Oblivion.

"Then my parents died, and I needed a job and a place to live. Becoming sheriff offered both."

"And your Arlene couldn't handle you being sheriff?" Arlene guessed.

Now I did face her. "You really did just skim my journals, didn't you? No, she had no problem with that once the worry for me wore off. Was proud of me, I think, once she came to terms with sharing me with the whole town, though she kept an eye on me when I worked. But that was part of the problem. I was busy. Busy all the time. If I hadn't accepted the job, she might have been willing to run away with me someday. Maybe. There was a small enclave of women… women like us who—"

"Lesbians," Arlene supplied.

"Right, sure." Couldn't quite bring myself to say the word out loud. I'd hidden who I was for so very long. But it was nice to hear her say it without prejudice or shame. "They owned and ran a nearby ranch. We could have joined them. But I liked being sheriff. I got to help and protect people, and for the most part folks respected me, which was nice too. Hard to earn respect out here, at least back then, and especially if you were a woman working a man's job. And Arlene, well, she had needs too. Even when she cheated, we stayed friends of a sort. And then the Eye Killers came, and they took her." I paused, swallowing hard. "They took her because she was helping me. And I had to stop her before she killed me or hurt someone else. It was my responsibility. *She* was my responsibility."

"You take responsibility very seriously. I respect that about you. It's a rare thing where I come from."

"Tell me about Vegas," I prompted. And she did. She told me about the huge hotels and massive casinos, about the shows and lights and crime, about the winners and the losers, and I listened, trying to soak it all in, though a lot went beyond my comprehension. "I'd like to see it someday," I said when she finished.

"I'd like you to see it too," she said, capturing my hand once more. "And, God help me, I believe you. It's insane, but I believe you." Her fingers squeezed mine, my riding calluses rubbing the showgirl-smooth skin.

"Then God help us both." A wave of exhaustion hit me then, and I covered my mouth to hide a yawn.

"Come on." Arlene pulled me to my feet, then snagged the bag she'd brought and dragged both me and it into my tent. She deposited me on the tarp and passed me a new bedroll and a small lantern from the bag. "Maybe you want to show off how tough you are, but I prefer a sleeping bag when I camp."

I lit the lamp and spread out the blankets, nodding my thanks.

The tiredness left me as fast as it had come while I watched her strip off her shirt, hat, and boots. No saloon upstairs girl attire, which made sense if she'd planned to walk and camp. When she reached for her belt, I knelt up and stopped her, preferring to slide the denim over her curvaceous hips all by myself.

Once again, I admired the taut stomach muscles and the general great shape she kept herself in, but being a dancer, I supposed she'd have to be physically fit. She caught me staring and grinned. "I dance every day and work out," she explained.

Wasn't sure what that second part meant. Maybe, like the Arlene of my time, she had a second occupation in the daytime hours. When the saloon was closed during the morning, the Arlene of old had worked at the general store, helping shelve goods and batting her eyelashes to encourage customers to buy more.

Profits went way up.

The jeans pooled around her ankles, and she stepped out of them. That left her in nothing but socks and lacy underthings in very tempting smooth-fabric black. Sure hoped I could finagle the thing with the straps that held up her full breasts. She looked down and saw my lips mere inches from the triangle of downy hair between her legs.

I couldn't disappoint her.

I took the edges of her… "What are you calling these things?" I asked, breathless.

"Panties," she murmured, eyes heavy-lidded as she watched me.

Good name. They sure were making *me* pant.

I drew them down over her hips and legs, careful not to let go so the strange waistband wouldn't snap against her skin. With her half-naked before me, I found her irresistible, and I leaned forward and darted my tongue to brush her most sensitive spot.

She jerked convulsively but didn't break contact.

"Cali," she growled.

My tongue teased the sensitive protrusion, tasting the evidence of her extreme arousal.

Here, in the lamplight instead of the dark, it was impossible not to make comparisons, and I had to admit, this Arlene was even more attractive, her soft dark curls trimmed to reveal full engorged lips, her pleasure center hardened and throbbing with each touch of my tongue. I sucked and teased her, reveling in her moans and the feeling of ultimate power my control over her body brought me.

Arlene's hands came down on my head, caught in my hair, and tried to pull me away. "Stop," she begged, voice hoarse, breath ragged.

I'd already discovered during our previous lovemaking that she could reach ecstasy more than once in an evening. But as tired as I was, I wasn't up to a full night of ongoing intense sex.

I paused to grin up at her unrepentantly, then ignored her plea and returned to my arduous endeavors. If she refused me again, I'd stop. I hadn't forgotten her words about consent… or what had likely happened to her when others ignored that… but she didn't refuse a second time.

"Ah damn," she groaned, then stiffened and jerked, hips bucking.

With her eyes closed and her head thrown back, she'd lost herself and never looked so beautiful. Gradually, she regained her senses, coming down from her peak and gently pushing my head away. She studied me for a long moment in the flickering lamplight.

Her fingers eased my vest off my shoulders, then found the buttons on my white shirt and undid them one by one. The shirt followed my vest into the corner of the tent. Reaching behind me, she deftly removed the crazy contraption Malek's prop elves had provided to support my breasts, even without turning me around. Impressive. I exhaled with relief at the release.

Arlene chuckled. "Not a fan of modern lingerie?" Her hands cupped me, fondling both sides.

I sucked in a gasp. "Better... than binding them... with fabric, I suppose."

"Ouch."

"Riding horses gets bouncy."

Arlene laughed, then knelt next to me and stripped away the rest of my suddenly too restrictive clothing. I assisted with the holster, belt, boots, and jeans, then reached behind her and took off her contraption as well. Okay, I got it on the third try.

"Your turn," she said, low and sultry.

What I got wasn't quite what I expected.

Arlene lay me down on the spread-out bedroll, my head pillowed on her discarded shirt. We didn't have much side-to-side space in the confines of the one-person tent, so she had to move in increments or risk collapsing the canvas upon us.

The lantern sat beside my head, just far enough from my skin to not produce uncomfortable heat and close enough I could watch and admire her. Even with the break in stimulation, the wetness between my legs told me I was more than ready for her. Desperate would have been a better word.

When she lay over me, arms braced on either side of mine, muscles taut to hold up her weight, I waited for her to lower herself. Instead, she kissed me, long and slow and deep, and then worked a trail of nips down my neck, across my breastbone, and between my breasts.

And kept working downward.

Her tongue teased my belly button, making me arch up against her, forcing me to wonder if I'd ever get any sleep tonight and if I really wanted any after all. She kept teasing, and I writhed, bucking and heaving, finding no escape.

Then she went lower.

I'd used my mouth on the real Arlene plenty, but she'd never done so to me. She preferred her hands, or to rub against me full length to full length. One more reminder this wasn't the woman I'd lost. She was the woman I'd found.

I yelped, actually yelped, when her mouth found the juncture between my thighs.

"Oh my God."

A war erupted inside me, half my soul not wanting her to stop, in fact wanting her to go a lot farther and a lot faster, while the other half wondered if I'd faint dead away if she kept this up.

Swirling and flicking, tasting and stroking, she drove me to frenzied motion. My hips bucked, and the tent flaps shook, making a sound like skin slapping skin. I groaned with need. I had my fingers buried in her hair, alternating smoothing and pulling it as she increased and decreased her tempo, but always pressing her lips and tongue as hard to my center as I could stand.

Guess the war was over.

With one final cry, I reached my peak and toppled over it, falling and falling as my vision whited out and tears crept from beneath my squeezed-shut eyelids. Arlene continued to apply stimulation, tickling with the tip of her tongue against me in gradually decreasing pressures and speeds, and I rewarded her by climaxing a second time.

Panting and heaving, we flopped down together, the sides of the tent billowing out and back with our motion and the displaced air. That's when I noticed the play of a small beam of light across the exterior of the canvas.

CHAPTER 32

"ARLENE!" I whispered, gripping her shoulder.

"Shh. Come on."

She grabbed up one of the blankets, wrapped it around both of us, and we crawled to the mouth of the tent and peered out. Ford stood beneath a tree, munching grass. I spotted Pandora in the same tree, and since she wasn't squawking, I could assume we weren't in immediate danger. A few dozen yards along the lake shore, a man strolled casually in our direction. He carried a long stick that emitted a steady beam of light, like a torch without flame, and he pointed it at us. With the moon shining directly down on him, I could make out a uniform with glinting gold buttons.

"It's the security guard I warned you about," Arlene reminded me. She glanced at my face, probably noting the fading panic there. "Don't shoot him."

Arlene raised a hand and waved, and the guard waved back. "Sorry to bother you folks," he called out. "Just stay away from the cars. That area's been rented."

"Not a problem, sir!" Arlene returned. "Good night!"

The guard nodded to us both, turned, and marched off the way he'd come. I exhaled, only to catch my breath at the sound of rustling in the nearby scrub.

This time the man who appeared wore a woven shirt and brown trousers with black suspenders and leather boots. I relaxed against Arlene. "Al," I said.

"Yep."

"No more sleep or sex." I sighed.

She sounded as disappointed. "Nope."

We hurried into our clothing while Al chuckled to himself outside, obviously aware of what we were doing and what we'd been doing. Together, we crawled out and seated ourselves beside the dying embers of the campfire. I grabbed a stick from the pile of dry branches I'd collected and prodded the glowing wood until it rekindled and burned bright. Introductions came and went, and we got down to business, Al's military background showing through his bartender facade.

"So, you wanna blow stuff up," Al said, pacing around my campsite and studying everything. "You know anything about explosives?"

"Not a damn thing," I said. "But I hear you're something of an expert."

His chest puffed out at that, stretching his suspenders to their limits. "Demolitions specialist for the Marines, ma'am. I can make a bomb out of less shit than MacGyver. What do you want blown?"

I gave him the rundown of the church, the storage closet, and the blocked stairwell leading into the basement cavern. When I finished, Al let out a low whistle.

"Well, that's gonna take some finesse." He seated himself and picked up a discarded twig, then twirled it between his fingers. "You wanna blow through that closet floor and clear those stairs without bringing the whole church down on your heads. Nothing homemade is that precise. A well-placed C-4 charge would do it, but I'll need to get a hold of some. You sure about this treasure cave?"

"Positive. I found it while exploring the mine. Treasure, and some religious items like hymnals and such. And there were old documents referencing a storeroom under the church and stairs leading down from the closet. Sam had them. He's the local expert, a park ranger at the mine. His family's lived here all their lives, but they didn't know about the treasure. I just put it all together." I made all this up, but I couldn't explain how I really knew about Xanthis's horde.

"And why, again, don't you just go back in through the mine?"

I'd had time to come up with this story too. "I nearly got killed the first time. Pits, rockslides, it's all unstable. But the original blueprints clearly showed the stairs under the church. They've got to connect. And with someone experienced like you, I figured that route would be safer."

Yeah, I could turn on the charm when I needed to. It wasn't my strong suit, but a woman batting her eyelashes and playing to a man's ego still worked, even if that woman wore a sheriff's star.

"This is your way of getting back on the show, is it? I could get in a lot of trouble for helping you, not to mention arrested for the explosives and damage."

"If it looks good on camera, Taz won't mind," Arlene put in. "In fact, he'll probably hand us all bonuses."

Al considered for a moment. "Too risky. I'm gonna need some other payment besides the promise of fame and a potential bonus… like some of that treasure of yours."

Shit. I couldn't promise him that. I had no idea how much gold had been taken in the initial strike, and no idea what Xanthis's treasure was worth or if it would be enough. That it was *Xanthis's* treasure had to count for something with the Elementals. His hiring of the miners to dig his escape tunnel was what had kept the gold mining going on for so long and extended the amount of damage. Regardless, I intended to drop every scrap of the preacher's valuable horde down that hole and hope for the best, and if I gave a piece away and the offering didn't work, I'd question myself for the rest of my likely short life.

I shook my head. "No treasure. I've already promised it to… others. But," I said, thinking fast. What would a military man value? "There were weapons. Dozens of them. Antiques. And probably worth a fortune in themselves. Swords, guns, throwing stars, you name it. You can have your pick of them."

The Marine-turned-bartender nodded once. "Done." He reached down into a boot and removed a small rectangular black… thing.

"A cell phone? You smuggled in a cell phone?" Arlene said.

"A Marine is always prepared."

"And you've got a signal way out here?"

"I do," he bragged, "with a little help from a signal-boosting device." He pulled a short, thin rod from his pocket.

"Nice," Arlene said. "It's a more powerful antenna," she explained to me. "Works with his cell phone."

Al nodded. "I wasn't gonna be completely cut off. Two hundred bucks and worth every penny. Never know when you might have an emergency. Besides, the director knows I've got it. He had to borrow it the night poor old Miss Josephine passed on. Couldn't reach a damn soul with his own phone. How do you think I've been getting my cigarettes?" He waved at the parking lot on the far side of the lake. "I figured, cigarettes, right? They had them in the 1890s. So I brought a couple cartons with me. Then Taz tells all the smokers he's been getting heat from the antismoking organizations to not show it on TV. Influences the little kiddies. Said we could manage a week without them. Huh. Spoken like a true nonsmoker. Asshole confiscated my stash." Al's hands clenched into fists. Damn, he must have really needed a smoke. "Anyway, I call my buddy Chris, and he drives up every two nights and meets me out here with a couple of packs of my brand. Couldn't coordinate without the phone."

He tapped on the black screen, kind of like the glowing boxes I'd seen in the video room upstairs in the courthouse but much smaller. "Let me make a quick call."

Al liked to pace while he talked, leaving me and Arlene at the fireside.

"It'll work," Arlene assured me, giving me a quick kiss. Her touch warmed me from head to toes. "He'll come through."

"We're running out of time. The Eye Killers are taking more and more lives, and Friday morning, everyone leaves, and I lose all my resources." *And you*, I thought, tightening my hand on hers.

When this ended, what happened? Did Pandora bite me again and move me to some other time period to fight a new evil? A tremor passed through me at the idea of another death by fire. And to think I used to find watching the flames relaxing. I'd loved those rare occasions when Pa came home and we had a cookout under the stars. But burning to ashes changed one's perspective somewhat. I shivered again. Arlene, probably thinking I caught a chill, let go of my hand and rubbed my arms to warm me.

Or did I stay here? I couldn't take over Sandra Meadows's life. We had similar appearances, but we weren't identical twins. Anyone who actually knew her would recognize me as false. And I didn't belong here, didn't understand this world with its TV and microphones and cell phones. I'd have to distance myself from civilization, be an outcast, unless....

Unless Arlene was willing to keep helping me and teach me what I needed to know to survive in this world. We could move in with Sam and Beth. They had an extra room. I could turn Sam's place into a working ranch again, bring in more income and send Beth off to cooking school. And if they really did plan to make Oblivion a tourist attraction, my intimate knowledge of the place would be invaluable.

I glanced at Pandora, perched at the peak of my tent like a gargoyle looking down from the top of a great cathedral. She cocked her head at me.

Leave me here, I silently begged her. *Leave me here to live out a life. Don't take me away from these new friends I've made. From Arlene, again. Go choose someone else. In fact, you could stay here with me. There's got to be somebody else capable of fighting evil.* And I'd grown to like her company, whether I admitted it out loud or not.

She shook herself, fluffing out all her feathers, and I got the uncanny and distinct feeling that not only had she heard me, but her answer was no.

Well, when the time came, we'd see about that. She couldn't send me on if she couldn't bite me, and I had to be stronger than that bird. Not that I'd hurt her, but, well, there had to be some alternative.

Maybe I could tie her beak shut.

Al returned, strutting and grinning up a storm, and I knew before he opened his mouth that he'd succeeded.

"We're all set," he announced, rubbing his hands together. "Thursday morning, 2:00 a.m., we meet here and go in through the graveyard. Before heading out here, I'll cover up any cameras I can find around the church."

I had to assume he'd be better at finding them than I'd been.

"That should buy us enough time to take care of that stairwell. Once we're through the debris, we can turn 'em back on and we'll all be famous."

Or arrested, I thought.

Al took his leave after that. Arlene wanted to stay, but I wouldn't have it.

"It's too dangerous out here alone," she argued.

"I've got the phoenix alarm," I said, smiling. "And you'll be missed if you don't go soon. Probably have been already." I gazed at the eastern sky, where a soft glow had appeared. "It'll be daylight in a bit. Get in touch with Sam and Beth and see where we are with that climbing gear. I don't know a thing about skunking, or whatever she called it, so I'll need some time to look over the equipment."

"Yes, ma'am!" she said, grinning and tossing off a snappy salute. "And it's spelunking, not skunking."

"Whatever." I shoved her in the direction of Oblivion. "Go on, git."

She came back in for one last kiss, her mouth lingering on mine, her arms tightening around me, and for a moment, I clung to her, too, my hands clenched in the fabric of her shirt. Then I pushed her gently away.

"I'll be fine."

Arlene nodded once and disappeared into the shadows. Pandora flew down to land on my arm.

"Just you and me," I told her. "Maybe we can get some sleep now?"

She bobbed her head in response, and we slipped inside the tent. But I kept the lantern Arlene had brought lit, leaving it just outside the tent flaps to ward off any animals or anything else, for that matter, since Eye Killers got distracted by fire, and my gun stayed within arm's reach.

I SLEPT hard and well into late morning until the sound of clanking metal woke me. Sticking my head out of the tent, I saw Beth and Sam, their horses picking their way over the rocks and brush and carrying rope and what looked like some contraptions of thick cloth straps and metal fasteners tied to their saddles. Sam rode an aging mare, slow and docile and much more suited to his equestrian ability than his barrel-racing mount.

Beth also had a basket, and my growling stomach and I sincerely hoped it contained breakfast. The scents of bacon, biscuits, and sweet rolls told me it did.

My little fire had burned to ash, but the morning was warm with only the slightest nip in the air, so we didn't need it.

"No eggs today," Beth apologized as she and Sam dismounted and tied their horses beside Ford. The three exchanged nose nudges and companionable whinnies. "They don't travel well. Nothing more disgusting than cold eggs."

"No coffee, either," Sam said, shaking his head. He stretched and bent from side to side, a small groan of pain escaping him. The man definitely needed more riding practice if he got sore after such a short time in the saddle. Then I remembered the back injury he'd referred to. Really, he just needed to stay off horses, period. I didn't want to see him get seriously hurt.

I took a biscuit, shoved a couple of pieces of bacon in the middle, and chewed gratefully. "This is more than plenty. Thank you."

"As you can see," Beth said, "my friends came through. Brought the climbing gear out to the house this morning, but they'll be pretty pissed if we break anything, so hopefully we won't tangle with Eye Killers for the next couple of days."

I figured that to be unlikely, so I kept it to myself. This would become a struggle, even if I was trying to appease them. They wanted revenge, and they'd make things as difficult for me as they could. And replacing the ropes and such would be the least of my problems.

"I've got enough equipment for two people," she continued, "and I brought a couple of backpacks too. Figured you'd need something to carry the treasure in while you were rappelling down the side of the pit. We can ride out to the reservation this afternoon and practice on the cliffs. That's where my friends live. Well, not in the cliff dwellings. Not anymore. Not since well before *your* time. Those are for the tourists. They have modern houses and all. Anyway, I wanted to bring the stuff here first so you could familiarize yourself with it and not look like a total idiot or get hurt. I, um, told them you'd done this a couple of times so they wouldn't worry so much about lending things to me. It's expensive gear."

The reservation? The cliff dwellings? Two plus two still made four, even in the year 2019. "Your friends are Indians?"

A flicker of a frown passed over her face before it cleared. "Yep. And they would have loved what you said to Taz yesterday morning. Modern media still paints them all in a bad light half the time. Oh, and I realize you didn't know better, but we call them Native Americans now, because, well, they are. Or at least more native to this country than we are, depending on which source you believe."

So, Indians. Or Native Americans. Huh. And white men were friends with them. Judging by the way Beth spoke, this wasn't unusual, either. Well, good for them. I'd been curious about how things had fared in that area over the intervening years. Looked like I'd find out.

"What about Arlene?" I asked, staring into the brush. I'd expected her to show up before we finished breakfast but saw no sign of her. In my head, she had been the one helping me cart the treasure from the secret church basement to the pit and carry it down. But experience should have taught me that what went on my head didn't always come to pass.

Sam scowled. "Taz has her dancing and singing at the saloon, watching her like a hawk. She'll slip away when she can, probably tomorrow morning. Taz mentioned something about having to go to a production company board meeting. Besides, she told me she'd done some climbing before, not in caves, but the equipment is the same."

I tried to mask my disappointment and failed. Beth touched me gently on the arm, but I shook her off and straightened my shoulders. It wasn't like she was abandoning me. She was stuck, plain and simple. She'd be there when I needed her. I knew she would.

Sam walked to where I'd left my makeshift fishing pole. "You all go on. I'll watch over the camp."

Beth poked her dad in the arm. "Yeah, and maybe catch a few fish while you're at it?"

I got the impression Sam disappeared a lot on Sundays and came home with a catfish dinner for Beth to prepare.

"Guilty as charged. You don't mind?" he asked me.

"Not so long as I don't have to cook it." I grabbed my hat from the tent and whistled for Pandora, who remained perched at the tent's peak. "You coming?"

She shook herself, a negative response, and I shrugged.

"Suit yourself."

WE HEADED out on horseback, Beth leading, though I knew the way to the long-abandoned cliff dwellings. When we got close, we came upon a barbed-wire fence with a huge swinging gate and a sign warning that we'd entered private property. We left the horses outside the gate keeping one another company and nibbling the taller grass there and proceeded on foot.

At the base of the cliffs, someone had erected a small booth advertising passes for sale to climb to the cave homes, but the wooden structure stood empty. Beth pointed at the advertised hours. "Closed on Wednesdays and Mondays. They couldn't get enough tourists to come out on the off days, so we've got the place to ourselves. And if anyone notices us, I can just smile and wave. They all know me around here." Regardless, she pulled a couple of dollars from her pocket and tucked them under the grimy glass window hanging askew at the front of the booth.

I followed her up the cliff, taking a well-worn path someone had gone to great pains to make safe with guard railings and steps carved into the steeper stretches. Every few dozen feet would be a signpost explaining a different aspect of Indian, er, Native American life, and I smiled at their accuracy. Unlike the "historical" attractions on white man's land, these were actually correct.

"We going all the way up?" I asked. We passed the empty cliff homes, devoid of all life, and a hollow pit formed in my stomach. Though I'd never seen these residences occupied in my original lifetime, it still felt like the massacre at the mining camp all over again, even though at heart, I knew no one had likely been murdered here in many generations. Whoever maintained the site left artifacts of Indian life—an unlit cooking fire, some blankets, a few crude handmade toys, but nothing breathed, nothing moved.

A Native American ghost town.

"Makes more sense to work down than up, since you'll be using this gear on a pit," Beth said, answering my question.

These cliffs weren't all that high, and we achieved the summit within fifteen minutes or so. From there we paused, catching our breath and taking in the vista. In the distance I could see a well-developed little city right where the Pueblo village had once stood in my time, with dozens of identical homes, their orange-tiled roofs glowing in the sunlight. Instead of a haphazard scattering of structures, more recent planners had laid out the streets at perfect right angles, and the whole thing made a nice, neat square with a pretty green park in the center. From here, I couldn't judge things like maintenance or the sizes of the homes, but it looked as fine as anything we'd had in Oblivion, which, admittedly, wasn't much to compare to in this modern age.

I had a sudden urge to travel to a city, to see the wonders a hundred and twenty-five years must have produced. I couldn't even begin to imagine what New York must look like now, or Chicago. Or Arlene's Las Vegas. Later. When my work was done.

"That's where they live," my companion explained. "Now it's all SUVs and satellite TV."

Whatever those were. But they lived in white man homes. A couple of cars made their way along the streets. They'd adapted to our presence and existed in our world while still maintaining this history of their past.

Over time, they'd continued to adjust, as all people did when faced with a new living environment, and I'd need to follow suit if I remained out of my element.

We donned the "harnesses," Beth adjusting and tightening the straps on each of us, assigning names to each piece and showing me how it worked. No way would I keep all the doohickies straight, but I got the basics.

She secured the top end, and we bounced down the side of the cliff, her in the lead and me a few hops behind. Beth called it "rappelling," and under other circumstances, it might have been fun. Growing up amongst the mesas, I'd never developed a fear of heights, and I found the process fairly simple. Of course, I didn't currently have a weighted backpack on, or Eye Killers threatening me from above or below. Advantages, to be sure.

Over the next couple of hours, we repeated the process three times, and climbed back up using the ropes as well, since I'd have to get *out* of the pit once I'd delivered my offerings. I decided not to go for a fourth try. My arm and leg muscles burned, and I'd need my strength for tomorrow.

We disconnected from the guide ropes, retrieved the equipment from the top of the cliff, removed our harnesses, and carried the heavy gear down the trail.

That's when I spotted the fast-moving shadow ducking into one of the abandoned cliff homes.

CHAPTER 33

I DROPPED my share of climbing apparatus, ignoring Beth's squeak of protest, and drew my pistol.

"Don't shoot. It's probably just Robbie. She's always skulking around up here, but she's harmless." Beth tried to take the lead, but I blocked her with an outstretched arm.

"Let's just make sure, okay?" I left the gear and stepped off the tourist trail to walk along the well-worn plateau fronting the cave homes.

Beth was most likely right. What I'd seen had moved fast, and though the more recent Eye Killers had picked up some speed and agility, they still didn't move like living, breathing, unpossessed human beings.

I crept to the entrance I'd seen the figure duck into and leaned my head around the corner to take a quick look. Sure enough, a solitary woman stood inside.

The lone woman, Robbie I presumed, proceeded to kneel in the exact center of the cave dwelling. She upended a large sack on the floor and discarded it to the side, leaving a pile of corn, wheat, flowers, and a variety of other homegrown goods before her.

I sucked in a sharp breath, making her jump and whirl to face me.

"What're you doing?" we asked, our identical words tumbling over each other.

She recovered first, standing and striding toward me with quick, angry steps. She wore jeans and the white canvas shoes with ties that Beth favored off-camera. Her simply cut shirt had no buttons and depicted a dog standing atop a wooden board at the crest of a wave. I placed her at about thirty-five or so with short-cropped black hair and tan skin. I saw no weapons on her, and with my gun hand still out of her sight, I slipped my pistol back into its holster.

"You shouldn't be here. The site's closed today," she said, coming almost nose to nose with me.

I felt Beth's presence behind me and shifted so the woman could see her.

"Beth?" she asked, focusing over my shoulder. Robbie's tension eased, and some of the anger left her expression. "She with you?" She jerked a thumb at me. "Where are Thomas and Joseph?"

We stepped fully into the cave home, the top of my head coming to about Robbie's chin. Tall woman, and muscular. She fixated on my holstered weapon, tearing her eyes from it after several long seconds.

"You some kind of cop?" she demanded. "This is sovereign land. You have no jurisdiction here."

"Joseph and Thomas aren't with me," Beth interrupted in an attempt to distract her. "They lent us some climbing gear, and we've been rappelling off the mesas."

"What were you doing?" I already knew the answer, but I had to ask.

Robbie backed away toward her pile of offerings, protective of the stash.

Beth placed a hand on my arm and whispered, "Personally, I'm all about 'to each his own,' but most people think she's crazy. Always performing these weird rituals. She works here, helping to maintain the site, but she does this too."

Yeah, well, she wasn't the only one being called insane. I could sympathize.

Robbie's head jerked in Beth's direction. "There's nothing crazy about doing this for--"

"The Eye Killers," I finished for her, thinking back to my conversation with Robert so, so many years ago. Robert. Robbie. I wondered....

"You know the legend?" Her tone held a modicum of respect I hadn't heard before.

Beth looked from me to Robbie and back again, eyes wide. Strolling past Beth, I stood beside the collection of gifts and studied them. "I know it." I touched an ear of corn with the toe of my boot. "This working?"

"You believe?" Her voice dripped with sarcasm and scorn.

"I believe," I assured her. "More than you'll ever know."

Whatever tension remained fled with that statement. She seemed to collapse in on herself, sinking down beside her pile. "It works," she said, "for the most part. We lost a tourist last week, a teenager. She wandered off, turned up beaten to death. The county police started questioning all the staff. I said I had no idea what had happened, but I know the truth. Her eyes were wide open."

Beth huffed in disbelief. "Don't you watch *CSI*? Lots of people die with their eyes open."

"But not this time," I said softly. Too much coincidence here. I could understand how allowing tour groups to tromp in and out of these cliff dwellings might anger the Eye Killers. Large numbers of constant visitors would do quite a bit of environmental damage to the earth Elementals' sacred mesas and caves.

"You sound like you speak from personal experience," Robbie said.

"I do."

Her eyes begged me to explain. So I told her my story, every bit of it.

By the time I finished up the long tale with an outline of my plan to appease the Eye Killers, the three of us had seated ourselves cross-legged in a circle around the offerings. The sun had sunk low in the western sky, and the evening chill had come creeping into the otherwise empty cliff homes.

Robbie nodded in agreement with my decisions. "That treasure you're talking about should work fine. It's the same type of stuff, and from what you say, probably more valuable than the original gold the miners took from that pit. It should make up for the damage to the stone too, in theory." She thought for a long moment before continuing. "You know, stories about Oblivion and what happened there have circulated through the ranch inhabitants for generations."

"The ranch being Paradise Found?" I asked.

She straightened with pride. "Yep. Still there. Still a safe haven for lesbians, but also gay men, trans people, pretty much every part of the LGBTQ community is represented there."

Wasn't sure what all the letters stood for, but I got the gist.

"When my parents threw me out for being a lesbian, I went there. Didn't want to keep my real name, so they gave me Roberta's chosen one and I shortened it. Robert's a legend. They did so much to protect marginalized groups, even if they weren't called that at the time, and not just the lesbian population. After Oblivion fell, they and the others at the ranch worked to forge bonds with the Native Americans as well. And all the ranch leaders have kept meticulous records and journals. Back then, after you vanished, Robert wrote that the local Native Americans named you the time walker."

"The what?"

"Time walker," Robbie repeated. "That's what they called Xanthis, and now you—time walkers. Oh, that preacher probably thought he'd hidden well, pretending to be a shaman from another peaceful tribe, but they knew better. The stories say he could walk the path of time the way I'd walk a cliff trail."

She spoke with such assurance, I couldn't bear to tell her it wasn't as easy as all that. Fighting walking dead, shooting your lover, burning to a crisp, rising from the ashes, losing all your loved ones, and having no control over your destination were details best left out.

"May you continue to have good fortune in your endeavors," she said. "And if you need anything, send someone with a message. I might be called crazy, but I can handle a gun, and I'm good in a fight."

Considering her solid build and callused hands, I didn't doubt it. I thought about Al and his need for payment for his services. "What will I owe you in return?"

Robbie shook her head. "Nothing. Absolutely nothing. Do you have any idea how amazing it is to meet you? To maybe help you? It's an honor."

I nodded my thanks and hoped this honor wouldn't get anyone else killed.

CHAPTER 34

A HORRIBLE high-pitched, repetitive sound screamed in my ear. Rolling over, I focused bleary vision on glowing red numbers that read 1:00 a.m. and shook my head.

Beth had been right to lend me this "battery-operated alarm clock." I had fallen asleep despite two cups of the strong black coffee Sam had brought with dinner and one head-dunking in the lake.

I considered hurling the foul, noisy thing out the tent flap, but I restrained myself. It didn't belong to me, and Beth might want it back, though why, I couldn't fathom.

My muscles ached from the climbing lessons as I struggled to sit upright in the tent. Beside me, Pandora pecked her beak at the clock. She hit one of the buttons on its shiny black surface and the obnoxious noise ceased.

Smart bird.

The lit clock face illuminated things enough for me to find the lamp just outside and relight it. Sometime during the night, it had gone out, and I shuddered to think about what could have come upon me in the darkness. Damn, I'd slept hard. I'd even missed the night watchman's pass through the parking lot. Now I had an hour to get myself to the cemetery and meet up with the others.

Ford waited outside, and I fed him a spare apple while I hurried to saddle him. Then I secured the climbing gear, which took a few more precious minutes. I double-checked that my pistol was fully loaded and swung myself up on the horse's back. Scanning the campsite, I saw nothing else essential to take with me. One more home left behind, and each one becoming more and more temporary.

Riding one-handed was how I'd been taught, Western-style of course, and I used the other to hold the lit lantern. No way would I leave that. I had a box of matches in my pocket, but the lamp cast more light. Pandora settled on my shoulder, and we rode into the very early morning.

Any other night, I would have loved a ride like this one. The temperature had cooled. An almost full moon hung overhead. It cast a glowing reflection that shimmered and shifted with the lake water. Small insects darted about my face, drawn by the lantern. In the distance, a coyote howled. Ford whinnied at the sound.

"Easy, boy," I soothed. He quieted, his hooves making soft clopping noises on the dirt and stone.

The closer I drew to Oblivion, the more surreal it felt, like I'd ride into town and time would have shifted back one hundred and twenty-five years. The mayor's snoring would pour through his open

window. Al would be chasing the last drunken strag-
glers out of his saloon and closing up. Miss Josephine would be silhouetted in her kitchen window,
hard at work on the breakfast buns.

I resisted a sudden urge to lean over and check
under Ford to see if he'd magically turned into my
Chessie. Besides, I'd grown to know his gait. It
hadn't changed, and neither had this insane world I
now lived in.

Pandora nuzzling my ear broke me from my
mind's wanderings. "Right. Here and now. No 'then.'
Then is gone." She cooed softly in agreement.

Three more lamp lights appeared as bright spots
ahead of me, coming from the rear of the church.
I could just make out the gravestones in their rows
extending across the cemetery toward me.

I didn't like the sacrilegious feel of riding a
horse through a graveyard, but we had much to accomplish before daybreak, and time ran short. I also
wanted Ford close at hand if I needed to make a
quick getaway.

Though where I'd get away to, I had no idea.

The rotting wooden crosses called to me as I
passed, voices of friends and family, acquaintances
and strangers, some pleading, some accusing, and I
shook myself hard in the saddle.

Don't lose it now, Cali. This will be hard enough
completely sane.

The three small lights broadened as I got closer
to reveal their holders: Sam, Arlene, and Al. Al had a
pouch in his hand containing what I assumed would
blow a hole in the back of the church closet.

"Where's Beth?" I asked while Arlene secured Ford to a tree and retrieved the climbing gear and backpacks from the saddle.

"On the porch of the post office, across from the church," Sam clarified, as if I didn't know every inch of Oblivion's main street, even in its rebuilt state. "Sorry," he added at the roll of my eyes. He cleared his throat and continued, "Beth's our lookout. I didn't want her inside in case things went bad, from one end or the other."

Right. Sam didn't want his daughter to go to jail if we got caught destroying public property, and he didn't want her dead if some Eye Killers happened to be waiting for us down those hidden stairs. I nodded my understanding. Al didn't know anything about the Eye Killers, and we hoped to keep it that way. To him, this was all a big publicity stunt.

"Pretty sure I found all the hidden cameras around the church and covered them, so we're safe to head in."

"Remember," I told them all while we still could speak without too much worry of being overheard, "if this goes wrong, use the show as your excuse. Don't try to make anyone believe in treasure—" I focused on Sam and Arlene. "—or anything else. No one will take you seriously." And I didn't want my friends labeled insane like I'd been and give Doc an excuse to target them.

They nodded, though Arlene's mouth compressed into a thin line and Sam looked like he was biting his lip to keep from arguing. Al turned and marched to the side of the church, and we fell into

step behind him, his military training moving to the
forefront as our mission got underway. Before we
could go far, Arlene pulled me into her arms, careful
not to clank the lanterns together. She'd passed Sam
the climbing gear and backpacks.

"Sorry I couldn't join you sooner," she said,
voice husky and low. This close, I could make out
a black eye forming and some other bruises on her
cheek. She grimaced at my sharp look. "Taz," Arlene
explained. "Got some boys to try to get me to take
them upstairs. Don't know how far it would have
gone, but I didn't take kindly to it."

"So I see." I touched the bruising with my fingertips. "I'm betting you won the fight."

"Damn straight." She kissed me quickly, and we
hurried after the others.

Up the church steps like that night so long ago.
From there, I caught a glimpse of Beth's shadow
across the street and raised a hand in greeting. The
shadow waved back. Pandora detached herself from
my shoulder and flew to join Beth. I nodded in approval. Her squawking would make a great additional warning alarm. Then the two of them melted into
the dark doorway of the post office.

We passed through the creaking door and used
our lamps to find our way across the main space to
the rear storage closet.

For several minutes, Al hemmed and hawed inside, removing sticky things from the pouch he carried
and placing them along the floor by the back wall's
bookcase. He pulled out a few more unrecognizable

items and turned to us. "Go find a place to hunker down. I'll be joining you in a second or two."

We followed his orders, Sam, Arlene, and I crouching low behind the pews about five rows from the pulpit and setting aside our lanterns. More time passed. "Everything all right in there?" Arlene called, exchanging a look with me.

Yeah, I felt it too, like Al was stalling us. I cast a furtive glace toward the front church entrance but saw no one.

"It's all good," Al called back. I heard a pop and a faint fizzing sound. Then Al came tearing out of the closet, raced toward us, and dove, headfirst, over the pews to land in a heap beside me.

A blast of light, sound, and smoke poured from the open storage area, driving my hands to cover my ears. Even so, they rang and rang well after the debris settled and the dust cleared. Arlene reached over and shoved my head down lower, but I pushed her aside. No time to be overly cautious. I stood and grabbed my lamp.

"Come on!" I shouted, knowing they'd all be as deaf as I was. I picked my way over toppled seats and scattered Bibles to the closet with its door now hanging by one hinge, Arlene and Sam on my heels.

We extended our lights to peer into the small space. A dark hole in the floor gaped open in front of where the shelves had been. Leaning farther, we could make out debris-choked stairs, spare prayer books, shelf pieces, and rocks scattered across each step. But the way was clear enough, for the first time in a hundred and twenty-five years. Arlene and

I grabbed handfuls of books, candles, some torn robes, and tossed them over our shoulders to land at Sam's feet. I'm sure he would have helped, too, but the closet wasn't large, and his hands were full of climbing gear waiting to be used.

I shifted my way forward, pushing aside some fallen candleholders with my boot.

"Holy shit," a voice breathed behind us. "You were telling the truth. It's really there."

Al. And where had he been while we'd dug through the piles of stored religious articles? I guess a few relics weren't payment enough to dirty his hands more than he had to.

"Shit, shit, shit," he muttered. "Is the treasure there too? And the antique weapons? You weren't shitting me?"

"She wasn't lying," Arlene snarled. "She has a job to do."

"Too bad she won't be able to do it."

We all turned at the sound of the new voice. Doc's voice, melodramatic as usual.

Doc and Jake stood blocking the doorway. My thoughts flitted to Beth and Pandora. What had happened to them?

No time to worry about them now. My hand dropped to my holster, but Al's got there first. He took the pistol and tossed it to the wood floor, then kicked it away with his boot. "Lady, it's that damn gun made me think you really were wacko like the doc here said. All those years in the service, you think I can't tell a real weapon from a fake one?

Now, real stairs or no real stairs, I think you'd better come along quietly."

"Where's my daughter?" Sam asked. He threw the climbing gear to land on the floor with a series of loud clangs and thunks.

"Don't worry," Jake said, twirling a set of keys on his fingers. "She's safe. Got her locked up for aiding and abetting, though. Won't look good on her culinary school application."

"You'll never make that stick. Not with the reality show to use as an excuse. You're out of your jurisdiction, anyway." Sam had his hands raised high in the air.

"Sam, that's a paint-shooter Jake's holding," I whispered to him.

He flushed red and put his hands down.

Jake shrugged. "Maybe. Maybe not. I'm pretty sure Taz intends to press charges with the local authorities for all this damage." He glared at Al. "You weren't supposed to really blow anything up, you know, but it's more for us to put on the arrest form. Taz is watching right now, filming everything, for the show and evidence."

Al grinned. "Taz said I could if I had to, and I'm sure he's editing out our conversation right now, so don't think for one minute you're putting me on that arrest warrant. You were late. Besides, with her really armed, I can always claim she threatened me into doing it."

"And here I thought you'd decided I wasn't so bad," I said, making one last attempt to win over my fellow lawman.

"You've crossed the line, Sheriff. I don't know what kind of mental breakdown you've had, but it's not safe for me to let you run around loose. If it hadn't been for Al, we'd never have known just how far around the bend you'd gone."

Arlene turned on the traitor. "You bastard. You had us sold out from the beginning." She dove at Al, surprise on her side, and the two hit the floor, rolling over broken glass and shredded prayer books. Arlene came out on top, slamming her fist into Al's face, but he drew in both legs, kicked her off him, and pinned her arms behind her back.

Al hauled her to her feet. Panting heavily, she fixed me with a quick look. "Go, Cali." Then she stomped on Al's instep, forcing him to release her, turned, and drove her knee into his groin. He staggered backward, taking down more rows of seats with a resounding crash that bounced off the high church ceiling.

I bolted for the closet even as Doc shouted for me to stop, and made it three steps down the debris-choked stairs before the click of a gun cocking brought me up short.

Real or paint-shooter? I had no idea, but I couldn't take the chance. If I got shot here, everything was lost. I turned slowly, the lamp I still clutched illuminating Al and the very real gun he'd taken from me, his other hand holding his privates. Behind him I made out a struggling Arlene held back by Jake and Doc together.

So close. So goddamn close. Son of a fucking bitch.

CHAPTER 35

THEY SEPARATED us at the church and hauled me to my room above the jail again, past the cells where the kids and now Beth pressed themselves against the bars to watch us pass.

I exchanged a glance with Beth, taking a tiny bit of heart from the grim defiance I saw there, but what could she do? What could any of us do now?

Once in my tiny living quarters, they bound my wrists together in front with my own handcuffs and threw me on my bed. As the hours passed, I pleaded desperately with whomever stood close by: Doc, Jake, then later Taz and Danielle. I tried everything, even the truth. They'd looked at me with mixtures of distaste and pity, mostly distaste from Doc and Taz, pity from the others. But no one believed me, and when I got violent, Taz secured my ankles to the bedposts, leaving me with my legs spread wide in a most uncomfortable and vulnerable position. The ropes made sense, though. I'd never had more than one set of handcuffs. Wonderful.

Eventually they left me alone, and I slept, throat raw and body exhausted.

The growling of my stomach roused me. Hunger—one more annoyance.

My captors had left the window open. Sunlight streamed through, and the slight breeze carried the sounds of typical Oblivion morning activity—wagons, horses, the metal awning pinging in the sun's heat, people stopping on the street to chat about the weather or exchange the latest gossip. With so many folks up and about, the hour had to be pretty late. It was Thursday. *Harsh Reality* was still filming.

And I'd failed.

Tears welled up in my eyes, and I fought the urge to let them spill. Not now. Not until they carted me to some psychiatric facility or put my cold body in the ground.

Knowing I couldn't break metal, I tested the ropes on my ankles instead. Whoever had tied them knew what he or she was doing but hadn't thought things entirely through. I couldn't pull free of the bonds, but I pressed my cuffed hands together against the mattress on one side of my body and managed to shove myself into a seated position. Using both hands, I grabbed one ankle at a time and, working each one upward, slipped the looped ropes over the tops of the foot-high bedposts, freeing my feet.

So, I could stand. Now what?

I took stock. Fully clothed, good. Empty holster, bad. Hat on the chair by my dressing table. I put it on.

I walked to the door of my room, grateful the motion caused nothing to blur or spin. Testing the knob, I found it locked from the outside. And while I had an open window, I didn't think I could make the jump safely while my hands remained cuffed.

I had sunk onto the mattress to ponder possible solutions when I heard a key in the lock. I grabbed a white vase from the nightstand that I would never have actually owned and held it between my palms, crept to hide behind the opening door, and raised the pottery high above my head.

"What the hell?"

"Where'd she go?"

"You sure they put her up here?"

I knew those voices. The Davidson trio of teens I'd locked in the downstairs cells. Clearing my throat so as not to startle them too badly, I stepped into view and handed off the vase to the girl, Katherine.

She grinned as she placed it on the table. "Should've known they couldn't hold you, Sheriff."

"They were doing a pretty good job of it, actually," I admitted. "You the cavalry come to my rescue?"

All three beamed with pride. "That's us," Alex proclaimed, pointing a thumb at his chest.

I remembered Beth had also been jailed. "Wasn't there another young lady with you?"

"Yep," Patrick replied. "She told us she had to go find her dad, but she said we could handle getting you out."

Ah, the confidence of youth. I held out my wrists. "I don't suppose…?"

"Oh, sorry, right." Katherine blushed and pulled my spare keys off her belt to unlock the handcuffs. I hooked them on my belt where they belonged. "You wouldn't have believed it, Sheriff," she chattered as we all filed downstairs. "First they locked Beth in with me. Then the bird showed up."

"Pandora?" I'd wondered what happened to her.

"Yep," Patrick said, picking up the tale. "She picked the freakin' lock! With her beak! That's one—"

"—smart bird," I finished for him. "Yeah, I know."

"Anyway," Alex jumped in, "the girls let us out with the extra set of keys you kept on that wall peg. Then Beth told us what happened and took off with Pandora, and we came after you. You're really lucky, you know. Doc used that Al guy's cell phone to call for some people from the Los Alamos mental hospital to come pick you up, but it was so early, they couldn't get out here right away."

I snorted. Yeah. Lucky. That's me.

We'd reached the office, which stood empty, thank God. After the night I'd had, I didn't think I was up to a fight just yet. I went straight to my desk, retrieved the spare knife Malek had sold me, and slipped it into my boot.

"So, now what?" Katherine asked, looking from me to the boys.

Any trace of earlier fear from their encounter with the Eye Killers had vanished. She'd wanted to become a sheriff, or go into some kind of law enforcement, and now I could see her itching to join the action.

There was no way I was taking these young folks into an even more dangerous situation than they were already in.

"Sorry, gang," I said, spreading my hands in apology. "Where I'm headed, there's likely to be zombies. Lots of them. Some of them folks you know."

That had the instant effect of dampening their enthusiasm. "More people have disappeared," Alex said. "At least ten more. Cast, crew, and extras. No one knows where they've gone or what's happened to them, but we know. Don't we?"

I nodded. "Afraid so. Look, I'd like to put you back in the cells, where you'll be a little safer. The zombies can't attack you physically from outside the bars, and so long as you don't look at them, they can't stare you to death, either."

"They can kill by looking at you?" Alex asked, eyes wide.

Patrick's mouth dropped open.

Katherine didn't care about my revelation. "No, no way." She shook her head. "Look, I'm not ready to go up against the walking dead, but I want to be free to run if I need to or fight if I haven't got a choice. You can let us have that much, can't you?"

I studied her face: young, determined, a little scared. The boys were working hard to match her. Kids might have grown up faster in my time, but these three had aged a lot over the past couple of days. "I'll leave you loose," I agreed, heading for the door, "but stay inside, lock up after me, and keep a lookout from upstairs. If things start to go bad, make a run for the stables and get out of here. You can all ride, can't you?" I knew Katherine could, from the barrel-racing competition, but I wasn't sure about the boys.

Three heads nodded.

"Good. And good luck. You all made a great cavalry." I closed the door, waiting beside it until I heard the lock snick and pausing on the front porch until an unfamiliar feeling passed. When I identified it, I almost laughed at the irony. It was the first time in my life I'd ever thought I might enjoy children of my own.

Great time for parental instinct to kick in, right before I charged to my death or got jumped to some other place a hundred years from now in one direction or the other.

Keeping to shadowed doorways, I set off searching for the rest of my Eye Killer fighting team, one particular showgirl's face at the forefront of my thoughts.

Settling down sounded pretty good to me right now.

CHAPTER 36

WITH THE jail full, Jake and Doc would have had to put Arlene and Sam somewhere else. The next most logical place was the hotel, so that's where I went.

The few people I passed stared at me but said nothing. Some even nodded greetings, so I guessed my status as a mental patient hadn't gotten around and they were just surprised to see me back. In general, the streets stood emptier than I'd seen them all week, and I hated to think where all the residents had gotten to.

The hotel turned out to be a good bet, and I spotted Jake in a rocking chair outside the front doors, though he couldn't see me from my position in front of the general store. He sat alone, his only company the occasional flirting townswoman. I didn't see Doc anywhere, or Taz for that matter.

Well all right, then. The time for professional courtesy had ended, and this showdown had been a long time coming.

I turned and slipped into the general store.

All my morals screamed at me when I pulled the knife from my boot, crossed the otherwise empty shop, and shoved it in Malek's face, where he stood behind the counter.

The small man froze, hands hovering over a package of dried beans he'd been tying up with twine. He stared at the shining blade, then my face, then the blade, and his Adam's apple bobbed as he swallowed hard. "Um, Sheriff, what are you doing?"

"I'm robbing your store," I said, matter-of-factly. "Actually," I amended, "I'm taking back property that belongs to me, my S&W. I left it in exchange for a horse, but since you've no doubt reclaimed the horse…?"

He nodded, and a wave of relief passed through me. I'd worried that poor Ford still stood tied behind the church, hungry and neglected. I'd miss that animal, sweet and gentle as he was, but I needed the gun more.

"I'd really rather not hurt you, but I'm crazy, you know. Unpredictable. So, if you'll open the safe, I'll take my pistol and be going."

Malek obliged by heading for the back room, with me skirting the counter to follow him. "You know they're coming for you, right? The doctors? They'll be here any minute. They're not playing anymore. And all this is on camera."

"Yep, just a little more great reality TV." I knew better than to harm Malek or admit I was doing anything other than acting, even if he claimed the others had stopped. If I failed against the Eye Killers but somehow survived the encounter, I'd use the show

as an excuse for my behavior. Just playing my role
to the hilt. History said I'd gone insane. Who was I
to argue with history?

Besides, I liked the man. And hurting innocent
people went against everything I'd sworn when I
took my oath as sheriff.

With the cameras filming, I didn't have much
time. Sooner or later Taz or Danielle would notice
what I was up to on their little glowing boxes and
send someone to alert Jake at the hotel. I gave Malek
a gentle shove to hurry him up. He knelt before the
safe.

Malek tried to stall, fumbling the dial and claiming he had to start over. I could feel them coming.
The hairs were standing up on the back of my neck.
When the rear door to the storeroom creaked open, I
felt no surprise.

Without looking to see who'd arrived, I held the
knife closer to the prop manager's neck and tried to
ignore his squeak of fear.

"Stay where you are," I told Malek's rescuer. "I
just want what's mine."

"Malek," came a woman's voice, "quit messing
around and give it to her."

We both turned toward the door in shock, and
I had to yank the blade away to avoid accidentally
cutting into Malek's flesh.

Danielle, the assistant director, stood just inside
the storeroom, her normally impeccable business-
like clothing torn and dirty, her face bruised, and her
hands scraped and bleeding. Sticks and brambles
stuck out of her matted hair, and she'd lost one of

her high-heeled shoes. The redness in her eyes and tear stains on her cheeks completed the tormented picture.

"Dani!" Malek said. He attempted to stand, but I pressed him down with a hand on his shoulder. He glared up at me, then focused on her. "What happened to you?"

I figured it out before she could speak again and pulled back, dropping my knife hand to my side. "I'd like to hear the answer to that too. But I think I already know. And I don't have much time."

Malek scrambled away on all fours, searching for an escape route, but I stood between him and the exit to the public area of the store, and Danielle had the rear door covered.

She nodded at me, seating herself on a crate of canned goods. "Don't worry. There aren't any cameras back here. Too many anachronisms." She gestured at the modern safe. "And Taz and Ryan were in Doc's office when I went by. No one's watching the monitors right now. No one knows you're here." She turned to Malek. "Cali never intended to hurt you," Danielle told him. "But she needs a gun. A real gun. Dear God, I wish I had an Uzi." She closed her eyes and took a shuddering breath, then opened them again. "Make that two Uzis."

I found a stool and sat down. Malek stayed on the floor.

"This morning, after we tied you to the bed..." She winced. "I'm so sorry about that. If I'd known...."

I waved my hand dismissively. "Forget it. If I'd been you, I wouldn't have believed me." That earned me a small but grateful smile.

"Anyway, I didn't want to be alone. What you said was pretty frightening, even though I thought it was all crazy ramblings. You seemed so certain, and it freaked me out. I went to find Lucinda."

"Ah. Damn." I closed my eyes and sighed. I'd wondered who it would be. Now I knew. Poor woman.

"We knew about your tent by the lake and figured it would be empty, so we hiked out there for some privacy. Not long after we got inside, we heard the security guard moaning, or groaning, or, well, something. We thought it was weird since his shift ended hours earlier, and Lucinda said she'd go check and make sure he hadn't hurt himself."

Danielle trembled where she sat, and I stood and fetched some empty flour sacks to drape around her shoulders.

"Thanks." She pulled them tight across her torn blouse. Flour remnants spotted her dark clothing, but she was clearly beyond caring about anything that trivial. "A long time passed, maybe a half hour, maybe more. Then she came back into the tent."

At this point, reality sank in, and the tears outweighed her restraint, flowing down her cheeks and tracing the same paths they'd previously taken.

"I really liked her. I did." Danielle choked with emotion, and it took several deep breaths for her to continue. "We'd exchanged contact information. I invited her out to LA. But she…."

"She was dead," I supplied, hating myself for rushing her but feeling the weight of time pressing me to move faster.

"Wait, what?" Malek stared at Danielle as if she'd grown a second head.

The assistant director glared at him. "How else would you describe it? Blue lips, pale skin, split skull, blood pouring everywhere. I couldn't bear to look her in the eyes."

"And a good thing too," I told her.

Her head jerked up and she stared at me. "God, you're right. That would have done it, wouldn't it? She would have killed me too." She inhaled, the air shuddering through her. "She tried, tried to make me look at her. She grabbed me and threw me down. She pulled my hair, my clothes. They tore." Danielle held up her arm, missing half a sleeve. "That's how I got away. Thank goodness for designer knockoffs." Her sarcastic laugh sounded borderline hysterical. "I ran here, saw you sneaking around, and followed you."

"This is some kind of joke," Malek said.

Danielle's voice lost all trace of humor. "Give her the damn gun."

"Taz will fire me!"

"I'll take the fucking responsibility. Think of it as a stunt if that's what you've got to do to convince yourself, but give her the fucking gun."

Faced with two indomitable women, Malek accepted his defeat. He quit his fumbling with the combination lock and opened it with three quick turns of the dial. From inside the steel safe, he produced my pistol and the spare bullets I'd handed over to him what seemed like weeks but had only been days ago. Once in his hands, though, he hesitated again.

"You use this to kill someone, I'm an accomplice."

Before I could react, Danielle came at me, reached, and swiped the blade from my hand. She had it under Malek's chin in a heartbeat. "Give. Her. The fucking. Gun."

Malek handed me the gun and bullets.

"What's your plan?" she asked, holding Malek in place.

"To get Arlene and Sam out of the hotel. I'm assuming that's where they are?"

Danielle nodded.

"Then I need to find our climbing gear. I think I have a way to stop all this, but I've got to get into the church." And God help me if they'd found and moved the treasure, if they'd decided to believe that little part of my "crazy" story.

"Whatever you need from me, you've got." She passed me my knife, and I put it in my boot. Her hand caught my arm. "I'm not sure I buy that you're the real Cali McCade, like you were saying this morning, but then, with real Eye Killers, who the hell knows? Regardless, you're our best chance. Jake might be a cop, but he doesn't *know* and he won't *believe*. It has to be you."

It had to be me. Whether I wanted it or not. Whether I believed in myself or not. It had to be me. From the moment Pandora bit into my flesh, it had to be me. No. Longer than that. From the moment I accepted the sheriff's star, my choice sealed my fate.

"Stay here," I told them both. "Don't involve yourselves more than you have to. You've got to live in this world after whatever happens, happens. Find a place to hide. Sooner or later, the Eye Killers are going to show up en masse. I'm surprised they haven't already. If I'm successful, they should stop." Actually, I had no idea how my success in replacing the treasure would affect the Elementals. Would it be immediate? Would they take a few more lives first? I could only do my job as I saw it and hope for the best.

I left them there, believer and nonbeliever, and used the rear exit to wind up behind the general store. Empty barrels and crates littered the property, with some sparse trees and scrub and the desert stretching out beyond. In my time, there'd have been cigarette butts and a collection of empty bottles waiting to be returned for the deposit money. A lot of the older men had liked to hang out in the back, smoking and drinking sarsaparilla.

I used the brief walk around the building to check that the pistol was loaded. Still was. And I put the remaining bullets in my vest pocket.

At the corner, I caught myself. This couldn't happen. Pa always taught me never to draw a gun I wasn't willing to use. Jake was a bastard and a fool, but he thought he was protecting people from a crazy woman, whether he liked me or not. There had to be another way.

But I couldn't think of one.

One moral stain to wipe out a mess of evil? Was stopping the Eye Killers worth my soul?

I holstered the S&W. Maybe some smooth talking could get him to let the guys out of the hotel. The gun would be my last resort. I turned the corner.

Jake had left his chair on the hotel porch. It rocked, empty, in the breeze, or in the wake of a recent occupant. I searched doorways and the small spaces alongside buildings where he might hide himself.

I needn't have looked so hard.

CHAPTER 37

JAKE STOOD a few businesses down, in the center of the street between the stables and the telegraph office. He had his feet braced apart, and his hand twitched above the grip of his pistol like some sharp-shooting gunslinger. One last try for fame. One last attempt to snag that acting job he'd told me he wanted. I wasn't the only crazy one around here. This whole damn town had been nuts since the moment I came back.

"You lookin' for me, Sheriff?" he called, taunting, sneering.

Somewhere inside the hotel I heard a crash like a door shattering and footsteps pounding down wood stairs. A moment later, Arlene and Sam appeared in the doorway. They must have been watching from the windows, waiting for an opportunity, a moment when Jake was drawn away from the front doors. I motioned for them to stay put.

"This isn't a paint-shooter," I informed Jake and nodded at the gun hanging at my side.

The other police officer hesitated, a flicker of uncertainty he quickly overcame. "Neither is mine."

Well, damn. Now I knew what had become of the gun Sam had given me. The one Al had held when he stopped me from getting to the chamber beneath the church. It figured that the lawman would confiscate it.

"You're going to point a weapon at a fellow officer?" I eased my way to the center of the street, facing off with him. Jake wanted a showdown, I'd give him one. Talking time had passed. But I didn't want to kill him. I didn't think I could.

Jake watched me move, focused on my hand more than the rest of my body. "I'm bringing in a fugitive. *You're* the one threatening a policeman with a loaded gun."

Movement in my peripheral vision drew my attention from him for a second, and I saw townsfolk gathering along the boardwalk. Just another theatrical performance for them. Taz stood in their midst, doing nothing to stop this farce. In fact, he was grinning, the bastard.

This had to violate every rule in Jake's book, but if he succeeded in bringing me in, especially alive and unharmed, he'd be a fucking hero. Goodbye police work. He'd have his choice of theater parts.

"I made a few calls, pulled a few strings, got a look at your job performance record," Jake said. "Your accuracy with firearms is barely above the minimal department requirements."

Well, that explained the risk he was willing to take. Sandra Meadows couldn't shoot.

I wasn't Sandra Meadows.

And I was done pretending to be.

From the age of eight on, hours upon hours of practice in the backyard, with shotguns, with pistols. Shattering bottles. Knocking down cans. Setting them up again. Better, better. Moving targets. Hit 'em in the air. Riddle 'em with holes.

Can't I go inside to paint? To draw?

You can draw your damn pistol. This is dangerous territory. A young woman should know how to protect herself. And when you're faster than me, better than me, then you can stop.

Then years later, hours upon hours of practice behind the sheriff's office, from the age of twenty-five on, aiming at the knothole, firing box after box of ammunition into that poor defenseless tree.

Jake's fingers twitched again. A trickle of sweat ran down my neck, tracing a chilled trail under my collar and across my breastbone.

He went for it a half second before I did.

Jake's bullet passed by my right ear so close I could hear the whistle it made. Had he gone for a head shot, or was his aim that far off? I didn't want to think about it too much.

My shot hit right where I'd aimed it, in his gun hand, ripping through flesh and shattering tiny bones.

Jake gave a shout of pain and surprise, his pistol flying off into the dirt street several feet from where he stood. He cupped his injured hand with his good one. Blood trickled from between his fingers.

"One," I whispered. And, "Thanks, Pa."

When the initial shock wore off, Jake scanned for the weapon.

I shot at it a second time, sending it skittering all the way to the side of the road. It came to rest against the edge of the boardwalk, where Arlene picked it up. The two of us met in the center of the street with Sam trailing behind.

"Two."

Some of the onlookers applauded. Many just stared.

"Um, now what?" Arlene muttered under her breath when she got close enough for me to hear.

"Now we finish what we started this morning." I raised my voice. "And anyone who tries to stop us is going to find himself with a leg wound."

Taz and the doc, who'd joined him at some point, took a couple of steps backward into the crowd, putting several other bodies between us and them.

I nodded at the gun in Arlene's hands. "You any good with one of those?" I didn't want innocents winding up dead, and I couldn't judge by her paint shots outside Sam's place. She hadn't really been trying then.

"I live in Las Vegas. Of course I'm good with it. Lessons and everything."

I blinked at her.

She shook her head. "Keep forgetting who you are and when you're from. Las Vegas. Half the population carries concealed weapons. I have a permit for small firearms and a nine-millimeter Glock at home."

I assumed that was a pistol. Fair enough. We formed a triangle, Arlene, Sam, and I, and hurried to the church at the end of the street. As soon as we stepped through the front doors, we ran right into Beth, Pandora, and of all people, Robbie from Paradise Found ranch.

"Where have you been?" Sam asked, embracing his daughter.

"Right here. When I saw Deputy Baylor outside the hotel, I figured I'd leave him to Cali and come guard the climbing equipment. Everything's untangled and ready to go. Then I spotted Robbie sneaking into town and I snagged her to help."

Robbie shrugged. "Thought you might need some additional assistance. Here." She passed a small black rectangular thing with a long thin rod sticking out of the top over to Arlene and pointed to a second one clipped to her belt. "I've got some friends from the ranch ready to stir up a ruckus outside the mine entrance. When you're about ready to do your thing at the pit, give me a holler and we'll try to draw any Eye Killers out of the mine."

Arlene nodded and attached the communication device to her own belt.

"Say, no offense, but I didn't think you had a lot of friends who believed you," I commented.

Robbie smiled. "Some old-timers whose grandparents talked about Robert all the time and treat anything they wrote in their journals as gospel. Some upper teens who grab on to any excuse to be weird or different from the norm. Enough to get the job done."

Worked for me.

I turned back to Beth. "Anyone else come by?" I didn't know how many people Al had told about my treasure claims.

"Not while I've been here, but that hasn't been too long. When they were leading me to the jail, Taz mentioned something about wanting to investigate the hidden basement, but Al convinced him it would all be too unstable and dangerous and he should wait for professionals," Beth said. "Al didn't mention the treasure, either, and I can't believe the 'unstable' excuse would have kept Taz out if he knew about it."

So, just in case I wasn't completely crazy, Al had kept the possibility of riches to himself. Good. I wondered what insane reason he *had* given Taz for me wanting to blow a hole in the church closet's floor. Historical exploration, I supposed. Something that might interest the TV audience and get me back on the show.

"Taz also told everyone to keep the discovery hush-hush so he could reveal the hidden room on TV," she finished, confirming my suspicions. "You know, like Al Capone's vault."

"Al's last name is Capone?" I asked. "And he has a vault?"

Beth laughed. "Never mind."

"Repent! Repent!"

We jumped at the booming voice behind us, and Preacher Xanthis found himself with two guns in his face.

"Cali, my child, give yourself up. Let the good doctor take care of you. You're sick."

I didn't like him now any more than I'd liked his counterpart one hundred and twenty-five years ago.

Arlene looked at me. "Can we just shoot him?"

The preacher seemed genuinely frightened, but whether it was because he didn't want to be paint-splattered and kicked off the show on this last day or because he recognized real guns when he saw them up close, I didn't know.

I sent my gaze heavenward. "Sam, Robbie, get him out of here," I said. Sam took one arm and Robbie got the other, and they muscled the preacher outside. "You go too," I told Beth. "You've done everything you can. No sense risking more, and the longer you can stall everyone here from coming after us, the better."

Pandora launched herself from the girl's shoulder and landed on mine, and Beth nodded, taking off after her father.

Arlene and I holstered our guns and hefted the pile of climbing gear and the two backpacks still lying in a pile by all the debris and the blasted-out closet. The lamps were gone or shattered, but we grabbed candles and lit them.

"You ready for this?" I asked.

Arlene leaned over and kissed me, hard and hungry. Pandora nuzzled us both, cooing softly, and we broke apart, laughing.

Together, we squeezed into the tight space of the storage room and picked our way over the rubble down the ancient staircase.

CHAPTER 38

WE FUMBLED our way down, candlelight flickering off the rough-hewn walls. Despite rocks and debris tripping me twice, the path looked too clear, and I worried Al hadn't heeded his own advice to wait for help with the unstable staircase.

If the treasure was gone, what the hell would I do?

The tunnel grew brighter the farther we descended, and I paused, then blew out my candle. Arlene did the same. With the smoke remnants wafting around us, we could still see the stairs ahead.

"Lanterns in the basement," I whispered in explanation. I made out the rising of her eyebrows and shrugged. We had company. We just didn't know who, though I had a pretty good idea.

Pandora took off ahead, and for a terrible minute we heard nothing. Then she squawked. It didn't sound panicked, but I wasn't taking any chances.

We placed our unnecessary candles in our pockets and drew our guns, trying to step without making noise but crunching small pebbles beneath our boots. At the bottom, the room opened up as I remembered, and I scanned the larger space but found no one except my feathered friend perched on top of the wardrobe. The treasure chest stood open, but I couldn't recall if I'd left it that way or not. The collapsed weapons cabinet still had blades and guns scattered all around it.

Yet a living human being had lit every unbroken lamp still attached to the walls with rusting clamps. The Eye Killers would have preferred to leave fire out of it.

I strode to the chest, expecting an empty box but finding the gold coins and jewels instead. At my side, Arlene whistled low and long. "Nice haul."

"Don't get attached to it." I slung my backpack off and stuffed the booty in by the handful while Arlene followed suit. When both would barely close and the chest stood empty, we put the packs on and proceeded to check out the weapons.

This close, I spotted several gaps where items had lain but were now missing.

When I lifted my boot, it clung to the stone floor, and my next steps tracked half-dried blood in nasty reddish-brown footprints.

"Everyone who knows about this place is accounted for except—"

Pandora screeched a second before a moan echoed from the dark tunnel leading into the mine. To my relief, she fluttered to the farthest corner. Guess she wasn't taking on any more Eye Killers, which was fine by me. I didn't want to risk her now.

Shambling steps brought Al into the basement, or what remained of him. A blade had taken off the

left side of his face, and the skin hung in a nice even
dangling flap below the white of his visible jawbone.
Blood soaked his shirt on that side, and his left eye
seemed bigger than the other without a cheek to
balance it. I looked quickly away before our gazes
locked.

"Avoid meeting the eyes," I reminded Arlene.

"Yeah, learned that lesson the hard way."

Al bore other wounds as well: a dislocated shoulder, a slice across the belly that had some intestines
hanging between the buttons of his shirt. Traitor or
not, I wouldn't have wished the gruesome death and
possessed afterlife on anyone.

Well, maybe Taz. But I didn't need another zombie to fight, so I made no secret wishes.

Arlene brought her gun up, but I pressed her arm
down to her side. "Let me do it. You don't need this
on your conscience, even if he is already dead, and
I've got plenty there to keep him company."

The Eye Killer advanced two more paces, and
I raised my pistol and eyes and fired fast. The shot
took him in the center of the forehead. The body fell,
and gemstones trickled from his pants pockets when
he hit the floor.

"Three." And time to reload. While Arlene
scooped up the glittering pretties, I added three bullets to my S&W. Experience had taught me where
one Eye Killer roamed, more would follow. Something had done all that damage to Al.

We stepped over the mutilated corpse and relit the candles, then entered the dark tunnel, where

we found a scattering of antique weapons and more blood on them and the floor.

"He must have been jumped here, trying to get away. Didn't want to take the treasure through town and figured this tunnel went somewhere useful." Arlene kicked at a shining sword, the hilt carved with ornate triangles and swirls.

"Big mistake. Let's go."

"We're making the same mistake, you know."

I paused, turning to face her. It wasn't easy with climbing gear over my shoulder, a stuffed pack on my back, and my hands holding a pistol and a candle, but I managed. "You don't have to do this," I said. "I don't want to lose you again."

"I don't want to lose you, either."

I could tell she wanted me to hold her, but we were both carrying too much. Instead we nodded in solemn agreement.

Pandora flew behind us as we pushed onward, passing the tunnels that branched off left and right and taking the straight shot toward the mine entrance.

We encountered no one else before I judged us to be almost at the pit. "Can you contact Robbie?" I asked, tilting my head toward the thing on Arlene's belt. "This would be a good time to start that diversion."

She passed me the second candle so that I clutched both in one hand and activated the black rectangle. A burst of screeching and noise erupted from it, so loud I felt certain a horde of zombies would descend upon us at any moment. Arlene fiddled with the knobs and dials and the horrible sound decreased.

"Damn, I'm not sure I can reach her from in here." She turned a dial with numbers on it, pausing at each one in succession, depressing a button on the side and speaking into the box. "Anyone there? Anyone copy?"

Copy what? I wondered.

When I thought she might throw the thing against the stone, a thin voice forced its way through the background noise. It sounded like Robbie. I hoped it was.

"…hear you… stirring up some trouble… now…."

"Best we can do," Arlene said, shutting it off. She took two steps forward and gave a shout as her right foot slipped out from beneath her.

"Woah, there." I dropped the candles, mentally cursing when they both went out, and grabbed for her blindly. I caught her shirt, and we both hit the tunnel floor and slid. Pandora screeched, and I felt her wings pass my face, but I could see nothing. Scrambling, I dug in with my boot heels, knowing if more than half Arlene's body weight went over the pit edge, we'd be lost. I tossed my pistol behind me, hearing it clatter to safety, and got a second handhold on her. The metal fasteners of the climbing gear clanked and rattled against the rock as we moved.

We stopped. Our harsh breathing echoed in the darkness.

"Shit," Arlene breathed. "Shit."

"Back up. Slowly," I added. "It's a long way down."

Together we shifted backward, dragging ourselves and our gear away from the jagged rim. My palm fell on one of the candles, and I snatched it up and lit it with a match from my pocket. Well, I tried to light it. My hand shook so badly I couldn't hold the flame to the wick. Arlene wrapped her free hand around mine and held it steady until the fire caught.

"I still have my gun," she said. "Lot of good it would have done me if we'd fallen."

Together we located my own pistol, and Pandora brought me the second candle in her beak.

"Wish Beth had packed us some flashlights. This candle stuff is ridiculous." Arlene took the equipment from my shoulder and set about attaching the ropes to some boulders and old timbers at the top of the pit. Meanwhile, I held both candles so she could see what she was doing.

"Who knows how fast she had to get everything together and who was watching? She probably didn't have a lot of time to plan or access to everything she thought we might need."

When Arlene had thoroughly tested the ropes, she helped me slip into my harness and tightened the straps over my body, letting her hands linger around my waist and hips.

"I can think of some fun things to do in these, when all this is over," she said, grinning, confirming one more thing this Arlene had in common with the original who'd enjoyed playing with, and in, my handcuffs.

I said nothing. The sudden lump in my throat prevented it. When all this was over, who knew where I'd be?

Instead, I nodded, ignoring her look of confused concern, and assisted her with her harness. I pointed out the wall of boulders separating this tunnel from the main cave of the mine and the place where I'd blocked the last hole in the wall after passing through.

"Hmm." Arlene skirted around the pit's rim, hugging the side of the cave to prevent another close call. She stopped before the most recent additions to the rock wall and leaned her weight on the stones, pushing hard with her shoulder until several fell outward with a loud crash into the space beyond. Light poured in, dim and hazy but much more than the tiny candle flames had provided.

Sound followed. I could make out shambling footsteps, dozens of them, though they seemed nowhere close by, and in the distance, screams and shouts and a few explosions. So the main entrance had filled with zombies, and Robbie's friends were keeping them busy for us. Another explosion shook the walls.

"Dynamite?" Arlene guessed.

I shrugged. Due to my phobia, I'd rarely visited the mine, and I'd never been present on blasting days. "If so, let's hope they're keeping it outside the main cavern. These tunnels aren't entirely stable. It would be a good way to lure the zombies away from us or kill a few."

With the extra light, we could see the pile of skeletons, Oblivion's original citizens, whom I'd discovered my first time through here. The ones who must have been uncovered in some rockslide after Sam closed off this section of the mine to tours. The ones who'd never been properly buried. Arlene knelt and examined them for a few moments. "Poor bastards." She glanced at me. "I'm guessing the Eye Killers guided their bodies down here?"

I nodded. "After me and Xanthis. When the preacher died and I went up in flames, they must have made it this far before deciding to abandon their hosts." Enough innocents had suffered. No more, dammit. I eyed the ropes and the black hole they disappeared into. "Let's get this over with."

Arlene studied everything, then took off her hat and lit the brim with the candle flame. I thought she'd lost her mind until she tossed the burning material into the pit. We leaned to watch it drop, fluttering and flickering as it went, and for a moment, I was certain it would go out. But it didn't, and at last it landed beside a bulky shadowy object at the bottom far below.

"Wonder what that is," Arlene mused. "I can't quite make it out."

I didn't answer. I knew exactly what it was. And I had no choice but to take Arlene down there with it. With her.

"Ah well, at least we have a landing site." She grabbed the ropes, attached her harness to one, and leaned back, slowly easing herself over the edge. I followed her lead, and soon we were side by side, hanging in space, feet pressed to the wall of the pit.

As we went down, I imagined the original gold miners, without the benefit of harnesses and metal clamps, hanging by nothing but ropes to lower themselves into the pit in their mad search for a rich vein of gold.

For gold, some folks would do anything.

Inch by inch, foot by foot, we descended, with Pandora keeping pace between us. The sounds of mayhem increased in volume above, but I couldn't tell if they were really getting closer or if the tunnels' acoustics played tricks with our hearing.

The ropes abraded the skin of our palms, and I wished for gloves Beth likely hadn't had time to pack for us. Thank goodness for calluses formed from years of riding, target practice, and other good, hard, honest work. I doubted Arlene would fare as well.

All Arlene's attention focused on the wall in front of us, but when we'd almost reached the bottom, I risked a glance back and down. Sandra Meadows's sightless eyes stared up at me. When I shoved her in, she'd fallen against the side of the pit, landing in a seated position with her head leaning against the wall. One arm had broken on impact, or maybe it had been already (I couldn't remember). It hung twisted from her shoulder with the bones protruding. Dark streams of clotted blood covered her cheek and matted her hair—hair pulled back like mine but in that horsetail style she apparently had preferred. At least she didn't smell too bad. It hadn't been that many days, and the cooler air of the caves had kept rot to a minimum so far.

I shivered, and when my boots hit bottom, my knees nearly buckled beneath me.

"Are you all right?" Arlene grabbed my arm and steadied me. Then she turned to see what had shaken me up. "Oh… Jesus." She looked from me to her and back again, then released me to bend and pick up a small card from the floor—one of the cards I'd taken from Sandra's pocket and tossed into the pit. She studied the photograph on it for a long moment before speaking again. "When you said—" Arlene paused to clear her throat. "When you said you'd taken over her life, I didn't really believe you meant literally. Did you—?"

"I didn't kill her. She was already dead. The Eye Killers did this."

"But you knew she was down here. You weren't surprised, just disgusted." It wasn't a question. She'd learned to read me too well.

I nodded, watching for her reaction. "I hid the body. I needed a reason to be here so I could fight them. She was a sheriff. I'd like to believe she would have wanted me to succeed."

Arlene considered that, and I watched the emotions play out on her face. I could read her, too, and they shifted from horror to acceptance to determination while I waited and the sounds of battle above us raged louder. Her mouth set in a thin line. "Let's do this, then."

The light from the still-burning hat showed us the "small cave" Sam had mentioned where the gold had been found. It looked naturally occurring, not man-made, as did the pit itself, and he hadn't been kidding about small. The opening looked barely large enough for Arlene or me to crawl into. We'd have to do it one at a time and take off our gear to even make an attempt.

I slipped off my backpack, then unfastened my harness and let it hang from the climbing ropes so I could maneuver more easily. Then I squatted and peered into the dark, narrow opening. "Sure hope there's nothing alive, or, um, sort of alive in there," I muttered, trying to pierce the darkness with my tired eyes and making no move to push my way in.

Some rattling behind me drew my attention to Arlene, giving me further excuse to stall. I looked back to see her harness had gotten caught on her pack and she struggled to disentangle herself from all the various straps. "I doubt it," she said while working a piece of her shirt out of the whole mess. "Eye Killers would have a hard time getting in there too. And there's nothing to attract them, like fresh meat."

"And thank you so much for that thought."

She grinned a little. "Happy to oblige. Look," she went on, yanking so hard she tore the shirt free, "you go on and make your... offering. By the time you're done, I should have my pack detached from this maze of ropes. Oh, and give me your hat."

I glanced at our makeshift fire. The flames had eaten through half of Arlene's headwear. I tossed mine next to it and watched until it caught. Damn, I'd kind of liked that hat. We had no trouble with the smoke, though. The updraft of the pit and the tunnels above acted as a natural chimney.

Arlene was right. We needed to get a move on. But I froze again, staring into that tiny crawlspace.

Pandora gave a quick squawk and dove into the darkness. I heard scrabbling and fluttering as her talons and wings moved about. She emerged, hearty and whole. All clear, then.

Now to decide how to do this.

I didn't want to give up carrying my pistol or a candle, and I found I could hold both in one hand if necessary, though I'd need to drop the light to fire the gun. I couldn't fit into the space while wearing my backpack, so I hooked the straps around an ankle to drag it behind me.

Then I crawled into the dark, narrow tunnel.

CHAPTER 39

THE TINY passage went straight for about thirty feet, so no twists or turns to navigate while dragging the heavy backpack, thank God. I held the candle up to the unusually smooth walls, as if this path had been made by running water eroding the stone away over centuries. Even with the smoothness, the crawling wore at the skin on my palm and bruised my knees through my dungarees, and I hit my head twice. I paused to rub at the forming lump, joining several others I'd earned in my struggles with the Eye Killers. My skull had taken a lot of abuse this past week.

A blood-curdling howl, similar to others I'd heard coming from the mine in the past and the present, carried to me from up ahead, and I stopped, shivering until the sound ceased.

"Cali?" Arlene called.

"No idea," I answered her unspoken question. Pandora had proclaimed the little tunnel to be Eye Killer free. I had to trust her assessment.

I guess that explained why the miners had never widened the passage, gold or not. If they'd heard the same strange and horrible howls, they might have thought better of this particular digging spot.

At last the tunnel opened up into a slightly larger space where I could pull my feet in front of me and sit up straight, though not stand. Dead end, so this had to be the spot where the first miners had struck gold. And no sign of what had made the noise. Not that I was complaining.

My instinct told me to dump the backpack and get the hell out of there, but I remembered the reverent way Robbie had placed her offerings in a neat circular pile, so I did the same. While shoving them into the backpack, I hadn't had a chance to take a look at Xanthis's collection, but as I set out each item, I marveled at the way the candlelight reflected off the gold coins with foreign writing on them, how it made the red, green, and blue gemstones sparkle, some of them almost as large as my fist. A small and somewhat surprising part of me itched to pocket just one, and I got a little taste of what gold fever must have felt like. If I remained in this time, I'd have no job, no resources. A single emerald this size would give me a nice start. Surely one wouldn't make any difference.

But I'd never been much for baubles or jewelry, and I wasn't taking chances now.

"Cali?" Arlene's voice echoed through the crawlspace. I jerked in response. "Can you hurry a little? Things sound like they're getting hot up top." Around me, the walls trembled from more distant explosions, small rocks and pebbles pelting me from above. No doubt about it, they were using dynamite up there. If this tunnel caved in….

"Coming!" I finished placing each treasure, every single one, and scurried out the way I'd come, as fast as my aching knees would allow.

When I got back to the pit bottom, Arlene was staring at her harness in disgust. "Broken," she said, kicking a piece that lay on the floor. "We're gonna have to share yours. But I got the pack free. Go on and head up while I dump the other half of the treasure in the tunnel. You can drop the harness down to me once you reach the top. I should be out here by then." She got on her knees, mimicking my trick of tying the pack to her foot and holding the candle and gun in one hand.

"You sure you don't want me to do the second run too?"

Arlene cocked an eyebrow at me in response. I thought about the howl and the oppressive closeness of the walls and shivered.

"Nah," she said gently. "I've got it." She squeezed her way into the space.

"Watch your head!" I called after her.

I heard a *thunk*. "Thanks for the warning."

Ah, sarcasm. One more thing this Arlene shared with the one of my time.

Pandora cackled from where she sat on Arlene's abandoned climbing gear. Beth's friends wouldn't like getting only half their equipment returned intact. Then again, they were probably outside with Robbie and who knew who else, trying to keep the Eye

Killers, Doc, Taz, and Jake off our backs, so they wouldn't be paying much attention to the state of their gear for a while. And that was assuming they survived.

The guilt of having strangers fight for me cut deep, but what choice did I have?

Another thunderous explosion sounded from above, shaking the stone beneath my feet and sending small pebbles cascading down the sides of the pit. In their zealous defense of us, I hoped our friends didn't collapse the entire mine on our heads. I heard some shouting, too, and gunfire, and knew they, whoever they were, were getting closer.

"Uh, hurry it up in there," I urged, tugging my harness on and fastening the clamps. I holstered my gun and extinguished and pocketed the candle, needing both hands for this effort. Grasping the main rope, I began walking up the side of the pit. Pandora chose to stay at the bottom and wait for Arlene.

About halfway up, I glanced down. Still no sign of her. Dang it, what was taking her so long?

I reached the top and disconnected myself, threw the harness down, and waited. I relit the candle from my pocket, the faint glow of the distant burning hat and the light coming through the gap in the rock wall not nearly enough to banish the shadows. The sounds grew closer, shuffling and moaning, the occasional scream—a voice I thought I recognized but couldn't be sure with all the echoing in the caverns. Then a beam of light, bouncing off the stone walls, shifting and moving everywhere at once as its bearer moved. I drew my gun.

"Cali! Sheriff McCade, you in there?" Beth's voice. Dammit, I'd told her to stay in town. But hearing her made my heart leap. If she was talking, she was breathing.

"Here!" I shouted.

A moment later, she tore into view, coming from one of the other side tunnels I'd never explored and never intended to. She must have found another mine entrance. And she wasn't alone. Even as she reached my side, three Eye Killers, including one of the fake Native Americans from the *Harsh Reality* crew, shambled into view. Makeup mixed with dried blood stained the victim's cheeks. His two companions bore a number of gaping, grievous wounds.

"Watch out!" I screamed, then fired a shot that went wild and ricocheted off the rock walls. "One," I grumbled. We both ducked as the bullet flew over our heads, finally embedding itself in the stone. "Arlene, we've got company!"

Beth pointed her light (must have been that "flashlight" thing Arlene had been wishing for earlier) first at the Eye Killers, then into the pit. I took a quick glance back and spotted Arlene coming out of the side tunnel, Pandora screeching at her. She saw me and waved, then stuck her thumb in the air. I had no idea what it meant, but her smile reassured me… a smile that vanished as one of the walking dead got close enough to grab Beth and haul her backward from the pit's edge. Beth's light went flying off to the side, landing with its beam pointing at the two of them grappling on the stone floor, the other Eye

Killers staggering about in an effort to get past them and attack me.

I scrambled for a clear shot, crawling on my knees, searching for an opening, but there was none. They rolled over and over, Beth locked in the Eye Killer's deadly gaze. In the brief instances I could make out her face, I recognized the wide-eyed panic of knowing she was suffocating and not being able to do a damn thing about it. Behind them, more shadows appeared, and the sound of many, many uneven footsteps.

"Cali, it's done! What's happening up there? You hear me? It's done!" Arlene shouted.

One clear shot. That's all I needed. Just one clear shot.

Yeah, and about a dozen more, considering what was coming. *One thing at a time*, I told myself.

And then I had it, an opening. I sighted the pistol, ignoring two more sets of grasping hands that had finally reached me… and that suddenly fell away.

Everything stopped. Just stopped.

The two closer Eye Killers dropped like run-down wind-up toys, crumpling slowly to the stone floor. Behind them, Beth and the dead actor ceased their rolling around, coming to a halt just shy of the pit's edge. With a grunt and a gasp, she shoved her way out from beneath him and crawled to my side. A series of dull thuds resounded from the side tunnel, and I could just make out the toppling shadows as the approaching horde fell where they'd stood.

Then, silence.

"Is… is it over?" Beth panted, gripping my shoulder with a trembling hand.

"I reckon," I said slowly, not quite believing it myself.

She laughed, an almost hysterical sound, but sobered fast. "Gotta get moving," she said. "The cops are coming. And the hospital guys Doc called. I let loose all the horses except mine so they couldn't follow me here, but the medical people brought a car, and they'll be driving up any minute. Since the zombies were all hellfired desperate to get in here and there was no way we could keep holding them back, Robbie has plans to blow the entrances. I snuck past them to warn you. We don't have a lot of time, and we've got to get you out and hidden somewhere."

"Arlene's still down below. She'll be up soon." I eyed her sideways. "Your pa let you come after us?" I wasn't buying that, not for one damn minute.

Her face broke into a sheepish grin. "He doesn't exactly know. We weren't doing too well. Dad broke an ankle, and Robbie got some bad cuts. I was the only one close by who could still run fast and knew the mine well enough from all those tours." Her smile faded as she glanced at the fallen mound of bodies. "Lots of dead folks from *Harsh Reality*. Some we didn't even realize were missing. And other people we don't recognize. Maybe tourists—campers and hikers. But I think that's all of them. They must have sensed you, somehow. Nothing was keeping them out."

"All right, then." I gave her a gentle shove. "You go on and get back to Sam before he worries himself sick about you. And try to stall Robbie as long as you're able. We'll be out as soon as Arlene gets up here."

Beth nodded and stood, passing me another flashlight she'd had hanging off her belt. I turned it over in my hands, found a button on the side, and pressed it, sending a bright beam of light across the tunnel. Excellent.

"Just hurry," she called, then turned and frowned. "If you don't get out before the cops arrive...."

Right. They'd have to blow the mine anyway or risk all the bodies being discovered and having a lot of fast talking to do. How could they possibly explain the time that had passed since these folks' deaths and how they'd all gotten here? Every single one of the people who'd helped me would wind up arrested.

"You tell Robbie to do what she has to do," I said. "Don't worry," I added when she opened her mouth to protest. "We'll be out of here in no time."

Beth nodded again, her lips forming a grim line, and headed off into the darkness. Her footsteps retreated until I couldn't hear them anymore.

I lay down on my stomach. Peering over the edge, I shone the light around, searching out Arlene. She'd finished strapping on my harness and readjusting the straps to fit her larger... chest. She grinned up at me and grabbed the climbing rope in both hands.

Behind her, something moved.

Pandora set up a series of screams to deafen us all as Sandra Meadows rose up and grabbed Arlene, wrapping both arms around her. Grievously wounded or not, Sandra managed to wrestle Arlene to the stone floor, and I winced at the sound of Arlene's head hitting rock.

"Arlene!" I aimed the pistol down, but with the distance, the dark, and their proximity to each other, I couldn't get a clear shot here, either. Besides, in such close quarters, and rock all around them, a miss might mean another ricochet. I didn't want to take a chance on making things worse.

"I thought it was over!" Arlene rolled with her attacker, then flipped herself so they ended up face-to-face, blood pouring down the side of Arlene's. For a second she froze, fixated on Sandra's unblinking gaze.

No, no, no.

Arlene reached out and pressed her palm over Sandra's eyes.

Damn, why hadn't I ever thought of that?

Even with one of Sandra's weapons disabled, Arlene still seemed to be at a disadvantage. Sandra clawed at her with her fingernails and drove a knee into her ribs. As an officer of the law, she would have known how to fight. The Elemental possessing her had learned to tap that knowledge and add its strength to hers.

If Arlene wanted to protect her body, she had to release Sandra's face. Arlene let go and swung her fist into Sandra's jaw, then staggered away. "What the hell?" She grabbed for the rope, but her hands slipped.

Pandora took the opportunity to dive in, raking the Eye Killer's cheeks with her talons, leaving long red streaks and flitting away before the zombie could grab at her.

I aimed the light at Sandra's eyes, blinding the Eye Killer as much as I could, though from my height and distance, I couldn't keep it focused for long without losing her.

Dammit, I hated being helpless. With my harness on Arlene below, I had no way of getting to them. I thought about free climbing it down the guide rope, but my arm muscles burned from the previous day's practice and today's exertions. Falling on top of Arlene and breaking my neck in the process wouldn't do either of us any good. All I could do was watch. And pray.

Sandra shambled at Arlene from behind, slamming her into the pit wall. I swore I could hear Sandra's broken bones grinding together when she moved, but it didn't slow her any. When Arlene shoved her off, blood poured from her nose and mouth. Sandra proceeded to promptly slam her again.

What had gone wrong? If all the other Eye Killers had been appeased, why would Sandra Meadows still be possessed? Unless....

"Arlene!" I couldn't get her attention right away and had to shout her name several times while she grappled with Sandra. When she had a spare moment to glance my way, she seemed disoriented and confused. "Arlene, did you keep anything? Even something small?"

She blinked at me.

"Dammit, Arlene!" She had. I knew she had. If I'd felt a twinge of greed and desire over the pile of precious gemstones, I could only imagine what an out-of-work showgirl who'd put all her hopes on getting paid for this role, now lost, would have felt. And the Elementals knew it too. They knew we'd brought an offering and she'd kept a piece of it for herself. And that offended them.

Sandra hit Arlene again. She kicked Sandra off, but Arlene's movements were sluggish, her punches haphazard. She reached one hand into a pocket and pulled forth something large and shiny and green.

Fuck.

"I'm sorry," she said, looking up at me. Limping, she went to the small branch-off tunnel and drew back her arm to toss it in underhanded.

At the same moment, Sandra hefted a huge boulder from the floor of the pit and raised it over her head.

"Look out!" I took a chance and fired my pistol. It hit Sandra Meadows, but in the neck, not the head, and did nothing to stop her. A small detached part of me realized I'd lost count of my bullets and didn't care.

Sandra brought the rock down on Arlene's skull. I heard the crunch of rock meeting bone, watched my lover sinking to her knees. The priceless jewel slipped from her fingers, bounced against the stone floor, and stopped a foot shy of the smaller tunnel's entrance. Arlene fell onto her side and lay there, unmoving, while I desperately tried to focus the light on her.

What I saw in the beam turned my stomach.

Sandra, standing to the side, her broken arm bones even more prominent, jagged and splintered after her last attack, torn flesh and clothing hanging in strips off her. Her body wavered as the Elemental within her regathered its strength. I shifted the light a little farther left.

"Arlene…." Her eyes were closed. Her breathing came in uneven gasps, and I knew it wouldn't continue for long. I swung the light around, scanning frantically for Pandora, and found her between them, watching both with her intense black eyes. She took two hops in Arlene's direction, stopped, and turned her face to me, cocking her head with the question she didn't have the ability to ask.

"Do it!" I screamed, nodding frantically. "Bite her. Leave me. Take Arlene. One mistake doesn't mean she deserves to die. Please. Before Sandra gets her strength back. Before Arlene—Please—" My sobs choked my words. Tears streamed down my cheeks. I couldn't look at Arlene anymore. Couldn't breathe. Couldn't think.

I was losing her again.

You'll lose her either way.

But some ways were better than others.

"Do it," I begged.

Pandora hopped the short distance to Arlene's side and sank her beak into her hand.

Maybe the closer to death a person was, the faster the effects took hold, because Arlene's body jerked spasmodically. The skin of her hand glowed, and the glow spread up her arm, beneath her shirt and the rest of her clothing so she appeared to be lit from within. She'd lost consciousness, so she didn't react to the horrible tingling/burning sensations I'd experienced, didn't get to watch her body burst into flame and consume itself. But I did.

The fires engulfed her, reducing her to ash. Even from behind my closed eyelids, I could see the brightness.

A piteous cry wrenched me from my misery and forced my eyes open. Pandora. Dear God, Pandora.

The possessed Sandra made a futile attempt to swipe at the phoenix with her good hand, but Pandora was already out of range, halfway to me, wings afire, straining to keep herself aloft even while her beautiful red-and-gold feathers blackened and dropped one by one from her body. The more she lost, the harder her flight became, and her continuous cries conveyed the horrible pain of her struggles.

Her struggles to reach me, to take me too.

But my job wasn't done.

"No," I told her softly. "Let yourself go…. Watch out for Arlene."

She shook her head, more burning feathers dropping away, her determination evident in every furious beat of her half-stripped wings. But I knew. I knew from the way she faltered, the way she rose, then fell, then rose again, that she'd never make it. Even if I stretched and reached, even if I swung out on the rope and tried to climb down to her, she'd never get to me in time.

Pandora gave one last scream of agony and frustration. The fires enveloped her, and she tumbled away from me, a ball of flame turning quickly to ash.

An unnatural silence fell over the cavern.

They'd left me. They'd left me behind.

God only knew when they'd rise again.

CHAPTER 40

IT'S WHAT I'd wanted. But telling myself that did nothing to lessen the utter loneliness and despair.

Holding back further tears, I clenched my jaw and looked into the pit. Sandra Meadows stared back, eyes unblinking, body still as a statue as she waited. Because somehow, the entity within her knew.

I was going down there. And I was going to finish this.

I holstered my pistol and attached the lit flashlight to my belt so that the beam shone downward and wouldn't blind me but might distract the Elemental. Harness or no harness, I swung out onto one of the two climbing ropes, got my boots flat against the rock wall, and descended.

I slipped, I skidded, kicking small stones free to send them tinkling and clinking to the bottom. Without the extra gear, it was much harder going. Even with the calluses, my palms tore from my strangling grip on the rope, blood slicking it and making my hold even more tenuous. I never looked down, but every nerve, every sense in my being was fully aware of Sandra staring up, watching my approach, awaiting my arrival for what would be our final showdown.

When my boots hit bottom, it came faster than I expected, and I let out a gasp at the sudden impact with solid ground. I wiped my palms down my dungarees, leaving reddish brownish streaks on the denim.

Then I turned.

I tried to focus on the wall behind her, but her eyes, they glowed from within like blue fire, an eerie, otherworldly light unlike anything I'd seen from these beings before. It compelled me to look upon her, to meet that steady, unwavering, ancient gaze in a face so like mine.

A battered, bloodied, lifeless mirror image, showing me my future if I failed again.

It took me a full minute of staring before I realized I hadn't strangled to death.

"Put it back," Sandra said, voice harsh and grating. I knew it must be partially hers, but it echoed off the stone walls, overlaid with a hundred or more others. "Repay the debt. Let us rest."

I wrenched my eyes from hers, searching out the single green gem beside the side tunnel entrance. Keeping her in my peripheral vision, I stepped to it, crouched, and took it into my bleeding palm. Some bits of ash covered its gleaming, faceted surface. Pandora or Arlene? I wondered, letting them flutter away as I lifted the emerald to cup it against my breast.

A shuffling, scraping sound came from above. I turned my face upward. The zombies had arisen once more, forming a silent, solemn ring around the edge of the pit. Their dead eyes tracked my every move, prepared to pronounce judgment.

I held the gem out to Sandra. My hand shook. I ignored the shaking. "Will this end it?" I asked, croaking out the words.

Her head nodded, lolling sideways on what must have been a broken neck. "We accept the worthiness of your offering of blood—" It gestured first at the now sticky gem in my hand, then at the piles of ash on the floor where Arlene and Pandora had fallen. "—and sacrifice."

I nodded back, only slightly less grotesquely than she had. Tired. So tired. It took almost all my remaining strength to hurl the emerald into the side tunnel. It clattered down the dark, narrow passage, then fell still.

A deep rumbling echoed through the walls. The side tunnel caved in upon itself with a final expulsion of dust and debris, burying Preacher Xanthis's treasure in the heart of the mine, the heart of the Elementals' home, hopefully forever.

A sigh escaped Sandra's body, like the weight of a century had been taken from her shoulders. And given when all this started, perhaps it had.

She slumped against the stone wall, slid down it, and stopped. The blue light in her eyes flickered and went out, leaving her as nothing more than the corpse she should have been. Above me, the others fell like dominoes, one by one, encircling the pit with their empty husks.

I hoped their hosts' souls found peace at last.

I wondered how long before mine would.

Having no idea how much time had passed, I retrieved my harness from the pile of ash and tried hard not to think about its source. I hooked myself in and walked up the side of the pit, muscles burning, hands bleeding, until I flopped over the top edge in the only spot clear of bodies.

Before I even had time or strength to remove the gear, a thunderous rumbling shook the walls and floor, the roar growing louder and louder, and I knew Robbie had held off the authorities as long as she could but had finally set off her dynamite.

I understood. Keep people out to prevent offending the Eye Killers ever again.

Erase the evidence.

Part of me no longer cared about being buried alive. I'd already died once. I'd lost everything and everyone. This time I wouldn't have phoenix magic to bring me back, but what did I have to come back for?

However, another, stronger part saw the walls of flames barreling down the tunnels at me, converging on the pit from three different directions.

With a scream of defiance not unlike Pandora's final cry, I threw myself back over the edge of the pit, scrambling down the rope as far as I could and hanging there as the fire passed overhead, incinerating everything in its path.

The other rope, the one I wasn't attached to, caught fire and burned through, dropping away. The air grew choked with smoke and the acrid stench of burning flesh. I coughed and wheezed, dangling in near darkness broken only by the now faltering beam of my flashlight.

I had no idea how long I hung there, how much time passed before the flames became flickers, then smoldering, glowing, human-sized mounds above.

Even then, I continued to dangle, knowing the rope might be fraying, knowing I should move but possessing no energy to do so. So I waited for what seemed like hours until I had the strength and hauled my weary body one more time over the edge.

I pulled the light from my belt and shook the dang thing, which actually worked to steady the beam. Then I shone it over the blackened stone, the bodies with their melted skin, visible bones, and unrecognizable faces. I nodded my silent thanks to the one that had fallen across my climbing rope, protecting it from catching fire and preventing me from being dropped to my own death.

Then I wandered, up and down every passage, every tunnel, running up against blocked passage after blocked passage until I was near certain Robbie had done her job all too well. Occasionally, I found shafts leading up, air passing through them, howling all the way, but too steep to climb, even if my gear had been salvageable after all the battering it took. At least they sucked out the smoke and I wouldn't suffocate.

A semihysterical laugh escaped me. All that effort to keep from dying, only to be trapped in the place I'd always feared most. I checked my pistol, glad that a few bullets remained. If worse came to worst, I wouldn't go slowly of starvation or dehydration.

When the tiny pinprick of sunlight in one of the crumbled walls finally registered to my senses, I was certain I was hallucinating, but no. It was truly there. I tore away what remained of my fingernails pulling out stone after stone until I could squeeze my body through into the brightness of day.

I had just finished plugging up the hole once more when the local authorities found me.

CHAPTER 41

THE NEXT days, weeks, months, passed in a blur. Between injections of a variety of mind-numbing drugs, I had bouts of terrible clarity ripe with flash memories: Arlene and Pandora burning to ash, capture by the police, rocking back and forth in my cell-like room so drained of emotional energy I couldn't cry anymore.

Doctors tossed terminology around like a dealer dealing cards—paranoid delusions, multiple personality disorder, severe depression. Some I understood. Some I didn't. I'd been charged with Sandra Meadows's murder and theft of her identity. My fingerprints were all over her car. I'd been wearing her vest when I got to the *Harsh Reality* set. I grasped that investigators had traced my path back into the mine. I'd been in no state to cover my tracks. They'd found the pit. They'd found her unburned body, and I'm sure I left evidence all over that too. I was still awaiting my trial. My lawyer was seeking an insanity plea. I refused to speak to him.

The one thing they knew for absolute certain was that I wasn't Sandra Meadows. Friends and family had come forward to denounce me and identify her remains, and if that hadn't been enough, that hair sample taken by the police at Sam's ranch house had somehow proven I couldn't be her.

They'd tried to pin Arlene's death on me too, but without her body or any other definitive evidence, the cops had dropped that one.

As for the rest of the Eye Killers' victims? A publicity stunt gone horribly wrong, according to the TV news I watched in the common room at the mental hospital. I didn't get to go to the lounge much, but once in a while, I played nice enough to earn the privilege. The fire had destroyed the rest of the bodies, as I well knew, making their identification almost impossible and throwing investigators for a loop. Sam and Beth and those who'd fought alongside them had gotten off. Taz went to jail for criminal negligence. They thought he'd set up the whole thing for the ratings.

Sam and Beth hadn't tried to come visit me. They'd done as I'd asked and not let themselves be dragged down alongside me. I missed them, though.

Oblivion had a whole new reputation as a ghost town. The local tourist industry was thriving. Good for Sam, anyway.

I sincerely hoped blowing the mine hadn't angered the Elementals further, but once the investigation was complete, the police had put warning signs all around the final entrance I'd used for my escape. I saw it in the image on the news—yellow tape, bright red placards pronouncing the area hazardous and unstable. Hopefully, no one would be going in there anytime soon. And I had a feeling the Eye Killers would appreciate the efforts to preserve their privacy rather than retaliate.

I hadn't cleared my name. Hell, I'd done everything possible to make the way history remembered me worse, even if no one believed me to be Cali McCade. But I'd stopped the Eye Killers, so far as I could tell. I'd made a difference. And that was all any lawman, or woman, could really hope to accomplish.

A chime sounded, and I glanced up from my sticky plastic chair in front of the TV. Chimes meant food, medication, or visitors. The digital clock on the wall told me it wasn't food or medicine time. Which meant do-gooder guests.

Some of the other patients grumbled. They'd rather watch sitcoms than listen to a high school chorus, play cards with Girl Scouts, under careful supervision of course, or take an art or dance lesson from the nice old ladies from the community center.

"Oh, you're in for a treat," said the perky blond orderly in the too short white dress. Her singsong voice grated on my nerves. I'd lost television privileges last week for telling her to fuck off. "We've got the people from the animal shelter here to let us play with some of the pets." Her eyes fell on me. "You like pets, don't you, Cali? You had a bird, didn't you?"

The staff had taken to calling me Cali, since I had no identification and refused to refer to myself as anything else.

I swallowed the lump in my throat. "Yeah, I like pets. Know a lot about them. I could spot you as a real bitch right off." Time in a mental institution had brought me up to speed on modern sarcasm and pretty much wiped out my sense of humor.

She pressed her lips together and ignored my comment, turning instead to the door to welcome our visitors. We had a pimple-faced teenager with a cat carrier, a portly older man walking a poodle on a leash, and….

My heart stopped.

It was Arlene. Animal shelter blue uniform, black hair instead of brown, sunglasses hiding her eyes, and a baseball cap, but there was no mistaking her. And even if I'd had a doubt, I couldn't mistake the red-and-gold beauty on her arm—Pandora.

Her head turned toward me, and she frowned. I knew I looked awful. The place had mirrors, unbreakable ones (I'd tried), and I'd seen myself: stringy hair, sunken eyes, and I'd lost a lot of weight. But she was the most beautiful thing I'd ever seen.

Arlene didn't approach right away, and it was all I could do to remain in the chair and wait quietly for her rounds to reach me. When she did, she crouched down in front of me, her hand gently resting on my knee. "Apparently Pandora didn't think the two of us should go off to fight evil without you," she said quietly. "Smart bird."

So Arlene thought the same thing I had, that Pandora selected when her time travelers got reborn. Clearly there was a lot more to this phoenix than even high animal intelligence could explain. I was struck once more with the oddest image of a dark-haired woman overlaying her beak and feathers, and memories of a torchlit room with columns and cages flickered in memory, but I shook it away. Those were questions for another day. I had more pressing current concerns.

"How? The pit… I took the other harness. And why wait so long?" I fought down a burst of anger at them both. If Pandora could have come back for me at any time, why leave me in an institution for months?

Arlene had the good grace to duck her head. "I'm guessing she had to wait until the time was right. When I came back—" She shivered, and I sympathized. "I was completely healed, though still wearing the same filthy bloodstained clothes."

Sounded familiar.

"Sandra Meadows's body had already been removed. Lots of signs the police had been there, though. And they left a rope ladder in case they needed to go back down to investigate some more. Made it easy for me. I'm sorry you had to wait, but Pandora timed it just right to have the detectives gone but my escape equipment still in place." She gestured at her uniform. "Then I had to do some research, volunteer with Animal Control for a while."

Behind her, the poodle barked, scaring the fluffy white cat, which jumped out of the teenager's arms. Two of the orderlies scrambled to catch the terrified feline. We weren't going to get a much better distraction.

The phoenix hopped onto my shoulder, but I stopped anything else she might have done with my upraised hand and turned to the woman I only knew as Arlene.

"You came back for me. You could have gone and done anything you wanted after you… got reborn… but you came here. I think…." I forced words around a sudden lump in my throat. "I think I'm ready to know your real name now—ready to let her go."

She moved her hand to cover mine, then gripped it tightly. A couple of tears trickled from beneath the sunglasses. "It's Allison," she said. "Allie for short."

"Allie," I repeated. A good name.

Pandora cooed into my ear and bit me. She then jumped to Allison and bit her as well. I reached out and stroked her soft feathers. She'd suffered a lot since meeting me. I prayed I'd continue to be worthy of her company.

It took some time, since neither Allison nor I was close to death. As the familiar tingling began in my neck and arm, I silently hoped the hospital had a good fire insurance policy, and I wondered what hell we were getting ourselves into next. But whatever time period Pandora was sending us to, I knew we'd have the best possible odds of success. And as long as we faced evil with honor and not ego or greed, she'd stick by us. Both of us.

The End

Keep reading for an excerpt from
Threadbare
by Elle Ire!

CHAPTER I
VICK
Not Quite Up to Specs

I am a machine.

"VC1, YOUR objective is on the top floor, rear bedroom, moving toward the kitchen. Rest of the place scans as empty."

"Acknowledged." I study the high-rise across the street, my artificial ocular lenses filtering out the sunlight and zooming in on the penthouse twelve stories up. A short shadow passes behind white curtains. My gaze shifts to the gray, nondescript hovervan parked beside me. In the rear, behind reinforced steel, my teammate Alex is hitting the location with everything from x-rays to infrared and heat sensors.

Our enemies have no backup we're aware of, but it doesn't hurt to be observant.

I switch focus to Lyle, the driver, then Kelly in the passenger seat. Lyle stares straight ahead, attention on the traffic.

Kelly tosses me a smile, all bright sunshine beneath blonde waves. My emotion suppressors keep my own expression unreadable.

Except to her.

Kelly's my handler. My counterbalance. My… companion. My frie—

I can't process any further. But somewhere, deep down where I can't touch it, I want there to be more.

More what, I don't know.

Midday traffic rushes by in both directions—a four-lane downtown road carrying a mixture of traditional wheeled vehicles and the more modern hovercrafts. As a relatively recent colonization, Paradise doesn't have all the latest tech.

But we do.

Shoppers and businessmen bustle past. My olfactory sensors detect too much perfume and cologne, can identify individual brand names if I request the info. I pick up and record snippets of conversation, sort and discard them. The implants will bring anything mission relevant to my immediate attention, but none of the passersby are aware of what's going on across the street.

None of them thinks anything of the woman in the long black trench coat, either. I'm leaning against the wall between the doctors' offices and a real estate agency. No one notices me.

"Vick." Kelly's voice comes through the pick-ups embedded in my ear canals.

She's the only one who calls me that, even in private. I get grudgingly named in the public arena, but on the comm, to everyone else, I'm VC1.

A model number.

"The twelve-year-old kidnap *victim* is proba-bly getting a snack. He's hungry, Vick. He's alone and scared." She's painting a picture, humanizing him. Sometimes I'm as bad with others as Alex and Lyle are toward me. "You're going to get him out." A pause as we make eye contact through the bullet-proof glass.

"Right," I mutter subvocally.

Even without the touch of pleading in her voice, failure is not an option. I carry out the mission until I succeed or until something damages me beyond my capability to continue.

Kelly says there's an abort protocol that she can initiate if necessary. We've never had to try it, and given how the implants and I interact, I doubt it would work.

"Team Two says the Rodwells have arrived at the restaurant," Alex reports in a rich baritone with a touch of Earth-island accent.

The kidnappers, a husband and wife team of pros, are out to lunch at a café off the building's lobby. Probably carrying a remote trigger to kill the kid in their condo if they suspect a rescue attempt or if he tries to escape. They're known for that sort of thing. Offworlders with plenty of toys of their own and a dozen hideouts like this one scattered across the settled worlds. Team Two will observe and re-port, but not approach. The risk is too great.

Which means I have maybe forty-five minutes to get in and extract the subject.

No. *Rescue* the *child.* Right.

"Heading in." My tone comes out flat, without affectation. I push off from the wall, ignoring the way the rough bricks scrape my palms.

"Try to be subtle this time," Lyle says, shooting me a quick glare out the windshield. "No big booms. We can't afford to tip them off."

Subtlety isn't my strong suit, but I don't appre-ciate the reminder. Two years of successful mission completions speak for themselves.

I turn my gaze on him. He looks away.

I have that effect on people.

The corner of my lip twitches just a little. Ev-ery once in a while an emotion sneaks through, even with the suppressors active.

I'm standing on the median, boots sinking into carefully cultivated sod, when Kelly scolds me. "That wasn't very nice." Without turning around, I know she's smiling. She doesn't like Lyle's attitude any better than I do.

My lips twitch a little further.

Thunder rumbles from the east, and a sudden gust of wind whips my long hair out behind me. Back at base, it would be tied in a neat bun or at least a ponytail, but today I'm passing for civilian as much as someone like me can. I tap into the local weather services while I finish crossing the street.

Instead of meteorological data, my internal display flashes me an image of cats and dogs falling from the sky.

This is what happens when you mix artificial intelligence with the real thing. Okay, not exactly. I don't have an AI in my head, but the sophisticated equipment replacing 63 percent of my brain is advanced enough that it has almost developed a mind of its own.

It definitely has a sense of humor and a flair for metaphor.

Cute.

The house pets vanish with a final bark and meow.

The first drops hit as I push my way through glass doors into the lobby, and I shake the moisture from my coat and hair. Beneath the trench coat, metal clinks softly against metal, satisfying and too soft for anyone around me to pick up.

The opulent space is mostly empty—two old ladies sitting on leather couches, a pair of teenagers talking beside some potted plants. Marble and glass in blacks, whites, and grays. Standard high-end furnishings.

"May I help you?" Reception desk, on my left, portly male security guard behind it, expression unconcerned. "Nasty weather." A flash of lightning punctuates his pleasantries.

Terraforming a world sadly doesn't control the timing of its thunderstorms.

My implants reduce the emotion suppressors, and I attempt a smile. Kelly assures me it looks natural, but it always feels like my face is cracking. "I'm here to see…." My receptors do a quick scan of the listing behind him—the building houses a combination of residences and offices. If we'd had more time, we could have set this up better, but the Rodwells have switched locations twice already, and we only tracked them here yesterday.

"Doctor Angela Swarzhand," I finish faster than the guard can pick up the hesitation. "I'm a new patient."

The guard smiles, and I wonder if they're friends. "That's lovely. Just lovely. Congratulations."

"Um, thanks." I'm sure I've missed something, but I have no idea what.

He consults the computer screen built into the surface of his desk, then points at a bank of elevators across the black-marble-floored lobby. "Seventh floor."

"Great. Where are the stairs?" I already know where they are, but I shouldn't, so I ask.

The guard frowns, forehead wrinkling in concern. "Stairs? Shouldn't someone in your condition be taking the elevator?"

"My condition?"

"Vick." Kelly's warning tone tries to draw my attention, but I need to concentrate.

"Not now," I subvocalize. If this guy has figured out who, or rather *what* I am, things are going to get messy and unsubtle fast. My hand slips beneath my coat, fingers curling around the grip of the semiautomatic in its shoulder holster.

"You're pregnant." The giggle in Kelly's voice registers while I stare stupidly at the guard.

"I'm what?" Sooner or later this guy is bound to notice the miniscule motions of my lips, even speaking subvocally.

Alex replaces Kelly on the comm. "Dr. Swarzhand is an obstetrician. She specializes in high-risk pregnancies. The guard thinks you're pregnant. Be pregnant. And fragile."

Oh for fuck's sake.

I blink a couple of times, feigning additional confusion. "My condition! Right." I block out the sound of my entire team laughing their asses off. "I'm still not used to the idea. Just a few weeks along." I don't want to take the damn elevator. Elevators are death traps. Tiny boxes with one way in and one way out. Thunder rumbles outside. If the power fails, I'll be trapped. My heart rate picks up. The implants initiate a release of serotonin to compensate, and the emotion suppressors clamp down. Or try to.

In my ears, one-third of the laughter stops. "It'll be okay, Vick." Kelly, soft and soothing.

Of course she knows. She always knows.

"Just take it up to the seventh floor and walk the rest of the way. It's only for a few seconds, a minute at most. It won't get stuck. I promise."

"Thanks," I say aloud to the guard and turn on my heel, trying to stroll and not stomp. "You can't promise that," I mutter under my breath.

"It'll be okay," she says again, and I'm in the waiting lift, the doors closing with an ominous *thunk* behind me.

The ride is jerky, a mechanical affair rather than the more modern antigrav models. I grit my teeth, resisting the urge to talk to my team. Alex and Lyle wouldn't see the need to comfort a machine, anyway.

Figures the one memory I retain from my fully human days is the memory of my death, and the one emotion my implants fail to suppress every time is the absolute terror of that death.

When the chime announces my arrival on seven and the doors open, I'm a sweating, hyperventilating mess. I stagger from the moving coffin, colliding with the closest wall and using it to keep myself upright.

There's no one in the hallway, or someone would be calling for an ambulance by now.

"Breathe, Vick, breathe," Kelly whispers.

I suck in a shaky breath, then another. My vision clears. My heart rate slows. "I've got it."

"I know. But count to ten, anyway."

Despite the need to hurry, I do it. If I'm not in complete control, I can make mistakes. If I make mistakes, the mission is at risk. I might fail.

A door on the right opens and a very pregnant woman emerges, belly protruding so far she can't possibly see her feet. She takes one look at me and frowns.

"Morning sickness," I explain, grimacing at the thought on multiple levels. Even if I wanted kids for some insane reason, I wouldn't be allowed to have them. Machines don't get permission to procreate.

The pregnant lady offers a sympathetic smile and disappears into the elevator. At the end of the hall, the floor-to-ceiling windows offer a view of sheeting rain and flashing lightning, and I shudder as the metal doors close behind her. I head for the stairwell—the nice, safe, stable, I'm-totally-in-control-of-what-happens stairwell.

"Walk me through it," I tell Alex. I pass the landing for the eleventh floor, heading for the twelfth.

"The penthouse takes up the entire top level," his voice comes back. "Figures. No one to hear the kid call for help. Stairwell opens into the kitchen. Elevator would have let you off in a short hallway leading to the front door."

Which is probably a booby-trapped kill chute. No thanks.

"Security on the stairwell door?"

A pause. "Yep. Plenty of it too. Jamming and inserting a playback loop in the cameras now. Sensors outside the door at ankle height, both right and left. Not positive what they trigger. Could be a simple alarm. Could be something else."

Could be something destructive goes unsaid. I might have issues with my emotions, but that doesn't make me suicidal. At least not anymore. Besides, with the kid walking around loose in the penthouse apartment, all the doors have to have some kind of aggressive security on them. Otherwise he would have escaped by now.

"Whatever it is, I won't know unless you trip it," Alex adds.

Oh, very helpful. I'm earning my pay today.

My internal display flashes an image of me in ballet shoes, en pointe, pink tutu and all.

Keeping me on my toes. Right. Funny. I didn't ask for your input.

The display winks out.

I take eight more steps, round the turn for the last flight to the top floor, and stop. My hand twitches toward the compact grenade on my belt, but that would be overkill. No big booms. Right. Give me the overt rather than the covert any day. But I don't get to choose.

I verify the sensor locations, right where Alex said they'd be. He's right. No indication of what they're connected to.

And time's running out.

If it's an alarm, it could signal the Rodwells at the restaurant. If they have a hidden bomb and a trigger switch….

"Wiring on the door?" I weigh the odds against the ticking clock. They don't want to kill their victim if there's any chance they can make money off him. If I were fully human, if the implants weren't suppressing my emotions, I wouldn't be able to make a decision. Life-or-death shouldn't be about playing the odds.

"None."

"Composition?" Some beeps in the background answer my request.

A longer pause. "Apartment doors in that building were purchased from Door Depot, lower-end models despite the high rents. Just over one inch thick. Wood. Medium hardness."

"The door at the bottom of the stairwell was metal."

"But the one on the top floor isn't. It's considered a 'back door' to the apartment. It's wood like the front entries." Alex's info shifts the odds—odds placed on a child's survival. I try not to think too hard on what I've become. It shouldn't matter to me, but— The suppressors clamp down on the distraction.

"Give me a five-second jam on those sensors," I tell him and count on him to do it. Damn, I hate these last-minute piecemeal plans, but we didn't have much time to throw this together.

"Vick, what are you—?"

Before Kelly can finish voicing her concerns, I'm charging up the last of the stairs, past the sensors, and slamming shoulder-first into the penthouse door. Wood cracks and splinters, shards flying in all directions, catching in my hair and driving through the material of my jacket.

Medium hardness or not, it hurts. I'm sprawled on the rust-colored kitchen tiles, bits of door and frame scattered around me, blood seeping from a couple of cuts on my hands and cheek. The implants unleash a stream of platelets from my bone marrow and they rush to clot the wounds.

I raise my head and meet the wide eyes of my objective. The kid's mouth hangs open, a half-eaten sandwich on the floor by his feet. I'm vaguely aware of Kelly demanding to know if I'm okay.

Her concern touches me in a way I can't quite identify, but it's... good.

"Ow," I mutter, rising to my knees, then my feet. "Fuck." I might heal fast, but I feel pain.

The kid slides from his chair and backs to the farthest corner of the room, trapped against the gray-and-black-speckled marble counter. "D-don't hurt me," he stammers.

I roll my eyes. "Are you an idiot?"

"Oh, nice going, Vick."

I ignore Kelly and open my trench coat, revealing an array of weapons—blades and guns. "If I wanted to hurt you...."

His eyes fly wider, and he pales.

A sigh over the comm. "For God's sake, Vick, try, will you?"

My shoulder hurts like a sonofabitch. I try rotating my left arm and wince at the reduced range of motion. Probably dislocated. I'm in no mood to make nicey nice.

"You're not the police." Oh good, the kid can use logic.

"The police wouldn't be able to find you with a map and a locator beacon."

My implants toss me a quick flash of the boy buried in a haystack and a bunch of uniformed men digging through it, tossing handfuls left and right.

"I'm with a private problem-solving company, and I'm here to take you home," I continue. "Will you come with me?" I pull a syringe filled with clear liquid from one of the coat's many pockets. "Or am I gonna have to drug and carry you?" That will suck, especially with the shoulder injury, but I can do it.

Another sigh from Kelly.

I'm not kid-friendly. Go figure.

My vision blurs. We're out of chat time. A glance over my shoulder reveals pale blue haze filling the space just inside the back door, pouring through a vent in the ceiling. A cloud of it rolls into the kitchen, so it's been flowing for a while. "Alex, I need a chemical analysis," I call to my tech guru. I remove a tiny metal ball from a belt pouch and roll it into the blue gas. Several ports on it snap open, extending sampler rods and transmitting the findings to my partners in the hovervan.

A pause. "It's hadrazine gas. Your entry must have triggered the release. Move faster, VC1."

Hadrazine's some fast and powerful shit. A couple of deep breaths and we'll be out cold, and not painlessly, either. We'll feel like we're suffocating first. If I get out of this alive, my next goal is to take down the Rodwells.

"Report coming in from Team Two." Alex again. "You must have tripped an alarm somewhere. Rodwells leaving the restaurant, not bothering to pay. They're headed for your location."

A grin curls my lips. Looks like I might get my wish.

I know I'm not supposed to *want* to kill anyone. I know Kelly can pick up that urge and will have words for me later. But sometimes… sometimes people just need killing. But not before I achieve my primary objective.

I'm in motion before I finish the thought, grabbing the kid by the arm and hauling him into the penthouse's living room. Couches and chairs match the ones in the lobby. "Tell Team Two not to engage," I snap, not bothering to lower my voice anymore. The boy stares at me but says nothing. "They may still have a detonator switch for this place." And Team Two is Team Two for a reason. They're our backup. The second string. And more likely to miss a double kill shot.

"You're scaring the boy," Kelly says in my ear.

I'm surprised she can read him at this distance. Usually that skill is limited to her interactions with me.

"Jealousy?" she asks. "What for?"

Or maybe she's just guessing. Where the hell did that come from, anyway? I turn up the emotion suppressors. Things between me and Kelly have been a little wonky lately. I've had some strange responses to things she's said or done. I don't need the distraction now.

"Never mind," I mutter. "Alex, front door. What am I dealing with?"

"No danger I can read. Nothing's active. Doesn't mean there isn't some passive stuff."

"There's a bomb."

I stare down at the boy by my side. "You sure?"

He nods, shaggy blond hair hanging in his face. I release him for a second to brush it out of his eyes and crouch in front of him. He's short for his age. Thin too. Lightweight. Good in case I end up having to carry him. "Any chance they were bluffing?"

The kid shrugs.

"The café manager stopped them in the lobby, demanding payment," Alex cuts in. "Doesn't look like they want to make a scene, so you've got maybe five minutes, VC1. Six if they have to wait for the elevator."

Maybe less if the gas flows too quickly.

Right.

I approach the door, studying the frame for the obvious and finding nothing. Doesn't mean there isn't anything embedded.

There. A pinprick hole drilled into the molding on the right side of the frame. Inside would be a pliable explosive and a miniature detonator triggered by contact or remote. Given the right tools and time, I could disarm such a device. I have the tools in a pouch on my belt. I don't have the time.

"Um, excuse me?" The boy points toward the kitchen. Blue mist curls across the threshold and over the first few feet of beige living room carpet.

I race toward a wall of heavy maroon curtains, shoving a couch aside and throwing the window treatments wide. Lightning flashes outside the floor-to-ceiling windows, illuminating the skyscraper across the street and the twelve-story drop to the pavement below.

Oh, fuck me now.

"Lyle, I need that hovervan as high as you can get it. Bring it up along the east side of the building. Beneath the living room windows."

"Oooh. A challenge." He's not being sarcastic. Lyle's the best damn pilot and driver in the Fighting Storm.

Too bad he's an ass.

The van's engines rev over the comm, and the repulsorlifts engage with a whine.

"Vick, what are you thinking?" Kelly's voice trembles when she's worried, and she rushes over her words. I can barely understand her.

"I'm thinking my paranoia is about to pay off."

I wear a thin inflatable vest beneath my clothes when we do anything near water. I carry a pocket breather when we work in space stations, regardless of the safety measures in place. I'm always prepared for every conceivable obstacle, including some my teammates never see coming.

So I wear a lightweight harness under my clothes when I'm in any building over three stories tall.

Alex teases me about it. Lyle's too spooked by me to laugh in my face, but I know he does it behind my back. Kelly counsels that I can't live my second life in fear.

Sorry. I died once. I'm in no hurry to repeat the experience.

Using my brain implants, I trigger an adrenaline burst. The hormone races through my bloodstream. I'll pay for this later with an energy crash, but for now, I'm supercharged and ready to take on my next challenge.

The hadrazine gas is flowing closer. I shove the kid toward the far corner of the room, away from both the kitchen and the damage I'm about to do.

For safety reasons, high-rise windows, especially really large floor-to-ceiling ones, can rarely be opened. Hefting the closest heavy wood chair, I slam it into the windows with as much force as I can gather. My shoulder screams in pain, and I hear Kelly's answering cry over my comm. With her shields down, she feels what I feel. They're always down during missions. I hate hurting her, but I have no choice. I need her input to function, and I need the window broken.

The first hit splinters the tempered glass, sending a spiderweb of cracks shooting to the corners of the rectangular pane. Not good enough.

I pull my 9mm from a thigh holster and fire four shots. Cracks widen. Chips fall, along with several large shards. There's a breach now. I need to widen it. I grab the chair and swing a second time, and the glass and chair shatter, pieces of both flying outward and disappearing into the raging storm.

Wind and rain whip into the living room. Curtains flap like flags in a hurricane, buffeting me away from the edge and keeping me from tumbling after the furniture. I'm soaked in seconds. When I take a step, the carpet squishes beneath my boots.

"VC1, I think the Rodwells made Team Two in the lobby…. Shit. I'm reading a signal transmission, trying to block it…. Fuck, I've got an active signature on the bomb…. It's got a countdown, two minutes. Get the hell out of there!"

Alex's report sends my pulse rate ratcheting upward. Other than not being here in the first place, no paranoid preparation can counter a blast of the magnitude I'm expecting.

Judging from the positioning of the explosives, anyone in the apartment will be toast.

I take off my coat and toss it into the swirling blue gas, regretting the loss of the equipment in the pockets but knowing I can't make my next move with it on. The wind is drawing the haze right toward the windows, right toward me. I grab gloves from a pocket and yank them on. I unsnap a compartment on my harness and pull out a retractable grappling hook attached to several hundred coiled feet of ultra-strong, ultrathin wire.

Once I've given myself some slack in the cord, I scan the room. The gaudy architecture includes some decorative pillars. A press of a button drives the grappler into the marble, and I wrap the cord several times around the column and tug hard. I'm not worried about the wire. It can bear more than five hundred pounds of weight. I'm not so sure about the apartment construction, given the flimsy back door.

The cord holds. I reel out more line, extending my free hand to the kid. "Come on!"

He stares at me, then the window, then shakes his head. "You're crazy. No way!" He shouts to be heard over the rain and thunder.

My internal display flashes my implants' favorite metaphor—a thick cable made up of five metal cords wrapped tightly around each other. Over the last two years, I've come to understand they represent my sanity, and since Kelly's arrival, they've remained solid. Until now.

One of them is fraying, a few strands floating around the whole in wisps.

Great. Just great.

The image fades.

"Die in flames or jump with me. Take your pick." The clock ticks down in my head. If the boy won't come, I'm not sure I'll have time to cross the room and grab him, but my programming will force me to try.

He comes.

I take one last second to slam myself against the pillar, forcing my dislocated shoulder into the socket. Kelly screams in my ear, but I've clamped my own jaw shut, gritting my teeth for my next move.

One arm slides around the boy's narrow waist. I grip the cord in the protective glove.

"Five seconds," Alex says.

I run toward the gaping hole and open air, clutching the kid to me. He wraps his arms around my torso and buries his face in my side.

"Four."

"Oh my God," Kelly whispers.

"Three."

Lyle and the hovervan better be where I need them. The cord might support our weight, but it won't get me close enough to the ground for a safe free-fall drop.

"Two."

The sole of my boot hits the edge and my muscles coil to launch me as far from the window as I can. There's a second of extreme panic, long enough for regrets but too late to stop momentum, and then we're airborne. Emotion suppressors ramp up to full power, and the terror fades.

My last thought as gravity takes hold is of Kelly. My suppressors have some effect on her empathic sense, but extremely strong feelings and emotions like pain and panic reach her every time.

If she can't get her shields up fast, this will tear her apart.

ELLE E. IRE resides in Celebration, Florida, where she writes science fiction and urban fantasy novels featuring kickass women who fall in love with each other. She has won local and national writing competitions, including the Royal Palm Literary Award, the Pyr and Dragons essay contest judged by the editors at Pyr Publishing, the Do It Write competition judged by a senior editor at Tor publishing, and she is a winner of the Backspace scholarship awarded by multiple literary agents. She and her spouse belong to several writing groups and attend and present at many local, state, and national writing conferences.

When she isn't teaching writing to middle school students, Elle enjoys getting into her characters' minds by taking shooting lessons, participating in interactive theatrical experiences, paying to be kidnapped "just for the fun and feel of it," and attempting numerous escape rooms. She is the author of *Vicious Circle* (original release 2015, rerelease 2020), the Storm Fronts series (2019-2020), the Nearly Departed series (2021-2022), and *Reel to Real Love* (2021). To learn what her tagline "Deadly Women, Dangerous Romance" is really all about, visit her website: http://www.elleire.com. She can also be found on Twitter at @ElleEIre and Facebook at www.facebook.com/ElleE.IreAuthor.

Elle is represented by Naomi Davis at BookEnds Literary Agency.